328

FINDING ASHLYN

SEAL Team Hawaii, Book 6

SUSAN STOKER

CHAPTER ONE

"I like your apartment," Slate said after Ashlyn had shown him around. She was giddy with nerves. He'd never been to her place before, even though they'd known each other for over a year.

"Thanks. It's not super fancy, but I like it," Ashlyn said.

She'd met Slate when Lexie had started dating Midas. At first, she hadn't liked him all that much, but the more time she spent hanging out with him and his team, the more he grew on her. He had a tendency to think bad guys were waiting around every corner to pop out and attack not only her, but all of her friends as well...which she couldn't blame him for, since a lot of bad shit *had* gone down with Monica, Lexie, Kenna, Carly, and Elodie.

But unlike those ladies, Ashlyn's current boss or her ex-boyfriend weren't going to be an issue. She'd moved to Hawaii because of a guy, yes, but Franklin had turned out to be a lazy mooch. She couldn't see him summoning the energy to bother her for any reason. As for work, Food For All was a dream job. She met a ton of interesting people and wasn't tied to an office from eight to five every day. And she loved the people she worked with. Lexie was amazing, of course, and Elodie was a genius when it came to creating dishes from the donated food.

While Ashlyn might've developed a small crush on Slate over the last year or so, she also never really expected anything to happen between them. She wasn't the kind of woman that tall, gorgeous, badass Navy SEALs looked twice at. She wasn't hideous, but she also wasn't anything special, in her opinion. Her best feature was her long, straight, sleek brown hair. Her eyes were a more boring shade of brown...her face didn't really boast any standout features.

She was tall at five-ten, but continually struggled to take off the extra fifteen to twenty pounds she carried on her frame. Long, curvy legs, not much ass, a little *too* much extra padding around her waist...

In short, she wasn't hideous, but she also wasn't the kind of woman people turned around to watch as she walked by.

And beyond her ordinary looks, Slate frequently seemed to be annoyed by her.

Despite that, a short while ago, when he'd brought her home from one of the many barbeques his SEAL team had thrown, he'd shocked the shit out of Ashlyn by asking her out. She'd immediately said yes, of course, but with the caveat that she didn't want anything serious. Slate had agreed...so she'd invited him up to her place to test out their new friends-with-benefits arrangement.

Ashlyn hadn't been nervous when she'd invited him up, but now, standing in her small apartment with Slate, she suddenly wasn't so sure. She'd just given him the two-cent tour, which included showing him the extra bedroom she used for doing step aerobics, and which held a hodge-podge of stuff that didn't fit anywhere else in the apartment; the master bedroom; the small half bath in the hallway; the functional kitchen; the laundry room, which was more like a closet; and now they were standing in her surprisingly spacious living room, which included a tiny balcony she never used, overlooking the parking lot. The living room was what sold her on the apartment. She liked how open it was to the kitchen, and that she didn't feel hemmed in.

Now, as she stood in that room feeling awkward, Slate walked toward her. Ashlyn couldn't read the look on his face. He looked...determined. But then again, he *always* looked that way. He was taller than her by about four inches, his black hair was cut fairly close to his head and, since it was late in the day, he had a five o'clock shadow. His dark brown eyes were pinned on her, and Ashlyn couldn't look away as he approached.

He put his hands on her shoulders and squeezed gently. "You change your mind?" he asked quietly.

Ashlyn immediately shook her head. "No."

"Then what's wrong? You look like you want to bolt."

She should be used to Slate's bluntness by now, but somehow he could still surprise her. "I'm just trying to wrap my head around everything. Us. How we went from two people who never really got along to...this."

Without a word, Slate wrapped an arm around her shoulders and pulled her to the couch. He sat, taking her with him and pulling her against his side. Then he grabbed the remote from the table next to the couch, pulled the square ottoman closer—she didn't have a coffee table, preferring the big cushioned ottoman—and clicked on the television.

"Um, Slate?"

"Yeah?" he asked, seemingly unconcerned.

"Aren't we going to...um...you know?"

He nodded. "Oh, yeah, we're gonna, um, *you know*, but not while you're freaking out about it."

"I'm not freaking out," Ashlyn protested.

He turned and looked at her while raising one eyebrow.

Ashlyn couldn't help but chuckle. "Okay, I'm a tad bit nervous, but that doesn't mean I don't want you."

Slate grinned. "That's good, Ash, because I want you too. But there's no rush."

Ashlyn burst out laughing at that.

"What?" Slate asked when she had herself under control.

"I can't believe *the* Duncan Stone just said there's no rush," Ashlyn teased. "You're the king of impatience."

The grin that crossed his face now made Ashlyn's belly clench. The man was way too damn gorgeous for his own good.

"For stupid shit, I don't like waiting," he agreed. "I don't like to be late anywhere. If there's a plan, I'd rather just execute it and get it done. But when it comes to intimacy... I'm absolutely not in any hurry. Anticipation is half the fun. And I have to say, babe, I've waited for over a year to taste you, to get between those long legs of yours...so I can wait a bit longer."

Ashlyn shifted in his grasp. Damn, this man was lethal. "I wasn't sure you even liked me."

"I liked you. *Like* you," he said simply.

And just like that, Ashlyn's nervousness disappeared. She was horny as hell, and the thought of Slate between her legs like he'd just described made her nipples harden. "You really want to watch TV?" she asked.

Slate didn't take his attention from her face. "I want to do what *you* want to do."

"I don't want to watch TV."

"Spell it out, Ash," he demanded.

She could feel his muscles tensing. Gaze locked with his, she said boldly, "I want you. I have for a very long time. Even though you annoy me sometimes, that doesn't mean I haven't imagined you in my bed."

"Lead the way," Slate replied in a low, rumbly voice that made Ashlyn's girl parts tingle.

She smiled and stood up, Slate at her heels, and headed for the hallway that led to her room. She supposed she should still be nervous, but she knew without a doubt that Slate was about to rock her world...in all the ways that counted.

She walked to her bed and turned to face him.

He lifted a hand and ran the backs of his fingers over her cheek. Goose bumps broke out on Ashlyn's arms. "Nothing serious," she reminded him. "If we do this, you can't go all uber protective on me. Well...any more than you already are. We're just having fun."

Slate nodded. "I'm perfectly all right with that. I'm not ready to settle down."

"Do you have a condom?" Ashlyn asked.

"Yes."

That was good, because she didn't. It had been a while since she'd been with a man, and she definitely wasn't prepared for Slate to be standing in her bedroom tonight.

"Last chance to change your mind," he warned in a deep voice.

"I could say the same to you," Ashlyn said.

"No fucking way."

"Then strip," she challenged. She had to admit, she liked this. Liked the freedom of their arrangement. They were two people attracted to each other, who were about to have sex. No declarations or promises of any kind and no pressure.

Without another word, Slate reached for the hem of his T-shirt. He had it up and over his head before Ashlyn blinked.

She stared, awestruck by all the muscles. There was a smattering of hair covering his chest and she wanted to taste the small nipples on his pecs. Her hands moved without her brain telling them to. She flattened her palms on his skin, and he inhaled sharply at her first touch.

Oh, yeah, this was gonna be good.

His hands went to the hem of her own shirt, and she raised her arms, helping him. Her hair cascaded around her shoulders as soon as the material cleared her head. The strands tickled her skin, but she forgot about anything but Slate's hands as he reached behind her and deftly unhooked the clasp of her bra.

"Beautiful," he murmured as he bent his head.

Ashlyn groaned and her head fell back when he suckled on one of her nipples. Hard.

When he finally lifted his head, their eyes met—then the race was on to see who could get their clothes off the fastest.

Before Ashlyn knew it, they were on her bed completely naked, and Slate was kissing her as if he'd never get enough.

She scratched her fingernails down his back and tried to pull him closer, which was impossible, as they were already touching from chest to knees. Ashlyn could feel his hard erection against her stomach and lust blossomed inside her. She needed him. Deep. Fucking her hard.

She tore her mouth from his and ordered, "Inside me. Now."

"Need to make sure you're ready for me," he retorted, even as his hips bucked against her.

"I'm ready."

But Slate didn't take her word for it. One of his hands snaked between them, and Ashlyn jerked as his fingertip brushed her clit. She knew what he'd find. She'd never been this turned on in her life.

"Soaked," Slate whispered with a small, somewhat conceited smile.

Ashlyn rolled her eyes. "Yeah, yeah, yeah. I told you I was ready."

He didn't say anything else, just moved his fingers lower. He ever so slowly pushed one inside her, and Ashlyn closed her eyes and groaned. It felt amazing, but she needed more.

Her eyes opened when she felt him moving off her. His finger slid out of her wet folds as he reached for the condom he'd thrown onto the bed when he took off his pants.

"Hurry," she said as she ran her hands up and down his biceps.

"Now who's impatient?" he joked.

"Oh my God, you're seriously gonna be a pain in the ass right *now*?" she huffed.

Slate chuckled as he rolled the condom over his cock, and Ashlyn realized at that moment that she'd never laughed while having sex before. In the past, she and her partners had been all business. Sex had never been about fun, just satisfaction...which was kind of sad.

But then all thoughts of laughter and fun flew from her mind as Slate notched the head of his cock between her legs.

Ashlyn understood for the first time just how big he was. He wasn't much longer than most, but he was thicker than anyone she'd ever been with. Looking down, she held her breath as he inched his way into her body. Her muscles tightened at one point as pain began to overtake the pleasure she'd been feeling only moments earlier.

Slate seemed to realize it. His jaw flexed as he held himself halfway inside her body.

"Give me a second," Ashlyn whispered as she willed her body to relax and accept him.

The hand that wasn't holding the base of his cock moved, and he used his thumb to manipulate her clit. Ashlyn bucked, inadvertently taking more of him inside her.

"That's it, babe. You can take me. You're so fucking gorgeous. Laid out for me, taking my cock. It's so goddamn hot."

She barely registered his words as pleasure swamped through her when he strummed her clit faster. Her fingers tightened on his biceps as he played with her body.

"You ready for more?" he asked.

Ashlyn couldn't speak if her life depended on it. She was overwhelmed with sensation.

"You're ready," Slate decided, the satisfaction easy to hear in his tone. He didn't stop caressing her clit as he slid all the way inside her.

They both moaned when his balls pressed up against her ass. He grabbed her hips and pulled her in tight, gaining another fraction of an inch inside her body.

"Holy shit, Slate. I...you...*damn*," Ashlyn stuttered.

He chuckled, and she felt the reverberations rumble through her from where they were connected.

"I know you aren't laughing at me," she said, frowning at him.

"Nope. No way," Slate said, clearly still amused.

In retaliation, Ashlyn tightened her inner muscles, feeling vindicated when the smile dropped from his face and he gasped.

"If you're done laughing at me, maybe we can fuck?" she said a little snarkily.

Slate's gaze met hers, and he rested his elbows on either side of her body. They were plastered together now as he stayed planted inside her as far as he could get.

"You want me to move, Ash?"

"Yes!" she exclaimed.

"You feel amazing," he told her as he rocked his hips, pulling back, then sinking back inside her.

"So do you," she told him.

"I'm not going to last long," he warned. "You're too tight. Too fucking hot. And it's been too long for me."

Ashlyn was surprised at that. She didn't think Slate was a

manwhore, but she figured he had to be getting some fairly regularly.

"Need you to get there too," he begged.

Ashlyn panted, "I will."

"No, babe. I mean before me. Wanna feel you squeeze my dick."

His words were raw, and they turned her way the hell on. She nodded.

"Touch yourself," he ordered.

"Bossy," she murmured, even as she let go of one of his arms and slid a hand between their bodies.

"You haven't even seen bossy yet," he told her.

Ashlyn couldn't help but roll her eyes. "Please." She began to stroke her clit. "Your middle name might as well be bossy. You love to tell me what I should and shouldn't do."

"Right now, you should be getting yourself off," he shot back.

Ashlyn couldn't help but grin at him.

Slate shook his head. "Fuck, you're gonna be the death of me. Faster, Ash. I want to see and feel your orgasm. Next time I'll be better, and I'll get you off with my mouth and hands before I get inside your soaking-wet body. I couldn't wait this time. Didn't help that you practically ignited as soon as I touched you."

Ashlyn couldn't even feel embarrassed by that. She was wet from the second he touched her. Hell, even before that, just talking on the couch. Slate turned her on as no man ever had before. She grinned wider.

"You always gonna be this hot for me?" he asked.

"Probably."

"Good. Get there, babe. Now."

"Yes, sir," she teased and moved her fingers faster over her clit. She didn't have a lot of room, but the feel of Slate inside her body as she masturbated was more than enough to ramp her desire into overdrive.

Slate lifted himself up enough so he could watch what she was doing, and began to lazily push in and out of her body.

"So damn hot," he mumbled. His gaze locked on where their bodies met.

That was all it took for Ashlyn to explode. As the first wave of her orgasm went through her, Slate slammed inside her body. He did it again and again, prolonging her pleasure. Ashlyn had never felt anything quite like this moment. It was almost overwhelming.

It didn't take long for Slate to grunt, press himself as far inside her as he could get, then hold still, his muscles tensing as he came. The veins in his neck stood out as he threw his head back and groaned.

Ashlyn squirmed under him, wanting more. *Needing* more.

Slate seemed to sense that she wasn't done, because as soon as he recovered, he leaned back to sit on his heels and hauled her ass onto his lap. He was still inside her, holding her against him with one hand while the other began to roughly stroke her clit.

"Slate!" she exclaimed, trying to squirm away from his touch.

"Give me another," he ordered.

"Too sensitive," she croaked, even as she thrust into his touch.

"You're not done. *Again*," he said.

"Oh, God!" Ashlyn moaned, feeling another orgasm welling inside her.

"My horny girl," Slate said with pride. "This is gonna work out just fine."

Ashlyn wanted to respond but was concentrating too hard on breathing.

"Gonna eat this pussy next time," Slate went on as he

stared at her. "Seeing my cock inside you is hot as fuck. I can feel you all around me. I was too fast this time, but I'll make up for it later."

Slate was a dirty talker. She'd had no idea, and Ashlyn couldn't believe it was turning her on as much as it was.

"Stop fucking around," he said gruffly. "Come, Ash. That's it. Almost there. Fuck, you have no idea how good it feels when you squeeze my dick."

Ashlyn flew. She arched her back and let out a strangled scream as she came again. It was even more intense this time. Her internal walls clenched hard, still stuffed full with Slate's cock. Her muscles twitched and she couldn't do anything but lie in his arms and tremble.

When the extreme pleasure passed, Ashlyn saw the satisfied smile on Slate's face before he pulled out, making them both grunt in displeasure. He manhandled her up the mattress so her head was lying on the pillow. He covered her with the sheet and gently ran his hand over her sweaty forehead.

"Feel good?" he asked.

"Fishing for compliments?" she teased.

"Nope. I know the answer, just wanted to hear you say it," he retorted.

Ashlyn chuckled. "Right, I'll give you this one. Yes, I feel good. Fucking fantastic, in fact."

"Good. I need to get rid of this condom."

Ashlyn nodded, but her eyes closed. She was exhausted. Probably because she hadn't had an orgasm that intense in years. Maybe ever. And Slate had just given her two. She vaguely felt him leaving the bed and then heard water running in her small bathroom.

It wasn't until she felt the bed shifting once more that she opened her eyes. Slate was sitting next to her, fully dressed.

She supposed some women would take offense to the man

they'd just had sex with leaving so soon afterward, but she and Slate were only casually dating. And she was kind of relieved he was heading home. She liked her space and didn't want to deal with an awkward morning after. "You going?" she asked sleepily.

"Yeah."

"Okay."

He stared at her for a moment, then nodded. "This is gonna work."

Ashlyn couldn't help but roll her eyes once more. She felt as if she'd rolled them more tonight than she had in a decade. But Slate just seemed to bring it out in her. "Yeah, it is," she agreed.

"I'll last longer next time," he told her.

"You've said that already. Do you hear me complaining?" she asked.

"Nope. But it's a pride thing," he said with a shrug.

"Whatever," Ashlyn said.

"You need to get up and lock the door behind me."

"Just lock the knob when you go," she told him.

"No. You need to get up and put the deadbolt and chain on."

"Slate, I'm comfortable. And warm. And you just gave me two orgasms. I'm not moving from this bed."

He stood up, and Ashlyn closed her eyes and snuggled down into her covers. But a second later she screeched as Slate picked her up, blankets and all.

"Slate!" she protested, even as she threw her arm around his neck to hold on.

He didn't respond, just carried her through her apartment toward the front door. He put her down on her feet, and Ashlyn grabbed the blanket to keep it from falling and leaving her butt-ass naked in her foyer. Yes, she and Slate had just fucked, but now that he was dressed and leaving, she wasn't all that psyched about being naked in front of him.

"Lock the door behind me," he ordered.

"*God*, you're annoying," Ashlyn complained.

"Anyone could kick in the door with just the knob locked," he said without raising his voice. "I'm sure Senior Chief Petty Officer Albertson taught you that."

Ashlyn couldn't help but chuckle. She and her friends had been going to self-defense lessons with Elizabeth, but the guys couldn't call her that. They always used her full name and rank out of respect.

"Fine," she grumbled, knowing Slate was right, but still not liking that she was no longer in bed, enjoying her post-orgasm high.

"You want to do something next weekend?" Slate asked.

Ashlyn nodded. "Sure. I don't think the girls have anything planned."

"You need anything this week, don't hesitate to let me know," Slate ordered.

"I will."

Then he surprised her by palming the back of her neck and pulling her close. Ashlyn stumbled a bit, trying to keep hold of the blanket while bracing herself against his chest with the other hand.

His gaze was intense as he looked at her. "I'll follow your lead as to what you want to tell the others about us."

"What do you mean?"

"You know as well as I do the second Elodie and the others hear that we're dating, they're gonna get ideas. Hell, even my team will. So if you want to keep this on the down low for a while, I'm all right with that."

Ashlyn swallowed hard. "You want to keep us a secret?"

"No."

She blinked at his immediate answer.

He went on. "I don't give a shit if the others know we're goin' out. Our relationship is none of their business regardless. But the last thing I want is you being stressed out if you get the third degree from the women. *We* know that we're just having a good time, but I don't want you being anxious if they give you grief about our choices."

Ashlyn relaxed. "I can handle them. Can you handle the guys?"

"Yes."

She shrugged. "Then I'm okay with telling them. Besides…I might want some sex advice. Will it bother you if I talk to them about us?"

Slate grinned. "First, you don't need any sex advice, babe. With how hot you blazed for me, *I'm* probably gonna need tips on keeping *you* satisfied."

Ashlyn knew she was blushing, but he continued before embarrassment could take over.

"Second, I don't care if you talk to your girls about what we do in the bedroom, but you also shouldn't feel awkward about discussing anything regarding our relationship or sex with *me*."

"Okay," Ashlyn told him. "Slate?"

"Right here, babe."

"I…when we decide that we're done…I don't want anything to hurt our friendship. Or make things awkward for the others."

"When this runs its course, we'll be good," Slate said. "I give you my word."

Ashlyn knew it wasn't that easy, but she was still feeling too damn blissed out after her orgasms to worry about the future of their relationship right this moment. "Okay."

"Okay. You might want to take a bath tonight," Slate said.

"What?"

"A bath," he repeated. "You were really tight. And I wasn't

exactly gentle. A bath might ease some of the soreness you could feel tomorrow. Especially since I have a feeling it'll take a while before I'm ever able to go easy on you."

"Right," Ashlyn said. Now that he mentioned it, she was a bit sore between her legs. And a bath sounded heavenly.

"I'll pick up some more condoms too. We can keep some here and at my place."

"I can get them," Ashlyn offered.

He looked amused. "You know what size I am?"

"Um...triple extra-large?" she guessed.

Slate burst out laughing. When he had himself under control, he promised, "I'll pick up the condoms."

"Fine."

"Friday night. I'm pickin' you up. We'll go out to eat, then back to my place," Slate told her.

Ashlyn wanted to protest his bossiness, but she was just as eager to repeat what had happened earlier in her bed as it seemed he was.

"Why don't I meet you at your place? That way you won't have to take me home afterward."

He stared at her for a long moment, then nodded. Leaning down, he kissed her forehead and let go of her neck. "Lock up after me," he said again, then turned and, without another word, walked out of her apartment.

Ashlyn did as he ordered and put both the chain and the deadbolt on. Then she wandered back to her bedroom and headed straight for the bathroom. She started the water in the bath and stared at herself in the mirror as it filled.

She didn't look any different on the outside, but she *felt* different.

This relationship with Slate was the start of a new Ashlyn. No more was she going to allow herself to fall headfirst into love blindly, like she had with Franklin. The craziest thing she'd ever done was move to Hawaii with a man she'd just met, but she'd actually thought he was "the one." He was that charming at the beginning.

Now, it was liberating to be in a relationship with no expectations on either person's part.

There were too many things about Slate that irritated the hell out of her to ever fall in love with him easily. He was impatient, bossy, and controlling; too macho, too into his job, and definitely on the surly side. Yes, he could be funny at times, and his bossiness and protectiveness were a result of what he did for a living, but still. Combined, it was all too much.

But she could put up with those flaws for a physical relationship because he was damn good in bed. And he was easy on the eyes too.

In a few months, when they tired of each other, they'd go back to being friends. Buddies who saw each other when the rest of their group got together. Not feeling the pressure to find someone to spend the rest of her life with was practically cathartic.

Ashlyn smiled as she stepped into her bath, pleased by the unexpected turn of her evening.

CHAPTER TWO

"Anyone up for another fishing trip this weekend?" Aleck asked after PT a few days later.

"When were you thinking?" Jag asked.

"Saturday."

"Sure," Midas said.

"I'm in," Mustang agreed.

"Can't," Slate said.

Everyone turned to him with identical expressions of disbelief.

"Why not?" Aleck asked. "You're *always* free."

He shrugged. "Goin' out with Ashlyn on Friday, and I'm thinking I'm not going to be able to get up early on Saturday to go with you guys."

Now his five teammates' mouths were all hanging open.

"Wait, what? You and Ashlyn?" Pid asked "When did that happen?"

"Took her home from the barbeque last weekend. Asked her out. She said yes," Slate said evenly.

"Wait, wait, wait. You and Ashlyn are *dating*?" Midas asked. "Do you guys even like each other?"

"Of course we like each other," Slate said.

"Could'a fooled me. You're always at each other's throats," Mustang said. "The other day, when Ash was leaving to deliver some meals, you once again growled at her and mumbled something about her job not being safe. She lost her shit and tore you a new asshole, then stomped out."

"Yup," Slate said. He couldn't help but grin at remembering the look of irritation on Ashlyn's face. He knew he was being an ass by constantly harping on the fact that he wasn't happy she was gallivanting around the island, delivering food to people's houses. But he couldn't stop thinking about all the things that could happen to her...including if someone decided they wanted more than just the meals she delivered.

"What gives?" Jag asked.

"We're dating casually," Slate told his friends. "We aren't gonna get married. We aren't having kids. We aren't moving in together. Unlike you guys, we're just interested in some fun."

"So you're using her for sex?" Mustang asked.

Slate didn't take offense. His team leader's question wasn't said in a disrespectful tone, he genuinely sounded curious. Besides...how could he be offended when that was essentially what he and Ashlyn were doing? "Believe it or not, I enjoy spending time with her. And shocker, she seems to like hanging out with me too. Yes, there's sex involved...you all have eyes; you know how pretty she is. Why *wouldn't* I want to go there? But it's a mutual thing. We agreed we weren't looking for anything serious. That we'd be friends with benefits."

"Slippery slope, man," Midas warned.

"We're good. When the chemistry wears off, we'll go back to being friends. It'll be fine," Slate said.

"Famous last words," Aleck drawled.

"No, seriously, we're just hanging out. Believe it or not,

two people *can* have a relationship that doesn't go from zero to four hundred and sixty-seven in a week," Slate told his teammates. "We aren't going into this blindly. We both know the score."

"But things could get weird if it doesn't end well," Pid warned.

Slate started to get irritated. "They aren't going to get weird. We talked about it."

The other guys chuckled.

"Right, you talked about it, so that's that, huh?" Midas asked.

"Yes," Slate said. "And I think I'm done with this conversation. I know you guys don't believe me, but we're both cool being casual. We're not keeping it a secret, and if Ashlyn hasn't already told your women, I'm sure she will soon. Nothing changes with the group dynamics."

"Except you aren't free to go fishing on Saturday," Aleck said dryly.

Slate rolled his eyes at his friend.

Mustang clapped Slate on the shoulder. "Well, I hope it works out the way you both want it to," he said. "Ashlyn is great. Elodie loves her, and the others are all just as close to her. For the record, I think you guys make a great couple. You're serious and she's more laid-back. It works."

Slate nodded. "Yeah, it does."

"Fine. We can put fishing off until another weekend," Aleck said.

"I probably wouldn't have been able to go anyway," Jag told them. "Carly and I are working on wedding plans."

"How's that coming along?" Midas asked.

"Good. We're trying to nail down a date that will work to rent out Duke's. It's not as easy as you'd think to take over a restaurant. Especially one as popular as Duke's," Jag said with a small shake of his head.

Talk turned to Jag and Carly's upcoming wedding, and Slate couldn't help but let his mind wander. There was a time not so long ago when none of the guys on the team would be caught dead talking about wedding shit, but now that the others were all madly in love, things had changed.

His thoughts turned to Ashlyn, as they had frequently over the last few days. He'd never been so preoccupied with a woman. Honestly, she'd shocked the shit out of him when she'd suggested a friends-with-benefits relationship, but he was all over that. He definitely wasn't ready to settle down like his teammates. He was only thirty-three. He had plenty of time to get married and start a family after he was out of the Navy.

Still, he was impressed that his friends were making it work, because being in a long-term relationship when you were a SEAL was hard as hell. He'd seen it firsthand with other SEALs and Navy sailors. Spouses who couldn't handle being by themselves on long, or even short, deployments. Who cheated the second their spouses left for another six-month tour.

Slate didn't want that for himself. He wanted to find a woman he could trust implicitly not to cheat on him, but until he was out of the Navy, he didn't see a relationship happening.

So a casual thing with Ashlyn worked out just fine. They hadn't talked about being exclusive, but he was fairly sure she wasn't interested in anyone else right now. And he wasn't either. They could cross that bridge when they came to it.

"How's Monica doing with the pregnancy?" Jag asked Pid.

Slate turned his attention back to the conversation.

"She's good. She's got the weirdest cravings right now, but from everything we've read, that's normal," Pid said. "Six more months to go, and I can't fucking wait."

"Elodie's already bought what seems like a hundred

_ your kid," Mustang said. Pid and Monica had
_ut recently they were having a girl, and both were
.-the-moon excited.

"And Kenna's picked up a bunch of jeans and T-shirts,
saying that girls shouldn't always be forced to wear frilly shit
all the time," Aleck added.

Everyone laughed.

"She's gonna be so damn spoiled," Pid said.

"Right, like you aren't going to be the king of spoiling
her," Jag said with a shake of his head.

"True," he agreed.

"You guys think of a name yet?" Midas asked.

"We're still discussing it," Pid said.

"Which means they're fighting about it and, in the end,
Monica will name her whatever she wants," Mustang
surmised with a chuckle.

"Honestly, her name doesn't matter to me. I already love
her so much it's almost scary," Pid said.

Slate listened as his friends bantered back and forth. He
was happy for Pid, and for the rest of his teammates, but he
was definitely glad he didn't have to worry about things like
baby names and wedding plans.

Yet again, his thoughts returned to last weekend. To the
fun he'd had with Ashlyn. The woman who burned so hot, so
quickly. She was ready for him in a heartbeat. He was looking
forward to seeing her on Friday night and exploring their
chemistry some more.

"All right, enough chitchat," Mustang said, cutting
through Slate's musings. "I'll see you guys at nine sharp. We're
going over the intel about the nuke North Korea said they'd
tested. Things are getting tense over there, especially with
China announcing their support of North Korea's nuclear
program."

"You think we'll be sent over?" Jag asked.

"Not sure. It's a possibility. Right now, we just have to wait and see. You guys know as well as I do that we could be researching North Korea one day and the next, we're on a plane headed to Bulgaria."

Slate nodded. That was true. It was one of the things he liked best about being a SEAL. The excitement and having to stay on his toes at all times.

The group said their goodbyes and headed to their vehicles. Slate got into his Trailblazer and drove toward his small house near the beach. It wasn't right *on* the beach, there was no way he could afford something like that, but close enough. When he'd moved into the place, it needed a lot of work, and the owner cut him a huge break on the rent when he agreed to fix what needed updating in his spare time.

Now the house was as good as it was going to get for a rental. There were still improvements Slate could make, but he wasn't going to put any more energy and work into a place that didn't belong to him. When he got out of the Navy, he'd buy a place of his own and put as much blood, sweat, and tears into it as necessary until it was his dream home.

He got home, showered, changed into his uniform and, after glancing at his watch, saw he had some time to kill before he needed to head out to the base. On a whim, he picked up his phone and clicked on Ashlyn's name. It was early, but she was a morning person and would likely be up.

"Good morning," she said as she answered the phone.

"Hey," Slate said. "I thought I'd call and see how you were this morning."

"I'm good. Is anything wrong?"

"Does something have to be wrong for me to call?" Slate asked.

"Well, no, but since it's not something you've done this early in the morning before, I thought I'd check."

"We weren't dating before. Now we are," Slate said simply.

Ashlyn let out a small laugh, and Slate couldn't help but smile hearing it. No matter what his mood, after he talked to her—even when they argued—he always felt better.

"True," she said. "How was PT?"

The question wasn't unexpected; they'd known each other long enough for her to understand his schedule. She knew he got up early most days to work out with his team, and she knew the time he usually got home each day. She also knew about his tendency to be impatient and stubborn, that he drove a bit too fast, and that he loved Hawaiian food.

In turn, he knew that she had a passion for her job, a tendency to trust people a little too much, that she didn't care much for most Hawaiian food, and that when she was upset, she got quiet and introspective, rather than crying or ranting and raving.

There was definitely a plus side to being friends with a woman before dating. And Slate could honestly say he'd liked Ashlyn as a person from the moment they met. He didn't always like some of the decisions she made, as he felt she was taking needless risks with her safety, but he'd still enjoyed their friendship over the last year.

"Slate?" she asked. "You there?"

"Sorry. I'm here," he said, jolted out of his introspection. "PT was good. Mustang went kind of easy on us today and only made us swim three miles before running a 5K in the sand."

"Jeez, you're such a slacker."

Slate could picture her rolling her eyes, and it made him smile again.

"I thought I was doing good getting my twenty-minute intermediate step workout finished before snarfing down the cinnamon rolls I made in my air fryer."

Slate chuckled. "You need to eat more vegetables."

"Yeah, yeah, yeah," she bitched. "Let me guess, you're having a protein shake for breakfast."

"Nope." He paused a moment, then said, "A protein bar."

Ashlyn burst out laughing, and Slate closed his eyes. He could hear her laugh every day for the rest of his life and it wouldn't be enough.

An instant niggling of worry hit him at that thought. This might be a friends-with-benefits kind of arrangement, and neither of them planned on anything more...but less than a week in and he knew he felt more for this woman than simple lust. Probably always had. He wasn't in love. But he cared about Ashlyn.

Her next question pushed those thoughts to the back of his mind.

"Right, of course. I should've known. Got anything interesting planned for today?"

"Nope," Slate said. "Just meetings. You?"

"Not really. I'm meeting a new client though."

"Be careful," Slate said, the words coming out without him even thinking first.

"Slate," Ashlyn warned.

"I know, I know. You've told me time and time again that you're a grown-ass woman. That people deliver packages and food and even groceries every damn day without any issues. But I'm not dating them, I'm dating *you*. And I know you—you aren't just dropping off the meals at people's doors, ringing the bell and leaving. You're going into people's houses. You're staying to chat. The thought of anyone getting their hands on you makes me kind of crazy. So wanting you to be careful isn't me just being an asshole. It's me knowing first-hand how much evil there is in the world, and not wanting that evil to touch one hair on your beautiful head."

Slate took a deep breath after his tirade. Ashlyn hated when he gave her shit about what she did for Food For All.

Yes, there were more dangerous jobs she could have, but he definitely didn't like her going into strangers' houses.

"Okay," she said after a brief silence.

"Okay?" he asked, confused by her simple response. Ashlyn fought him on *everything*.

"Yes. I'm well aware that you aren't thrilled with what I do. And believe it or not, I *am* careful. Lexie always knows my route and who I'm going to be visiting. I always have my phone with me, and she has a tracker app so she can look me up and see where I am at all times. When I go to a new client's home, I text her when I arrive and when I leave. All things considered, I'm as careful as I can be, Slate."

He hadn't realized she and Lexie had such a logical system, but he should have. It made him feel a little better. "What app?" he asked.

Surprisingly, Ashlyn laughed. "That's what you got out of all that?"

"What I got is that you're doing what you can to mitigate any danger you might be in, which I appreciate more than you know. I didn't know you had a tracker app, and I'm fucking thrilled you and Lexie have a system in place when you go out to meet a new client for Food For All. I also figure it wouldn't hurt for someone *else* to track you, just in case Lexie isn't around to have your back. And I wouldn't mind being that person. I won't abuse your trust if you give me access, Ash. But it would give me peace of mind."

She sighed. "Do I get to track you too?" she asked sarcastically.

"Yes." A few months ago, there would be no way in hell Slate would give that kind of access to anyone other than his teammates. But he'd gotten to know Ashlyn, and knew she *also* wouldn't abuse the privilege of knowing his location at all hours of the day and night. He had no problem with reciprocating with the tracking app.

"Wow, you didn't even hesitate," she said.

"Just because we aren't out shopping for engagement rings doesn't mean I don't respect you and want this relationship to be as real as it can be for the time we're together," Slate told her.

"True. Okay. I'll send you the deets on the app," Ashlyn said.

"Thank you. And there's something else you should know."

"Oh, shit, what?" she asked.

Slate chuckled. "Nothing bad. I just wanted to give you a head's up that I told the guys about us this morning."

"So I should expect the third degree from Lexie and Elodie at work this morning," she surmised.

"I don't know about that. I mean, we *do* know how to keep shit to ourselves," Slate said dryly. "You know, national security and all that."

As expected, Ashlyn laughed. Slate loved how easy it was to amuse her. And he much preferred her laughing than scowling at him. When they'd first met, they'd definitely rubbed each other the wrong way, and he could admit that he'd said shit on purpose fairly regularly just to rile her up. But he was finding it was much nicer to see her laughing than pissed off at him.

"Yeah, right. You guys are the worst when it comes to gossip," she said when she had herself under control.

Slate didn't disagree. The guys were very into each other's lives, no doubt. His teammates were quick to talk about their relationships and what was going on with everyone. He'd always kind of felt as if he was on the outside looking in during those conversations, so it felt surprisingly good that morning to tell them something they didn't already know. He just didn't want his friends getting the wrong idea about him and Ashlyn.

He obviously took too long to respond, because yet again, she said, "Slate?"

"Yeah, babe?"

"You aren't mad about the gossip comment, are you? I mean, I know you guys can keep secrets, obviously. I'm guessing there's a lot of shit swirling around in your head that you'd love to talk to someone about, but you can't."

"I'm not mad," Slate said in a gentle tone. "And the guys and I made a vow a long time ago that if shit got too deep, we'd talk to each other."

"Good."

"I just wanted to give you a head's up, just in case."

"I appreciate it. And just so you know, I haven't said anything to the girls yet because, well...they know how long I've liked you, and they're most *definitely* going to jump to the wrong conclusion. Especially with all the baby and wedding stuff happening recently."

"You've liked me a long time?" Slate asked, knowing he had a goofy smile on his face but not giving a damn.

"Maaaaybe," she drawled.

"So when you were calling me names and rolling your eyes at me for being overbearing and annoying, secretly you really wanted to jump my bones?"

"I wouldn't say that I liked you all that much every time you overstepped your boundaries and told me I was stupid for risking my life by delivering a few containers of food. But when you weren't busy being overbearing, I thought about what it would be like to have you in my bed."

Slate felt his dick twitch in his pants. "You ever masturbate to the thought of what I could do to you?"

"Yes," she said, without hesitation or shame. Her openness was one of the hundred reasons why he'd asked her out.

"What about you? You ever get off thinking about me?" she asked.

27

"Every fucking time," Slate practically growled.

"Well, shit," she said.

"What? What's wrong?"

"Now I'm gonna be late to work because I'm so turned on, I just might need to take care of myself before I leave."

"Shit, woman, you're killin' me," Slate groaned.

"Hey, I'm all for phone sex if you are."

"No."

"No?" she echoed, sounding surprised.

"We don't live even ten minutes apart. You get horny, just text or call and I'll come over. We aren't in a long-distance relationship, babe."

"You don't think phone sex is hot?" she asked.

"It can be," Slate said. "But it's also frustrating as hell. Especially now that I've been inside you and know how good you feel wrapped around my cock. I much prefer *you* to my hand."

"Wow, um...okay. Right."

She sounded flustered, and Slate loved that. "I know we made plans already for Friday night, but do you mind if I stop by tonight after work?" he asked.

"Not at all."

"Good. I'll text you to let you know when I'm on my way."

"You want me to make something for dinner?"

"Nope. I'll be hungry for something other than food." Slate knew he was coming on strong, but after the turn in their conversation, he couldn't help it. The thought of her lying in bed with a hand between her legs, getting herself off, was stuck in his head. If he thought Ashlyn touching herself while he was deep inside her was intense, the thought of her fantasizing about him while masturbating was just as hot.

"Right. Then I guess I'll see you later."

"Yup. Ash?"

"Yeah?"

"I like this."

"Like what?"

"Us. Saying what we think. Not being ashamed to admit that we want each other."

"Me too," she agreed.

"Good. Tell your girls about us. Text me the name of that tracker app. And be careful today."

"Bossy," she said with a snort.

"You knew what you were getting into when you agreed to go out with me."

"True again. Okay, Slate. Have a good day yourself. I hope the terrorists don't pick today to lose their shit, because I'm gonna be pissed if anything keeps you from coming over later."

"Nothing's gonna keep me from you," Slate told her. "You really gonna be late this morning?"

"Oh, yeah. Definitely."

"Shit," Slate said again with a shake of his head. He shouldn't have asked. He'd never get the vision out of his head of Ashlyn taking care of herself before leaving for work.

"Later," she said with a giggle.

"Later," Slate said.

He clicked off his phone and closed his eyes. It took a moment for him to get control of his body. But once he could walk without his hard-on trying to bust through his pants, he grabbed the protein bar he'd planned on eating for breakfast and headed for the door.

CHAPTER THREE

"Oh my God!" Elodie screeched later that morning.

Ashlyn winced, but couldn't keep the smile off her face.

"You're telling me that you slept with Slate four days ago and you waited until *now* to tell us?" Lexie asked.

Ashlyn nodded. "Yes. Because I knew you'd react this way, and it's just casual. Don't go getting all mushy and starry-eyed over the two of us," she warned her friends. "Just because you guys are disgustingly happy with your SEALs, doesn't mean that Slate and I are gonna end up the same way. We're dating. Having sex. That's it. People can just date without it being a serious thing, you know."

"Of course we know that," Elodie said. "But I still remember a while ago when you told us that you *liked* Slate."

"I do like him," Ashlyn insisted. "But just because I like someone doesn't mean that I'm secretly sabotaging his condoms so I get pregnant and he has to marry me. We're hanging out. Having fun. Hell, we already know each other really well from all the get-togethers we've been at with the team."

"There isn't a part of you that, deep down, wants more?" Lexie asked.

Ashlyn shrugged. "Let's put it this way, this past weekend, after he blew my mind and gave me two orgasms, then immediately got dressed to leave, I wasn't upset in the least. I like living by myself. I like sleeping in bed by myself. I know the score going into this, you guys. Slate's a good guy, but long term, he'd annoy the hell out of me. Just as I know I'd annoy him. We're too different in a lot of ways. We're hanging out and doing the dating thing, but I don't know how long it'll last. I'm just gonna enjoy the hell out of it while it does."

"So that's that?" Elodie asked. "You wouldn't even consider getting more serious?"

"I have no *idea* where things between us might go. But for now, we're both happy being laid-back and casual. There's no pressure. We both like sex, and sex with each other is pretty damn spectacular. Is Slate gonna one day get down on his knee and tell me he's fallen head over heels in love and can't live without me? I very highly doubt it. And I'm okay with that. Honestly."

"Well, I'm happy for you guys," Lexie said. "Slate's always seemed a little uptight, but if you're both content with dating casually, then good for you."

"Thanks," Ashlyn said, feeling more relieved than she'd expected to. She liked and respected these women, and she wanted them to be okay with the fact that she wasn't serious about a man they all admired.

It wasn't lost on her that Slate could get any woman he wanted. He was a hero, honorable, fucking gorgeous, and that protective streak could be damn appealing at times. So the fact that he wanted to go out with her was still somewhat surprising. She was going to go with it though, until their relationship ran its natural course.

And Ashlyn had no doubt that it *would* end. But she was determined to enjoy the hell out of being with him while it lasted.

"So...was it all you hoped it would be?" Lexie asked with a gleam in her eye.

"You did hear me say two orgasms, right?" Ashlyn asked with a smile.

Elodie and Lexie grinned.

"Only two? Seriously, you need to hold out for more," Elodie said.

Ashlyn burst out laughing. "Well, he called this morning to tell me that the cat was out of the bag, so to speak, and that he'd told the guys about us. And somehow by the end of the conversation, I'd admitted to touching myself while thinking about him, and he reciprocated by telling me he masturbated to thoughts of me. And now, instead of waiting until Friday to take me out to dinner, he's coming over tonight...and told me not to bother with dinner at all."

Elodie fanned herself with her hand.

Lexie smiled. "Right. Well, brace yourself, because it sounds like those two orgasms are gonna seem kinda lame after tonight."

"Is this weird?" Ashlyn said. "Talking about sex with Slate like this?"

Her friends answered at the same time.

"Nope."

"No way."

"Here's the thing," Elodie said. "Our guys? They're sexual. *Very* sexual. Maybe it has something to do with testosterone and having to be in complete control when they're on missions. I don't know. There's probably been studies on it, for God's sake. But why should we *not* talk about sex? Men do, freely and openly. It's only women who, even in this day and age, are still told they should be all prim and proper and not talk about sex. Which is stupid. Sex is amazing. It's totally natural. And sex with someone who loves and respects you and wants you to have as good a time as he is while in bed? That's outstanding."

"I never knew what true intimacy was until Midas," Lexie admitted. "Being with someone who wants you to get off even before he does is..." Her voice trailed off.

"Special," Ashlyn finished.

"Exactly."

"Don't ever settle for mediocre sex," Elodie said. "If Slate isn't giving you what you need to get off, help him understand what you *do* need."

"Neither of us could wait. I swear, all he has to do is look at me and I'm wet," Ashlyn admitted. "And he was inside me in like five seconds. But he insisted that I orgasm first. Then a second time while he was still inside me, even though he already came," Ashlyn said.

Lexie and Elodie smiled at her.

"Yup. You're good," Lexie said after a moment.

"I'm thinking you're not gonna need any advice. But we're here anyway if you need it," Elodie added.

"Thanks, guys," Ashlyn said. How she'd found such good friends, she had no idea.

"Seriously though, I'm happy for you. And you're right," Lexie said. "There's nothing wrong with having a good time with Slate. As long as you both know the score from the start, I think you guys dating each other is awesome."

"Me too," Elodie added. "Now, if we're done talking about sex—which is making me miss my husband even though I just saw him this morning—maybe we can pack these boxes so you can get on with delivering and I can start on tomorrow's meals."

"Ma'am, yes, ma'am!" Lexie teased.

Elodie balled up a napkin and threw it at her.

The next half hour was spent with the three women working together to package up the meals that Ashlyn would deliver. The new client on today's route was a single mom. Her husband had died in a construction accident. He hadn't had any insurance, and they'd moved to Hawaii specifically for the job, so she didn't have any family on the island. She was struggling to find a decent-paying job that would cover the rent for their small apartment, food, the payments on the medical bills that were coming in, as well as all the other expenses that popped up on a day-to-day basis.

Lexie had talked to her last week when the woman first called, desperate for food to feed her child. She'd been put into the rotation immediately, and today was the first day Ashlyn would stop by her place.

When she'd first started delivering meals, she had maybe ten stops. But as the months went by, and people became more familiar with Food For All's new service, the requests for deliveries had increased quickly. Now Ashlyn was bringing meals to at least thirty people every day. That was about all she had time for. She carefully planned her route so she wasn't backtracking and wasting time. She really couldn't keep increasing her workload, but it was so hard to say no to people who truly needed the assistance and couldn't make it down to one of Food For All's two locations.

As Slate had guessed, Ashlyn did have favorites on her route that she spent extra time with. The Turners were a young family; Brooklyn was only twenty-one and Trey was twenty-four. They'd moved to Oahu from Maui, hoping for more work opportunities. They had two children; Curtis was three and Briar was two. They were barely scraping by, but with the help from Food For All, they were managing.

James Mason was an eighty-eight-year-old man who relied

on his social security benefits and a small pension he received from the Navy. He'd served two tours in the Vietnam War and had been injured, ending his service, but not his love for his country. He was hilarious, and always had fascinating stories to tell. Ashlyn did her best to sit with him for as long as she could, not only because it was obvious he was lonely, but because she loved hearing him talk about being a boy during World War II and how much the world had changed since then.

Christi Dryden was in her late twenties and handicapped. She was living in an apartment with her sister. Their parents had died a few years ago, and Lori was doing all she could to keep Christi with her. Ashlyn respected the hell out of the woman for taking on the responsibility of caring for her sister. It wasn't easy, her medical needs were expensive, so the meals they got from Food For All really helped when it came to having money to pay for the aide who stayed with Christi during the day, while Lori worked.

Everyone Ashlyn delivered meals to was struggling. Some days it was depressing, doing what she did. Seeing the level of poverty people were living in. But for the most part, her clients were making the best of what they had and were grateful for any help they could get.

After she, Lexie, and Elodie got the food packed into her RAV4, Ashlyn took a moment to text Slate the name of the tracker app she used. She wasn't expecting a response, but before she'd even pulled out of the alley behind Food For All, her phone vibrated.

Slate: Got it downloaded. Add me, babe.

. . .

Shaking her head at his impatience, Ashlyn took a minute to send a request to his email, adding his number to her circle of friends on the app. As much as she bitched about his overprotectiveness, she couldn't deny it felt good. She had absolutely no qualms about delivering meals to her clients. They were all good people, from all walks of life and all ethnicities and ages. She'd never once felt as if she was in danger when she went into their homes.

But after all the shit that had gone down with her friends, she also appreciated having someone who cared about her well-being. Who would sound the alarm if something went wrong. Not that she expected anything untoward to happen.

Her phone pinged with a notification, and Ashlyn saw that Slate had indeed downloaded the tracking app and was now able to see her location. She unlocked her phone and pulled up the app, smiling when she saw the new icon on her map that said DS. Duncan Stone.

She could see that Slate was on the Naval base, and even what building he was in.

A goofy smile crossed her face. She clicked her phone off and put it in the drink holder next to her. She didn't need to look at a map to get to the first ten or so houses on her list. She'd been to all of them enough times to know the routes by heart.

* * *

By the time Ashlyn finished with her deliveries and got back to Food For All, she was tired, but also a little giddy about seeing Slate later. Her thoughts were filled with the fun they'd have this evening, so when she walked into the building, she wasn't expecting to be ambushed by Kenna, Monica, and Carly. Lexie was also there, trying to hide a smirk. Elodie was the only one missing.

"Giiiiirl!" Kenna said as soon as Ashlyn walked into the main room at the front of the building.

Ashlyn shook her head. "I guess you all heard?"

"Heard that you and the last man standing finally hooked up? Hell yes, we heard!" Kenna said enthusiastically.

"That's really great, Ash," Carly said a little more sedately.

"Happy for you," Monica added. Little by little, the most quiet woman among them was coming out of her shell. Monica would never be the kind of person to enjoy being the center of attention, but at least with their group of friends, she was opening up more.

"Thanks, guys. I'm pretty happy too," Ashlyn said.

"You looked pretty chummy at Monica and Pid's wedding out at Kualoa Ranch," Kenna said. "Are you sure you weren't already..." Her words trailed off as she bumped her fists together suggestively.

Ashlyn rolled her eyes. "Good Lord, what are you, twelve? And no, Slate and I weren't having sex back then. Honestly, even though he annoys me sometimes—"

"Sometimes?" Lexie interrupted.

"Right, fine, even though he annoys me a lot, he's also funny, and I like hanging out with him. Of course, it's not like we had much of a choice. As a group, we hang out all the time, and the rest of the guys are spoken for," Ashlyn said, winking at Carly, the last woman to fall for one of the SEALs. She and Jag hadn't gotten together until fairly recently, but everyone knew he'd had his eye on the pretty waitress for a long time. "It was kind of inevitable," she finished.

"I think it's great!" Kenna exclaimed. "Can you imagine if Slate brought someone into our inner circle who was a bitch?"

"You *did* hear that we're just dating casually though, right?" Ashlyn asked before everyone could get all excited about the possibility of another future wedding. They were neck deep in planning Carly and Jag's ceremony, which would take place at Duke's restaurant down in Waikiki, and she wouldn't put it past her friends to try to plan a double ceremony or something.

"What does that mean, exactly?" Carly asked.

"Just that we aren't in love with each other," Ashlyn said.

"Yet," Lexie muttered under her breath.

Ashlyn ignored her. "We just like hanging out. We're doing what millions of other couples do around the world... getting to know each other better, enjoying spending time together, and taking things one day at a time."

"So, you can see other men, and he can see other women?" Monica asked.

Ashlyn shrugged. "I guess."

"You guess? You haven't talked about it?" Kenna asked in bewilderment.

"Guys, it's been like two-point-three seconds since he asked me out for the first time," she insisted.

"Kenna's got a good point though. Knowing if you're exclusive or not is important," Monica said.

"Right? What if he fucks some random chick, then comes to your place for seconds?" Carly asked.

Ashlyn pressed her lips together in agitation. "Slate's not like that."

"I know," Carly said. "I was just trying to create a scenario."

"Would it bother you if he was dating someone else at the same time he was seeing you?" Monica asked.

Ashlyn tried not to get irritated at her friends. They were just looking out for her...but it was still kind of annoying. What part of "casual" didn't they understand?

"And what if you meet someone you like? I'm guessing he wouldn't he happy to know you were with someone else at the same time you were with him," Kenna added.

"Look, it's a moot point. I'm *not* seeing anyone else.

Neither is Slate. Jeez, neither of us has time to even meet people. Most weekends we're hanging out with you guys and his team. And it's not like guys were knocking down my door to ask me out before now, anyway. We'll figure that out if it becomes an issue," Ashlyn said.

"We're just trying to protect you," Lexie said softly.

"I know, and I appreciate it. But I'm good. Slate's good. I'm excited about this, about not having the pressure of wondering if he's 'the one' and if he wants to have kids and all that stuff. We're just being chill about things right now—and I need you guys to be that way too."

"We are."

"We will be."

"No problem."

Ashlyn was relieved at her friends' immediate support.

"When are you seeing him again?" Carly asked.

"Well, we had plans to go out to dinner on Friday, but when he called this morning, he asked if he could come over tonight."

"Oooooh," Kenna purred.

Ashlyn rolled her eyes. "And before anyone asks, yes, we've had sex. Yes, it was amazing. Yes, I had multiple orgasms. And yes, we'll do it again tonight. Anything else you want to know?"

Everyone burst into laughter.

"I think that about covers it," Kenna said, still chuckling.

"Can we change the subject and start talking about someone else now?" Ashlyn asked. "Carly, what's the latest with your ceremony?"

Thankfully, her friends were content to let her off the hook and started talking about Carly's wedding. They'd finally nailed down a date, two and a half months from now. It was a little sooner than Carly wanted, but since they were at the mercy of the schedule at Duke's and when they could rent out the entire restaurant for a few hours, they couldn't be picky.

Ashlyn had a feeling Jag probably thought two and a half months wasn't nearly soon enough, but she didn't say anything.

Lexie and Midas were the only ones not already married or actively planning a wedding. Neither was in a rush to tie the knot or have children, though Lexie admitted to Ashlyn recently that Midas had added her to his life insurance, so she'd be taken care of in case anything happened to him.

The thought of any of the guys being hurt struck fear in Ashlyn's heart. She'd gotten to know them all very well over the last year, and it would be devastating to everyone in their circle if someone was killed.

After half an hour or so, she discreetly looked at her watch. At least she'd *thought* she was subtle about it. Lexie came over and hooked her arm with Ashlyn's. "I can finish things up here. Go home."

"But—" Ashlyn started.

"Nope. I got it," Lexie told her firmly. "You want to get home and get ready for Slate. I can tell."

Ashlyn smiled. "I'm being silly."

"Nope. You're in a new relationship. It's not silly at all. Go." Lexie winked at her. "Don't do anything I wouldn't do."

"Which leaves me wide open to do whatever I want," Ashlyn retorted.

"Yup." Lexie hugged her. "Have fun."

"I will. Thanks." Ashlyn returned the hug then waved at the others. "See you guys later! I'm outta here."

"Bye."

"Say hi to Slate for us."

"Orgasms are your friend!"

The last came from Kenna, and Ashlyn couldn't help but laugh. She loved her friends. They were all so very different, but they all wanted the best for her and for each other. Ashlyn had a feeling they were still secretly hoping she and Slate would suddenly fall madly in love, but for now, and for the foreseeable future, she was happy to settle for lots of mind-blowing orgasms.

CHAPTER FOUR

Slate checked the app for what seemed like the four hundredth time that day. He'd set it up so he got notifications when Ashlyn moved after being in one place for more than fifteen minutes. He'd watched as she went through her rounds for the day, delivering food to all her clients.

It was kind of embarrassing how obsessed he was with making sure she got back to Food For All safely.

When Mustang called him out on his distraction during one of their meetings, Slate did his best to pay attention. When he'd gotten the notification that Ashlyn had arrived at her apartment, though, time seemed to slow to a crawl. All he could think about was everything he wanted to do to her once he got to her place.

Finally, Mustang wrapped up their last meeting and they were all free to head home. Without hanging around to chitchat with his teammates, Slate headed down the hall for the exit. It was almost ridiculous how badly he wanted to see Ashlyn. His cock stiffened in his pants, and Slate swore. He was acting like a horny teenager, not a mature man of thirty-three.

He drove too fast, as usual, on the way to her place. His stomach rumbled, but food was the last thing on his mind. He'd gone hungry plenty of times in the past—it wasn't always easy to stop to eat while on a mission—and he was used to going without when he was in the zone. And Slate definitely felt in the zone right now. He was focused on getting to Ashlyn and picking up where their phone call had left off that morning.

He parked and headed up the stairs to her floor in the apartment building without remembering much about the trip. Then he was there. Knocking on the door he'd gone out of a few days ago feeling more satisfied than he could remember being in a very long time.

The door opened almost immediately, and Slate's gaze devoured Ashlyn as he stepped inside. She had on a pair of leggings and an oversized long-sleeve shirt. He could tell at a glance that she wasn't wearing a bra; her nipples were already hard behind the pale pink cotton.

"Hi," she said as she shut the door behind him, turning the deadbolt.

The second the door was secure, Slate grabbed her shoulders and spun her around, putting her back against the wall.

She stared up at him with huge brown eyes, and he loved the way her breath hitched. Her long, shiny hair was down around her shoulders, brushing the tips of her tits. Her cheeks were flushed, and she immediately lifted her hands to his biceps.

"Hey," Slate belatedly returned her greeting. "Did you have a good day?" He forced himself to speak before falling on her like a panther in heat.

Her lips twitched. "Yeah. Got the third degree from the others, but they're cool."

Slate nodded. "No trouble with your deliveries?"

"Nope. Everyone behaved themselves. There wasn't an ax murderer in sight all day."

Slate shook his head in exasperation.

"Did you get the app working okay?" she asked.

"Yup." He wasn't about to mention how he'd been tracking her ass all day. Some people might think wanting to see his woman's every movement was creepy. But after everything that had happened to Carly, and Monica, and all the others, he didn't want to take any chances. He was sure that, as time passed, he'd get less obsessed with making sure Ashlyn was safe. Maybe.

"Are you hungry? I know you said not to bother with dinner, but I roasted some veggies earlier. I've got leftovers. I can heat up some noodles and throw them together, since I know you'd probably explode if you just had vegetables for dinner."

"Starved," Slate said.

She looked surprised. "Okay, step back and I'll go put the water on."

"Not for food. *You*," Slate clarified, running his hands down to her hips. He wasn't even speaking in full sentences, but he couldn't help it. The thought of getting his mouth between her legs was making him feel a little Neanderthal-ish.

The small, sexy smile that crossed Ashlyn's face made him feel a lot better about the slight obsession he was developing with her body.

Her hands tightened for a moment on his arms, then she slid sideways, grabbing his hand and heading for her bedroom.

Slate's eyes focused on her ass as they walked. She was curvy in all the right places. Her tits were large, but she wasn't top heavy because her sexy hips balanced everything out. They were perfect for grabbing. Her gorgeous lips were plump, and he couldn't wait see them wrapped around his cock. Her straight brunette locks were soft and silky, and he could just imagine how the thick mass would feel, tickling his chest as she rode him. Her soulful brown eyes always seemed to sparkle with some sort of emotion...humor, compassion... irritation at his high-handedness.

Yeah, there wasn't anything about Ashlyn that didn't turn him way the fuck on. He wasn't sure why it took him so damn long to ask her out, but he was thrilled he finally had.

She pulled him into her room. After dropping his hand, and without a word, she peeled her shirt up and over her head.

For a moment, Slate was struck dumb. All he could do was stand there and stare at her in awe. Women tended to overthink things when it came to their looks. Men were simple creatures at heart. They liked tits. Period. And Ashlyn's breasts were perfect.

Slate took a step forward and his hands reached out without conscious thought. He palmed her and ran his thumbs over both nipples, loving how they became even harder under his touch.

"So damn sensitive," he murmured.

In response, Ashlyn arched her back, encouraging him. As it had the other night, an overwhelming sense of urgency overcame Slate. He needed this woman. It felt as if he didn't get inside her in the next sixty seconds, he was gonna die.

Taking a deep breath and vowing not to repeat the way he'd come too damn fast last time, without truly appreciating Ashlyn, Slate forced himself to let go of her and take a step back.

"Everything off and get on the bed," he said in a raspy tone. "Legs spread."

Ashlyn didn't comment, merely smiled and leaned over to

push her leggings off. Her tits bounced with the action, and once again Slate had to force himself not to pounce on her.

He removed his own clothes in what seemed like record time. He took a second to throw a few condoms on the table next to her bed and stroke himself. His cock jerked at his touch, more than ready to burrow inside Ashlyn's hot, wet, tight body.

But not yet.

She got on the bed just as he'd ordered and spread her legs, knees bent and feet flat on the mattress. Slate didn't miss the way her cheeks turned pink as she exposed herself.

He crawled onto the bed, immediately settling between her legs. He leaned in and kissed her slightly rounded belly tenderly. Feeling guilty that he hadn't said much to her since he'd arrived—hell, he hadn't even kissed her—Slate looked up and asked, "You good?"

"I'll be better if you stop fucking around," she retorted.

Grinning, and relieved that she wanted to get to the good stuff just as fast as he did, Slate licked his lips. Then he scooted down a bit and lowered his head.

From the first taste of her slightly tangy musk, Slate was a goner.

He already couldn't get enough. The way she sighed, the way her hips tilted up toward him, encouraging him to continue, the way every muscle in her body tightened when he hit a spot she liked...He could spend all fucking night between her legs.

He teased her at first, licking her folds and barely paying attention to her clit. While he was sure what he was doing felt nice, he wasn't going for nice. He wanted to drive Ashlyn out of her mind with lust.

He put one hand on her belly to hold her still and inserted a finger deep inside her as he latched onto her clit and sucked. As he expected, she jerked under him.

"Slate!" she exclaimed.

Smiling, Slate didn't lift his mouth from her clit. He could feel her inner muscles tightening around his finger as she squirmed. He lashed the small bundle of nerves with his tongue, and when his finger began to slide more easily in and out of her slick channel, he knew she was getting close.

"Yes, right there! Oh my God, yes! Holy shit, Slate..."

Her words were breathy and he could hear the desperation in them, so he redoubled his efforts, sucking hard on her clit.

And just like that, she exploded. Her orgasm seemed even more intimate with his mouth on her and his finger inside her. She trembled uncontrollably and her thighs slapped against his shoulders when she tried to close her legs...and couldn't because he was between them.

"Too much, Slate...enough!" she breathed.

But it wasn't enough. Not nearly enough. Lifting his head, Slate used the hand that had been pressing on her belly to manipulate her clit.

Ashlyn shrieked and jerked violently. She made a strangled sound in the back of her throat as she once more flew over the edge. Forcing a woman to orgasm had never been his kink, but there was something so damn satisfying about seeing Ashlyn lost in pleasure at his hands. She was at his mercy—and he fucking loved it.

She was still trembling when he removed his finger from inside her still-spasming channel and greedily sucked it into his mouth. Fuck, she tasted so damn good. He rose to his knees and grabbed a condom off the table. He rolled it down his cock before glancing at Ashlyn's face.

The dazed look in her eyes made him smile. It was a great look on her. And *he'd* done that. "You ready?" he asked.

She was still nodding when he lined up his cock between her folds and pushed. He was thick, and the feel of her body yielding to him was enough to make his head explode. But just like the other night, the second he felt her tighten around him, Slate knew he was in trouble. There was no way he was going to last long enough to build her up to another orgasm. She felt too good. Was squeezing him too hard.

"Fuck, woman," he bit out, as he felt his balls draw up closer to his body in preparation.

She chuckled, and Slate felt the movement around his cock. He'd never fucked someone while laughing before, had no idea how incredible it could feel. "Maybe after I've had you a hundred times, I'll be able to last more than two fucking seconds," he grumbled, even as he pulled out and thrust back inside her body.

She didn't respond verbally, just lifted her hands and gripped his biceps, digging her fingernails into his skin as he began to fuck her hard and fast.

It didn't take long before the pleasure became too much for him to hold back. He pushed deep inside her and groaned, goose bumps breaking out on his arms as he came.

For a moment, shame filled him. Once again, he hadn't been able to last when he'd gotten inside her. He was a grown-ass man, not a fucking teenager.

But Ashlyn made a contented sound deep in her throat. "That was amazing," she whispered. "I've never gone off that fast before."

At least he wasn't alone. Slate lowered himself on top of her, not ready to pull out yet. He knew he needed to take care of the condom, but he couldn't make himself leave her. "Yeah?" he asked.

She smiled up at him. "Yeah."

"And once again, I came like that was my first time," he said in disgust.

"I'm gonna tell you a secret, big man," Ashlyn said. "When a guy can't hold back, it's kind of a compliment."

"Right," he said skeptically.

"I mean it. And I'll go even further and say for a lot of women, thrusting for ten, twenty, or however many minutes, isn't all that pleasurable. We get to a point where we just want you to get off and be done with it. For me personally, it's about clit stimulation."

Surprisingly, Slate felt his cock twitch at her words. He loved that she wasn't afraid to tell him what she liked. "Noted," he drawled.

"Am I ever gonna get to have my hands and mouth on you?" she asked.

His cock began to show even more signs of life. He wanted that. Ashlyn on her knees in front of him, or between his legs, giving him a blowjob, was one of his frequent fantasies.

Reaching down, he held on to the condom as he slipped out of her. Ashlyn wrinkled her nose adorably. Slate scooted over so he was sitting on the edge of the mattress, then twisted at the waist to hover over her, leaning on one hand. He kissed her long, deep and easy, kicking himself for not doing it earlier. Then he drew back and just stared.

"Slate?"

"You want my cock, Ash?"

She blushed, but nodded.

"As soon as I can control myself from jumping you the second I see you, you'll get your chance."

Predictably, she rolled her eyes. "So, like, never," she huffed.

Slate burst out laughing. He couldn't help it. She sounded so put out over the fact that he couldn't keep his hands off her. "I'll be back," he said as he stood to take care of the condom.

"Um...now are you hungry? My offer to whip you up some noodles with veggies still stands."

Slate considered it for a moment before nodding. "Yeah, I'd like that."

She beamed. "Great."

He couldn't stop himself from leaning over the bed once more and kissing her forehead before heading for the bathroom, scooping up his uniform on the way, which he'd left in a heap on the floor.

Twenty minutes later, he was sitting at her small table off the kitchen eating a simple meal of penne noodles and some really fucking good vegetables. Whatever she'd seasoned them with when she roasted them was awesome. They had a little bit of heat, and the garlic might've been overpowering but the noodles balanced everything out.

"Good?" Ashlyn asked.

"Delicious," Slate told her. "So, your visits today went well?" he asked.

Ashlyn's face lit up. "Yeah. There's this one family who's working so hard to give their kids everything they need, but they're young. I can't imagine having two kids under four and only being twenty-one years old. But Brooklyn is a really good mom, from what I can see. And Curtis and Briar are so damn adorable. Some people would think what I do is depressing... seeing people struggling all the time. But I don't usually see it that way."

Of course, she wouldn't. Ashlyn was definitely a glass-half-full kind of person, another one of the reasons why Slate was attracted to her.

"Yes, the people I see every day are struggling, but aren't we all? Struggle isn't always about money. It's about feeling worthy, about wanting to be loved, about having a chronic illness. There are a million different ways people struggle, and if I can take away just one of those by bringing healthy, free meals to their door, then I feel as if I'd made a difference in their lives, even if it's a small one."

Slate nodded. "I've seen people so poor they literally have only the clothes on their backs, are sleeping in the dirt, and the only roof over their heads is a couple of boards they scavenged from a junk pile. But they're quick to offer a space under a threadbare blanket for someone who needs it more than they do. They'll give away their last piece of bread to someone hungrier, and they'll greet strangers with a smile. So yeah, I totally understand what you mean. Being poor doesn't make someone a bad person, just as being rich doesn't make someone a good person."

"Exactly."

Slate couldn't take his eyes off the woman sitting across from him. For a long time, Ashlyn had been merely a friend of his teammates' women. The pain in the ass who loved to snipe at him. After spending more time with her, he was surprised the first time he realized bickering and sarcasm were actually signs that she was comfortable with someone. He witnessed the same dry wit and verbal sparring when she was hanging with her friends.

It was around the same time as that revelation when he realized he was physically attracted to her, as well. Now, sitting across from her, eating a meal Ashlyn had gone out of her way to prepare for him, he could admit they were more compatible than he'd first thought.

Slate also never cared about money. Yes, he was glad he had enough to rent his house, to eat, and to buy the few material things he wanted, but he never aspired to have the kind of wealth Aleck had, for instance. Like Ashlyn, he was just as keen to make a difference in people's lives where he could. And hearing her talk about her clients with such respect made him even more grateful he'd finally gotten up the nerve to ask her out.

Between the way she lit up for him between the sheets and the fact that they could actually have an intelligent conversation, Slate was certain dating Ashlyn would be awesome for however long it lasted.

Just as he finished putting the last forkful of pasta in his mouth, his phone rang.

"Sorry," he told Ashlyn, reaching for it.

"It's fine," she said breezily as she stood and reached for his plate.

"Slate," he answered, noting it was Mustang.

"Hey. You got time to talk? I was thinking about the North Korean situation, and I had some thoughts that I wanted to run them by someone."

"Yeah, can you give me ten minutes or so?" Slate asked.

"Of course. It's not a big deal. I'll wait till tomorrow if you're busy."

"It's fine. I'm happy to be your sounding board."

"Great. Call me back when you can."

"Will do. Later," Slate said.

"Later."

As soon as he clicked off the connection, Ashlyn said, "You need to go."

Slate nodded, standing and joining her in the small kitchen. "Mustang has some things he wants to talk to me about. Work stuff."

"I get it. No problem."

Slate studied Ashlyn's expression carefully for signs that she was annoyed or pissed that he was leaving so soon after eating. He found none. "I appreciate the dinner."

"Of course. It's the least I can do. You're feeding me on Friday night, yeah?"

"Yes," Slate said.

"Can I ask where you're taking me?"

"No."

Ashlyn pouted. "But it's not Hawaiian, right?"

CHAPTER FIVE

Ashlyn couldn't remember when she'd had a better week. Her sex life was suddenly amazing. All her clients were doing well at the moment. Even her relationships with Elodie, Lexie, and the others seemed to somehow be better just because she was dating Slate. She was happy. Very happy.

And tonight he was taking her out to dinner. She'd proposed the friends-with-benefits arrangement because she'd had the hots for him for what seemed like forever, but she hadn't thought they would click as well as they had. She figured they'd continue hanging out with their friends in a big group like they always had, throw in sex maybe every once in a while, and that would be that.

But she was finding that Slate had more depth than she'd given him credit for. She felt kind of bad about that. He was more than the cocky, good-looking Navy SEAL that she'd labeled him.

Yes, there were things about him that rubbed her the wrong way, but she was discovering she could overlook those things when his good traits were so much more important. He was still impatient and bossy and overprotective, and somewhat gruff. But he was also considerate, appreciative of the little things—like when she made him dinner—and he could turn his more irritating quirks into positives in bed.

Of course, good sex wasn't the only key to a successful relationship, but it sure went a long way toward making it better.

Ashlyn pulled up to Slate's small beach house and smiled. She loved his place. It wasn't fancy; from the outside it looked pretty rough, in fact. But she'd been inside a time or two, and he'd done a great job of making it homey and comfortable.

She parallel parked on the street in front of his house and made her way up to the door. It opened before she could even knock.

She'd spent way too long trying to decide what to wear on their date. Slate had seen her in everything from jeans to shorts to bathing suits, but since this was their first official date, she wanted to look nice. She'd decided on a flowy skirt that ended just past her knees, a V-neck light blue blouse, and a pair of strappy sandals that she thought accentuated her calves.

It had only been a couple days since Ashlyn had last seen him, but when he opened his door, he looked even better than she remembered. Instead of his uniform, he wore a pair of jeans and a navy-blue collared shirt. His black hair framed his square jaw perfectly. He had a slight hint of five o'clock shadow, and Ashlyn couldn't wait to feel the scratchy skin against her sensitive thighs once again.

Blushing at how her thoughts immediately turned to sex, she smiled up at him. "Hi. I hope I'm not late."

"Only a few minutes," Slate said in the deep rumbly voice she knew so well. "Come in."

Ashlyn was well aware that Slate hated when people were late. It seemed to be ingrained in his DNA to be on time or early. But she didn't hear even one iota of irritation in his voice. It was somewhat surprising, but she wasn't going to look that gift horse in the mouth.

His hand was warm on her lower back as she walked into his living room, and it was all Ashlyn could do not to spin around and jump the man. God, she'd turned into a sex fiend after just two times together. It was almost embarrassing. But when she caught a glimpse of the bulge in Slate's jeans, she didn't feel so guilty.

"I made reservations for seven-thirty, so we've got a bit of time before we have to leave. You want to sit on the roof deck for a bit?"

"Yes." Ashlyn didn't even have to think about her answer. His roof deck was the best part of the place. He'd built it himself, after getting approval from the owner. The house was a block back from the beach, but when sitting on the roof, it almost seemed as if they were right on the sand. The last time she'd been at his place with a few of their friends, the sun was setting and it had been one of the most beautiful things she'd ever seen.

Then, something else he said sank in. "Wait, seven-thirty? I thought you said reservations were for seven."

"I lied," he said without remorse. "I knew you wouldn't be able to get here on time, so I gave us a cushion."

Ashlyn frowned and put her hands on her hips. "I think I'm offended," she told him.

"No, you aren't," he retorted, wrapping an arm around her waist and yanking her close.

She landed against him with a small *oof*. When he leaned down and took her lips with his, she forgot about being irritated. In fact, she forgot about everything.

They'd kissed before, but this one seemed more leisurely. He took his time, teasing with small nips and licks before enticing her to open for him.

By the time they pulled apart, Ashlyn didn't even remember what they'd been talking about. But he quickly reminded her.

"I hate being late, so I figured I'd give us some breathing room, just in case."

Ashlyn couldn't muster up the energy to be pissed. He'd mellowed her with a single kiss. He'd already figured her out… and that didn't bode well for her in the future.

"Whatever," she huffed.

Slate grinned. "Come on, I brought glasses and wine up right before you arrived."

Okay, that was sweet. And he couldn't have thought she'd be too late if he'd already brought the wine up to the deck.

She walked up the stairwell with Slate at her heels. Under ordinary circumstances, she would've been a bit worried walking up the stairs, but she knew without a doubt that Slate wouldn't let her fall. The only other time she'd gone up to the deck she'd been a nervous wreck because the steps were both small and steep, but she didn't have Slate at her back that time.

She opened the door at the top of the stairs and sighed in contentment as she walked into the warm evening air. Slate had built a small alcove of sorts, with a roof in case it was raining and he wanted to sit up there, but for the most part it was a simple design. A flat surface of thick boards with a couple of chairs and a small table. There was a short railing around the deck, maybe four feet high at most, making the area feel safe but not hemmed in at all. In the distance, over the rooftops of the houses on the other side of the street, was the ocean. If she listened carefully, Ashlyn could hear the waves breaking on the shore.

"I love it up here," she said on a sigh.

"I know."

She turned to look at Slate. "You do?"

"Yup. I watched you when you were up here last time, and it was obvious how much pleasure you got from the view."

It somewhat surprised Ashlyn that he'd taken notice, since that had been at least three months ago, but it warmed her heart knowing that he'd paid attention to her even back then.

"Here, sit. I'll get you a glass of wine," Slate said, gesturing to one of the extremely comfortable Adirondack chairs she would have considered snatching the last time she was there if she could figure out how to get it off the roof and into her car without Slate noticing.

Ashlyn never drank anything if she knew she'd be driving —ever—but she didn't want to make a big deal out of her quirks. She sat down and immediately sighed in contentment as she stared into the distance at the rolling waves.

Slate handed her the glass of white wine, and she took a tiny sip as he settled into the chair next to hers. He'd poured himself a glass as well.

"You like wine?" she asked, not able to remember seeing him drink any before.

He shrugged. "Yeah. Why?"

"I don't know, it just seems...not you."

"It wouldn't be my first choice of a relaxing drink, but I know you like it, and sharing a glass while sitting on my deck with a beautiful woman seemed appropriate."

She smiled. God, that was such a nice thing to say.

"I could go downstairs and get a can of beer, guzzle it, then crush the can on my forehead if that would make you feel more comfortable," Slate said with a grin.

Ashlyn burst out laughing. "No, this is perfect. Thanks." And it was. Seeing the delicate glass in his large calloused hand was somehow sexy. She knew firsthand how gentle those hands could be, and how good they felt on her skin.

"How private is this deck?" she asked, looking around,

trying to figure out if people could see them from the windows in the surrounding houses.

Slate snorted. "Not private enough."

"Damn," Ashlyn said under her breath.

Slate didn't say anything, just took another sip of his wine and stared at her over the edge of the glass. His gaze was intense, and Ashlyn had a feeling all she had to do was give him the smallest sign and dinner would be forgotten.

But as much as she loved sex with Slate, she'd been looking forward to going out with him all week. Every time previously, they'd hung out with the whole group or at least a few other people. She wanted to get to know him more, one-on-one.

Breaking his gaze, she turned and stared off into the distance. "If I had this kind of deck, I'd live up here," she said after a moment.

"I come up here all the time," Slate admitted. "Especially after a tough mission. Watching the stars, hearing the ocean... it helps recenter me."

Ashlyn nodded. She could understand that. One of her favorite places was the balcony in Kenna and Aleck's condo. Her friends' place was beautiful and more expensive than she'd ever be able to afford, but that view overlooking the ocean was worth every penny the place cost.

They sat in companionable silence for a while, Slate sipping his wine, before he eventually looked at his watch and asked, "You ready to go?"

"What if I say I'm not? And I want to sit here for the rest of the night?" she asked.

"Then we'll sit here for the rest of the night. I'll call and order something to be delivered. You can sit your ass right here for as long as you want."

"That's a good answer. But I want to go out. I'm dying to know where you're bringing me tonight."

"Admit it, you don't trust me," Slate said.

Ashlyn frowned in surprise. "I trust you," she told him. "I do," she insisted when he raised a brow. "I mean, if I can't trust you, who the hell *can* I trust?"

"I'll always have your best interests in mind when I do something," Slate assured. He didn't give her time to question that declaration. He sounded much more serious than the conversation warranted. He stood and held out his hand. "Come on, let me feed you."

Ashlyn stood up and grabbed her glass.

"Leave it. I'll come up later and grab everything. I don't want you going down those stairs without having both hands free to hold on to the railing."

Since Ashlyn wasn't all that pumped about trying to hold a glass of wine while negotiating the stairs, she nodded.

"I'll go first," Slate said as he opened the stairway door.

"So you can break my fall?" she teased.

"Yes." His answer was immediate and sincere. "Put your hand on my shoulder if you need to," he continued as he waited for her to approach.

Ashlyn swallowed hard. Man, he was making it hard to remember any of his faults by being so sweet. They made it down the stairs without her making a fool out of herself by tripping, and she grabbed her purse as they headed for the front door.

Slate held open the passenger door to his Trailblazer, and Ashlyn couldn't help but marvel at how polite and solicitous he was being. She was more used to his quips and gruff orders than the side of him she was seeing tonight. But she didn't hate it. Not at all.

To her surprise, instead of heading in the direction of Honolulu and Waikiki, he headed for the west side of the island, getting on 93 toward Waianae.

She so wanted to ask where they were going, but managed

to contain her curiosity since she knew he wouldn't tell her anyway. After a lovely scenic drive up the coast, he pulled into the parking lot of a restaurant called Staxx Sports Bar & Grill.

He cut the engine and turned to her. "It's nothing fancy, but I don't think you're a fancy kind of woman."

"I'm not," she agreed immediately.

"They've got some delicious traditional Tongan dishes, but also steak, wings, fish tacos, burgers...and we're definitely getting an order of their tater tots. After that meal you made me the other night, I'm guessing the garlic tots are something you're gonna want to try."

Ashlyn grinned. "I like garlic. Sue me."

"Lucky for you, I do too," Slate told her. "There are also a ton of TVs, dartboards, and sometimes they have live poker and trivia tournaments."

"Ooooh, trivia," Ashlyn said with excitement. "I love trivia! I suck at it, but I love it."

"For the record, babe, I didn't pick this place because I'm a guy who's only comfortable in sports bars. I chose it because they've got damn good food. And because I wanted to share it with you."

"Okay." Honestly, the thought hadn't crossed her mind, but she was glad he clarified.

"Come on. I swear I've been listening to your stomach growl for the entire drive."

Ashlyn rolled her eyes. "You have not."

He grinned at her, and Ashlyn swore she could feel her ovaries explode at the heat she saw in his gaze.

"Food first," he muttered before climbing out of the vehicle, proving he was definitely on the same page as she was when it came to what they were *most* hungry for.

She didn't wait for him, but popped out before he could get to her side of the car.

He didn't comment, which kind of surprised her, just took her hand in his and led her toward the entrance.

An hour later, Ashlyn sat back against the pleather booth and sighed in contentment. "Those tater tots were literally the best thing I've ever eaten," she said happily.

"I guess so, since you ate about twenty pounds of the things," Slate teased.

He was a great dinner companion. The conversation had been steady, he hadn't let his eyes wander around the crowded restaurant as if bored, and Ashlyn loved how interested he seemed in everything she had to say. But then again, she'd been just as fascinated by the stories he told about some of his deployments. She was well aware he wasn't telling her anything classified, but it was a side of Slate that she hadn't previously allowed herself to think about.

Like the time he and his team had been cut off from their extraction point and they'd literally had to crawl three miles to stay undetected by the enemy. Or when he'd eaten spiders and a snake when they ran out of MREs after a mission went on longer than they'd expected.

He was trying to keep his stories light and funny, and while Ashlyn laughed in the expected places, the thought of how much danger he and his friends were in every time they were deployed wasn't exactly a laughing matter.

They'd just finished their entrees—she'd gotten the Staxx burger, and he'd devoured his braised pork belly bao—and were now waiting for the deep-fried ice cream they'd ordered for dessert.

"Can I ask you something?" Ashlyn started.

"Of course," Slate said, leaning forward and putting his elbows on the table, giving her his undivided attention.

"I could use some advice...but not if you're gonna go all uber protective on me."

"Can't promise that, as I *am* protective of you," Slate said calmly. "But I'll do my best to temper it, since this is just a discussion."

Ashlyn chuckled. It was such a Slate answer, she couldn't take offense. "Okay, you know how we were talking about some of my clients earlier?"

"Yup."

Ashlyn had been pleasantly surprised at Slate's interest in the men and women she brought meals to. She'd been reticent to talk about them, since she knew he didn't exactly approve of her job, but he'd listened carefully, asked appropriate questions, and he honestly seemed curious about the people she interacted with on a daily basis.

"Well...I've been thinking about Christi."

"She's the one in the wheelchair, right?" Slate asked.

"Yeah. That's her. I don't know exactly what her disability is; I feel kind of weird asking. I mean, if I spent more time with her and her sister, I'm sure they'd open up, but I suppose that isn't important. Anyway, I was thinking about seeing if I could arrange for her to get out of the house. Like, bring her down to the beach for some fresh air or something. I'm sure I can figure out how to transport her, but I don't want Lori to feel bad if I offer. Her nurse's aide would obviously come with us, but I just don't know how to broach the subject.

"She's always in the house when I get there. Usually sitting in front of the TV. I just feel awful that they're in Hawaii, and Christi never gets out. What do you think?"

Slate reached across the table and took her hand in his. "First, I think you've got the biggest heart out of anyone I've ever met. Most people would do their job of delivering meals and that would be that. They wouldn't get to know the Turners, wouldn't sneak in extra treats for the elderly clients, and they definitely wouldn't care about a handicapped girl needing more fresh air."

"But?" Ashlyn prompted when he paused for a long moment.

"I'm not saying it's a bad idea, but maybe Christi is perfectly happy with her life as it is. Maybe she doesn't like the smell of the sea because it reminds her of things she can't do because of her handicap. Maybe she doesn't like being stared at when she's outside the house. Obviously talking to Lori is a very important step, because she's ultimately in charge of her sister's well-being. You've already told me how hard she's working to keep Christi with her, and the last thing you want is her thinking she's not doing enough."

"Very true," Ashlyn said.

"But even if you talk to Lori and she agrees, and you can arrange for transportation, and you check to make sure wherever you want to take Christi is wheelchair friendly, and the home health aide gives her approval for the trip and agrees to accompany you...there's still something big you're missing."

"What?"

"Asking *Christi* if she wants to go to the beach. You've said she's non-verbal, but she has to have some way of communicating. She's a human being, and she deserves to be asked her opinion, not for decisions to be made without her input."

Ashlyn stared at Slate. He was right. One hundred precent right—and she was an idiot. She hadn't expressly said otherwise, but it *had* been her intention to discuss it with Lori and the nurse...not Christi. She closed her eyes, feeling awful.

Slate squeezed her hand. "Hey, look at me."

She didn't want to, but opened her eyes and met his gaze.

"She's lucky to have someone like you in her life."

Ashlyn swallowed hard. She'd been all gung-ho to try to make Christi's life better, without a clue as to whether the woman was content or not. She wasn't seeing her as a *person*. Not really. She just got an idea in her head and started planning stuff without thinking of all the angles. Asking Christi if she wanted to go to the beach should be the *first* thing she did, not the last.

Slate leaned forward and brought their clasped hands to his mouth. He kissed her fingers gently. "You're an amazing advocate, Ashlyn. You *care* about your clients, which is fucking awesome."

She chuckled. Leave it to Slate to make her laugh when she felt like shit for being so thoughtless.

Their waiter appeared then, holding a giant plate with three scoops of fried ice cream. He put down the plate and two spoons, and said, "Enjoy!"

Slate kept hold of her right hand and reached for a spoon. Ashlyn tugged on her hand. He didn't let go. Without acknowledging her slight struggle, he scooped up a bite of ice cream and ate it.

"Hey, big guy, I need my hand to eat," she told him with a grin.

"You've got another," he said, seemingly unconcerned.

"Yeah, but I'm right-handed," Ashlyn reminded him.

"I know. If you have to eat with your left hand, I'll get more."

"Hey!" she complained, laughing now and tugging at her hand with more effort.

Slate's lips curled up into a grin. "You know you'll eat more than your fair share if I don't give you a handicap."

"I will not!"

"Babe, you've got the biggest sweet tooth of anyone I've ever met. I don't care that you've eaten twice your weight in tater tots and gobbled that burger like you've got a stomach parasite. If you get the chance, you'll inhale this ice cream and leave me only a few slurps of melted goo."

Ashlyn couldn't help it, she laughed even harder at the

vision he painted. "Fine. I promise to only eat my half if you give my hand back."

He eyed her skeptically.

"And aren't you supposed to be worried about eating all healthy and shit? Mr. I Only Eat Protein Shakes and Bars For Breakfast."

"It's Friday. My cheat day," he said without missing a beat.

"Come on, it's melting!" Ashlyn whined.

Slate squeezed her hand once more, then let go. She didn't hesitate to reach for a spoon and dip it into the dessert. Taking a huge bite, she glared at Slate.

"Fuck, you're cute," he muttered, before turning his concentration back to the treat between them.

Ashlyn had never in a million years thought being called "cute" would get her motor revving...but then again, she'd never imagined the words coming from Slate either. The smile never left her face as they finished their dessert.

CHAPTER SIX

When they pulled up to Slate's house after dinner, Ashlyn was feeling extremely mellow. The night had been awesome. She'd loved spending time with him one-on-one. He was a great conversationalist. When they were out with their friends, he stayed in the background, often saying very little. When they'd first met, she'd actually pegged him as being moody and a bit of a downer, but that wasn't the case at all. He just preferred letting his friends take the spotlight.

"You comin' in?" Slate asked when he turned off the engine.

It was fairly late, but neither of them had to work in the morning, so Ashlyn nodded. "If that's all right."

"It's more than fucking all right," he answered, leaning in and snagging her behind the neck, pulling her close. He kissed her hard right there in his truck, his tongue twining with hers, immediately making Ashlyn squirm with lust.

"Inside," he growled after abruptly pulling back and opening his door.

Ashlyn grinned and followed suit, once again meeting him

at the front of the vehicle. Slate put his arm around her shoulders and led her to the front door.

Surprisingly, he didn't immediately push her against a wall and strip her naked. Instead, he gestured to the couch with his chin after locking the door. "Have a seat. I'll grab us something to drink."

Still turned on, but letting the mellow mood she'd fallen into on the drive back settle over her, Ashlyn headed for his couch. It was a tan micro suede and extremely comfortable. She'd looked into getting one just like it after she'd seen it the first time, but it had been out of her price range.

When Slate appeared next to her with a glass in hand, she opened her mouth to tell him she didn't want to drink anything because she had to drive later, but he spoke before she could.

"It's Sprite. I figured you wouldn't want any alcohol."

"Thanks," Ashlyn said, pleased—but not surprised—that he was considering her safety.

He sat next to her, putting the bottle of beer he'd taken out of the fridge on the coffee table. Next, after waiting for her to take a sip of soda, he took the glass from her hand and set it next to his own drink. Then he reached for her.

But instead of pulling her closer, he turned her body to face him and eased her back, pulling her legs up and putting her feet in his lap. Then he slipped off her sandals and began to massage her soles.

"Holy crap. Don't ever stop that," Ashlyn groaned.

Slate smiled and kept rubbing.

It was hard to believe she was here. In Slate's house. Her belly full and with the man she'd crushed on for months, *hard*, giving her a foot massage.

He'd only turned the kitchen light on, so the room was fairly dark. And quiet. Sighing in contentment, Ashlyn pulled over a small pillow from the end of the couch and stuffed it under her head. Now she could see what Slate was doing and relax at the same time.

Several minutes went by with him massaging her feet before she spoke. "This is nice."

Slate's lips twitched.

"I don't mean the massage. I mean, that's great. Stupendous, in fact. But I mean...*this*...hanging out with you. Just being present together in the moment."

As soon as the words left her mouth, Ashlyn felt stupid. But she should've known Slate wouldn't make her feel uncomfortable.

"Yeah, it is. Sometimes with my schedule, and the things I see and hear at work, I forget to live in the moment. To take time to appreciate what I've got."

"You have a family?" she asked.

"Nope. Was hatched from an egg," Slate said without missing a beat.

Ashlyn nudged him with her foot. "Dork. You know what I mean. I haven't ever heard you mention your parents or any siblings."

"Don't talk much about them," Slate said as he resumed his massage. "But I've got 'em. My older sister is an aide to a Congresswoman in Washington, DC, and my younger brother works on a ranch in Montana."

"Wow. You guys couldn't be any more different, huh?" Ashlyn asked.

"Nope. Makes things very interesting when we all get together."

"And your parents?"

"They live in Idaho on ten acres of land. Mom was a schoolteacher and Dad was an accountant. They're both retired now, and are loving the quiet life," Slate said. "What about you?"

"I'm an only child," Ashlyn said. "I really missed having

someone to hang out with when I was growing up. My parents are still together...but I wish they would've gotten divorced a long time ago."

"They don't get along?" Slate asked. He stopped rubbing her feet and simply rested his arm over her ankles.

"No. For as long as I can remember, they've been at each other's throats. And not in a joking or healthy way. They'd fight, then make up, then a day later they'd be yelling at each other again. My dad spent a lot of time sleeping on the couch."

"That sucks."

Ashlyn shrugged. "It is what it is. Lots of kids have it worse than I did. They both had good jobs, so we were never hurting for money. We were solidly middle class. I always had food to eat and clothes to wear."

"But?" Slate asked.

Ashlyn looked at him. "But what?"

"I hear a but in there. You had your basic needs met, but what else? Where did you fall into the family dynamics?"

Dang, Slate was very observant. "A lot of times, they were too busy sniping at each other to remember they had a kid. And when they did take notice of me, it was to bitch at each other for raising me wrong." Ashlyn shrugged. "I learned it was better to stay out of their way than to bring attention to myself. I was independent at a pretty early age."

"Sucks, babe," Slate said.

"Yeah," she agreed.

Silence settled between them.

"Sorry for being a downer," she said after a moment.

"You aren't. On the contrary, you fascinate me."

Ashlyn looked at him in surprise.

"You may not have had the best childhood, but despite having bad role models, you're a loyal friend. You're a hard worker. You have ambition, and empathy for others. I have no idea where or how you learned all that, with the kind of parents it sounds like you had, but I'm impressed."

"I learned to pay close attention when I was very young. I needed to gauge the kind of moods my parents were in so I'd know how to interact with them. As I got older, that just continued with others. I observed everyone around me. Simply by watching people who were ugly toward others, and seeing the reactions when someone treated a person with kindness, I decided I wanted to be like the latter and not the former," Ashlyn explained.

"Well, you've definitely succeeded in that," Slate said.

He couldn't have said anything to please her more. Some women craved compliments on their looks or material possessions; hearing Slate praise her because she was kind meant the world to her. "Thanks."

They fell quiet again as Slate started massaging her once more. But this time he didn't stick to just her feet. His hands moved up her legs, caressing her calves, tickling the backs of her knees.

When he finally shifted his position on the couch, bending one knee and moving to face her, Ashlyn's heart rate picked up.

She'd worn a skirt to look nice for their first official date. It was loose and comfortable—and at the moment, was absolutely no barrier to Slate's roaming hands. They slid under the fabric until he was caressing her inner thighs.

Ashlyn couldn't keep the moan from escaping.

A small smile crept over his face, and when he pulled the gusset of her panties to the side, Ashlyn closed her eyes and spread her legs for him.

It didn't take long for an orgasm to creep up on her. Slate's hands were magic, and he knew exactly where and how to touch her to send her soaring.

Minutes later, when she was panting and had stopped

shaking from the pleasure he'd given her, Slate said, "I like this skirt."

Ashlyn couldn't help it, she burst out laughing.

"I'm serious," he said. "You have no idea how hard it was for me to keep my hands to myself throughout dinner."

Ashlyn sat up, ignoring how wet her underwear was now. She knew she'd be removing them soon. "Hard?" she asked, looking at his lap suggestively. His erection was clear to see behind the zipper of his jeans.

Slate stood and held out his hand. "Shall we move this to the bedroom?"

"Yes, please," she said politely as she reached out to take his hand. As soon as he had her in his grasp, Slate hauled her up, bending and leaning forward at the same time. He put his shoulder in her belly and hefted her over his shoulder.

"Slate!" she screeched.

"Hush, woman," he said as he turned toward his room.

Ashlyn couldn't help but giggle as he carried her off like she was a prize he'd won in a fight or something. When he got to the side of his bed, he dumped her onto the mattress. Ashlyn bounced and laughed some more. She didn't stay down for long though; she'd been dying to get her hands on Slate's cock, and now seemed like the perfect time.

While he was tearing off his shirt, she slipped off the bed. She had his zipper down and was palming his erection before he knew what she was doing.

"Shit!" he exclaimed as Ashlyn pushed his underwear down and pulled out his cock.

The head was dark purple, and the veins running up and down the length seemed to pulse with excitement. She looked into his eyes even as she leaned forward, running her tongue up the underside of his hard shaft.

A drop of precome immediately beaded on the end, and Ashlyn couldn't help but smile in satisfaction.

"Stop fucking around," Slate grumbled as he put his hands on her head, running them through her hair.

Ashlyn wanted to tease him about his impatience, but at the moment, she was just as eager to get started as he seemed to be. She opened her mouth and took him inside as far as she could. Which wasn't all that far, since he was so thick. She began to bob up and down slowly, taking a tiny bit more of him each time, loving his taste...and the constant groans that were coming from his mouth.

His hands tightened in her hair, but he didn't force her to move faster or take more of him than she could comfortably manage. He shifted, spreading his legs farther apart as she sucked him.

Ashlyn had never really enjoyed doing this in the past, but with Slate, she freaking loved it. Loved the control she had over this strong, dangerous man. She used her hand to jerk him off as she continued to move up and down his length.

"Holy shit, babe...that is so damn good! You have no idea. I love being inside your pussy, but this is—" He inhaled sharply and couldn't finish his thought when she moved her other hand down to cup his balls, bobbing faster on his cock.

Ashlyn was so into what she was doing, she didn't feel Slate let go of her hair. The next thing she knew, she was flying through the air once more. She landed on her back on the mattress and Slate quickly grabbed her thighs, pulling her ass to the edge of the bed. He threw her skirt up and ripped her lacy panties right off her like a wild man.

He grabbed the box of condoms on the bedside table, spilling them all over the place in his rush to get the box open. He managed to tear one open and roll the condom down his dick in record time. He pushed her thighs apart and notched his cock between her legs.

But then he took a deep breath and closed his eyes, obviously trying to get control.

"I'm ready," Ashlyn said. "Fuck me, Slate."

He looked down at her, and she could see the relief in his eyes. "You liked sucking me off, didn't you?"

"Yes." There was no use lying about it. He'd see for himself how wet she was as soon as he entered her.

"This is gonna be rough and fast," he warned.

Ashlyn smiled. It wasn't as if his words were a surprise. "Okay."

That was all the permission Slate needed. He entered her in one hard thrust, which made Ashlyn inhale sharply. Then he was fucking her hard.

It felt good, but it wouldn't be enough to get her off. She didn't mind. Knowing she'd made Slate lose it so badly was hot as hell. She had a feeling he rarely let go of the iron control he wore like a protective shield around him.

It wasn't long before he swore under his breath and shoved deep inside her, his whole body shuddering. Seeing him come was damn beautiful. The satisfaction and pleasure and awe on his face was worth not orgasming herself. His jeans were still hanging off his thighs, and he looked better than any half-dressed male model she'd ever seen.

And for now...he was all hers.

He finally opened his eyes, and when he met her gaze, Ashlyn shivered. She saw determination in his stare.

"Your turn," he said.

Ashlyn shook her head. "It's okay, I—"

Her words were cut off abruptly when he pulled out of her body and knelt on the floor next to the bed. He grabbed a pillow and shoved it under her ass.

"Slate?"

"Hush," he said gruffly. Then asked, "You ever have a G-spot orgasm?"

"Um, I'm not sure..."

"Then you haven't," he said. "Hang on, babe. I'm about to

rock your world like you just did mine."

Ashlyn didn't have time to comment before he leaned over and proceeded to blow her mind.

Thirty minutes later, Ashlyn felt completely boneless. Slate had proven that she hadn't, in fact, ever had a G-spot orgasm before, and how different and intense it could be. Then he'd stripped her naked, manhandled her limp body onto the bed, turned her onto her stomach and taken her from behind, making her explode once more—this time while he was deep inside her, fingers on her clit—before coming again himself.

Now they were lying sweaty and exhausted. Slate had pulled her close to his side, and she had her head on his shoulder. She'd never experienced *anything* as pleasurable as what Slate had done in the last hour. The man should definitely come with a warning.

"You okay?" he asked as he ran his hand over her hair.

She snuggled closer, practically purring. "I'm awesome," she said. "You?"

"Fucking perfect," he drawled.

Ashlyn smiled against his shoulder.

"Been wondering something," Slate said after a minute or two of comfortable silence.

"Yeah?" Ashlyn asked.

"I know you don't have a problem with drinking in general, but is there a deeper reason behind why you won't even have one drink if you have to drive? Besides the fact it's a smart fucking thing to do, obviously," he added.

God. He really *was* perceptive. "I worked at a bar in San Diego before I moved to Hawaii," she said. "Aces Bar and Grill. It's owned by a woman who's married to a SEAL."

"I know the place," Slate said. "Awesome atmosphere."

Ashlyn nodded against him. "Yeah. I loved it. There was this guy who was in there all the time. Like, every single day.

He was a veteran, and he'd come in fairly early and sit at the end of the bar and nurse a few drinks. Something clear, so I figured maybe it was a gin rickey or something...you know, club soda, gin, and lime. He was hilarious and told the best stories about his time in the Navy. I guessed his wife had died fairly recently, and he was lonely. He always left around ten, before the bar got too busy.

"Anyway, one day I came into work and he wasn't there. Jessyka, the owner, told me the bad news that he was killed in a drunk driving accident the night before. I assumed it was because he was driving drunk. But apparently, all he ever drank when he was at the bar was Sprite with a lime garnish. Someone *else* had been drunk behind the wheel of their car and hit him head on."

Slate hugged her with one arm and turned to kiss her forehead.

"I know life is short, and we don't know when our time will be up, but I never, *ever* want to do something stupid and be the reason someone else's life is cut even shorter. So I choose not to drink when I know I'll be driving. Even if it's only one drink, or if I know it'll be hours before I have to get behind the wheel of a car. I can't do it. I sincerely appreciated the wine earlier, and believe me, if I wasn't driving I'd have had a glass or two. But...anyway, that's why I only had a sip."

"I think that's very smart."

"I don't want you to think I'm judging you if you have a drink with dinner or anything. It's perfectly fine. I just can't do it. I think of that sweet old man and it still upsets me."

"One of the kids I went to high school with drove after drinking, crashed his car on prom night my junior year," Slate said quietly. "It was extremely sad. His date didn't die, but she ended up in a wheelchair. Her spinal cord was severed. So I get it. And for the record, I'm very careful. I limit myself to one drink if I'm driving."

Ashlyn petted his chest, loving the feel of the crisp hair there. "I know. I've noticed."

"And now that I've ruined the mood...can we talk about how revved up you got by sucking my cock?" Slate asked.

Ashlyn burst out laughing. With any other man, she'd probably be embarrassed, but Slate made it feel natural to talk about pretty much anything while lying naked in each other's arms. She propped her head on the hand on his chest and looked at him. "Couldn't help it. You're seriously hot, Slate."

"Back at ya, babe. Seeing your lips stretched around my cock was a dream come true."

She smiled. "Good, because I'll be trying it again, since as you stopped me before I was finished."

It was Slate's turn to laugh. "You want me to come in your mouth, Ash?"

"Um...maybe?"

He grinned. Huge. "Works for me."

Ashlyn abruptly yawned. "Sorry," she muttered. "I should get going."

Slate stared at her for a long beat before finally nodding. "You want to shower before you go?" he asked.

"No. It'll wake me up too much. I'm gonna go home and crash. Besides," she added, "I kind of like smelling like you."

"Like smelling you on me too," he told her. "You gonna be able to stay awake long enough to get home safely?"

"Sure."

"While you're changing, I'll make you a tea to go. Yeah?"

"Sounds good, thanks, Slate."

He sat up, taking her with him. Then he put his fingers under her chin and tilted her face up to his. He kissed her, longer, slower, and sweeter than any other kiss they'd shared so far. When he pulled back, his eyes roamed over her face and body.

"You have sex hair," he announced with a grin.

Ashlyn rolled her eyes. "Whatever. You have a sex *hickey*," she retorted, nodding to a spot on his chest she hadn't been able to resist sucking on earlier.

"Gonna wear it with pride, babe," he said, seemingly not embarrassed in the least that she'd marked him. He kissed her once more, hard and fast, then scooted out from under the covers.

Ashlyn admired his ass for a moment as he walked around the room gathering up the clothes he'd taken off earlier. It was muscular and round, and Ashlyn wanted to put her hands on him once more.

"Up," Slate ordered. "Before it gets any later. Not thrilled about you driving around this time of night, but I know if I say anything about it, you'd lose your shit on me and tell me I was being ridiculous and a Neanderthal."

"Um, you just *did* say something about it," Ashlyn informed him.

Slate ignored her as he pulled on a pair of gray sweat-pants...without putting on any underwear. When he turned to face her, she had to swallow at the sight of him. She'd never understood women on the Internet going all ga-ga over pictures of men in sweatpants, but right then, she got it. She could clearly see the outline of his cock, and the suggestive-ness of it seemed even hotter than seeing him bare somehow.

"Eyes up here, Ashlyn," Slate said, the humor easy to hear in his tone.

She forced her gaze from his mouthwatering cock up to his face.

"Get up. Get dressed. I'll get your tea," Slate said.

Ashlyn nodded.

"Fuck. So cute," he muttered, before turning and heading out of the bedroom.

CHAPTER SEVEN

Ten days.

That's how much time had passed since their first date, and Slate had talked to Ashlyn every day since.

He was thrilled with how well things were working out. The sex was out of this world. He'd never been with a woman as passionate, enthusiastic, and sensual as Ashlyn. But it was more than that. He enjoyed hearing about her days. Was interested in hearing how her clients were doing. Looked forward to sharing the funny things his teammates said and did at work.

And he was utterly obsessed with that damn tracker app.

Pid have given him shit earlier that afternoon when he'd checked it for what seemed like the fiftieth time. He just wanted to be sure Ashlyn was progressing through her deliveries without any issues.

They'd had plans to hang out for dinner tonight, but after his workday, Slate was in no mood or condition to do anything but go straight home and sit on his roof deck and decompress. He didn't want to disappoint Ashlyn, and it wasn't as if he didn't want to see her. He just needed to sit in a quiet space for a while without having to talk to anyone.

He waited until he got home before calling her, so he could concentrate on the call and not try to drive and talk at the same time.

"Hi!" she said happily when she answered. "You on your way?"

Even though she could've seen his location on the tracking app, she didn't seem inclined to use it much. Slate didn't know whether to be pleased or irritated by that.

"I'm not going to be able to come over tonight," he told her.

"Oh." He could hear the disappointment in her tone.

"Frankly, work sucked," he said. "I wouldn't be the best company tonight, and I'm actually feeling a bit nauseous anyway."

"You're sick?" she asked in concern.

"No. But for four hours this afternoon, we watched bodycam and helmet cam videos for training. My head is swimming. I feel as if I've been on a boat in the pitching and rolling ocean for hours."

"Oh my God. Four hours of watching that stuff? I've seen some of those videos on police officer bodycams, and it makes me sick to watch more than like two minutes at a time. I'm so sorry, Slate."

"It usually doesn't bother me so much, but since we were trying to figure out what went wrong on the mission of a team we're analyzing, we had to watch each man's video over and over. So yeah, it was a bit much."

"I don't get seasick or carsick, but I sometimes get really bad headaches," Ashlyn said. "I'm not sure I'd call them migraines, because I only get them now and then, but they can make me super nauseous too. The only thing that helps is lying in a dark room with no sound. So I get it. Is there anything I can do?"

Slate wasn't surprised that Ashlyn was all right with the change in plans. She always seemed to go with the flow in just about every regard. Reason number two thousand why he liked being with her. "No, I'm just going to decompress. Probably go up to the roof and chill for a while."

"You should eat something," she said gently. "I know you probably don't feel like it after all those videos, but I'm sure you're hungry, and sometimes an empty stomach can make you feel even sicker than you already are."

"I'm okay, babe."

"Slate...seriously."

"I'm good. I'll grab something later," he told her, lying through his teeth.

"Okay. Was...Never mind."

"What?"

"I was just going to ask if the videos were bad in...other ways. You said you were trying to figure out what went wrong."

"Yeah. They were bad," Slate said without elaborating. "How about you? Did you have a good day?" he asked, deliberately trying to change the subject. He didn't want to think about his fellow SEALs lying in the dirt, dying from gunshots they'd received in the ambush the team had walked into.

After a while, all he could see was his own teammates' faces on those men. Mustang bleeding out from a gut shot. Aleck's eyes staring unseeing up at the sky as half his head was blown away. Jag's screams of pain as he tried to put a tourniquet on his own leg to stop the gushing from his femoral artery. And Pid's desperate calls for help over the radio as he and Midas did their best to hold back the enemy shooters.

"It was fine. I did what you suggested today."

"And what was that?" As much as Slate had wanted to be alone tonight, he found that Ashlyn was the one person he could handle talking to right now. Surprisingly, her voice soothed some of his weariness.

"Before I brought up taking Christi to the beach with her sister or caretaker, I asked *her* what she thought. And you know what? Even though Christi can't talk, she let me know in no uncertain terms that she did *not* like the beach. There were lots of hand gestures and grunting, but when I suggested maybe just taking her out to the backyard instead, she smiled. *Smiled*, Slate. And she kept smiling, tilting her head up to the sun as we sat outside. It was a good day."

"That's great, babe."

"It was such a small gesture. And I should've thought to ask her first thing. Instead, I got all wrapped up in the logistics of getting her into my car, and then to the beach, and talking to everyone else. Your advice was spot on. I think too many people talk *around* handicapped people instead of talking *to* them. So thank you for basically smacking me upside the head and getting me to see what an idiot I'd been."

"Wanting the best for someone isn't idiotic," Slate said. "Your huge heart is one of your greatest traits."

"Even though it drives you crazy sometimes?" Ashlyn asked.

Slate chuckled. He hadn't thought he'd be able to laugh today, after everything he'd seen, but clearly Ashlyn had done the impossible. "It's also the thing that keeps me up nights," he told her.

"I thought that was my winning...personality," she teased.

Slate laughed harder at that. "Oh, yeah, that too," he agreed.

"Okay, well...thanks for calling to let me know you aren't coming tonight. I'm really sorry you had a tough day and that you want to barf. Go up to your deck—but don't fall off. It would suck to have to admit to your friends that you broke your leg because you were walking like a drunken sailor and fell ass over head off the roof of your house."

Slate couldn't stop smiling. "Yeah, that *would* suck."

"I'll talk to you tomorrow?" Ashlyn asked.

"Yeah, babe, you will."

"Good. Later."

"Later."

Slate clicked off the phone and took a deep breath as he leaned against the kitchen counter. He felt better. Not great, but better. Talking to Ashlyn, he realized, always seemed to put him in a better mood. The images he'd seen today were still in his head, but they were muted now. With a small smile, he grabbed a bottle of water and headed up the stairs to his rooftop deck.

An hour later, Slate was feeling much more relaxed. The fresh air and the sound of the ocean had done their job, clearing his head. His nausea had faded as well, thank God.

A car vaguely caught his attention when it turned down his street—then even more so when it pulled into his driveway. Frowning, as he wasn't expecting anyone and he didn't recognize the vehicle, he stood up to get a better look at who it might be.

He saw the logo of an Internet delivery app on the side of the car.

Rolling his eyes, he knew immediately that Ashlyn hadn't been able to stop herself from trying to take care of him. He headed down the stairs to see what she'd ordered for his dinner.

The young man had already dropped off the bag and was headed back to his car.

"If you wait a second, I can grab a tip," Slate called out.

"No need. The tip through the app was more than generous. Enjoy!"

Shaking his head, Slate picked up the bag and went back inside. Putting the food on the kitchen counter, he started to unload it, and the smells from the covered containers made his belly rumble.

She'd ordered from Oahu Grill, a Hawaiian restaurant he loved. And she'd gone overboard.

There was squid lu'au, taro leaves slowly simmered and mixed with squid and coconut milk; chicken hekka, shredded chicken and long rice noodles cooked in a semi-sweet shoyu-based sauce with green beans and carrots; and a Ho'io salad, which was fiddlehead fern shoots with dried shrimp, tomatoes, and onions, again in a shoyu-based sauce. There was even Kona coffee ice cream packed with dry ice for dessert.

Everything she'd ordered were things he'd mentioned at one time or another that he loved. Not even directly to *her*, necessarily. But in conversation with their friends when they were all together.

Ashlyn wasn't kidding. She paid *very* close attention...and she went out of her way to show people how much she cared about them.

Slate didn't bother plating the food, he simply plunked the containers down on his small table and grabbed some utensils.

Before he dug into the delicious-smelling meal, he picked up his phone to send Ashlyn a text.

Slate: There's no way I can eat all this. But thank you for thinking about me.

Three dots immediately appeared at the bottom of the text string. And Slate waited impatiently for her to finish typing and hit enter.

. . .

Ashlyn: Please, I've seen you eat, and I'm sure what I ordered is nothing. I hope you're not feeling nauseous anymore.

Slate: I'm good.

Ashlyn: Yes, you are. :) I figured you needed some comfort food to help you feel better.

Slate: I appreciate it.

Ashlyn: And now you owe me, because you get all that ice cream to yourself. You don't have to fight me for it. I hope it's not too melted. When I called, the guy assured me they'd package it up so it would be good for at least two hours, but I was still skeptical.

Slate: It's perfect. And the next time we're out, I'll let you have all the ice cream.

Ashlyn: I'll just screen-shot that comment so when you forget and steal my spoon, I can show it to you.

Slate laughed out loud once more. He was about to reply when his stomach growled again. Shit, he'd only meant to send a quick thank you and now here he was, absorbed in a conversation rather than eating.

Slate: Gonna go so I can eat before everything gets cold. Thank you, babe. Means the world to me that you'd go out of your way to send me dinner.

Ashlyn: You're welcome. Enjoy your slimy, gross Hawaiian food, Slate.

Once again, he laughed as he shook his head.

. . .

Slate: Sleep well.

Ashlyn: You too.

Ashlyn: Oh, and...I don't think I said it earlier, but thank you for what you do, Slate. I know it's not always easy, and in fact a lot of times it sucks huge monkey balls, but I appreciate you and your teammates. Talk to you tomorrow.

Slate was used to people thanking him for his service. Often it felt insincere. As if the people were just reciting something they felt they should say, rather than something they truly felt. But Ashlyn's words seemed genuine. Hilarious in her unique way, but truly sincere. And they were just what he needed to hear tonight. After everything he'd seen earlier, her words were able to soothe the images in his head.

Picking up his fork, Slate tucked into the lu'au first and sighed in contentment when the flavors burst on his tongue. Yeah, Hawaiian food wasn't everyone's cup of tea, but he fucking loved it.

Looking down at the meal, Slate couldn't remember the last time someone had gone out of their way to take care of him like Ashlyn had tonight. Most of the time, it was him taking care of others. It felt...really nice.

CHAPTER EIGHT

Ashlyn relaxed on Slate's couch, tired and content, thinking about tomorrow. Carly and Jag had invited everyone to Duke's on Sunday to try out different options for their wedding meal. Though, it was really just an excuse to get everyone together and have a good time, because everything Duke's served was delicious. No matter what they chose, it would be perfect. Ashlyn was excited to spend time with all her friends.

Almost two weeks had passed since Slate had called to cancel their dinner date. Ashlyn knew she'd ordered too much food for him, but she'd wanted to get him everything he loved to try to make him feel better. If she couldn't be there for him in person, she'd send food.

Luckily, it had worked. The next time Slate saw her, he'd shown her *exactly* much he appreciated the gesture. She hadn't thought she could orgasm that many times in one night, but he'd proven just how much her body could take.

Their relationship seemed to be going strong. Even though they sometimes bickered over little things, she never felt as if Slate was truly irritated—or getting tired of her.

For her part, she was proud of his work as a SEAL, and the man made for great arm candy, but most importantly, she just liked being with him. It made her happy. They didn't see each other every day, but they talked and texted frequently. Sometimes he'd call after he did PT, and other times he'd wait until they were both home from work. He always asked about her clients and continued to seem genuinely interested in the stories she shared about the men and women she served.

This morning, Slate had picked her up early and they'd spent the day hiking the Kealia Trail. It was on the north side of the island, and while it had lush scenery and beautiful ocean views from the summit, it had also kicked Ashlyn's butt. She hadn't thought she was out of shape, but apparently she was. When she finally ascended the mountain ridge, she felt as if she was gonna die.

Of course, Slate had no mercy for her, and instead of being overly concerned about how loud her breathing had become, he'd teased her and egged her on. It was just what she needed, though, to finish the hike.

Ashlyn couldn't remember a better date with a guy. It was refreshing that she didn't always need to be perfect around Slate. She could be sweaty and grumpy, wear a pair of sweats with her hair in a messy bun, and he didn't care. He seemed to like her just as she was. Which was awesome.

Now, she was stiff and sore from the hike, but content. She and Slate were currently vegging on his couch after he'd made burgers for dinner, and she'd eaten two. She felt full and relaxed.

"Today was good," she said after a moment.

Slate had turned on the TV and started the movie *Red* with Bruce Willis and Morgan Freeman. It was good, but Ashlyn was having a hard time keeping her eyes open. The exertion from the day, and the food in her belly, made her extremely sleepy.

"It was," Slate agreed.

"I was thinking..." she started.

"Lord help us all," Slate teased.

"Shut up," Ashlyn said with a shake of her head. She did her best to elbow him, but because she was plastered to his side with his arm around her shoulders, it wasn't very effective.

"Sorry," he said, not sounding very sorry. In fact, he sounded amused. "Go on."

"I was thinking about how much things change, yet still stay the same. The other day, I was talking to James Mason—you know, the Navy vet I deliver to—and he was talking about how he and his wife used to go on long hikes around the island. He'd always bring a picnic lunch for them. Nothing fancy, usually sandwiches and potato chips. They'd find a good spot on the trail and sit and just enjoy each other's company as they ate. Today reminded me of that."

Slate squeezed her shoulders and kissed the top of her head. "Yeah. It really was a good day."

"I bet James would have some suggestions for other hikes we could do. Maybe ones that wouldn't kick my ass as much as today's did."

Slate chuckled. "You did fine, babe."

"Right. I was wheezing like an out-of-shape hippo."

"No, you weren't. Maybe an out-of-shape piglet—"

"Slate!" Ashlyn exclaimed, sitting up so she could elbow him properly.

"Kidding!" he said immediately, grabbing her arm. Then he shifted, lying down on the couch with her on top of him.

He was as hard as a rock beneath her, but surprisingly comfortable.

"You like him," Slate said.

It took a second for Ashlyn to get her mind off how much she loved being on top of Slate. She could feel his cock between her legs. He wasn't hard, but she had a feeling all it would take was a dirty comment or rubbing against him suggestively and that would change. She loved how responsive he was to her...just as she was to him. But for right now, she was enjoying the easy intimacy. The atmosphere wasn't sexually charged, it was comfortable.

"James? Yeah, I do. Some older people I deliver food to are grumpy as hell. They complain about what I've brought, even though they're getting it for free. They don't invite me in and they definitely have no interest in getting to know me. But James is different. The first time I knocked on his door, he insisted I come inside. He got me a glass of ice water and told me how pretty I was."

"He's probably lonely. Didn't you say his wife died recently?" Slate asked.

"Yeah, but I honestly think it's just his personality to be welcoming and kind. He's told me several times how his wife always used to get irritated with him because he befriended everyone he ever met. The guy behind the cash register at the grocery store, waiters and waitresses, clerks at the hardware store.

"He's also told me about every single one of his neighbors. The man knows everything about *everyone*. Even the dirt," Ashlyn said. "He told me about how the woman who used to live three doors down was having an affair with her son's surfing instructor. One day her husband came home early from work, and the surfer guy had to bail out the window butt-ass naked."

Slate chuckled. "James sounds like quite the character."

"He is. He's got quirks of his own too...including some that worry me."

"Like what?"

"Well, last week when I got there, a handyman was just cleaning up after fixing a leak in the roof. Instead of writing a check, James walked over to a decorative jar on his kitchen table and pulled out a stack of hundred-dollar bills. He peeled off three and handed them to the guy. Then he put the rest back in the jar." She shook her head. "After the man left, I asked why he had so much money hanging around, and he told me he didn't trust banks. That after hearing what his parents had to do to survive the depression and the various crashes that happened throughout the years, he was more comfortable having his money close at hand."

"That's not smart," Slate said with a frown.

"I know. I tried to convince him the world is very different now, and told him about the protective measures in place for money in the bank, but he just shrugged and told me he was old and set in his ways," Ashlyn said. "It worries me for sure. But he's eighty-eight, it's not like he's gonna earn much interest if he puts everything he has in the bank. I'm assuming, since he was approved to get deliveries from Food For All, that he's not swimming in cash."

"Maybe you should mention the next time you see him to at least not pull out a wad of cash like that in front of anyone again. It's possible flashing money around will be too much temptation for someone and they'll come back to rob him."

"I already did," Ashlyn said. "He laughed and said that he might be old, but he still knows how to shoot."

She felt more than heard Slate chuckling under her. "I think I like this guy."

"You would," Ashlyn said. "I have a feeling he was bossy and overprotective as a younger man, just like you."

Slate smiled at her. "I love how concerned you are for your clients," he said. "You're a good person, Ashlyn Taylor."

"So are you, Duncan Stone."

"How'd you ever find out my full name, anyway?" he asked.

Ashlyn mimicked zipping her lips shut. "I'll never tell."

The truth was, during a conversation with the other women about the guys' nicknames, she'd asked what Slate's real name was. No one knew, and Elodie had made it her mission to find out. Within two days, she'd texted Ashlyn with Slate's name.

"Doesn't matter, really. It's not like I'm ashamed of it or anything," Slate said.

"It's a good name. Strong, like you. Although I don't know why people didn't call you Stone instead of Slate."

"Think it was because of my black hair. You know, black as slate," he said.

Ashlyn thought it was kind of funny how his team all had nicknames. It seemed silly to her, but since she'd known him as Slate for so long, she couldn't think of him any other way now.

Ashlyn opened her mouth to tell him how much she liked that thick black hair, but a huge yawn overtook her words.

Slate's hand moved to the back of her head and he gently eased it down to his chest. "Rest, babe. You're tired."

She was, but she felt horrible about being bad company. "I'm okay," she said.

"You can't keep your eyes open," he retorted with a small shake of his head. "Rest your eyeballs for a second."

"Are you sure?" Ashlyn asked, already snuggling into him. Slate was always so warm, and she loved how they fit together so perfectly.

"Yup. I'm just gonna watch the movie."

"Okay, wake me up when it's over."

He hummed in the back of his throat.

Ashlyn must've been more tired than she realized, because the last thing she remembered was the feel of Slate's hand lightly caressing her hair...then nothing.

* * *

Ashlyn shifted, then grimaced as it became clear she'd overdone it on the hike with Slate. She was sore all over. She tried to roll to her other side to look at her clock and see what time it was—but a strong arm around her waist prevented her from turning.

Opening her eyes, she realized she wasn't in her own bed.

The night before, talking with Slate, then falling asleep on his chest, came back to her in a flash—and she panicked.

Shit, she and Slate hadn't done a sleepover before. They'd never even discussed it! If they had dinner together, they usually had sex afterward at one of their homes, then whoever didn't live there got up and left. That routine was just fine with Ashlyn. She wasn't offended when Slate left, and he never seemed upset to let her go.

But she had no idea how he would feel about her staying the night. Guys could get weird about that sort of thing. She didn't want to rock the boat when everything between them was still so new.

She liked how things were going. She liked Slate, and she didn't want him to think she needed to change their routine. Get more serious. Spending the night was definitely a big shift in the unspoken rules they'd been operating under for the last month or so.

"Morning," Slate said sleepily.

Ashlyn wasn't sure what she should do. Leap out of bed, apologize and hightail it out of there? Pretend it was perfectly normal to wake up in his bed, in his arms?

But Slate being Slate, he took the decision out of her hands. He gently tugged her shoulder until she was on her back next to him. Then he propped himself up on an elbow and kept his other arm around her waist. "What's wrong?" he asked with a small frown.

For once, Ashlyn wished he wasn't so freaking perceptive. "Nothing."

"Babe."

That was it. Just one word, but it was so full of skepticism, Ashlyn couldn't help but blurt out her thoughts.

"I'm sorry! I didn't mean to fall asleep on you. I mean, I did. You said I could. And you were so comfortable and I was tired from hiking. You should've woken me up. I would've left. I didn't mean to alter our agreement."

"Breathe, Ash, it's fine. First of all, I encouraged you to sleep. I liked holding you while you conked out. You snore, you know."

Ashlyn frowned. "I do not."

"Yeah, you do. It's not a full-on snore, but you kind of snuffle in your sleep. It's adorable."

"Focus, Slate. And not on my non-snoring," she told him.

"Sorry. I knew you were tired and had no problem with you taking a nap. When the movie ended, I tried to wake you up, but you were out. And I mean, *out*. I'm not even sure if sleeping that soundly is safe. Like, what if someone breaks into your apartment? Or if a fire breaks out? You'd probably sleep right through it."

"I've always been a really deep sleeper," Ashlyn admitted sheepishly.

"Right. One more thing I learned about you last night. That, and your snoring."

"Stop it with the snoring thing," Ashlyn griped. "I do *not* snore!"

"Riiiight. Okay. Anyway, I did try to wake you, and you slapped at me, told me to hush. So I carried you in here, stripped you naked, made long slow love to you, then went to sleep myself."

Ashlyn stared at him blankly for a solid five seconds.

"You did not. I wouldn't have slept through that."

Slate had been keeping a straight face, but at her words, he laughed. "Damn straight, you wouldn't have. I mean, what a slap in the face that would've been. Seriously though, I brought you in here, got you comfortable, then climbed in next to you. Slept fucking awesome too. You were like a rock. Once you're out, you're seriously out, babe. Works well for me, actually, since I'm a light sleeper. If you were the kind of sleeper who tossed and turned all night, it would've sucked because I'd constantly be waking up every time you moved."

Ashlyn could only stare up at him. For the first time, she realized that all she had on was her panties. Slate had taken off her shirt, bra, and leggings. She wasn't upset. It wasn't as if he hadn't seen her naked before. He'd seen everything she had to offer up close and personal. It was an intimate thing to do, getting her ready for bed, but she couldn't deny that it was nice of him to take care of her when she'd been so tired.

"So you're not upset that I stayed the night?" she blurted.

"Did you not hear anything I just said?" Slate asked.

"Um...yeah."

"Then you weren't paying close attention, because nothing I said could in any way indicate that I'm upset you stayed the night."

"Okay."

"Okay. You sore this morning?"

"Yes."

"How sore?"

"Um, on a scale of one to ten, about a twelve."

Slate nodded, leaned down, and kissed her forehead, then began to roll away.

"Slate?" Ashlyn asked, putting her hand out and touching his bare back. He was wearing a pair of boxer shorts and nothing else. The muscles in his back rippled as he turned around to look at her.

"Yeah?"

"Where are you going?"

"Gonna get you some painkillers. Then start a bath for

you. It'll help your muscles relax a bit. How do you like your water? Warm, toasty, or boil-noodles hot?"

Ashlyn swallowed hard. She'd invaded his space without giving him a choice, and now he was continuing to take care of her because she'd overdone it the day before?

"Babe? How hot do you like your bath water?"

"A shade under boil-noodles hot," she told him.

"Got it. Stay here and relax. I'll be back in a moment with some water and the pills."

"Will you be joining me?" Ashlyn blurted.

"Nope. Don't do baths."

"What about sex?"

"What about it?" Slate asked with a small tilt of his head.

"I...um...do you want it?"

A wicked smile crossed his face. "Hell yes. But you're sore. I'm not going to wither away and die if I don't get inside your delectable pussy this morning. While you're in the bath, I'll make us some breakfast. Maybe we can take a leisurely walk along Waikiki Beach before we meet the others at Duke's. Stretching your muscles will also help. But if you've got things you need to do this morning, that's okay too."

Something had suddenly changed between them, and Ashlyn wasn't quite sure how to process it. "It's Sunday. I'm usually lazy on Sundays, so no, I don't have anything I need to do before we meet everyone at Duke's."

"Great. Stay put. I'll be back."

Then Slate twisted a bit more, kissed her on the lips briefly, and stood.

Ashlyn kept her gaze on his back as he disappeared inside his small walk-in closet. He reappeared a few seconds later wearing a pair of black sweatpants and headed for the bathroom door. She heard the water turn on and in a minute or so, he came back into the room. He gave her a smile, then left without a word to go to the kitchen and get her some painkillers.

The second he was out of sight, Ashlyn flopped back on the bed and let out a long, slow breath. She was happier than she could say that he hadn't flipped out over her still being there this morning. She felt bad that she hadn't woken up when he'd carried her into his room, but relieved that things between them still seemed to be all right.

She liked Slate. He was a good man. She wasn't ready for things to end. And it seemed as if she didn't need to worry about that yet.

Ashlyn had no doubt that eventually they'd get sick of each other. She'd find herself becoming more and more annoyed at things he did. As he likely would with her. It always happened.

But for now, she was going to enjoy Slate taking care of her...and her hot bath.

* * *

"You look great!" Lexie exclaimed later that day.

The day had been relaxed so far, and Ashlyn couldn't remember a better "morning after" than the one she'd shared with Slate. He'd brought her a glass of water and pills —bossily ordering her to drink all the water. She humored him, and only blushed a little when he took her hand and led her to the bathroom. She might've had sex in countless positions with the man, but walking around mostly naked in the light of day was a different thing altogether. But he didn't make it weird. Simply pointed out the extra tooth- brush he'd unearthed from a drawer and left her alone in the bathroom.

The temperature of the bathwater was perfect, and she stayed in the tub until she felt like a prune. Then she showered, washed her hair with Slate's shampoo, and got dressed before joining him in the kitchen.

He'd made a potato, egg, and spinach casserole and pulled it out of the oven as soon as he saw her. They'd talked more about James and the Turner family over breakfast, as well as a new Japanese couple who'd moved to the island and hadn't quite gotten on their feet yet. He talked about how things were currently pretty intense at work, and that there was a chance he and his team would be deployed soon.

She didn't like to think about that, but as it was a part of who Slate was, she didn't shy away from asking him a million questions. He couldn't answer most of them, and she understood why.

After breakfast, he'd followed Ashlyn to her apartment so she could change and get ready for their outing at Duke's. They'd walked up and down the Waikiki beach, people watching and making up stories about some of the more flamboyant characters they saw. And now they were at the restaurant with the rest of their friends.

"Seriously," Lexie repeated. "You're glowing. If I didn't know better, I'd say you were pregnant."

Ashlyn nearly spit out the sip of mai tai she'd just taken. Slate had handed it to her when she was talking with her friends earlier. She had no plans to drive for the rest of the day, so she felt comfortable imbibing a bit...and obviously Slate knew that.

"Jeez, I'm not pregnant," Ashlyn said when she had herself under control.

"I'm with Lexie. You look different. Not bad different, just...*different*," Kenna said as she took a sip of her own drink.

"I'm the same person I've always been," Ashlyn told them.

"Things with Slate are going well," Elodie said. It wasn't a question.

"Yeah."

"I'm glad," Elodie added.

"And the casual thing is still the plan?" Carly asked.

"Of course. Why?" Ashlyn asked.

"No reason. I just... Never mind."

"Seriously, what?" Ashlyn insisted.

"Okay, but you can't get mad. I was just thinking that I've never seen Slate look so...calm. Usually, he seems as if he's on the verge of throwing up his hands and saying 'fuck this' and storming out of the room."

"I agree," Monica said. She had a glass of water in her hand instead of a cocktail on account of her pregnancy. "His eyes used to roam the room pretty constantly, as if he's always looking for danger or some excuse to leave. Lately, his gaze has been glued on *you*."

Her friends' words made a warm glow spread within Ashlyn. She shrugged. "He's a protector. You guys know that because your men are the same way. It's just who he is."

"You're right," Lexie said. "But it seems more intense now."

"He's always watched you, but lately it's different," Elodie agreed.

"Well, we're having sex," Ashlyn said matter-of-factly. "Our relationship has changed. It's more personal. And maybe he's just watching me more intently today because we didn't have sex last night or this morning, and now he's horny." She tried to blow off her friends' words, because thinking about any kind of permanent relationship with Slate was dangerous. They both knew the score, and she wasn't going to mess with that. It wouldn't be fair to either of them.

"Wait, wait, wait," Lexie said as she narrowed her eyes. She looked around then leaned into Ashlyn. "Last night *or* this morning? Did you stay the night? Or did he?"

Ashlyn sighed. She loved her friends, but they were way too observant sometimes. And had memories like elephants when it suited them. "Yes. I didn't mean to, but I fell asleep on his couch. He couldn't wake me up because of how heavy I sleep, so he carried me to bed."

All five of her friends sighed as if that was the most romantic thing they'd ever heard.

"You do sleep like the dead," Kenna said after a moment. "That first sleepover we had, I felt bad because we were all being so loud while you were sleeping, but you didn't even flinch."

"But things are okay?" Lexie asked, putting her hand on Ashlyn's arm.

She nodded. She'd confided in Lexie not too long ago that she and Slate had never spent the entire night together, and that she worried about how it could affect their relationship for the worse if they took that step.

"It's good. Really good, actually," Ashlyn said.

"Hey, guys, they're ready for us!" Jag called out. They'd all been hanging out in the bar area at Duke's until the food was ready. Alani, the manager, had set up a few tables in one corner of the restaurant for their party.

The women all headed for their men, but Elodie caught Ashlyn's arm, holding her back for a second. "I'm happy for you," she said.

"Thanks," Ashlyn said with a smile.

"I know you plan to keep things casual, but I just have to say...don't be afraid to go after what you want."

Ashlyn stared at the other woman. Elodie had been through hell, and somehow she'd managed to come out the other side with not only her sanity intact, but with a man who would move heaven and earth to make sure she was safe and had everything she'd ever wanted.

"What I want is to have a good time. Date a man who isn't a jerk, isn't trying to mooch off me, and who likes me for who I am. So far, Slate is that man. I'm not ready to settle down. I don't want to get married right now, and I definitely don't want children at this point in my life."

"I just don't want you to be too stubborn. Or regret giving up what could be the best thing to ever happen to you," Elodie said.

"Slate's a good man. Actually, he's a *great* man. But I'm not sure he's 'the one.' How can I know when I've been in so few serious relationships?" Ashlyn said. "We're taking things one day at a time. We're enjoying each other's company and the sex is out of this world. The last thing I want to do is screw it up by moving too fast."

"I understand," Elodie said. "Just don't let your hormones overrule your good sense."

Ashlyn opened her mouth to ask what she meant by that, but an arm wrapped around her waist. "All the good shit'll be gone if you don't get a move on," Slate said impatiently.

Ashlyn rolled her eyes. "Always in a hurry," she teased.

"Hell yeah I am, when it comes to beating these guys out for food," Slate said.

"Lexie looks like she's ready to fight someone if they get too close to those chicken wings she's been salivating about since she heard they were going to be on the menu," Elodie remarked.

They headed for the corner, where everyone was filling their plates with samples. Slate leaned down and whispered, "You good?"

Ashlyn stopped and looked up at him. "Yeah, why?"

"You get uncomfortable when you're the center of everyone's attention, and it looked like things were kind of intense for a while there."

Ashlyn was surprised he knew that about her, but she supposed she shouldn't be. They'd known each other for quite a while now, even if they'd only been officially dating for a month or so. "I'm fine. They just wanted to know if you were good in bed."

Slate blinked.

Ashlyn couldn't keep a straight face. She burst out laughing. "Oh my God, if you could only see your face."

"Brat," Slate growled. "I was trying to be nice."

Ashlyn sobered and put her hand on Slate's arm. "I'm sorry. I know you were, and I appreciate it. I'm good. They were just saying that they thought I looked really happy. And I am, Slate. I was worried this morning that you'd think I was overstepping the boundaries we'd put up as to how things should work in our relationship. But you made everything seem normal. It's been a really awesome day, and I'm very satisfied with how things are going between us."

"I don't like rules in my relationships," he told her seriously. "I have enough fucking rules I have to follow at work. I want things between us to progress naturally. I had no problem with you staying the night, Ashlyn. I was actually relieved you wouldn't be driving alone that late...something that bothers me every time you leave my place. And I wasn't lying when I said I slept really well. I'm not ready to move in together or anything, but staying the entire night, either at your place or mine, is definitely not off the table as far as I'm concerned."

Ashlyn grinned. "I feel the same."

"Good. *Now* can we go get something to eat?" he asked.

Even though he was trying to act put out, Ashlyn could tell he was relieved by her response. "Yes." Then she put her hand on the side of his face and waited until he met her gaze. "Thank you."

"For what?" Slate asked.

"For being you."

The words didn't accurately portray what she wanted him to know. How glad she was that he was the kind of man who worried about his girlfriend driving home late at night, even if she was perfectly capable of doing so. That he was concerned about her being sore. That he drew her a bath, then took her for a leisurely walk when he could've been doing something more productive. That he seemed worried her friends were giving her a hard time. That he listened to her stories about her clients when she was well aware he worried about her going to so many people's houses.

She was glad he was the man he was in so very many ways.

Slate must have understood the deeper meaning behind her words, because he didn't make a joke. He just nodded, then leaned down to kiss her. Right there in the middle of the restaurant, he covered her lips with his and demanded entry to her mouth. The kiss seemed...more intense than usual, for some reason. More meaningful.

When he pulled back, Ashlyn licked her lips and stared up at him. He brought his hand to her cheek and rubbed his thumb over her skin in a gentle caress before nodding again, grabbing her hand, then towing her toward their friends.

* * *

Later that night, after Carly and Jag had decided on what dishes to serve at their wedding, after she'd laughed with her friends until her stomach hurt, after stopping back at Slate's house so he could grab his PT clothes for Monday morning, after dinner—during which Slate had pulled out a gallon of Duke's mai tais he'd somehow conned Carly into letting him take out, even though it was illegal—after getting drunk on said mai tais, and after Slate had fucked her on her couch, against a wall, gone down on her until she begged for mercy, and then made long, slow, sweet love to her, Ashlyn lay boneless and completely relaxed against him in her bed.

"Still sore?" he asked softly as he ran his hand up and down the bare skin of her back.

Ashlyn couldn't help but laugh. "I can barely remember my name after all the alcohol and the orgasms. I wouldn't know if I was sore if my life depended on it."

Slate chuckled.

A comfortable silence descended between them for a minute or two. Then Slate said, "Had another really good day."

Ashlyn grinned against him, feeling his words warm her down to her toes. "Me too."

"Who's on your schedule tomorrow?" he asked.

She snorted. "No clue. And you don't really expect me to think right now, do you?"

"I think I like you like this."

"Like how?"

"Tipsy. And in a sex coma."

Ashlyn giggled. "Why does that not surprise me?"

"Gonna get up early to head to PT. You want me to wake you up before I go or let you sleep?" he asked.

"Wake me up," she said immediately.

"You gonna be *able* to be woken up?" he retorted.

"Yes," she said somewhat huffily. "I'm only a super-deep sleeper right after I lay down. In the morning, after I've gotten my beauty sleep, I wake up easily."

"All right, babe. I'll put a glass of water next to the bed. Be sure to drink it all without giving me shit about it, okay?"

"I'm not *that* drunk," she protested, even though it had been quite a while since she'd had as much alcohol as she'd had today.

"Still," he said.

"Fine, Mr. Bossypants. I'll drink it."

"Thank you."

It was nice to have him here. When they'd first started

dating Ashlyn remembered thinking she was glad to have her bed to herself after sex. But now she couldn't think of one good reason why she'd want to be alone. He was warm, he liked to snuggle, and despite his hard body, he made an excellent pillow.

"Ash?"

"Hmmm?" she said, on the verge of falling asleep.

After a long pause, he answered, "Sleep well."

She had the fleeting thought that those words weren't what he'd meant to say, but she was too tired and replete to question him. "You too."

CHAPTER NINE

Slate stared down at the sleeping woman in the bed. Yesterday...well, the last two days...had been enlightening. While the sex between them was the best he'd ever had, and he loved how enthusiastic she was when it came to anything in bed, he was finding that he actually enjoyed being with her when sex was off the table just as much.

It had been a long time since he'd slept with a woman. *Slept*, slept. As he'd told Ashlyn, he was a light sleeper. The slightest noise or movement typically woke him up. So staying with a woman after they'd had sex usually meant a shitty night's sleep. But with Ashlyn, because of how soundly she slept, he hadn't woken up once.

It was the ass crack of dawn on Monday, and he had to get to PT on time or Mustang would give him hell. But Slate couldn't make himself go. He had no idea what it was about Ashlyn that made him reluctant to leave. She was a good woman, he respected her, but he wasn't ready to settle down like his teammates had.

With that thought in his head, Slate leaned down and shook Ashlyn slightly.

SUSAN STOKER

She groaned.

He couldn't help but smirk. "Hey, babe. I'm headed out."

"Umkay," she mumbled.

"Wake up and drink some water," he ordered.

"I'm awake," she said in a tone that belied her words.

"Ash, *up*. You promised you'd drink this water."

Frowning, Ashlyn opened her eyes. "You're really annoying," she told him.

"And you'll feel better if you drink something. Trust me."

"Fine," she groused and reached for the glass he was holding out to her. She guzzled the water down without stopping to breathe, which only made his smile widen.

"There. Happy?" she asked in a huff as she flopped back down to the mattress.

"Yes. I was thinking..." Slate said.

Ashlyn groaned. "Thinking this early in the morning can't be a good thing."

"We've got water training this Wednesday, then we'll have the rest of the afternoon off. What would you think about me coming with you on some of your deliveries that day?"

Ashlyn's eyes popped open once more. "Are you serious?"

"Yeah."

"Yes! I'd love that. The Turners are on my schedule for that day. And James too. Oh, and Jazmin. Her son Henry gets home from school around three-thirty, and he loves everything having to do with the military. I'm sure he'd love to meet you."

Slate wasn't sure why he'd offered to go with her...probably to further put his mind at ease about her job. He was pleased with her enthusiastic response though. "Great. I can meet you at Food For All after lunch. Will that work?"

"Perfect."

"It's a plan then. Go back to sleep for a while. You want

108

me to call after PT and make sure you're up and moving?" he asked.

"Yeah, would you? I'm usually good at getting up, but I think I'm kind of hungover."

Slate wanted to laugh, but knew she wouldn't appreciate it. He figured she'd be hurting a bit, which was why he'd insisted on her drinking the water.

"Okay, babe. I'll talk to you later." Slate leaned down and kissed her on the lips gently.

"Later," she said, then reached out and grabbed his hand before he could walk away. "Slate?"

"Yeah?"

"I can't wait for Wednesday."

"Me too, babe. Me too," he said, then squeezed her hand and headed for the door. He turned around once more to look at the woman he couldn't seem to get off his mind, before forcing himself to leave.

* * *

"What's up with you and Ashlyn?" Mustang asked after PT. The others had all left already, and Slate was helping his team leader pack his car with the weights they'd used that morning.

"We're dating," Slate said.

"No shit, Sherlock," Mustang said. "But things look more serious now than when you two first started going out."

"Why?" he asked, crossing his arms over his chest.

"Look, I'm not trying to be an asshole here, but a blind man could see the intensity between you two. Especially when you claim to be merely friends with benefits."

"And *I* don't want to be an asshole, but what's between me and Ashlyn is between me and Ashlyn," Slate said. He wasn't ready to talk about his relationship with anyone. Hell, he wasn't sure what there was to say. They were dating. Period.

Not planning a fucking wedding like Jag and Carly, and not trying to figure out a name for their kid like Pid and Monica.

"Right, I can respect that. But I'm just trying to look out for her. Women are...not like us. They're more emotional. Elodie and I are both worried that things are gonna go bad if one of you falls in love and the other doesn't."

Slate couldn't help but laugh. "We aren't in love," he said without hesitation. "Hell, it was Ashlyn's idea to have a friends-with-benefits relationship."

"But you've been spending more time with her lately. And now you're spending the night," Mustang said.

Slate scowled. "So?"

"So, I'm just saying, be careful. I like Ashlyn. Elodie likes Ashlyn. Hell, *everyone* likes her. I just don't want to see things get weird in the future if this doesn't work out between you guys."

"They won't," Slate said firmly. He could see the skepticism on his friend's face. "We've already talked about this. We're good. Great, even. The sex is good—no, it's fucking phenomenal. She's fun to hang out with and we have a good time. But that's it, Mustang. Seriously."

"You know the saying about protesting too much, right?" his friend said sarcastically.

"I need you to get off my back about this," Slate retorted. "I respect you and would take a fucking bullet for you, but give this a rest. We're good. I like her. I don't love her, and I'm not ready to settle down like you and the others. If you can't handle that, I don't know what to say. I didn't get the memo that said I had to marry the next girl I had sex with," he said, feeling defensive now.

"All right," Mustang said, holding up his hands. "I'll lay off. I've said my piece anyway. Back to business. I haven't said anything to the rest of the team yet, will do just that this morning when we all get to work, but there's a chance we'll be headed to Bahrain later this week."

Slate winced. "Bodyguard duty?"

"Yeah," Mustang said with a nod. "Tensions are still high now that Israel is part of the Central Command instead of the European one. With the CENTCOM meeting in Bahrain next week, we've been asked to not only provide extra security for the US representatives, but to be there just in case things get messy."

"Damn," Slate sighed. Then he shrugged. "Better than crawling around the mountains of Iran or Iraq looking for insurgents."

"Very true. No one expects this to be anything other than what it is...standing around being bored out of our minds for a few days while politicians attempt to come to some sort of compromise on foreign policy."

"All right. I'll be interested in hearing the details later today. Oh, wait, you think we'll be headed out *after* Wednesday, right?"

"Most likely, why?"

"Told Ash I'd go with her on her deliveries Wednesday afternoon," Slate said.

Mustang grinned, but as promised, he didn't take the chance to sneak in another comment about his relationship with Ashlyn. "I suspect you should still be good to do that. The meetings don't start until Sunday, so we shouldn't have to head out until Friday. Thursday night at the very earliest."

"Great. You don't expect any complications on us getting back, do you? It would suck for Jag and Carly to have to reschedule their wedding."

"Nope. That was one reason I pushed the commander to let us take this mission instead of something else," Mustang said. "I know the wedding's not for another month or so, but we both know sometimes short and easy missions can turn out to be anything but."

Slate nodded in approval. Mustang was a good team leader. He wasn't afraid to make hard decisions when they were warranted, but he always had the best interests at heart for the SEALs under his command.

"Gonna head out. See you later," Slate said.

Mustang nodded and shut his trunk. "Later."

On the way back to his house, Slate refused to think too hard on what Mustang had said. He and Ashlyn were fine. They knew where things stood. Neither was ready for a permanent relationship, and neither was in love with the other. Things were good. Great, in fact.

Slate refused to let his friends' concerns get to him. Just because they wanted to see him settled down like they were, didn't mean that was going to happen right this second.

He let his thoughts turn to the night before. How hot Ashlyn had burned for him. His cock hardened, and Slate took a deep breath. For just a moment, he wished he was headed back to her place. He'd love to wake her up with his mouth between her legs, giving her an orgasm or two before getting off himself. But he'd have to be satisfied with his own hand in the shower.

After, he'd call Ashlyn to make sure she was awake and moving before heading into work. If the team was going out of town, there would be a lot of logistics to figure out ahead of time. The entire week would be busy with reports and intel gathering, not to mention their training Wednesday morning. Spending time with Ashlyn on her deliveries would be a nice break in what was shaping up to be a very hectic week.

CHAPTER TEN

"You look tired," Ashlyn blurted. She hadn't meant to be so rude right off the bat, but she couldn't take the words back now. She hadn't seen Slate since Monday, and she hated that he looked so exhausted.

Luckily, he didn't take offense. "Yeah, we've had a couple of long days."

Slate had told her about the upcoming mission when he'd called Monday night, and he'd reassured her that it wasn't anything dangerous. She wasn't sure she should completely believe him, but since he'd never lied to her so far, she figured she'd give him the benefit of the doubt.

But just because it wasn't going to be a life-or-death thing didn't mean he wasn't working his ass off. It wasn't until late last night that he was even certain he'd have this afternoon off.

Ashlyn had been looking forward to him meeting some of her clients, and even though she would've understood if he'd had to cancel, she was relieved he was still able to come with her. Regardless, she couldn't help but say, "If you'd rather not go so you can take a nap or something, I'll understand."

They were standing in the parking lot near Food For All, where she'd met him after lunch to continue her delivery route. Slate walked up to her and put his hands on either side of her head. "I've been looking forward to this for a while now. All the stories you've told me about your clients have hooked me. I want to come with you, Ash."

"Okay," she said with a huge smile.

He stared at her for a long moment before slowly lowering his head. "I haven't said hello properly, have I?" he asked. He didn't give her a chance to answer before his lips were on hers. Unlike some of their kisses, this one was slow and lazy, but it still had Ashlyn squirming.

"Now I'm ready to go," he said after lifting his head and licking his lips as if trying to capture her taste.

"And I'm horny as hell," Ashlyn mumbled. She was rewarded by Slate's chuckle. He walked around to the driver's side of her RAV4 and opened the door for her. She got settled in behind the wheel and watched Slate as he strode around the car to the other side.

Once he was in and had buckled his seat belt, he said, "Drive on, James."

Ashlyn rolled her eyes. "You're a dork," she told him as she started the car.

He simply grinned.

After she'd pulled out and they were on their way, she asked, "Does it bother you that I'm driving?"

"Why would it?" he asked, the confusion easy to hear in his voice.

"Well, men like you seem to like to be in charge all the time. In control. And letting a woman drive seems to go against that."

"I don't give a shit if you drive," he said easily. "There are times when I like to be in charge, and I can't deny that I've got a tiny bit of a control issue. But I've seen you drive, babe.

You're careful and not reckless. You don't speed and you've never honked your horn in anger at anyone. I know those things don't make you immune to accidents, but I'm comfortable with you driving."

Some women might not find his comments terribly important, but Ashlyn felt as if she'd passed some momentous test. It was silly, she was just driving, for goodness sake, but still. "Thanks," she said after a moment. "I've always thought it was crazy that a man thinks he's safer in a car when he's driving."

Slate smiled at her. "So, where are we going first?"

"The Turners. Trey is probably at work, but Brooklyn will be there with her little ones."

"The kids are two and three, right?" Slate asked.

Pleased he'd remembered, Ashlyn nodded. "Yup. And they're definitely a handful."

"You want kids?" Slate asked.

Ashlyn's eyes widened and she glanced over at him.

He laughed. "Relax. That wasn't an invitation. I'm just curious."

She breathed out a sigh of relief. "I guess so."

"Hmmm, that doesn't really sound like a yes to me," Slate noted.

Ashlyn shrugged. "It's not that I don't like kids. I do. But so far, I've never had a huge urge to have my own. Maybe that makes me selfish, but I like my life. I see Brooklyn, or Jazmin, or other parents on my route, and I see how hard they're struggling and how exhausted they always are, and it doesn't exactly make me anxious to enter motherhood myself."

"You don't think they're happy with their kids?" Slate asked.

"It's not that. They love their children, that's obvious. And I'd probably feel different if I had my own, but for now, I just don't feel that huge pull." She shrugged again, struggling to find the right words. "It's hard to explain."

"No, you're explaining it just fine. And for the record, I don't think you're selfish. Having children is a huge commitment. It takes time, a lot of effort, and yes, money. Not to mention the world is a scary place, and seems to be getting scarier with every day that passes. I understand."

Ashlyn glanced over at him. "What's your stance on kids?" She couldn't believe she'd gotten up the gumption to ask. But then again, he'd started the conversation.

"About the same as you. My reticence is more because I'd hate to leave a child fatherless if something happened to me. I'm good at my job, and I have five of the best men I could ask for at my back, but when your time is up, it's up. I wouldn't want a child of mine to have to deal with my death."

"But you won't always be a SEAL," Ashlyn pointed out.

"True. And my feelings on having children might change once I'm out." It was his turn to shrug.

They were silent for a while as Ashlyn drove.

"For what it's worth, I think you'd make a great mother," Slate said. "You'd find a way to make things work out if you had a kid. I'm guessing you'd probably strap him or her in a car seat and continue right on with your deliveries, charming the hell out of all your clients."

She smiled. "Thanks. And the same back at you. You'd be an awesome dad. I have a feeling you'd be totally hands-on and any child of yours would be a mini-you. Following you around and wanting to be just like their daddy."

Slate didn't respond, just reached for her hand. He squeezed it gently, then kept hold as they drove.

This was what Ashlyn had wanted in a relationship all her life. Someone she could be honest with, who would be a true partner, who she connected with sexually...and who could make her feel all tingly inside by simply holding her hand.

She held back an ironic sigh. Figures she'd find exactly what she wished for with a man she was only seeing casually.

Ten minutes later, she pulled onto the street where the Turners lived. She parked in front of their house and cut the engine. She and Slate climbed out of the car after she popped the hatch on the back. Slate grabbed the box with the meals and followed behind her as she walked up to the front door.

She knocked softly, not wanting to wake the kids if they were napping, but the excited screech from inside let her know they definitely weren't asleep.

Brooklyn opened the door, joining them on the porch when Briar and Curtis toddled out and grabbed onto Ashlyn's legs.

"Ash!" the little boy said with a huge smile.

His sister didn't say anything, just tilted her head up and grinned.

"Hey, kiddos! You doing good today?" Ashlyn asked.

The toddlers didn't answer, not that she expected them to. Ashlyn looked at their mom—and swallowed a chuckle at the way she was staring at Slate. He still had on the uniform he'd worn to work that morning, and he'd started growing his beard out a bit. He'd said it was in preparation for the mission they'd be leaving for in a few days; that in many places, a beard helped him blend in with the locals. But for now, it just made him even more gorgeous.

Brooklyn obviously agreed.

"Hey, Brook," Ashlyn said. "This is Slate. He's helping me with deliveries today."

"Hi," she said shyly.

"Hi," Curtis said, copying his mom. He walked over to Slate and grabbed his pants leg. "Up!" he demanded.

"Oh, I'm sorry," Brooklyn said, reaching for her son. "He has a thing with being carried recently. It's been hell on my back."

"It's fine," Slate said. "If you'll take this?" he asked, holding the box out to Ashlyn.

She grabbed it and watched as he bent over and picked up the little boy. He sat him on his hip and grinned. "Hey, Curtis. You been a good boy today for your mama?"

Curtis seemed mesmerized by Slate. He put a hand on his face and patted his beard.

Ashlyn swore her ovaries clenched at seeing Slate holding the little boy. She might've just told him that she wasn't ready to have kids of her own, but seeing him with Curtis was already making her rethink that decision.

"Come in," Brooklyn said, picking up little Briar and gesturing inside her house. "The place is a mess, but I've learned to just go with it and try not to be too embarrassed. Having two toddlers definitely doesn't make it easy to keep a clean house."

"It's fine," Ashlyn reassured her. "And we can't stay today. I'm behind schedule because I took a long lunch to meet up with Slate. But you'll love the food. Elodie outdid herself today with the meals. She made veggie pockets, which sound completely plain and boring, but somehow, like usual, she was able to make them gourmet. She thinly sliced red and green peppers, put some onions, mushrooms, zucchini, lettuce, and tomatoes inside a focaccia pocket. Then she added brie cheese and this delicious horseradish mayonnaise. Trust me, even if you don't think you like some of those ingredients, you'll change your mind when you taste them all together."

"It sounds amazing," Brooklyn said.

"And I know Trey isn't a huge fan of veggies, so I grabbed a lemon pepper chicken breast for him. Oh, and the seven layer dessert bars are to die for. I recommend you have a glass of milk handy when you eat them," she suggested with a grin. "It's a perfect pairing."

"I can't wait to try everything," Brooklyn said.

"I've also got some Pull-Ups in the car," Ashlyn said. "Someone came by and donated them, and I figured you could use them."

"Oh, yes, thank you so much!"

"If you take him, I'll go get them," Slate said.

Ashlyn immediately reached for the little boy. Curtis was smiling, happy to have another adult paying attention to him. In contrast, his sister seemed satisfied to hang out in her mother's arms.

As soon as Slate was off the porch, heading back to the car, Brooklyn said, "Giiiiirl!"

Ashlyn laughed. "I know, right?"

"I remember you said you were dating someone, but *damn*."

"Yeah, he's great."

"If the things you've said about him are true, he's more than great. You need to hang on to him, Ash. He's gorgeous, considerate, and he was great with Curtis."

"We're not serious," Ashlyn protested.

Brooklyn raised an eyebrow. "Does *he* know that? Because the way he keeps his eyes on you says differently."

"Of course he does. That's just how he is. He's very...intense."

"Uh-huh, keep telling yourself that."

Ashlyn opened her mouth to protest, but Slate returned before she could say anything else.

"Here you go. Can I bring them inside for you?"

"Yes, please," Brooklyn said with a smile, stepping out of the way and raising both eyebrows at Ashlyn the second Slate turned to place the box of Pull-Ups just inside the door.

She just smiled at the other woman.

"Thanks again for the meals. I can't wait to try them."

"Of course. I'll see you on Friday," Ashlyn told her, leaning over and carefully placing Curtis on the porch. When his mom opened the door, he ran into the house with a screech and didn't look back.

"Jeez, he's on a roll today. Thanks again, and I'll see you Friday," Brooklyn said as she headed inside to wrangle her toddler.

When they got back into the car, Slate was smiling at her.

"What?" Ashlyn asked.

"Nothing."

"Come on, what?" she cajoled.

"You looked good with him."

She knew exactly who Slate was talking about. "I could say the same about you. I stand by my earlier statement, you'd make a great dad."

"She's nice, but she's struggling," Slate said next.

"I know. I wish I could do more for her."

"You're doing more than a lot of people are. And I noticed you didn't tell her that you *bought* those Pull-Ups."

Ashlyn shrugged. "She's proud. And it wasn't a big deal for me to pick up a pack at the store when I was there last."

"I regret not doing this before now," Slate said.

"Doing what?" Ashlyn asked as she started the car.

"Coming with you. Seeing the people you help. If I had, I might not have given you such a hard time about the deliveries."

His words meant a lot. "Thanks."

"I mean it. They clearly care a lot about you, and you obviously worry about them. They're lucky to have you in their corner."

"Well, you've only met one client," Ashlyn said, almost embarrassed by his praise. "They aren't all as friendly as Brooklyn and her kids."

"Bet they're still appreciative though," Slate said. "Where to next?"

The afternoon passed quickly. It was nice to work side-by-side with Slate. As Ashlyn warned, not all her clients were overly friendly, but they all seemed glad to see her and grateful for the food.

It was close to five o'clock when she pulled up in front of the last house. "I saved James for last," she told Slate. "He's gonna be super excited to meet you and will probably want to talk about the Navy. Is that okay? Do you need to get back?"

"It's fine," Slate said. "I've heard you talk about him so much, I feel like I already know him. You want to grab dinner after we check back in with Lexie at Food For All?"

Ashlyn nodded. "Sure."

"Hearing you talk about the veggie pocket sandwich and lemon pepper chicken all day has my stomach growling."

She laughed. "Come on, I'm sure James is waiting for us. He has a chair right by the window in front so he can see all the people coming and going in the neighborhood."

This time when they walked toward the door, Slate held her hand as he carried the remaining meal with the other.

James opened the door before they'd reached it. "How's my favorite girl doing?" he asked with a grin.

Ashlyn dropped Slate's hand and carefully embraced the older man. His back was rounded with age and his white hair was in disarray on his head. He had scruff on his face from not shaving for a day or so, and there were stains on his shirt. But the welcome she got from him every time she came by was so genuine, his disheveled appearance didn't even faze her.

"Sorry we're late," she said when she pulled back. Ashlyn kept her hand on his upper arm to make sure he didn't fall over. For eighty-eight, he was surprisingly mobile, but she didn't want to take any chances that he'd stumble.

"You're not late, you're right on time!" James exclaimed. "I just made a new pot of coffee. Can you come in for a while?"

Ashlyn would've scolded him for how much coffee he

drank, but the one time she'd brought it up, he told her that he'd been drinking two pots of the stuff every day his entire life and he wasn't about to stop now.

"We'd love to stay for a bit," Ashlyn reassured him. "James, I want you to meet Slate. He's my boyfriend. I told you about him."

"He the SEAL?" James asked.

Ashlyn did her best to hide her smile. Slate had told her it would be okay to tell James what he did for a living, and it somewhat amused her that he'd yet to speak directly to him. "Yes. This is him."

James's gaze turned to Slate. He stood up a little straighter and brought his hand up to his forehead in a salute. "Pleased to meet you."

Slate returned the salute with one of his own. "I've heard you've got some damn good stories about your time in the service," he said.

Ashlyn felt James relax in her grip. It was obvious he'd been nervous to meet Slate. He'd told Ashlyn that he didn't get out much anymore and had a hard time connecting with younger people.

"I bet you've got some stories of your own," James said.

"That I do," Slate agreed with a nod.

"Well, come on, don't stand out here on the front stoop all day. I'll get us all some coffee and we can talk."

"How about you and Slate sit, and I'll get the coffee?" Ashlyn suggested. She knew from experience that James liked his coffee very strong and very black. If she was going to choke it down, she needed to doctor hers up a bit.

"Fine, fine. We'll just go and relax then," James said.

Ashlyn reached for the bag Slate was holding. He smoothly transferred it to her while taking hold of James's elbow at the same time, to make sure he didn't fall. The move was so casual, she suspected James didn't feel as if he was being treated like an invalid.

Slate nodded at her, and Ashlyn couldn't help but see the approval and admiration in his eyes when he held her gaze for a moment. He led James into the house. It was small and cluttered, but clean. Ashlyn knew he had someone who came in every other day to take care of small chores around the house, and to make sure James was eating.

Slate got him settled in the recliner he obviously preferred to sit in, and took a seat on the couch across from the older man. Ashlyn heard them immediately start talking about life onboard a Naval ship and what countries they'd been to.

Smiling, she put the bag with the lemon pepper chicken breast on the counter and opened the cabinet to get out two coffee mugs. James's mug was already sitting on the counter, stained brown from many years of use. Ashlyn had been appalled the first time she'd seen it and tried to scrub out the stains, but it was no use. She figured if drinking out of the mug hadn't done James in yet, it wasn't worth her worry.

She put his chicken on a plate, along with the sides, wanting to make sure James ate before they left, and after heating it in the microwave, she cut the chicken into bite-size pieces. James could cut up his own food, but had admitted once that his wife used to do the same thing for him, and how much he missed the small gesture. She poured the dark coffee into mugs. Fairly certain Slate wouldn't mind the strong brew, she added sugar only to her own.

She took the coffee out to the men first, smiling to herself when James barely even looked at her. She didn't mind though, it was nice to see him so excited to talk to someone who could truly appreciate his history.

Then she brought out the plate to James, and handed him a fork. He didn't miss a beat in the story he was telling Slate about his time on the USS *Maddox* and when they'd faced down three Vietnamese torpedo boats back in the sixties. Just shoveled the first bite of chicken into his mouth and kept talking.

Slate met her gaze again, his eyes twinkling with humor, before taking a sip of the coffee and returning his attention to the older man.

Ashlyn wandered back into the kitchen, not wanting to intrude on the "guy time" going on in the other room. She loved hearing James's stories, but had heard most of them more than once. Looking around the kitchen more closely, she frowned. It didn't seem as if James's helper had done much when he'd been there yesterday. From what she understood, Aiden Quinlan came on Tuesday, Thursday, and Sunday to help James out.

She'd met him only once, and Ashlyn wasn't sure what to think of the man. He was Slate's height, around six-two, and about the same age as well, in his early thirties. He had blond hair and blue eyes, had been pretty quiet when she met him... but for some reason, he just rubbed Ashlyn the wrong way. She couldn't say why, exactly. It was just a gut feeling. James seemed to like him, so she'd kept her opinion to herself.

But lately when she stopped by, it seemed as if the house wasn't being taken care of as well as it should've been. Peeking into the half bathroom off the kitchen, Ashlyn wrinkled her nose. The roll of toilet paper was empty, the trash was full, and the toilet lid was up. It was obvious the room hadn't been cleaned in a while.

She headed back into the kitchen to grab some paper towels and cleanser. While James and Slate were talking, she might as well pass the time by cleaning up a bit.

Half an hour later, the bathroom was clean, as was the kitchen. She'd washed the dishes sitting in the sink and had thrown away the spoiled food in the refrigerator. She'd even gone into James's room and collected his dirty clothes and started a load in the washer.

A knock on the door surprised her, and Ashlyn stepped into the living room where James and Slate had been talking nonstop. She blinked in surprise at seeing Aiden standing there. As far as she knew, he wasn't scheduled to come by on Wednesdays.

"Oh, hi. I thought you'd be gone already," Aiden said when he spotted Ashlyn.

She walked into the room and shrugged. "I rearranged my delivery schedule so Slate could meet James."

"Hey. Good to meet you," Aiden said, even though he hadn't been introduced yet. "I just stopped by to check on you, James, since you said your legs were hurting yesterday," Aiden continued.

"Your legs hurt?" Ashlyn asked in concern.

"It's not a big deal," James said, waving off their concerns. "I'm eighty-eight, I'm allowed to have aches and pains."

"Have you talked to your doctor?" she asked.

"Not yet. If it continues, I will," James reassured her.

"Well, since it looks like you're good, I'll be heading out," Aiden said, using his thumb to point at the front door he'd just entered.

"Can I talk to you for a second?" Ashlyn asked quickly.

A look of impatience crossed Aiden's face.

"It won't take long," she told him.

"Fine."

"We can talk in the kitchen," she said, when it didn't look like Aiden was going to move from his spot next to the door.

He sighed and nodded, walking toward her.

Slate's eyes were glued to the other man, and when Aiden glanced his way as he walked by the couch, Ashlyn saw him take a step to the side...as if to get farther away.

If he was a little leery of Slate, Ashlyn wasn't going to complain.

When they were in the kitchen, out of earshot of James, Ashlyn didn't hesitate to get right to it. "This place was kind of a wreck when I got here. The bathroom, kitchen, and bedroom were a mess. You're paid to help clean for him, right?"

"You don't get to tell me how to do my job," Aiden retorted nastily.

Ashlyn was a little surprised at the venom in his tone. She probably could've been a bit more diplomatic in her criticism of the state of the house, but still.

"You're right, I'm sorry," she said immediately.

It was the right thing to say. Aiden's shoulders slumped and he ran a hand through his longish blond hair. "No, *I'm* sorry. I didn't mean to be a dick. James didn't have a good day yesterday, and he wasn't himself last weekend either. I spent all my time just talking with him, trying to snap him out of the depression he seems to have fallen into."

Ashlyn frowned. "Depression?"

"Yeah. He was still in bed when I got here on Sunday, and he told me he didn't want to get up when I tried to encourage him to do just that," Aiden said.

Ashlyn wasn't happy about what she was hearing. She was also surprised. "He seems to be okay today."

"Yeah, he does, which is a relief," Aiden agreed. "I didn't have time to clean like I usually do, so that's why it's messier than usual. I'll make sure I get to anything you didn't on Thursday. Thanks for doing the dishes and stuff."

"You're welcome. I'm thinking we need to say something to his doctor about his legs and his depression."

"He's embarrassed about it. Says he should be able to keep himself together better," Aiden told her. "He's been talking a lot about his wife and how much he misses her. I think he'll snap out of it, and I'm not sure it's a good thing to get a doctor involved without his permission. Even if we do, you and I both know they'll just prescribe some pills that'll knock him out or something. It's why I stopped by today even though I'm not scheduled. I wanted to check on him. Make sure he'd gotten out of bed and was okay."

Ashlyn nodded. "I appreciate it. He's like my own grandfather at this point. I wish he didn't live alone, but I guess there's nothing we can do about that."

"Nope. Anyway, thanks again for picking up in here. As I said, I'll be sure to get to the rest of the house tomorrow," Aiden said.

Reassured, Ashlyn smiled at him. "Sounds good."

"Great." He smiled back before adding, "So...how serious are you with that guy out there?"

Ashlyn was surprised by the question. "Um...pretty serious." Not quite, but she wasn't about to explain her and Slate's relationship to Aiden. Not when she didn't know him at all.

"Too bad. You're pretty hot. If you ever want to go out sometime, just leave your phone number on the counter after a delivery. We can hook up."

"Uh...okay."

"Okay," he echoed, then knocked twice on the counter and headed back into the other room.

Ashlyn trailed behind him, making sure to keep her distance. She didn't want to lead Aiden on in any way. He had to be a decent guy, since he made a living being an aide to older people like James. The first and only time she'd met him, he'd talked about the three other elderly people he cared for. But she wasn't attracted to him...and there was still that gut feeling she'd had on their first encounter. She didn't want to go out with the guy.

Aiden nodded at James and Slate, then headed for the

door. "See you tomorrow, old man," he said off-handedly as he left. He didn't even give James time to say anything before he was out the door and headed for a beat-up old Chevy Chevette parked behind Ashlyn's RAV4.

"Come sit, babe," Slate said, patting the cushion next to him.

Unable to interpret the look in his eyes, she did as he asked. She was tired from the day, and from cleaning the kitchen and bathroom, and wouldn't mind a short break.

The second she sat, Slate's hand landed on her leg. His fingers rested against her inner thigh...a very possessive touch. She didn't say anything, though she saw James watching them carefully with a small smile on his face.

"So...you gonna take care of Ashlyn?" James asked.

"Yes," Slate said without missing a beat.

"I heard a saying once, and it stuck with me. A man doesn't protect his woman because she's weak, he protects her because she's important," James said.

Ashlyn nearly melted in her seat. She liked that. A lot. She thought about Elodie, and Lexie, and Carly, Monica, and Kenna. Her friends were strong and independent, but they'd all been in situations where they'd needed protecting from the evil in this world. And their men, Slate's teammates, had not only stepped up to the plate, they'd made sure her friends never felt as if they weren't capable or strong in their own right.

"Very true," Slate said, turning to meet Ashlyn's gaze. "One thing I've learned over the years is that many times the strongest person is the one who needs someone at their back the most."

"I like him," James told Ashlyn. "You need to keep him."

Ashlyn smiled at the older man. "I like him too." She wasn't touching the "keep him" comment with a ten-foot pole. She had the sudden thought that when she and Slate finally broke up, it might just hurt her friends, including James, even more than it hurt *her*.

"How was it?" she asked, nodding at the empty plate in front of James.

"Good, as usual. Your friend sure knows how to cook," he said.

"That she does," Ashlyn agreed. "I'll take your plate into the kitchen before we get going." As much as she wanted to stay longer, it was getting late, and Slate had been tired before they'd set out on her rounds. He had to be even more exhausted now.

"Is there anything we can do for you before we go?" Slate asked, after Ashlyn stood. She felt his fingers trail along the small of her back before she headed over to where James was sitting to grab his plate.

"I'm good."

"You sure? Your legs aren't hurting you today?"

Ashlyn paused long enough to hear James's answer.

"No. Aiden's a worrywart. I'm fine."

Satisfied with the insistence in her friend's voice, Ashlyn entered the kitchen.

She washed the plate and fork by hand and put them away before going back into the living room. James was standing with Slate's hand on his elbow once more. When they saw her, they moved toward the front door.

Ashlyn hugged James, feeling Slate's hand move to her back again as she did so. She pulled back a bit and hardened her voice. "You have my phone number, I expect you to use it if you're not feeling good. Even if you just want to talk, I'll listen, okay?"

"You don't need to spend your free time listening to an old man," he told her with a small shake of his head.

"It's not a hardship," she told him. "I love you, James. You know that, right?"

His lip trembled a bit, but he got control over his emotions and nodded. "I do."

"Good. So call me if you're feeling lonely or down, alright?"

He nodded.

"Aiden's coming tomorrow, and I'll see you on Friday. I have it on good authority that Elodie is making one of your favorites."

"Frittata?" James asked hopefully.

"Yup," Ashlyn said with a smile. "So be good, or I'll make sure I run out before I get here."

"You will not," James said with certainty. "Take care of her," he said to Slate.

"I will," he told the man.

They waited until he'd shuffled inside and locked his door before getting into her car. Ashlyn started it up and headed back toward Food For All.

"That asshole asked you out, didn't he?" Slate growled after a few silent minutes.

Looking over at him in surprise, Ashlyn didn't even think about lying. "Aiden? Yeah. How'd you know?"

"Because he was eyeballin' you hard. What'd you say?" Slate asked.

Ashlyn wasn't sure she was ready for this conversation, but she didn't shy away from it. "I told him I wasn't interested."

"Good."

"Um...we haven't talked about this. I know we're casual and all, but what are your thoughts about seeing other people?"

"I only date one woman at a time," Slate said.

Relief swept through Ashlyn. "Same with me. So we're exclusive?"

"Yes. If you meet someone you're interested in, all I ask is that you let me know first."

Ashlyn wasn't sure what that meant. Let him know so he could break up with her? Let him know so he could date others, as well? He'd said he only dated one woman at a time, but would that change if he knew she was seeing someone else?

She was too chicken to ask any of those things. For the moment, she was just pleased that he wasn't interested in dating someone else at the same time they were seeing each other. Just because they were casual didn't mean she liked to share.

She realized that she hadn't responded to his last statement. "I will. And same goes for you."

Slate nodded. His jaw was tight, but Ashlyn couldn't figure out if he was upset with her, or with Aiden, or what.

After a few more minutes, he reached for her hand and brought it up to his mouth and kissed her fingers. "I'm sorry, he just took me by surprise. I didn't like the way he was looking at you."

Deciding she needed to lighten the mood, Ashlyn smiled at him. "I think it was probably the smell of chicken that was turning him on more."

As she'd hoped, Slate chuckled.

"Speaking of which, I'm starved. What'd you want for dinner?"

"I could make something," she told him.

"How about we stop at Plantation Tavern and pick something up on the way to my place?" he asked.

"Your place?" she asked.

She caught the gleam in Slate's eyes. "You have a problem with that?"

"Nope. Not at all."

"Good. And I just realized I forgot about my car. After we

get to Food For All, I'll go to the restaurant and pick up dinner, you can go on ahead to my house." He reached into his pocket and pulled out his keys. He took one off the ring and held it out to her. "I'll meet you on the roof."

Ashlyn loved that he was comfortable with her being in his space without being there himself...but him giving her a key mildly freaked her out.

As if he could read her mind, he said, "You can put the key on the table inside the door once you're in. I'll put it back to my keychain when I get there."

Ashlyn nodded. "Okay."

"Anything you're in the mood for?" he asked.

"Surprise me. You know what I like." And he did. They'd eaten together often enough, both with their friends and now plenty of times by themselves. He'd learned what she preferred to eat, and what she couldn't stand.

Slate nodded. "Sounds like a plan. I enjoyed seeing what you do today, Ash. And at the risk of hearing you say 'I told you so,' you were right about not being in danger. Most of your clients would bend over backward for you."

"Thank you," Ashlyn said. She wasn't exactly surprised that Slate was the kind of man who could admit when he was wrong, but it still felt good.

"But that doesn't mean I'm going to stop worrying about you," he warned. "There are assholes everywhere, you need to stay on your toes."

Ashlyn rolled her eyes. Figures he couldn't resist giving her a safety lecture. "Yes, sir," she quipped.

"If only you were that respectful all the time," he deadpanned.

Ashlyn burst out laughing. Being with Slate was so comfortable. She could be herself, and it felt nice that he respected what she did for a living. It had been a long time since she'd felt so connected to someone.

"Maybe I'll show you how respectful I can be tonight after dinner..." she said in a suggestive tone.

"Maybe you should meet me in my bedroom instead," he replied.

"Nope. My badass Navy SEAL has to eat. He's gonna need his strength."

"If I get a speeding ticket driving home from the restaurant, it's your fault," he complained as he shifted in his seat, trying to get comfortable with the erection Ashlyn could now see.

"I can live with that," she told him.

Today had been a great day. But Ashlyn had a feeling the night was going to be even better.

* * *

Aiden Quinlan wasn't happy. He was getting dope sick and didn't have any money to score more heroin. It had been over twenty-four hours since he'd had his last hit, and the nausea was setting in. He hated feeling the effects of withdrawal more than anything in the world.

His plan had been to stop by the old man's house to get some money so he could meet with his dealer that night, but he hadn't counted on Ashlyn being there. As it was, it wouldn't have been easy to raid the old man's stash with James sitting in the living room, but Aiden had been desperate enough to try.

Luckily, he'd remembered James's complaint about his legs hurting, and was able to use that as an excuse as to why he'd shown up on a day when he wasn't scheduled.

The audacity of that bitch to complain about the state of the house! Who was she to judge him? It wasn't her job to clean up after a bunch of disgusting old people. They were slobs, and he was sick and tired of being a maid, working for so little.

When he'd first started as a home health aide, Aiden had been more than pleased with his salary. But after tweaking his back while helping one of his clients, he'd been put on some heavy-duty painkillers. He liked them. A lot. His back was still messed up when the doctor stopped prescribing the medication, and Aiden had no choice but to try something a little...*less legal* to keep the pain at bay.

Even though the pain in his back had finally gone, his drug habit hadn't.

And now the money he got as a home health aide wasn't enough. It was never enough. Drugs were expensive, especially when his body needed more and more with every day that passed. But he'd lucked out in getting assigned to James Mason. The man hated banks with a passion and refused to use them.

The first time Aiden drove him to the bank to cash his social security check, he hadn't thought much about it when James pocketed the money and took it home with him. But as his need for dope increased, his interest in what the old guy did with his cash grew.

James was a paranoid old bastard. He never accessed his stashes while Aiden was in his home. But one day, he'd lucked out. As he was leaving work, he'd glanced back to the front window...and watched as James pulled a wad of cash out of a vase of flowers in the corner of the living room. It was always obvious the flowers were plastic. Aiden had thought the bouquet was ugly as fuck. Now he loved the damn thing.

Stealing money from the old coot was easy after that. Aiden had come up with the perfect plan, and for the last couple of months it had been working without a hitch. He took small amounts of money, not enough for James to notice, but enough for him to get a few hits. But now, he needed more dope to get the same high, and getting a couple bills once or twice a week wasn't enough.

He needed a bigger score. Needed to find more of James's hiding spots. It shouldn't be hard; the house wasn't that large.

"Tomorrow," he reassured himself as he paced his nearly barren apartment. He'd already pawned most of the things worth a few bucks. Now, desperate times called for desperate measures, and James Mason was his own personal ATM.

For a moment, his conscience made a rare appearance and Aiden felt bad about stealing from the old man. In many ways, he reminded him of his own grandfather. But he pushed those thoughts to the back of his mind. The only way he was going to get the dope he needed to function was by taking that money. James didn't need it. He didn't go anywhere or do anything. Besides, he'd never miss it. There was no way he knew exactly how much money he had stashed around the house.

Aiden would have to be more careful though. He'd need to stay away from the house on the days Ashlyn was supposed to be there. Hitting on her was a spur-of-the-moment thing. The closer he was to her, the better he'd know her schedule. He didn't want to give up his cash cow *or* his job, and deep down, he had a feeling Ashlyn could be a problem. If he was fucking her, he could more easily control the bitch, maybe even get some cash off her too. But she hadn't taken the bait...damn it.

The last thing he wanted was for anyone to discover what he was doing. He'd just have to take more cash, enough to last him a little while. And definitely no more unscheduled visits.

Satisfied with that plan, Aiden nodded. He still had no money, but he needed dope. Bad. It looked like he'd have to go down to Waikiki and panhandle, which he hated. He disliked being dope sick even more. Maybe all the sweating and the way his hands shook would make the tourists feel even more sorry for him. He could always claim his blood sugar was low, that he needed money to eat.

Aiden headed out to his car. By this time tomorrow, he'd be flying high, and old man Mason would be a few dollars poorer.

CHAPTER ELEVEN

Ashlyn settled back in the chaise lounge on Kenna's deck in the drool-worthy condo she shared with Aleck. The men had left the day before on a mission. Slate claimed it shouldn't be a long one, and that he was ninety-nine percent sure there wouldn't be AK47s, sand, or RPGs involved.

He'd meant it as a joke, but Ashlyn hadn't exactly been thrilled with the statement. Because it meant in the past, and in the future, those things *would be* involved, a reminder that Slate and his friends were frequently in mortal danger. Intellectually, she'd known they weren't exactly skipping through towns spreading love and cheer when they were deployed, but hearing it put so frankly was hard to take.

Dating a SEAL meant taking the bad with the good. And so far, Ashlyn had experienced mostly all good things with Slate. Deployments were part of dating a military man. She just had to suck it up. She'd missed Slate in the past when he'd gone on missions, but in a more abstract way, like she missed anyone on the team while they were putting their lives on the line.

Still...it was no longer the same.

"Sucks, doesn't it?" Elodie asked as she plunked herself down in the chair next to hers. The sun was just beginning to set and the sky was lit up with oranges and purples. Ashlyn should've been focused on the beauty in front of her, but she couldn't concentrate on the view.

"Yeah."

"It's different when you care about him," Elodie said with certainty.

"Are we talking about how much deployments suck?" Kenna asked as she came out to the balcony. "Because I'm up for the conversation if that's the case."

"Try being pregnant and having your man putting himself in harm's way," Monica complained as she wandered out behind Kenna.

"Or planning your wedding and not knowing if your fiancé is gonna make it back in time for it," Carly complained. "I mean, I know it's weeks until our wedding, but SEAL missions can easily go from a simple weekend kind of thing to being gone for months."

Ashlyn turned to Lexie, who'd been sitting with her on the deck before the others came outside. "You want to add your two cents?" she asked.

Lexie shrugged. "Don't figure I need to. You're now part of an exclusive club. The one none of us really wanted to join, but knew we had no choice if we were going to be with our men."

"Lexie, Monica, and I are in the even more unique position of knowing *exactly* what our guys do for a living," Elodie said gently. "We were smack dab in the middle of their missions when they met us."

"Does that make it easier or harder when they leave?" Ashlyn asked.

"Both," Lexie said. "Easier because I've seen firsthand how good the team is. How well they work together and how professional they are. Harder because I know the bullets that are flying around are very real. And how things can definitely go wrong."

"Agreed," Monica said, as she rubbed her growing belly bump. She had about three and a half months to go before her baby was due, and both she and Pid were anxious for her to be born.

"Like Lexie said, our guys are good at what they do. We just have to trust that they'll come home to us," Elodie added.

"I may not have experienced their expertise overseas, but when I was on that beach and there was a chance I might be blown to pieces, I had no doubt Marshall would do whatever was necessary to get me out of the situation," Kenna said.

"But then you went and got *yourself* out of it," Carly retorted with a smile.

"Yeah, but honestly, that was luck," Kenna protested.

"Um, no, it wasn't," Carly said adamantly. "My douchebag ex was bound and determined to kidnap and torture someone. If he couldn't get to me, you would've been a good substitute."

"My point is that you and I, Carly, have still seen the team in action, even if we weren't in some foreign country," Kenna explained.

"No matter how scary it gets, no matter how worried you are and how freaked out you get when you watch the news, you have to stay positive," Elodie told Ashlyn seriously. "The last thing Slate needs is to be distracted while on a mission because he thinks you can't handle what he does for a living."

Ashlyn thought about that for a moment and knew her friend was right. Slate needed to keep his mind on what he was doing, not thinking about how she was coping with his absence.

"So...have things gotten more serious between you and Slate?" Carly asked. "Last I heard, you guys were still casual."

"We are," Ashlyn told her. "But that doesn't mean I can't worry about him."

"Oh, I know, I wasn't implying that," she said quickly.

"When we were just friends, I worried about him too," Ashlyn said a little defensively.

"It's different now though, isn't it?" Lexie asked. "No matter how much you try to tell us that things are super-duper laid-back between you guys, there's no way you can sit there and tell us that you don't feel differently about his deployments now that you're dating."

Lexie was right. It *was* different. But Ashlyn couldn't put her finger on why. She'd spent the night at his house the evening before he left, and the sex was more intense than ever. Still mind-blowing, and he'd still made her come several times before getting off himself. But it was more...intimate somehow. He didn't seem as rushed or desperate. Slate had taken his time, been gentler with her...as if he wanted to prolong everything, as reluctant to leave as she was to see him go.

"It's different," Ashlyn finally admitted.

All five women nodded, no explanation necessary.

"I do have to say, I never really understood the need for you guys to all get together when the team deployed. I mean, I was certainly happy to join you and hang out in Kenna's posh condo, but I didn't *get* it. I do now."

"What do you get, precisely?" Elodie asked.

"The need to connect with people who know what you're feeling. Who won't judge you for freaking out a bit about something you have no control over. About taking time, even if it's only one night, to admit that you're scared and worried and even a little depressed before putting on our big girl panties and getting on with life until the guys come home," Ashlyn said.

"Exactly," Lexie said softly.

"Yup," Carly agreed.

"Spot on," Elodie added.

Monica nodded.

"That's exactly why I want you guys here," Kenna said. "I know you're feeling the same things I am, and it's okay not to be strong all the time. We all know we need to suck it up and continue living our lives when the guys are gone, but it feels nice knowing we aren't alone in our fears."

"There are times when I want to say 'screw this' and go down to the justice of the peace to get married," Carly admitted. "I mean, yeah, we have some time until our wedding date, but what if something happens to Jag? What if he gets deployed again and it's a long-term mission? I just want to be his wife, and I feel selfish that I want to have some semblance of a traditional wedding."

"Don't feel bad about that," Elodie said immediately. "You know Jag wants the wedding as much as you do."

"I can't help but think about Stuart missing the birth of our daughter," Monica admitted. "Women have babies all the time without the dad being there, but he's just so excited about seeing her born that it would kill me if he missed it."

"Midas and I aren't in any hurry to get married, but I know he worries about something happening to him every time he leaves. He put me down as the beneficiary on his life insurance, which I can't stand to even think about, but he insisted that if we weren't going to get married right away, he wanted to make sure I was taken care of, just in case," Lexie shared.

"This military spouse and girlfriend thing isn't for wimps, that's for sure," Kenna said on a sigh.

Ashlyn nodded along with everyone else...but all of a sudden, she felt like a fraud. She'd felt more a part of the group tonight than ever before, since she was now dating

Slate. But hearing all of her friends' concerns, she once again felt kind of like an outsider.

"Okay, this conversation has gotten too depressing," Kenna declared. "We need to talk about something else for a while."

"How's the job going, Monica? Are you still loving working with the kids at the Head Start Center?" Carly asked.

"It's awesome," Monica said. "I'm actually going to miss everyone so much when I take time off after having the baby. But the good thing is that I can take her to work with me when I return, and I won't have to worry about finding reliable and trustworthy childcare."

After about thirty minutes of general chitchat about raising children in today's culture, how the planning for Carly's wedding was going, if anyone had seen or heard from the mysterious Baker recently (no one had), and discussing plans for an actual girls' night out instead of just holing up in Kenna's condo like they usually did, Lexie asked Ashlyn about one of their Food For All's clients.

"I forgot to ask you yesterday when you came back from your deliveries, did you see Marcus? Was he okay?"

Marcus was one of their regulars. He'd broken up with his ex-girlfriend a while ago, who hadn't taken the separation very well. In short, she went bat-shit crazy when he started dating someone else, and had decided if *she* couldn't have Marcus, no one could. After weeks of harassing him, she'd broken into his apartment and beaten the shit out of the man. Someone had called the cops, and his ex was arrested.

Ashamed, Marcus tried to cancel his deliveries. He was already struggling to make enough money to support himself, let alone to give his new girlfriend everything he felt she deserved. Ashlyn refused to let him cancel, persuading him to stay on the program until he found better-paying work.

"His ex really did a number on him, "Ashlyn said. "I mean, I'm not naïve enough to think that women can't abuse men, but I swear if the cops hadn't gotten to his apartment when they did, Marcus might not have survived. He told me that she'd just run into the kitchen to get a knife when the police arrived."

"Holy shit, seriously?" Elodie asked.

"Yeah."

"But she's in jail, right?" Monica asked, worry lacing her voice.

"For now. When I saw how badly injured he was, I made some calls," Ashlyn said. "There are battered women shelters that help in situations like this, but there aren't any battered men shelters that do the same thing. I get it, the majority of people in abusive relationships are women, but that doesn't mean men aren't in desperate situations as well. Anyway, after talking to three different organizations, I finally found someone who was willing to help. Marcus was reluctant to accept assistance at first, but I think his ex really scared him, and he knows if he doesn't disappear, next time she might finish what she started."

"The island's not that big," Kenna said. "Do you really think he can hide from her?"

"You're right, it's not. And no, I don't. Crazy people have a way of finding their targets, as I think we've all learned firsthand."

Carly winced and nodded, as did the others.

"He's going to the mainland. I don't know where, and I didn't ask. But the person I talked to is part of an organization that relocates abused women. They had no problem using their knowledge and connections to help Marcus start over somewhere else."

"Wow, that's awesome," Carly said.

"Sucks that he has to leave Hawaii though," Lexie said.

"Yeah," Ashlyn agreed. "But I could see the relief in his eyes the last time I delivered food, after he'd talked to the contact."

"You're amazing, Ash," Elodie said. "I'm proud to call you my friend."

"I felt bad that I didn't try to get him help *before* he was beaten up," Ashlyn said.

"You can only do what you can do," Monica said. "Sometimes, even if people do all the right things, they can still end up in a shitty situation. I'm a big believer in karma, especially after what happened to me. Those who do bad things will suffer for it eventually. And those who do good will be rewarded." The words were even more poignant because it was Monica who'd shared them. She wasn't one to talk a lot, but when she did, she made it count.

"I know. I just wish that karma worked faster," Ashlyn said.

"Sometimes it does," Monica told her.

"Like in your case," Carly said.

"Exactly," Monica said with a small smile.

Ashlyn couldn't blame Monica for being satisfied that the man who'd kidnapped her, and who'd planned for her and Baker to die horrible deaths in a lava flow, had instead suffered that fate himself.

"Anyone want a refill?" Elodie asked as she stood and stretched.

"Me!"

"Yes!"

"Count me in!"

"I'll help you," Ashlyn offered, standing and grabbing the other women's empty glasses.

Everyone but Monica was partaking in the extra-strong margaritas that Elodie had a tendency to make. Partly on account of her pregnancy, but also because she didn't often drink alcohol, even when she wasn't growing a baby in her belly.

In the kitchen, Elodie turned to Ashlyn and put a hand on her arm. "Are you okay?"

"Yes, why wouldn't I be?"

"I don't know, I just thought you looked kind of...lost there for a while."

Apparently Elodie was extremely observant even when drunk.

"For the record, I think you and Slate are closer than you're letting on."

Ashlyn opened her mouth to disagree, but Elodie held up a hand, stopping her.

"No, don't say anything. Just think about it. You and Slate were friends before you started dating. You've both been through all the shit that's happened recently with Carly, Monica, and Kenna. That kind of emotional upheaval has a way of connecting people. I know you guys were always sniping at each other, but I think that's because neither of you wanted to admit you actually liked each other more than you thought you should.

"And on Slate's part, all the harping on your safety is a huge sign that he cares about you a hell of a lot. If he didn't, he wouldn't care so much about your job and who you might come into contact with during your deliveries. I think it's great that you've moved your relationship forward. That you're having sex. But I would hate to see you lose Slate, or him you, because you're both too stubborn to admit that you want more than a casual relationship."

Ashlyn wasn't sure how to respond. It was a familiar argument from her friends.

She liked not having the pressure of being in a long-term relationship. She was enjoying not having to worry about telling Slate where she was all the time, or what he would think if she didn't want to spend the night, or if she wanted to go out with her friends, or even stay home and veg in front of the TV alone. So far, things with her and Slate were pretty perfect, and she didn't want to jeopardize that.

But Elodie wasn't exactly wrong either—which was disconcerting. This first deployment after they'd officially started dating was harder than she'd thought it would be...and it had only been one freaking day.

"I really don't mean to harp on you," Elodie said when Ashlyn didn't respond. "No pressure."

Ashlyn chuckled dryly at that. "Right. No pressure."

"Seriously. I love both you and Slate. Do I want things to work out with you guys? Duh, yes. But if they don't, they don't. It's not going to make me like you, or him, any less. Unless you turn out to be as psycho as Marcus's girlfriend. Then I'll have to hunt you down and put a major hurt on you."

Ashlyn had a feeling Elodie was trying to be funny, but she wanted to make sure her friend knew that she'd never, *ever*, be clingy and psycho with Slate. She respected him too much to hurt him in any way. "I don't know what the future holds for us, but if and when he decides he wants to move on, I'll let him," she told her friend. "I value his friendship, so I'd like to try to remain friends after we stop dating. I hope we can do that."

Elodie reached out and hugged Ashlyn hard. "Me too," she said softly. "But more than that, I'm hoping you guys pull your heads out of your asses and realize that you're actually perfect for each other." Then she stepped back and turned to the blender. "Hand me the bottle of tequila, would you?"

Ashlyn shook her head, knowing Elodie had purposely changed the subject so she could have the last word on her and Slate's relationship. She didn't want to let her or any of the other women down, but Ashlyn simply wasn't sure that she and Slate could last long term. Not when the biggest thing they had in common was an unwillingness to commit.

Putting that thought out of her mind for the moment, she grabbed the alcohol and watched as Elodie poured what was left of the bottle into the blender. They both grinned as she hit the blend button. The drinks were gonna be strong as hell...which was perfectly all right with Ashlyn. She needed to think about something other than Slate.

When the margaritas were mixed, Elodie filled each glass and grabbed two. Ashlyn managed to juggle the remaining three and they brought them back out to the balcony. They were greeted with cheers from Lexie, Carly, and Kenna.

"I'll be right back, gonna go to the bathroom," Ashlyn told the group.

"You need a buddy?" Kenna teased.

Ashlyn laughed. "Nope. If we were in a club, definitely, but I think I can make it to the bathroom and back without someone breaking in and kidnapping me."

"Never say never," Carly said, wagging a finger at her before taking a large sip of her drink.

Still chuckling, Ashlyn turned to head back inside.

The second she closed the bathroom door behind her, she couldn't resist taking out her phone and opening the tracking app. It was stupid, she knew what she was going to see the second she clicked on the map.

The icon for Slate's phone was right where it was the last time she'd checked...at the airport on the Naval base. He'd obviously turned his phone off before the flight and hadn't turned it back on since. It was one more reminder that Slate was out there, risking his life, and she had no idea where he was precisely or when he'd be back.

Ashlyn missed him. More during this deployment than any of the others. Even her bed seemed too big now without him in it. Which kind of sucked.

Sighing, she put the phone back in her pocket before doing her business. Afterward, she washed her hands, took a deep breath, and headed back out to the balcony and her friends. She needed to follow their lead. Get drunk, be sad her boyfriend was out of town, then tomorrow she'd straighten her shoulders and get back to living.

CHAPTER TWELVE

Ashlyn's phone rang just as she was pulling into the parking lot near Food For All. It had been a week since the guys had been deployed, and she'd just finished her deliveries for the day. Her hopes skyrocketed for a moment, thinking it was Slate calling to tell her he was home, but when she looked at the screen, she was surprised to see James's name on the display.

She cut off her engine and clicked on the green button. "Hey, James. Everything okay?"

"Of course. You said I could call anytime," the older man said.

"I did," Ashlyn agreed. "What's up?"

"I just realized that you brought too much food," James said. "I wondered what was taking you so long in the kitchen earlier, getting my lunch ready, and now I know. You're sneaky."

Ashlyn laughed. "Two of the people I was supposed to deliver to today weren't home when I got there, so I had extra," Ashlyn said, lying through her teeth. "And I didn't want the food to go to waste, and since I know how much you love Elodie's corn frittatas, I figured you wouldn't mind if I left the extras."

"Of course I don't mind. And yes, I love frittatas. Thank you. Although I'd prefer your company to the food," he said quietly.

Ashlyn's heart nearly broke. It was obvious the older man was lonely. And while she enjoyed spending time with him, she couldn't stay too long at his house and still get to all the other families and people she needed to deliver to. "Aiden's supposed to come on Sunday, right?"

"Yeah. But it's not the same. I napped the last few times he was here," James said.

"You did? I didn't think you were much of a napper," Ashlyn said in concern.

"I'm not. Or at least I didn't use to be. I'm an old man, and getting older every day."

"You aren't that old," Ashlyn told him.

He laughed. "I'm eighty-eight," he said as if she'd forgotten.

"I know. But you're a young eighty-eight," she replied, smiling at his chuckle.

"Right. Anyway, I just wanted to say thank you for looking out for me. I appreciate the extra meals."

"You're welcome."

"And you never know, maybe next time I'll send you a text thingy."

Ashlyn didn't have the heart to tell him that he couldn't send her a text message from the old-fashioned landline he still insisted on using in his house. "Sounds good. Have a good weekend, James. I'll see you on Monday."

"Looking forward to it. Try not to stress too much this weekend about your man. He's a SEAL, he'll be fine."

Ashlyn had admitted to James earlier how much she was missing Slate. "I'll try."

"See you next week."

"Bye." Ashlyn clicked off the phone and took a deep breath. She didn't have plans for the night, and she had a feeling she'd obsess about Slate's absence. Even though whatever mission they were on wasn't supposed to be dangerous, she still worried about him, and with every day that passed that he didn't return, she imagined all sorts of things going wrong.

She reached over and grabbed her purse off the passenger seat and turned to open her door—and saw someone standing right next to her car.

She let out a girly screech and jumped in fright. Then the person leaned down and smiled at her through the window.

"Slate?" she yelled, frantically trying to grab the door handle. It felt like she was all thumbs, but she finally managed to open the door. Slate had taken a step backward so she could get out, then she was in his arms.

"Oh my God! You're back!" she exclaimed.

"I'm back," he said with a chuckle.

His laugh was the best thing she'd heard in what felt like forever. She clung to him and closed her eyes. Simply breathing in his familiar scent made her world seem ten times brighter.

To her horror, she felt her throat closing up and her lip began to tremble.

"Just got back and I checked the app, saw you were on your way here. Thought I'd come and surprise you." Slate pulled back...then frowned when he saw her face. "Ash? What's wrong?"

"N-n-nothing," Ashlyn stuttered, doing her best not to burst into tears.

He gave her a skeptical look. "Babe. Talk to me."

"I'm just so happy you're back. And that you're safe," she managed to say.

"I told you this mission wasn't going to be a big deal. In fact, it was completely uneventful. We stood around all day trying to look badass and mean, when inside we were bored out of our skulls. I had a lot of time to think about all the things I wanted to do to you when I got back," he said with a sexy smirk.

Ashlyn took a deep breath, and that mostly worked to help her regain composure. "Yeah?" she asked. "Like what?"

"Like eat you out and watch you explode all over my fingers. Then when you're still coming, push inside you and feel you strangle my cock. Then fuck you hard and fast until you're begging me to let you come a second time. That's just for starters."

"Holy crap," Ashlyn said. The pictures he painted weren't anything they hadn't already done, but somehow, after a week of worrying about him and sleeping alone, she was more turned on than she could ever remember being. "Yes."

Slate beamed. "Your place or mine?"

"Don't care," Ashlyn said.

"Mine," Slate decided. "You need your car this weekend?"

"Um, I don't think so. I don't have any plans."

"You do now. To be with me...in my bed, my shower, on my couch, spread-eagle on my table while I eat you out, on your knees taking my cock down your throat... That okay?"

Ashlyn could barely speak. Her nipples were almost painfully tight under her shirt. She wanted Slate. Now.

"Yes. Slate?"

"Yeah, babe?"

"Kiss me."

"With pleasure," he said before lowering his head.

Ashlyn sighed in contentment the second his lips touched

hers. She tangled her fingers as well as she could in his short hair and held on. One leg lifted, and she pressed her thigh against his own. She couldn't get close enough. His hand moved down to grasp her leg, holding her against him as they made out in the parking lot.

"Guess you know the guys are back," Lexie called out.

Ashlyn pulled away in a daze, but Slate didn't let go of her leg. He had one arm around her back, keeping her close, and she was wrapped around him as if she'd never let go. As Lexie approached, he finally let her leg slide down his own, slowly, but he didn't release his grip around her back. Ashlyn suspected it was because he wanted to hide the erection she could feel against her belly.

"I left a note for you inside Food For All because I didn't know you were back," Lexie said. "It just says the guys are home and I'm heading out for the weekend."

"Slate surprised me," Ashlyn told her friend. "Do you think the others know? Should we call them?"

"They know," Slate assured her. "Mustang called Elodie from the airport, and Aleck and Jag did the same for their women. Pid's going to pick up Monica at work."

"All right then. Great," Ashlyn said. She hadn't thought much about how big a deal it was when the team returned from a mission, but after the tough week she'd had...she finally got it. Keeping the fact that they were home from her friends would have seemed cruel now.

"Have a good weekend," Lexie said as she headed for her car. "I'd say to call me later, but I'm guessing none of us are gonna come up for air before Monday."

Ashlyn felt Slate chuckling against her. "See you Monday!" she called to her friend.

Lexie waved and closed her car door and started up the engine.

Slate turned her and headed for his car, which Ashlyn

hadn't seen because she'd been too preoccupied talking with James when she'd parked. He opened the passenger door, but took Ashlyn into his arms for a long, heartfelt hug rather than letting her climb inside.

Ashlyn once more felt emotion clogging her throat, but she swallowed it down. She wanted to show Slate that she could be strong. That she hadn't fallen apart while he was gone.

"Missed you," he mumbled into her neck as he held her tightly.

"Same," she returned.

Another twenty seconds or so passed as they simply embraced, before Slate finally took a deep breath and pulled back. "You hungry?" he asked.

Ashlyn shook her head. "No. You?"

"No. I need you, babe."

"Then let go of me so we can get to your house and you can have me," she quipped.

Slate smiled. "Right." He gestured to the seat. "Your throne, my princess."

He was joking, but Ashlyn couldn't help but feel warm and fuzzy from his words.

"That's queen to you," she retorted.

Slate smirked, shutting the door once she was seated. Then he jogged around the front of the car—actually jogged, as if he couldn't stand the five extra seconds it would take to walk to the driver's side—and jerked open the door.

They didn't speak on the way to his house, but Slate reached for her hand and held it tightly the entire drive.

* * *

Hours later, Slate lay with his elbow on the mattress and his head in his hand next to Ashlyn, watching her sleep. It was late, after midnight, but he couldn't rest. He was still on Bahrain time and wasn't very tired, even with the long hours of travel.

Ashlyn had been ravenous when they'd finally gotten home. She'd started to strip him even before he'd had the door closed and locked behind them. She went to her knees right in the entryway of his house and took his cock in her mouth. She hadn't let him hold back either, keeping her mouth on him even when he'd warned her that he was going to come. She'd taken his load down her throat...then looked up at him with a satisfied smile, licking her lips.

He'd kind of lost it then, needing to taste her and return the favor. Eventually they'd made it to his bedroom, where he'd teased her, bringing her to the brink of orgasm over and over until she was both pleading and threatening his life if he didn't let her come.

Afterward, he'd put her on her knees and taken her from behind.

Slate couldn't remember a better homecoming than this one. He'd missed Ashlyn more than he thought he would. He hadn't lied earlier, he'd spent most of his time thinking about her. But it wasn't just sexual thoughts. He wondered how her deliveries were going, if the girls' night at Kenna and Aleck's place went all right, how the Turner family was doing, and if she had any new clients. He hoped she was eating enough and taking care of herself, because she had a tendency to forget about herself if someone else needed something.

Ashlyn sighed in her sleep and turned onto her side, snuggling into him. Slate shifted onto his back and pulled her closer. She didn't wake up, as she was out hard, as usual, but she still wrapped her arm around him and hiked her leg on top of his. She clung to him even in her sleep.

With any other woman, he might've been annoyed.

Ashlyn actually thought he was a cuddler, and he'd never corrected her. But in truth, before Ashlyn, he hadn't liked anyone touching him when he slept. So much about this relationship was different. He'd missed the way she gravitated toward him in her sleep. His bunk had seemed empty over the last week.

After landing, he'd instantly pulled up the tracker app to see where she was. Instead of calling or texting to let her know he was back, Slate had decided to surprise her at Food For All. Her happiness at seeing him was exactly what he'd hoped for. It was his *own* joy at seeing Ashlyn that was somewhat surprising. He hadn't realized exactly how much he'd missed her until she was back in his arms.

They hadn't been able to take their hands, or lips, off each other long enough to even eat since getting home, which Slate needed to make sure he rectified in the morning. He didn't know what he had in the house, but he'd figure something out. While sex was good, he didn't want Ashlyn to go hungry.

"It's good to be home," he whispered.

It was. But it was even better to be home with Ashlyn in his arms.

She sighed in her sleep but didn't loosen her hold on him.

Slate stared up at the ceiling, realizing he was completely content. Asking Ashlyn out had been one of the best decisions he'd made in a very long time. She was unlike any girlfriend he'd ever had. He loved to laugh with her, tease her... even their bickering turned him on. And she gave as good as she got. They were well-matched sexually, of course. Yeah, he didn't know if he'd ever been this content. This...settled.

He thought back to their conversation before he'd gone to Bahrain, about whether or not they were exclusive. He hadn't even thought about dating anyone else before she'd brought it up. He had no desire to seek out anyone either...not that he was in a position to do so. If he wasn't on the base, he was hanging out with his teammates or Ashlyn. Frankly, he didn't have time to give to someone else.

Slate could also admit—if only to himself—that knowing Aiden had asked her out made an uncomfortable feeling settle in his gut. He'd never been good at sharing, even as a kid. The thought of Ashlyn laughing and joking with another man like she did with him? The very idea made his jaw clench.

And the thought of her sleeping with another man, wrapping her gorgeous body around him, made Slate want to fucking hurt someone.

As far as he was concerned, they were exclusive. He'd asked her to let him know if she met someone else she was interested in, but Slate knew himself too well. If that happened, he'd have to let her go. He had no interest in half of Ashlyn's time and attention.

Blinking in surprise, Slate felt his whole body flush as it occurred to him that he wanted Ashlyn all to himself. He couldn't remember feeling this way before. If a woman got too clingy, he'd always found a way to gently back away and eventually break it off. Suddenly, it felt as if *he* was becoming the clingy one in the relationship.

But, Slate realized in amazement, he wasn't upset about that.

It still felt as if he and Ashlyn were casually dating. He didn't see her every day, even though they did talk most days. She didn't have an issue with him leaving after spending an evening together, although lately they were spending the entire night together, whether they had sex or not.

Closing his eyes, Slate decided he was thinking too hard about their relationship. They were good. Enjoying each other's company. It was inevitable that the connection he felt with her would taper off sooner or later. It always had in the past, so he expected nothing different.

And when it did, they'd still be friends, would still see each other when they hung out with his team and their women. This relationship was just fine as-is.

CHAPTER THIRTEEN

Ashlyn squinted as she drove. Her head was killing her. She hadn't had a headache this bad in a very long time. She'd considered calling Lexie earlier and telling her she needed to take the afternoon off, but her clients were depending on her to bring them food, and besides, Lexie was helping Carly with some last-minute details for her wedding, which was in a week and a half.

So she'd taken some aspirin and pushed through the afternoon, her headache getting worse with each minute that passed. By the time she'd walked up to Jazmin's house, Ashlyn thought she was gonna puke on the front porch.

The second the young mother saw her, she'd taken the food from her hand, then ordered her to go home. Of course, Brooklyn, James, and Christi's nurse aide had all said the same thing. Fortunately, because she hadn't stayed to chitchat with anyone today, she was actually done sooner than usual.

She'd sent a text to Lexie, letting her know she was done and heading home to nurse a headache, then concentrated on not wrecking as she made her way back to her apartment. She pulled into a space, not caring that her car wasn't perfectly straight between the lines. Grabbing her purse, Ashlyn breathed in through her nose and out through her mouth, attempting to stave off the nausea that was becoming overwhelming.

More thankful to be home than she could ever remember, Ashlyn shut her apartment door behind her. She dropped her purse on the floor, unconcerned about where it landed, and walked toward her bedroom. She stumbled, walking as if she'd drunk an entire bottle of tequila by herself, her only thought to get to her bed.

Without turning on any lights, and taking the time to pull her curtains closed, Ashlyn finally made it to her bed, sighing in relief. Before she could collapse, though, she knew she needed to get comfortable. Taking off her shorts and shirt—she'd already kicked off her flip-flops at the door—she reached behind her to unhook her bra. She knew from experience that any kind of clothing rubbing against her skin made her feel claustrophobic and seemed to exacerbate the pain in her head. It made no sense, but she was willing to do anything to reduce the throbbing in her skull.

Once naked except for her panties, Ashlyn carefully lay back. She didn't crawl under the covers. Simply closed her eyes and did her best to relax.

The ringing of her phone on the nightstand not only scared the crap out of her, but made her head throb harder when she jerked at the sound. Kicking herself for not putting it on silent mode, Ashlyn blindly reached for her cell.

"'Lo?" she said, not even looking at the display. The mere thought of keeping her eyes open made the nausea worse.

"Ash? Why are you home already?"

Slate.

"I'm okay," she said, even though it was a lie. She wasn't fine. She wanted to die. But there was nothing Slate or anyone else could do to help her. She just needed time to rest. She'd be all right. Eventually.

"That's not what I asked, babe," he said.

Ashlyn winced. His voice sounded extremely loud. Even the sound of her *own* voice made the pain worse.

"I have a headache," she whispered. "Finished deliveries and came home."

"Shit," Slate said, his voice lower than it had been, which Ashlyn was extremely grateful for. "I'm on my way."

"No, Slate, there's nothing you can do."

"Is your door unlocked?" he asked, ignoring her protests.

"Um..." Ashlyn couldn't even remember if she locked it after she'd arrived home or not.

"Never mind. If it is, I'll find a way of getting to you."

"I can get up and let you in," Ashlyn said, not sure if she actually could or not, but feeling like she should say it anyway.

"No. Stay put. I'm assuming you're in bed?"

"Yeah."

"Good."

"Are you gonna bust in my door like the badass Navy SEAL you are?" Ashlyn asked weakly. "Because I'm not sure my landlord will appreciate that."

Slate chuckled softly. "No. Close your eyes and relax, Ash. I'll be there soon."

"They're closed. The light hurts," she whined, wanting to kick herself for sounding so pathetic. "Wait, what time is it? Are you allowed to leave early?"

"Yes. I'm leaving now. I'll be there soon."

"Kay. Drive safe."

"I will. Bye."

Without opening her eyes, Ashlyn flicked the small switch on the side of her phone to put it on silent mode and put it back on the nightstand. She concentrated on breathing, in through her nose, out through her mouth, praying the pain would ease soon.

What seemed like a minute after she'd hung up her phone, the quiet sound of her front door opening made her jerk in surprise. She wanted to call out to make sure it was Slate, but knew if she raised her voice above a whisper, she'd definitely throw up.

A second later, the door to her room creaked as it was pushed open. Ashlyn opened her eyes to slits, sighed in relief that it was Slate and not a serial killer coming to chop her into itty-bitty pieces, and shut her eyes tight once more.

"Jesus, babe," Slate whispered.

Each footstep on the carpet sounded like little jackhammers against her aching head. He wasn't stomping, was merely walking, but every little noise seemed amplified a thousandfold.

Ashlyn raised a hand and put it against her lips. "Shhhh," she said in a barely there whisper.

A finger brushed against her cheek, and Ashlyn whimpered. He immediately drew back.

"I'm calling the doctor," he whispered.

"No. I'm okay," she told him.

"Like hell you are. You winced at the simple sound of my footsteps on your carpet. You're lying naked, spread-eagle, and the lines of pain in your brow make me want to fucking kill someone."

Ashlyn couldn't help but grin weakly. "It's just a headache," she told him.

"Right. And I'm just a sailor. Tell me what you need," Slate ordered.

"Dark. Quiet. And to lie here until the pain goes away."

"You take something?" he asked.

"Aspirin."

"That it?"

"Yeah. I don't get these often enough for a doctor to prescribe me something stronger."

"I'll take care of it," Slate said with confidence.

Ashlyn wanted to open her eyes to look at him but knew that would be a bad idea. She settled for reaching out blindly and squeezing his arm. "Like you picked my lock to get in?" she teased half-heartedly.

"Babe, your door was unlocked. I just waltzed right in. But for the record, my first plan was to find your landlord and make him or her open your door for me. If that didn't work, I was going to find a maintenance person. And as a last resort, yeah, I was gonna pick your lock. *Nothing* will keep me from getting to you when you need me."

Even though talking, and having someone talk to her, was painful as hell, his words made Ashlyn's inner romantic soul swoon.

"And I've got a few connections. I'll find you something more heavy-duty to take for the pain."

"Okay."

He gently pried her fingers off his arm and kissed the back of her hand, then placed it on the mattress. She wasn't really surprised that he was astute enough to immediately realize kissing her anywhere on her face or head would cause more pain. "Sleep, babe. I'll be back in later with something for you to take."

Ashlyn started to nod, then thought better of it. "Thanks."

She heard him walk over to the window, and the curtains made a shuffling noise. She assumed Slate was making sure they were as closed as they could be. Then he walked back to her side of the bed, stood there for a moment, and finally left the room. The door clicked as he closed it behind him, leaving Ashlyn alone once more.

Just knowing he cared enough to stop by made her feel

good. She wished she was in better shape to spend time with him. The days he'd been back since his last mission had been good. *Very* good. Their relationship seemed even more solid, as if the time away had proven the old adage right. Absence makes the heart grow fonder.

Except neither of their hearts were involved. Yes, they liked and respected each other, but that was it. They were lovers now...but when things ran their course, they'd go back to being friends.

A little voice in the back of Ashlyn's head was screaming that she was being naïve and not acknowledging what was right in front of her face. Then again, her head was screaming with pain as well, so maybe that was all she was hearing.

Now that she was home, in the dark, lying supine on her bed, Ashlyn let her mind go blank. Slate coming to check on her meant the world. And she'd thank him profusely as soon as she was able. In the meantime, she'd just take a little nap.

* * *

Slate sat at Ashlyn's table and ran a hand through his hair in agitation. She was in so much pain, she hadn't even thought to lock her door behind her when she got home, and dropped her purse on the floor just inside. And the way her brow was so deeply furrowed told him exactly how bad her head hurt. Not to mention the fact that she was naked except for her panties, as if the very idea of anything touching her skin made the pain worse.

In any other circumstance, he would've gotten turned on to see a practically naked Ashlyn lying spread-eagle on her bed, but not today.

When he'd absently checked the tracker app to see Ashlyn's progress on her delivery route, he was surprised to find her at the apartment. It was way too early for her to be done.

He'd stood up from his meeting without a word and stepped out of the room to call and check on her. He hadn't even thought about what he was doing. The team was researching an increase in hostilities in Afghanistan, and it was looking like they would most likely be heading out once again in a couple of weeks.

But his mind was as far from the desert as it could be when he heard the first word out of Ashlyn's mouth. She was hurting, and he needed to do whatever it took to make it stop.

Mustang had come out of the room to make sure everything was all right, and Slate had briefed him on what was happening and where he was going. Without hesitation, Mustang nodded and told him to take care of her, and let him know how Ashlyn was doing.

After making sure she was as comfortable as possible, Slate sent a text to Mustang, asking for a favor, and his friend had called immediately, saying he'd talk to a doctor they knew on base and would bring a stronger painkiller to Ashlyn's apartment after he left work.

Slate wanted the drug now, but he had no choice but to wait unless he wanted to leave Ashlyn alone again. He definitely didn't. So in the meantime, all he could do was sit and worry about the woman in the other room who'd tried to be so strong, to reassure him that she was fine, when she was anything but.

He couldn't turn on the TV. It would be too loud even with her bedroom door shut. He didn't want to cook anything because the smell might make her more nauseous than she was right now. Drumming his fingers on the tabletop silently, Slate impatiently waited for the minutes to pass until Mustang arrived.

He hated seeing Ashlyn hurting. He rubbed a hand over his tight chest. He wasn't used to feeling helpless. On a mission, there was always something to do. Decisions to make. But he literally couldn't do anything to help in this situation. He couldn't hold her, as that would cause her pain. He couldn't kiss her, because again, more pain. He couldn't sit and talk to her because...*pain*. Everything he wanted to do would literally just hurt her even more. The thought was enough to make *him* want to throw up.

The longer he sat there, thinking about what Ashlyn was experiencing, the more his mind whirled and his paranoia increased. Could she have a brain tumor? She needed to get a cat scan. Or MRI. He'd go with her to see a doctor and whatever was wrong, they'd deal with it together. If she thought he might break up with her because she had cancer, or a tumor, or whatever the doctor found, she was wrong.

Realizing how crazy his thoughts had gotten, Slate took a deep breath.

It was a headache. She said she got them every now and then. Yes, it was bad—*really* bad—but she didn't seem freaked out about it. He had to trust her to know her own body. He'd still encourage her to go to a doctor, if for nothing else than to get some pills in case it happened in the future, but he had to get his shit together.

Ashlyn's phone lit up with another incoming text. He'd grabbed her phone off the nightstand before leaving the room, not wanting to risk it ringing or vibrating while she was trying to sleep off the pain. He shouldn't have been surprised she'd already turned it to silent, but he wasn't going to go back into the bedroom and possibly disturb Ashlyn by returning it.

She'd been getting texts pretty much nonstop since he'd sat down. Elodie, Lexie, Kenna, Monica, and Carly had been sending her notes. Apparently, Lexie had told Carly that Ashlyn had a headache, and word had spread from there.

Slate read the texts the women had been sending. He could see them in the pop-up notifications without having to unlock the phone.

Elodie: Sorry you're sick. Let me know if you need anything. I'll make you some tomato soup. And before you say ick, trust me, I make kick-ass tomato soup.

Kenna: Carly told me you have a killer headache. That sucks. Call me when you feel better.

Carly: I hope you don't mind that I told the others you were sick. You need to concentrate on getting better so you don't miss my wedding. I know, that's selfish, but I can't imagine you not sharing my day with me. So get better soon!

Monica: Pid told me you weren't feeling good. I've had a few bad headaches, and I've found that lavender really helps. If you aren't better tomorrow, I'll bring you a sachet.

But it was the last text, from Lexie, that made Slate frown.

Lexie: I'm so sorry you've got another headache. You should've let me know earlier and I could've taken over your shift or something. I know how bad they can get. Last time you went three days without eating, and that's totally not cool. So if you're still feeling shitty tomorrow, let me know and I'll bring some stuff you can eat without having to cook. Okay? Love you.

He didn't even think about what he was doing. He picked up his own phone and clicked on Lexie's name. He hadn't ever sent her a text before, had no reason to communicate privately with Midas's woman. But he couldn't stop himself now.

Slate: This is Slate. I read the text you sent Ash on her phone. I'm at her place now. These headaches last for days?

Lexie: Oh! I'm so glad you're there with her! They don't usually last that long, but one time she was super sick, and she lost quite a bit of weight because she literally couldn't get out of bed to eat anything.

Slate: When?

Lexie: When what?

Slate: When was this long headache?

Lexie: I'm not sure. Maybe around six months ago?

Slate closed his eyes and took a deep breath. She'd had a killer headache, for *days*, and he hadn't known. For some reason, that irked him. No, they hadn't been dating six months ago, but they were friends, and he hated that she'd kept it from him.

Lexie: Make sure she drinks lots of water. She isn't going to want to, because moving hurts, but I read that staying hydrated can help.

Slate: I will. Anything she likes to eat when she gets like this?

He wasn't happy that he didn't know the answer to something as simple as what Ashlyn liked to eat when she didn't feel well, but he wasn't going to shy away from asking what he needed to know.

Lexie: I don't think she likes to eat anything. I'd keep it simple. Nothing too hot or cold, because that would probably exacerbate the headache. Plain bread, applesauce, maybe a protein shake if you can get one down her.

Her advice made sense. Slate's thumbs flew across the keyboard as he responded.

Slate: Thanks. I'll take care of her.
Lexie: I know you will. Seriously, I feel so much better knowing you're there. Please tell her that we're all thinking about her. And maybe you can text me later and let me know how she's doing?
Slate: I will.
Lexie: Thanks. Ash is always looking out for everyone else. It's good she's got someone to look after her for once. Gotta go, Carly needs me. Later.

Slate didn't bother to respond, knowing Lexie was busy. Another text popped up on his screen. Mustang, letting him know he'd just pulled into the parking lot. Slate got up and headed to the door, not wanting his friend to knock or ring the bell.

In a minute or so, Mustang was walking down the hall toward him. He had a small bag in his hand and handed it over.

"How is she?" he asked.

Slate shrugged. "Not good. Hurting."

"Right. Well, the doc said ibuprofen can help reduce symptoms of a migraine, but it's most effective if taken at the first signs of the headache. Once it takes root, it's usually too late for the medicine to work."

"Fuck."

"Yeah. But he did give me two Topamax tablets. He said sometimes they can help even if it's not taken within two hours of the start of the headache. He definitely recommends her seeing her doctor and trying to figure out what causes the pain, and to get a prescription for something that will work for her specific symptoms."

"Thanks. I appreciate this."

"Keep an eye on her. Since this is a new medicine for her, it's probably smart not to leave her alone."

"Wasn't gonna do that, even if you hadn't stopped by," Slate said, feeling irritated that his friend thought he'd do such a thing.

"I know, just sayin'. You need anything?" Mustang asked.

"If you can convince Elodie to give me some time before she storms the castle, I'd appreciate it. And I'm sure Ashlyn would too. I'm guessing by her reaction to me being here, that she hates for people to see her vulnerable and sick."

"I'll do my best. But you know my wife. And the others. They like to take care of their own. And Ashlyn is definitely one of their posse."

Slate nodded. "Sorry I left today without much warning. I miss anything?"

Mustang sighed. "Just the fact that there's a ninety percent certainty we'll be heading to the desert."

"Will Jag miss his wedding?"

"Not if I can help it," Mustang said firmly. "Of course, he might not get the honeymoon he was looking forward to."

Slate nodded. He wasn't all that surprised. But knowing Jag and Carly, they'd make up for not having a honeymoon right after their wedding ceremony when he got back.

"Keep me in the loop on how she's doing," Mustang said.

"Will do. Thanks again for coming by."

"She's a good woman," Mustang said earnestly. "Never has a bad word to say about anyone and is more generous than most. Besides, she's your girlfriend, which means she's important to all of us. Later."

As Mustang walked back down the hallway, Slate shut the door, still thinking about his friend's words. He loved the support his teammates showed each other when it came to their women. It made their group feel even more like a family.

He walked into the kitchen and got a plastic cup out of a cabinet. He dug around and was happy to find a drawer filled with plastic cutlery and straws from takeout she'd had in the past, and had saved.

Remembering Lexie's warning about giving Ashlyn anything too hot or cold, he filled the glass with tap water and stuck the straw in. He opened the bag Mustang had brought to find a sample pack of the migraine drug with two doses. He popped out one pill and headed for the bedroom.

He pushed open the door quietly and saw that Ashlyn hadn't moved. He walked over to the side of the bed and got down on his knees.

"Ash," he whispered.

She didn't move.

"Ashlyn," he said a little louder, hating that her brow scrunched upon hearing her name.

"Don't open your eyes, I've got a pill for you to take."

"Wanna sleep," she mumbled.

"I know, and you can, after you swallow this down. Can you do that for me?"

"Yeah."

"I brought you water with a straw so you don't have to tilt your head back to drink. Get up on one elbow and lean toward me. Good, just like that."

Slate kept his eyes on her face as he moved the cup closer. "Open."

She did as he asked without opening her eyes.

"Okay, stick out your tongue. I'll put the pill on it and you can swallow it down with the water I've got right here."

Her trust in him was humbling when she didn't ask him what kind of drug he was giving her or anything. She just did as he asked, letting him give her the pill. As she swallowed it, Slate said, "Keep drinking. Get as much of the water down as you can. It's good for you. Promise."

Ashlyn nodded slightly as she continued to drink through the straw.

Finally, she pulled away and carefully lay back down.

"Good girl. That tablet'll make you feel better soon, babe."

"Was it cyanide? Because right about now, that sounds like it would *really* make me feel better."

Slate was torn. He was happy to hear her trying to joke, but wasn't thrilled it was a joke about dying to make her pain go away.

"No," he told her.

"I was kidding," she said on a sigh.

"I know. And you should know I'd never give you anything, or do anything, that would hurt you."

"I *do* know. But head's up, while I'm really glad you're here right now, tomorrow when I'm better, I'll probably be embarrassed."

"No need to be embarrassed about anything. You'd take care of me if I was sick," Slate said.

"I would," she agreed.

"Okay then. I promised if you took the pill you could go back to sleep. I'm gonna go hang in the living room so you can do just that."

"Thanks again for being here."

"Nowhere I'd rather be," Slate told her, then he leaned over and, as gently as he could, kissed her temple. "Sleep," he whispered in a barely there tone.

Ashlyn sighed and visibly relaxed.

Backing away, Slate didn't take his eyes off her face until he'd reached the door. He closed it behind him silently and took a deep breath. She'd be fine. She was strong. He just hated seeing her so helpless and hurting. He had the thought that he was very glad it happened when he was there, and not while he was deployed. It would tear him up to come home and realize she'd been so sick while he was gone.

But it wasn't as if that could be helped. Soldiers and sailors missed a lot of important occasions in their families' lives. Births of babies, sicknesses, first steps, birthdays, holidays, deaths of friends and family. But they'd made oaths to serve their country, and unfortunately, missing things back home was a part of that.

Making a vow to live for the moment even more than he already was, Slate headed back to the kitchen table. It was going to be a long night, but he wasn't going anywhere.

CHAPTER FOURTEEN

Ashlyn woke up a few times in the middle of the night, but it wasn't until the next morning that she felt she could move without extreme pain. She looked over at the nightstand and saw a plastic cup with a straw sticking out of it. She recalled Slate bringing it to her and ordering her to drink and take a pill, but not much else.

Rolling over, she sat up slowly, pleased when her head didn't immediately begin to throb. Her mouth felt as if she'd been sucking on cotton balls all night, but amazingly, whatever she'd taken had done a good job of soothing the horrible pain.

She still felt a bit foggy headed and knew she wouldn't be running any marathons later that day, but she felt better than she usually did after one of her headaches. She remembered the last episode, when she couldn't get out of bed for three days. Yeah, that had been bad, but thank goodness she seemed to be past the worst of this one.

Ashlyn stood, carefully testing her balance. She needed to get her butt to a doctor soon. She might not get the headaches very often, but when she did, they were bad. Really bad. And it wasn't smart to ignore them any longer.

Shuffling toward the bathroom, Ashlyn grabbed an oversized T-shirt on her way. She peed, then brushed her teeth, deciding a shower would be pushing things a bit too much right now. It didn't really matter though, it wasn't as if she was going anywhere today. She planned to hole up in her apartment and regain her equilibrium. She'd call Slate later and thank him for coming over and getting her whatever that pill was.

She also needed to let Lexie know she was good, as well as the others.

Her belly growled as she padded into the living room, heading toward the kitchen—and stopped in her tracks at the sight on her couch.

The very last thing she expected to see was Slate, sound asleep.

He looked uncomfortable as hell. He'd left the night before...hadn't he? He said he was going to go so she could sleep...didn't he? She'd assumed that meant he was leaving her apartment, not just her room, but apparently she was wrong.

She must've made some kind of noise, because Slate's eyes popped open and immediately went to her own.

"Ash. You feel better?" he asked as he sat up, rubbing his face.

"Yeah. What are you doing here?"

"You were sick," Slate said as he stood and stretched. He put a hand on the small of his back and bent backward. He was still wearing the Navy uniform he usually wore to work, and somehow the sight of his bare feet made the moment seem intimate.

"But my couch sucks. And you're still wearing your uniform," she protested.

Slate grinned and walked toward her. "It's okay," he said

with a shrug. "I've definitely slept in worse places, and I'm used to sleeping in my clothes. It's not like I get naked and comfortable while deployed," he said. "How are you feeling this morning? For real? Does your head hurt? Your forehead isn't all furrowed with a million wrinkles, so I'm hoping that's a good sign."

Ashlyn was having a hard time wrapping her head around the fact that Slate stayed to...what? Watch over her?

"Ash? What's wrong? Talk to me," he ordered gently.

"I...you... I can't believe you stayed."

"Where the hell was I going to go? Back home? No fucking way. Not while I was worried about you. Babe, I couldn't even touch you without you flinching. You stripped off all your clothes, I'm guessing because they hurt your skin. Whispering was too loud. And your room was like a cave. You scared the shit out of me. I got up every hour to check on you last night. It took about four or five hours, but finally that pill I gave you seemed to take effect. You seemed more settled, and you'd even crawled under the covers at one point. You need to see a doctor, Ash. I can't see you go through that again."

Ashlyn nodded automatically. "I'd already decided this morning to call and see if I could get an appointment."

"Good. Come on, sit while I find you something to eat."

"I don't know that I'm ready to eat all that much," she warned.

Slate nodded. "I'm not surprised. But you need something. I'm gonna make you a vanilla protein shake, and maybe some applesauce."

Ashlyn frowned in confusion. "Um, I don't think I have either of those in my kitchen."

"You do now. I ordered stuff and had it delivered last night."

She was floored. "You did?"

"Yup. Along with other stuff I thought you might eat. Now sit and let me take care of you."

Ashlyn felt as if she'd woken up in another dimension. She'd been on her own for so long, she'd gotten used to taking care of herself. And while she'd used grocery delivery herself a time or two, she wasn't sure she would've thought of using it this morning. She would've just found something in her cabinet to tide her over until she could get to the store.

She sat on the couch, realizing the cushions were still warm from his body heat. When Slate went to walk away, Ashlyn reached out and took his hand in hers. "Slate?"

He turned back to her immediately. "Yeah?"

"Thank you for staying. I think you went above and beyond the friends-with-benefits thing."

His eyes narrowed and he leaned in, forcing Ashlyn back against the couch cushions. He put his hands next to her shoulders and braced himself over her. "We don't follow rules," he said sternly. "We're Ash and Slate. Period. You're my friend, but you're also my lover. My girlfriend. There's no fucking way I was leaving when you needed me last night, and I know you would've done the same if the roles were reversed."

She nodded immediately.

"We might not be running out to buy promise rings, but that doesn't mean I don't care a hell of a lot about you, and that I don't look after what's mine. And make no mistake—you're mine for as long as we're dating, just as I'm yours. Understand?"

Her heart pounding a million miles an hour, Ashlyn nodded for what seemed like the twentieth time that morning.

"You have a problem with that? Is this too much? If you want to go back to being just friends, I can do that. It would suck hard, but I'd do it. I just don't want you thinking this relationship is a half-assed one, even if it's casual. Casual doesn't mean that I ignore you when you're in pain. It doesn't mean we fuck then go our separate ways as if we're strangers."

"Okay."

"Okay?" he echoed with a tilt of his head.

"Okay," Ashlyn confirmed.

"Good. Now relax while I get you something to eat."

With that, Slate leaned forward, kissed her forehead gently, then stood and headed for her kitchen.

Ashlyn let out the breath she'd been holding. Slate was intense on a good day, but even *she* hadn't realized he could be *this* intense. She liked everything he'd said. She'd gone into this relationship thinking she could keep things light and easy, but she'd underestimated Slate's magnetism...and her own emotional tendencies.

Ashlyn had never been in a relationship only halfway. When she dated someone, she was usually all in from the get-go. Hell, she'd moved to Hawaii with Franklin after way too short of a time after meeting him.

She'd thought she could keep things easy and carefree with Slate. Had tried to convince herself for weeks.

She'd been wrong.

Still, just because she liked him a hell of a lot and enjoyed spending time with him, both in bed and out of it, didn't mean they were getting married. But they *were* in a relationship, and she admitted to herself now that people who were dating didn't just fuck and run.

He was right with his earlier assumption, if it was Slate who was hurt or sick, she'd definitely be there for him.

Feeling oddly relieved about everything—her relationship with Slate, how last night had gone down, and even this morning—Ashlyn relaxed against the cushions. She might as well enjoy being waited on, because there would come a time when she'd once again be on her own.

By the time Slate came back into the living room with a glass in one hand and a protein bar in the other, Ashlyn was feeling pretty damn good. She was still a little foggy from the migraine and probably whatever was in the pill he'd given her, but she'd take that over the headache she'd had last night.

He handed her the glass, then sat next to her. "You need to text your friends."

Ashlyn took a sip of the shake and was pleasantly surprised by how good it tasted. For some reason, she'd assumed it would be kind of nasty, maybe because it was supposed to be healthy. But she couldn't really tell the difference between what Slate had made her and one of the milkshakes she sometimes bought from her favorite ice cream shop.

"This is delicious," she said with a grin.

His lips twitched. "I know."

"It feels as if I'm eating dessert for breakfast."

"Yup."

She narrowed her eyes. "I can't believe you didn't tell me how good this was before now. You let me think you were being all healthy in the mornings when you have one of these for breakfast."

Slate burst out laughing, the sound filling Ashlyn with happiness. He was often so stoic, and knowing she could make him laugh made her feel warm and fuzzy inside.

"Babe," he said.

That was it. Just one word.

"What? I'm serious," she said. "Wait, are you sure this is one of your protein thingies? You didn't have some ice cream delivered and made this out of that, just to make me feel better?"

"It's a protein shake," Slate reassured her. "Ice, vanilla protein powder, some strawberries for a bit more flavor and skim milk to make it creamier."

"It's yummy," she said, taking another sip.

He grinned at her. "Yummy? Nobody says that."

"Apparently I do," she informed him.

"Right. But for the record, you should probably save some of that to wash down the protein bar. It's good, but not as good as that shake. They've come a long way toward making them not taste like cardboard, but I'm guessing you aren't going to be as big a fan of it as you are of that drink."

Ashlyn wrinkled her nose, but reached for the nutritious bar in his hand. "I think I'll feel better if it doesn't taste like a decadent treat. I feel guilty enough for drinking the shake."

Slate chuckled and watched as she tore off the wrapper on one end and took a bite. She chewed for a moment then shrugged. "It's not as bad as I was expecting. I'm not sure I want to eat one as a meal every day for the rest of my life, but it's not awful."

Slate hadn't taken his eyes off her since he'd sat down.

"What? Do I have something on my face?" Ashlyn asked, wiping her face on her arm, since both hands were full.

"No. I'm just so damn relieved to see you back to your normal self. You scared me, Ash."

"I'm sorry," she said softly.

Slate shook his head. "No, don't apologize. You didn't purposely get a headache. Just letting you know that I hope to never see you like that again."

"They aren't fun. Thank you for getting me some meds. What was it, by the way?"

Slate shrugged. "No clue. I mean, Mustang told me the name of the drug, but I wasn't really paying attention. All I cared about was that it would help you."

"How did he manage to get it?" Ashlyn asked.

"In our line of work, we know a lot of people," Slate said offhandedly.

"Oh my God, did he call Baker?" Ashlyn asked, sitting up

straighter in her seat. "I've heard so much about him! I mean, I know he came to Monica and Pid's wedding out at the Kualoa Ranch, but I didn't get to talk to him."

"What? No, Mustang didn't call Baker. Jeez."

"Oh. Darn."

He shook his head. "He called a doctor on base who's treated us in the past. Explained your symptoms, and he had a sample pack of the drug for you. He only brought over two. But since they worked, you can tell your doc what you took and that it seemed to be effective, and maybe he or she can give you a prescription."

"Well, that's no fun," Ashlyn grumbled.

"Besides that, I'm not sure I want you getting chummy with Baker," Slate said.

"Why?"

"Because apparently he's hot. All the other women say so."

"And?" Ashlyn asked.

Slate merely arched a brow at her.

"Oh, come on. It doesn't matter if he's hot, I'm dating *you*."

"And don't you forget it," Slate said, reaching out and tagging her behind the neck, pulling her toward him.

Since Ashlyn's hands were full, she couldn't brace herself, but Slate didn't let her fall. He kissed her hard, and way too briefly, before letting her go.

"From what I've heard from the others, he's got a thing for a woman named Jodelle, anyway," she said.

Slate nodded. "I'm also not all that fired up to get Baker involved with *anything* to do with you, because every time we've had to call him lately, it's because bad things are threatening our women. I'd be perfectly okay with you never meeting him if that means everything's good. Safe. Normal."

Ashlyn could understand that. She shivered a little,

thinking about everything her friends had been through. "Right."

"And...said it earlier, but we kind of got sidetracked. You need to text Elodie and the others."

"I know."

"No, you need to do it soon. They're worried about you, babe. Been texting you—and me—most of the night, checking in. And they've already started this morning." Slate turned and picked up her phone from the table next to his end of the couch. He held it out to her.

She leaned forward and put the shake on the coffee table, then took her phone. "Holy crap, they're acting like I was dying or something. It was just a headache," Ashlyn muttered as she scrolled through all her notifications.

"With our jobs, and with everything that's happened, no one takes anyone's health for granted."

Ashlyn sighed. After a moment, she said, "When I broke up with Franklin, I felt so stupid."

Slate frowned in confusion, and she hurried to try to explain her abrupt change of topic.

"I moved to Hawaii because of him, and we hadn't even been dating that long. I was excited about living here, and he gave me an excuse to do something I'd dreamed about but was too chicken to actually do. When I found out what a douche he was, I couldn't believe I'd been such an idiot. Who moves across the ocean for a guy they barely know? But it turned out to be the best decision I ever made in my life. I got the job at Food For All, met Lexie, then Elodie and Kenna, Monica, and Carly...and you."

"You weren't thrilled to meet me at first," Slate said with a chuckle.

"True. You were overbearing and obnoxious."

"But you like me now," Slate said, leaning toward her. Except he didn't stop, and Ashlyn laughed as she fell onto her back trying to get away from him. He hovered over her on the couch, smiling. "Say it," he ordered.

"It," she retorted sassily.

"Brat," Slate said as he lowered himself farther, pinning her in place. The smile faded from his face. "You weren't stupid," he told her. "You were optimistic. And that's one of your greatest assets. Do I think you're sometimes *too* optimistic? Yes, but if you weren't who you were, we wouldn't be here right now. And I know for a fact the other women are just as glad to have you, as you are to have *them*."

Ashlyn smiled up at him.

"Now, how about you finish that protein bar," Slate said, gesturing with his head to the half-eaten bar still in her hand, "and your shake, text your girls, then we'll hang out here and watch a movie or two."

"Are you...I figured you'd head on out, now that you know I'm okay. I'm sure you've got stuff you need to do today."

"It's Saturday, babe. I've got nothing to do but hang out with you and make sure you're good. That headache could come back, and I want to be here if it does."

That warm and fuzzy feeling rushed back. Ashlyn couldn't think of anything she'd rather do than hang out with Slate all day. "Okay."

"But I get to pick the movie," he said.

Ashlyn scowled. "No. You'll choose something boring."

"No, I won't," he protested.

"Yes, you will. You think *Full Metal Jacket* is a classic."

"Babe, it *is* a classic."

"But it's gory. And there's lots of yelling," Ashlyn protested.

Slate chuckled. "Fine. You can pick the first movie, but I get the second one. And if you choose *Legally Blonde* again, I'm gonna make you sit through the longest, most boring military movie I can find."

"Oh, all right," Ashlyn said. She didn't care what they watched, as long as she could be with Slate.

He lifted a hand and ran it over the side of her head tenderly. "Hated not being able to do this last night," he murmured softly. "Hated knowing my touch would hurt you."

Ashlyn hated that too. She tilted her head into his hand, giving him her weight. He smiled at her, then leaned down and kissed her forehead gently.

"We could go back into the bedroom and find something to do other than watch a movie," she blurted.

"No way," Slate said without hesitation. "No sex until I'm sure you're one hundred percent better."

Ashlyn pouted. "You're no fun."

"Nope," he agreed as he sat up. "Eat, text, then we'll snuggle and watch TV."

Ashlyn giggled.

"What's funny?" Slate asked.

"You, saying the word snuggle," she admitted.

"Just as funny as you saying the word yummy," he retorted. But he smiled as he said it.

Ashlyn took another bite of the protein bar and chewed even as she smirked at him.

She never would've thought Slate could be as...compassionate and tender as he was being this morning. She liked it. A lot.

As she finished chewing her protein bar, a new notification popped up on her phone. Elodie. Asking if she felt better, if she was up, and when would be a good time to bring over the soup she was already making for her that morning.

"I'm gonna go shower while you chat with your posse," Slate told her. He leaned over, kissed the top of her head, then wandered toward her bedroom.

Ashlyn watched him go, tempted to follow him into her bathroom and climb into the shower with him, but she knew how stubborn he was. If he thought not having sex was the best thing for her health, nothing she could do would change his mind.

She picked up her phone, eager to reassure her friends that she was feeling better, but she also wanted to be done with her texting so she could fully enjoy her day with Slate.

CHAPTER FIFTEEN

More than a week after her killer headache, Ashlyn was still feeling great. She'd seen her doctor and her MRI had come back clear. She had to admit, she was relieved she didn't have a brain tumor or something. Looking up reasons why she'd had such a bad headache on the Internet wasn't the best idea. According to the websites she'd looked at, she probably had brain cancer.

Luckily, it was neither. Her doctor had talked about some things she could do to try to stop the headache from getting so bad if it happened again, namely not pushing herself to finish out her workday and taking ibuprofen immediately. He'd also prescribed her some of the same drug Slate had given her, since it worked so well this last time.

It was a Tuesday, and Ashlyn was on her way to James Mason's house. It was his eighty-ninth birthday, and she and Slate had made him a special cake last night. It had killed her to not say anything yesterday, when she'd delivered his usual meal to him. She'd wanted to surprise him. And not only with the cake.

Ashlyn had talked to Carly, and she'd wholeheartedly

given her support for what she was going to talk to James about today.

When she pulled up outside his house, she saw Aiden's Chevette parked in the narrow driveway next to James's house. It wasn't surprising, since Tuesday was one of the days Aiden came over to help out, but it was early, and she didn't think he usually arrived until after lunchtime.

Too excited to be concerned about Aiden's schedule—she didn't always arrive at her clients' houses at the same time every day either—Ashlyn carefully picked up the cake from the passenger seat and closed the door with her foot, heading toward the front door.

Holding the cake with one hand, she knocked on the door.

Aiden opened it with a scowl on his face. "What are you doing here?"

Taken aback by his brusque greeting, Ashlyn didn't immediately respond. She took a moment to study the man. He looked a little worse for wear. His shirt was dirty and wrinkled, his face was pale, and he seemed a little...twitchy? He was clearly out of sorts.

Deciding to ignore his attitude, she said cheerfully, "It's James's birthday. I brought him a cake."

"I didn't know it was his birthday," he mumbled as he opened the door for her.

"Yup. Eighty-nine." Ashlyn stepped into the house and saw James standing in the doorway between the kitchen and living room. He didn't look very happy either...but as soon as he saw her, he smiled.

"Hi, Ashlyn. What brings you by today? It's not Wednesday, is it? I lose track of days."

"Nope. It's Tuesday. A very special Tuesday. I couldn't let it go by without coming to wish you a happy birthday and bring you cake!"

James beamed. "How did you know? I didn't tell anyone," he said.

"I know all," Ashlyn said mysteriously. She wasn't about to tell him she'd specifically asked Lexie to look up when his birthday was a while ago, because she was curious.

"I haven't had a birthday cake in a good while. Ever since my beloved Angie died," James said softly.

"Then I'm extra glad I came by today," Ashlyn told him.

"I'm gonna go," Aiden said from behind her.

She turned around. "Oh, you don't want to stay and have some cake? I didn't mean to chase you off—"

"It's fine," James interrupted.

Surprised at the stern tone of his voice, Ashlyn stood in the middle of the room between Aiden and James, suddenly feeling awkward.

"I'm sorry," Aiden said quietly, speaking to James. "It won't happen again. I'll see you on Thursday." Then he turned and opened the front door and let himself out.

"I'm so sorry, James. Did I interrupt something?" Ashlyn asked cautiously.

James looked sad for a moment, then shook his head. "Nope. It's good. Aiden hopefully learned a lesson today. Everyone makes mistakes. I'm willing to let bygones be bygones. Now...what kind of cake did you make me?"

Ashlyn wanted to ask more questions about what happened with Aiden. What "mistake" he'd made, precisely. But she also didn't want to upset James.

"Black forest, what other kind would I make for you?"

James beamed once more. "My favorite," he told her.

Ashlyn knew that, which was why she'd made it for him. She'd heard plenty of stories about the cakes his wife used to make him every year. His favorite one to tell was the time she'd sent him a box of black forest cupcakes for his birthday when he was deployed on a ship, and they got lost in transit and didn't get to him until a week after his birthday. They were stale and mostly crushed, but James still swore they were some of the best cupcakes he'd ever eaten.

Personally, Ashlyn was surprised he didn't get food poisoning, but she'd kept her mouth shut about it since it was obviously one of James's fondest memories.

She walked into the kitchen and put the cake on the small table. She held a chair out for James, and he sank into it gratefully. She scooted the glass of water that was on the table closer to him, but he shook his head.

"No. Get me a fresh glass. Please," he said a little belatedly.

Wondering what the problem was with the other water, Ashlyn simply nodded and brought the apparently not-good glass to the sink and dumped it out. "I've got a better idea," she said, opening the fridge. She pulled out a bottle of Bikini Blonde Lager, brewed by the Maui Brewing Company, from the back of the top shelf.

She held it up. "I think a birthday celebration calls for a beer, don't you?"

James looked at his watch. "It's not even ten," he said.

"So? I won't tell if you don't. Besides, you have big plans to drive somewhere today?"

He chuckled. "Nope. And a beer sounds great. I forgot I had that in there."

Ashlyn popped off the top and put the bottle on the table in front of him. Then she leaned down and kissed the top of his head. "Happy Birthday, my friend."

He grinned at her.

Ashlyn felt a little teary, and she turned away to get some plates and forks to hide her emotion.

A little later, as they were each digging into a second piece of the delicious cake, Ashlyn decided it was time to give

James his next present. "So, I was thinking. And before you say no, hear me out."

James tilted his head in curiosity at her words.

"My friends Carly and Jag are getting married on Thursday. It's a very laid-back thing they're doing at Duke's. You know, the restaurant down at Waikiki? I was wondering if you would go with me. Be my date."

James stared at her in disbelief. "What about your young man? I'm guessing he'll have something to say about me going with you."

"Yup, you're right. He does. He's all for it. I already talked to him about asking you to come. And Carly's excited to meet you. And Jag has no problem with you coming, either. I know you have to be bored, maybe even a little sad, sitting here in your house alone all the time."

She held her breath as James thought about her invitation.

"I don't want to be a burden," he said after a moment. "I don't walk so good, and I can't do stairs without help."

"You are *never* a burden," she said sternly. "And there will be tons of people there to help you if you need it. Have you been to Duke's before?"

"Been to Duke's? Girl, I'm eighty-nine years old and have spent most of my life on this island. Of course I've been there. Their hula pie is the most amazing thing—after black forest cake, of course. I met Duke Kahanamoku a few times, you know."

"You did?" Ashlyn asked, fascinated.

"Yup. He was the sheriff of Honolulu when I was a boy, and he liked to visit the beach and chat with the kids who were there surfing. He died in nineteen sixty-eight, and I was there when his ashes were scattered into the ocean he'd always loved."

"So? Will you come?"

James looked her in the eye. "Are you sure it wouldn't be an imposition?"

"Not at all. I promise. Carly and Jag are keeping things very relaxed. After the ceremony, a huge spread of food will be laid out, and I'm sure there'll be a ton extra. In fact, I *know* there will be, because Carly specifically told me she wanted lots of leftovers so some could be donated to Food For All. Heck, I'll probably be delivering Duke's entrees all of next week. Please say you'll come."

"I haven't been down to Waikiki in forever," James said wistfully.

Ashlyn held her breath.

"If you're sure I won't be a pain in the butt, I'd love to come," he said at last.

"Yay!" Ashlyn exclaimed. "Slate and I will be here to pick you up around eleven on Thursday. I know that's a weird day to get married, but that was the only day Duke's had the space available for rent. And don't dress up. This is Hawaii, and Carly's made it very clear that if anyone shows up in anything stuffy, she's gonna kick 'em out." Ashlyn smiled at him. "I actually bought you a Hawaiian shirt the other day for your birthday. It's in the car, I'll bring it in before I leave. I couldn't carry it with my hands full of cake. It would be perfect for Thursday."

James narrowed his eyes. "You had this all planned," he accused without heat. "What would you have done if I'd said no?"

"Convinced you otherwise," Ashlyn said without missing a beat. Then she got serious. "I'm not close with my parents, James. They fought a lot when I was growing up and preferred to yell at each other rather than try to get along for my sake. I never knew my grandparents. I might be overstepping...but you're like the grandfather I never had. I'm fascinated by the stories you've got of growing up here, and the wars you've lived through, and I'm only sorry I never got to meet your wife. I feel as if I lucked out when you signed up for Food For All meal deliveries."

James's eyes filled with tears, and he blinked quickly and played with the crumbs of cake on his plate. Ashlyn felt a little emotional herself. She gave him time to compose himself.

"I'm the lucky one," he said after a moment.

"We both are, then," Ashlyn said.

She stayed another half an hour or so, laughing and joking with James. He oohed and aahed over the shirt she'd bought for him, and said he loved it.

When she knew she couldn't delay leaving if she was going to finish up her food delivery rounds, she reluctantly stood. "Remember, eleven o'clock on Thursday. Wear the shirt I brought. No gifts are necessary, and be ready for a great time chillin' on the beach."

"And lookin' at pretty girls in bikinis," James said with a smile.

Ashlyn giggled. "That too." She hugged the sweet man, hating how frail he felt in her arms. "Happy Birthday, James."

"Best birthday I've had in years," he told her, returning the hug.

After Ashlyn got him settled in his chair and made sure his phone and the remote were within easy reach, and after she put another slice of cake on the table next to him for later, as well as a large cup of water with a straw, she finally left.

She sent Slate a text as soon as she got into her car.

Ashlyn: He said yes!

Slate: Good news, babe.

Ashlyn: Yeah. He even said he'd wear the shirt I got him. And he loved the cake.

Slate: You had a good morning.

Ashlyn: I did. How's yours going?

Slate: Busy.

Ashlyn frowned. She had a feeling she knew what that meant. Slate and the rest of the guys were getting ready to be deployed again. She hated that it was going to happen so close to the last deployment, but as Slate reminded her, they didn't get to choose when terrorists decided to be assholes. They just had to be ready to act when they were.

At least they wouldn't be leaving before the ceremony. It would be awful if Jag had to miss his own wedding, causing a delay.

Slate: Drive safe today.

Ashlyn: I will. Am I still coming to your place tonight?

Slate: Yes. I don't know when I'll be getting out of here though. Use the key I gave you this morning and make yourself comfortable. Don't worry about dinner for me. If I'm too late, I'll grab something on the way home.

Ashlyn grinned and looked down at her keychain. She'd been stunned when Slate had handed it to her that morning, before they'd left her house. They'd discussed her coming over to his place later that evening, and he'd nonchalantly taken the spare key off his keychain and given it to her. She wasn't moving in or anything, but it felt like a huge deal that he'd given her a key to his place.

. . .

Ashlyn: Don't stop and get crap. I'll make an egg casserole. It'll be full of protein and good stuff, and it'll keep until you get home. If you're too late, we can just heat it up.

Slate: Sounds good. But, babe, don't wait for me. You'll be hungry, so eat when the casserole is done.

Ashlyn: Fine.

Slate: And don't pout.

She laughed out loud. He knew her too well.

Ashlyn: I'm not pouting. How can I pout when it's James's birthday and he said he'd come to the wedding on Thursday?

Slate: You can't. See you later tonight.

Ashlyn: Later. Have fun storming the castle.

Slate: Babe, this isn't *The Princess Bride*. We aren't storming anything.

Ashlyn: But you're planning the storming.

Slate: You're a dork.

Ashlyn: Yup. I'll let you go. I need to burn some rubber to get all my deliveries in.

Slate: No one's gonna care if you're late. Be safe.

Ashlyn: I will. Bye.

Slate: Later.

Ashlyn was so happy, her mind busily poring over the deliveries she had to make, what ingredients she needed to get at the store after work to make the casserole, and how excited she was for Thursday.

She didn't think twice about the odd interlude between James and Aiden. But later, when she looked back on the day, she'd realize that she should've asked more questions.

* * *

Aiden sat in his car and scowled at the fuel gauge. He was almost out of gas and had no money to get more. Just as he had no cash to get his next hit. His dealer refused to give him his usual stash without payment. Just because he hadn't been able to pay him back when he said he would the last two times, that didn't give the asshole the right to deny him!

It was the old man's fault. If he'd drunk the fucking water Aiden had given him, instead of getting all paranoid, he would've been snoring away before the bitch arrived...and Aiden would have the money he desperately needed.

No one in his life understood how awful it felt to be dope sick. No one cared. He didn't need a thousand bucks, he just needed a hundred. Enough for a couple hits. And the old man didn't need the damn money. All he did was sit on his ass all day, letting the cash pile up from his Navy retirement and social security.

He'd just wanted the old bastard to sleep, so he could look for another stash in the house. Aiden had taken as much as he dared from the two places he'd already found. He knew there had to be other hiding spots.

But he'd gotten careless, and James saw him crushing a sleeping pill into his water. He'd confronted him about it. Wanted to know what the hell he was doing. Aiden had no choice but to admit to putting drugs in his water, but he was pretty sure he'd done a convincing job of making James think it was because he was worried about him, since he hadn't been sleeping well.

It was probably a good thing the bitch showed up. It gave James something else to think about other than Aiden's motives. But now the old man was suspicious, and would be more alert than ever.

If he got fired, Aiden was screwed. He *needed* the money hidden in James's house.

Since he couldn't go back until Thursday, he'd have to figure out some other way to get money. Probably panhandle again, which *sucked*! But he'd do whatever it took to get enough cash for a hit. He wouldn't be able to last until Thursday, when he may or may not be able to steal more money from the old fart.

Eighty-nine years old. Jesus, Aiden hoped *he* didn't live that long. What was the point? You couldn't walk well, couldn't do much but sit around and watch TV and sleep. Ridiculous.

Aiden would have to get sneakier about drugging the guy so he could search his place. There was more money hidden, Aiden had no doubt. And he needed to find it. *Would* find it. No one was going to stop him either. Not James, not the bitch...no one.

CHAPTER SIXTEEN

Slate couldn't keep his gaze from straying to Ashlyn. She was literally glowing. Usually that was a phrase reserved for the bride, but he couldn't help applying it to Ashlyn. She had a huge smile on her face, and she looked relaxed and happy.

The day had been perfect so far. From waking up with her mouth on his cock, and fucking her hard and fast, then soft and slow while in the shower, to witnessing her compassion and delight when they'd arrived at James Mason's house, and she saw him wearing the shirt she'd bought him.

She'd led the older man to his Trailblazer and gotten him situated in the front seat, then happily sat in the back, chattering their ears off all the way down to Waikiki. Slate had dropped them off in front of the Outrigger, where Duke's was located, and left to park. By the time he'd arrived at the restaurant, James was seated at a table, having the time of his life chatting with Kenna, Aleck, Midas, and Lexie.

Now, Ashlyn was at the bar getting drinks, most likely a mai tai for her and beers for him and James. She was laughing with the bartenders and had her arm looped around Elodie as they waited for their order.

Mustang wandered over and stood next to Slate. "Never thought I'd say this," he said with a small chuckle. "But I fucking love weddings."

Slate snorted.

"Seriously, what's not to love? Get to see my wife all dressed up, she gets tipsy, which means good things for me tonight when we get home. She's happy as a fucking clam, and I get to spend time with my favorite people on Earth. Gonna suck when you and Midas do the deed and we run out of people to throw these shindigs for."

"Jumping the gun a bit there, aren't you?" Slate asked. "Not sure Midas and Lex are ready to get married anytime soon, and I'm definitely not. Besides, we could both decide to go to the courthouse and do something quick and easy."

"True, but we could still have a big party afterward."

Slate shook his head at his friend. "But seriously, I don't want you to be disappointed when this thing with Ash and me cools off, and we end up just friends."

Mustang turned and rested his shoulder against the wall where they were standing, giving Slate his full attention. "I know you're getting sick of me bringing this up—"

"Then don't," Slate interrupted, but his friend ignored him.

"It's been almost three months since you two started dating. You both keep saying over and over that it's casual, that you've just got some sort of friends-with-benefits things going on, but I'm calling bullshit."

"It's not bullshit," he retorted gruffly.

"It is, Slate. Shit, you and Ashlyn danced around your attraction for each other for a whole damn year before you finally hooked up. And that is *not* like you. Name one other woman that you're just friends with."

"Elodie," Slate said without hesitation.

"Fine, one other *single* woman," his friend clarified.

Slate pressed his lips together.

"Exactly," Mustang said, but he didn't sound smug. "You don't do the friend thing with women. There's nothing wrong with that, but from the get-go, you and Ashlyn had something different. I hesitate to use the word special, because I don't want to sound like a pussy. But seriously, you and her are *not* casual. I don't know if the two of you will eventually end up walking down the aisle together or not, but I think you're disrespecting yourself, and Ashlyn, by insisting that you're just fucking. That you aren't in a real relationship."

Slate wanted to be irritated at his friend's attempts at psychoanalyzing him. But he had too many valid points. Slate hadn't ever been just friends with a woman. Not because he didn't like or respect women in general, but because he simply clicked with men better.

Until Ashlyn.

She made him laugh.

She exasperated him.

Sometimes she irritated the shit out of him. Exactly like his teammates did.

He also trusted her. Hadn't ever had a problem finding things to talk about with the woman. He enjoyed spending time with her...and not just in the bedroom. Yes, when they'd first started dating, they couldn't keep their hands off each other. Every time they met up, they ended up in bed.

But their relationship had morphed into...more. They didn't immediately jump on each other when they got together. They talked. They laughed. They even fucking cuddled on the couch watching TV. They weren't spending every night together, but when they did have sex, they slept together at whichever house they were at. Getting up and leaving right after orgasming was the last thing he wanted to do.

He might not want to admit it out loud, but Mustang was pretty much spot on.

Slate was still just as determined as ever to *not* change the nature of their relationship. But now...it was because he didn't want to fuck anything up. He didn't want to spook Ashlyn.

"And that woman doesn't look at you as if you're just a friend," Mustang continued. "Her eyes are constantly searching for you when you're not at her side. She's not checking out other guys, looking for better prospects, like some women do when they're in a casual relationship. And when you guys are close, you automatically reach for each other. You touch her back. She leans into you. You hold her hand or wrap an arm around her.

"You can both protest and tell everyone who'll listen that there's nothing serious going on between you, but it's all bull-shit. The sooner you own up to it, the better off you'll both be."

"Mustang, you know I respect and love you like a brother, but you need to back off," Slate said, feeling uncomfortable with the serious tone of the discussion.

"All right. But I've got one more thing to say before I shut up."

Slate braced.

"Elodie is the best thing that's ever happened to me, and I'm not bullshitting you by saying that. I never thought much about marriage before meeting her, but I literally can't imagine my life without her now. I thought I was content. I had a job I loved and was damn good at, I had great friends, money in the bank, was living in Hawaii...what else could I ask for? I can't explain how it feels to get off work at the end of the day, or when I get back from a mission, and know that when I walk through my front door, she's gonna be there. Ashlyn might not be your soul mate, but...what if she is? The last thing you want is to spend the rest of your life kicking your ass for letting her go. For not at least trying to see if you can make things work long term.

"At some point, she's gonna get tired of being a piece of ass. She's gonna want a deeper connection with a man—and she'll leave to find that with someone else. Deep down, if you're truly okay with that, fine. But if you aren't...you need to stop half-assing this relationship."

Slate's hands curled into fists. He wasn't upset with Mustang. It was the thought of Ashlyn being with another man that didn't sit well with him.

"I can see I'm finally getting through," Mustang said with satisfaction. He clapped his friend on the back and straightened from his position against the wall. He turned to look at Elodie and Ashlyn at the bar. They were both laughing hysterically at something one of the bartenders was saying.

"On another note," Mustang said, and Slate was more than ready to change topics, "looks like we'll be heading out on Sunday."

Slate nodded. He'd expected that. The situation in Afghanistan was volatile at best. Threats against the American base there had been declared credible and a few special forces teams were being sent overseas to see if they could ferret out the ones responsible.

"Does Jag know?" Slate asked.

"Yeah. Told him this morning. He's not thrilled he has to leave Carly so soon after their wedding, but he's relieved that she'll be wearing his ring before he does. Sucks I can't give him the next few days off though," Mustang said on a sigh. "We need him in on the planning sessions."

Slate nodded. Researching and planning their missions were the most important things the team did. No one liked going into a situation blind, and while they'd already been examining the town and trying to narrow down the locations of the major ISIL players, they needed to know every alley, every bad guy's house, and every escape route like the backs of their hands before landing in the country.

"Incoming," Mustang said softly.

Slate turned his head and saw Elodie and Ashlyn walking toward them with huge grins on their faces. Ashlyn had three drinks in her hands, doing her best not to drop any.

Slate took a step forward and took the two beer bottles from her, leaving her with just the mai tai. "Jeez, babe, did you leave any alcohol for anyone else?" he teased. He absently noted Mustang leading Elodie away.

Ashlyn's grin widened. "I told Kaleen I wanted a double so I didn't have to go back and get another anytime soon, and she gave me this huge glass."

And it *was* huge. Instead of being a double, it was more like a quadruple drink.

"Hope you weren't planning on walking by the end of the evening," Slate mused.

Ashlyn giggled. "Nope. Why walk when you can carry me? But seriously, I'm planning on drinking a lot of water too. The last thing I want to do is pass out at my friend's wedding and embarrass myself."

Slate couldn't help himself. He leaned forward and took her lips with his. The only parts of their bodies touching were their lips, as his hands were full and she was holding her big-ass glass. She tasted like the fruity drink—and Slate wanted her. Right then and there.

He forced himself to pull back, staring at Ashlyn as she licked her lips. She wanted him too. Her desire was clear to see.

Suddenly, Slate couldn't wait for the afternoon to be over. Sex with Ashlyn when she was tipsy was fantastic. He had a feeling that sex with her when she was drunk would be stupendous.

"Stop that," she whispered.

"Stop what?" he asked.

"Looking at me like you want to strip me naked and fuck me right here."

"Can't help it," he told her.

"I don't think this is normal," Ashlyn mused.

"What's not normal?"

"Us. We already had sex twice this morning. How can we want it again so soon?"

Slate grinned. "Because you're you," he said simply.

She wrinkled her nose. "That makes no sense. I've always been me, and I haven't been like this before."

"Fine, because we're us," Slate amended.

Ashlyn grinned. "That, I'll buy."

"Come on, babe. James needs his beer, and you being cute is only making me want to skip out on this wedding thing and take you back to my house and show you how normal we really are."

"We can't leave!" Ashlyn exclaimed in horror.

"I was kidding. I wouldn't miss Jag's wedding for anything," Slate told her. He switched one of the beers so he was holding both in one hand, and put the other on the small of Ashlyn's back. He leaned down and nuzzled the skin next to her ear. "Drink all you want, but not so much that you get sick," he said softly. "Don't like when you feel like shit."

She nodded and gazed up at him, her eyes swimming with emotion he couldn't read. "Thanks for going along with my idea to bring James."

"I like him. And not only because he's a veteran. He's got some interesting stories, he's funny, it's obvious that he's lonely. And I'd do just about anything to make you happy, Ash."

"I'm very happy," she said without missing a beat.

"Good. Me too."

"Good," she echoed, leaning into him as Slate put his arm around her shoulders.

They walked back over to where everyone was gathered, waiting for the ceremony, which was scheduled to start in about twenty minutes. Everyone would move out onto the sand at the back of the restaurant where a white gazebo had been set up. Jag hadn't been sure about getting married on the beach where Carly's ex had literally blown himself up while trying to kidnap Kenna, but she'd convinced him that it would help cleanse the area of his bad juju.

Personally, Slate agreed. The beach should be a happy place, and he was glad the awful memories of that night were being replaced by good ones...for everyone, not just Kenna and Aleck. But for every civilian who was at the restaurant that night when Shawn had lost his mind.

"Here ya go," Slate said, handing the beer to James.

The older man looked up, and it was easy to see the happiness in his eyes.

"Thank you. I've got money, I can pay you back."

"Nonsense," Ashlyn said, overhearing him. She leaned down and kissed his cheek. "Consider it a birthday present."

"You already gave me this," James said, tugging at the brightly colored Hawaiian shirt he was wearing.

"Yup."

"I've got a couple bucks for a beer," he said, quieter now. "I know I'm getting meals from Food For All, but I'm not broke."

Ashlyn squatted next to his chair and put a hand on his leg. She spoke just as quietly, so everyone around them couldn't overhear. But since Slate was standing right next to them, he was close enough to hear their discussion.

"I know you're not. And honestly, even if you called to cancel the service tomorrow, I'd still keep showing up. I already told you, James, you're like a grandfather to me.

Giving you gifts isn't an act of charity, it's because I love you. As far as I'm concerned, you're now a part of my family. And family doesn't bitch when someone buys them a beer. In fact, you should be manipulating me into buying you more. Because that's what family would do. Got it?"

It took a second for James to compose himself, but after a moment, he nodded. "Got it."

"Besides...I didn't buy your beer. Slate did. I opened a tab," she whispered, winking at James. "And told the bartender my hunky boyfriend would be paying it off at the end of the evening."

James chortled. "In that case...cheers!" he said, lifting his beer bottle and clinking it to Ashlyn's huge-ass mai tai.

Slate pulled Ashlyn against his side as soon as she stood. He kissed her temple and whispered, "You're amazing," into her ear.

She beamed up at him.

"Come on, guys," Kenna said, gesturing to everyone from a few steps down on the beach. "It's almost time, and we need to get into place!"

"Go on," Slate told her. "I've got James."

"You sure?"

"I'm sure."

She went up on her tiptoes and kissed him on the lips, soft and sweet, before grinning and hurrying to join her girl-friends.

James slowly stood next to Slate. "She's beautiful," the older man said.

Slate nodded. She was. She absolutely was. She wore a dark blue sundress that hugged her chest and hips, but blew around her calves in the sea breeze. She'd left her sleek, shiny hair down, and every now and then a few strands would blow across her face and she'd have to brush them back. She wasn't wearing heels; they weren't practical on the sand, and Carly wanted everyone to be casual and comfortable. Her toenails were painted a bright pink, which matched the flowers on the flip-flops she wore. Besides, she didn't need heels. Ashlyn was the tallest of all her friends, perfect for his six-foot-two height.

As Slate took James's elbow in his hand to steady him as they made their way down the few steps to the sand, he thought about how Ashlyn was perfect for him in just about every way. In the few months they'd been dating, he hadn't once gotten so much as annoyed with her. Truly annoyed.

"It's been a very long time since I've been on the beach," James mused.

Slate turned his attention from Ashlyn to the older man. "Heard you were quite the surfer back in the day."

"I was," James said without a hint of boasting. He was just stating a fact.

"You would've been a damn good SEAL," Slate told him. He wasn't just blowing smoke up the guy's ass. He'd heard James's stories about some of the things he'd done while in the Navy. And while he might not have been a SEAL, he'd certainly done some of the exact same things Slate and his team still did today.

There weren't any chairs set up around the gazebo, everyone was just standing to watch Carly and Jag's short ceremony. Ashlyn started to drag a beach lounge chair closer to the tent so James could sit, but Slate shook his head.

"He's fine."

"But—"

"He's fine," Slate said again, with a little more emphasis.

Ashlyn stared at him for a moment before nodding.

Slate did move into the shade of the gazebo with James, but he knew without having to ask that it would embarrass the veteran to be the only one sitting. He kept his hand on

James's elbow, giving him some support and making sure he didn't accidentally fall over in the sand.

Everyone's eyes turned to the steps leading down from the eating area at Duke's as Carly and Jag started toward them. There was no real aisle, no music, and no bridesmaids or groomsmen. It was simply two people in love, coming together to pledge that love to one another in front of their friends.

Ashlyn snuggled up against Slate's left side and hooked her arm through his, resting her head on his bicep. Slate felt James shift against him on his right, and he looked at the slightly stooped eighty-nine-year-old. The man was looking over at Ashlyn with a tender expression. Then he raised his gaze and met Slate's.

He nodded in approval before turning his head to watch Carly and Jag once more. They approached Paulo, who'd agreed to officiate, and turned to face each other.

It was crazy how content Slate felt right at that moment. He knew in a few days' time, he'd be sweating his ass off in Afghanistan, doing his best to kill insurgents before they killed him. But for now, he had the sand under his feet, the breeze blowing against his legs and arms, an amazing woman at his side, a man he respected a hell of a lot on his other side, and he was watching one of his best friends in the world marry the woman he loved.

Life was pretty damn good.

* * *

"Move, babe," Slate ordered late that night.

They were in his bed, and Ashlyn was indeed drunk. She'd attacked him as soon as they'd gotten inside his house. He'd let her take the lead. And apparently, what she wanted was to be on top.

Not that Slate had any problem with that whatsoever. Except for the fact that she wasn't moving fast enough for him. Ashlyn's cheeks were flushed from the alcohol and all the dancing she'd done earlier. After Carly and Jag had said their I do's and shared an entirely inappropriate kiss on the public beach, they'd all gone back into the restaurant and done their best to make a dent in all the food that had been prepared for them.

Then Ashlyn had joined Elodie, Lexie, Carly, and Kenna on the dance floor. Monica had mostly watched from the sidelines, saying that since she was pregnant, she couldn't dance. Of course, the girls had only let that excuse go for so long before they had her up and dancing with them...albeit a little less boisterously.

Slate and the rest of his team had watched their women with amusement, making sure to claim them when the music slowed down. James observed everything from his chair in the corner with a smile on his face, perfectly happy to be out of his house and watching the merriment.

They'd driven him home, and Ashlyn had taken him inside, made sure he was good to go, then proceeded to make Slate crazy all the way to his house. Her hands roamed up and down his leg, brushing against his cock every now and then. She had a sly grin on her face, and the second he'd parked his car, she'd flung off her seat belt and straddled him right there in the car.

And now they were in his bed. Ashlyn was as bare as the day she was born, grinding slowly on his cock. Slate put his hands on her hips. The pleasure was almost *too* intense.

"*Move*," he ordered once more.

Ashlyn seemed to be lost in her own world. A small smile lit her face as she used her inner muscles to grip his dick from deep within. "But I like this," she argued. "You feel so good..."

He was done. He needed her to come so he could fuck her

the way he wanted—hard and fast. One hand eased down, and he began to rub her clit with his thumb.

She jerked, and it was all he could do not to explode when her muscles clamped down on him even harder.

"Oh!" she exclaimed, finally undulating faster on his cock. It wasn't the up and down motion he needed to come, but it felt amazing all the same.

"That's it, babe. Come all over my cock. Let me feel you dripping down my balls."

"Slate!" she cried, as her entire body began to shake. She curled into him, one hand resting on his chest, holding herself up, and the other gripping his bicep, nails digging in, as if he was the only thing holding her together.

Slate continued roughly manipulating her clit, needing her to get off. But he couldn't deny he was enjoying the view. Her long hair brushed his chest and face, tickling him with every movement she made. Her nipples were hard and her tits bounced as she swayed. The pooch on her belly made her seem even more womanly, and he loved the feel of her soft thighs on either side of his hips.

Ashlyn bit her lip and closed her eyes as her trembling increased. He knew she was on the verge of coming, and he growled, "Open your eyes and look at me."

When she didn't comply, he stopped the motion of his thumb on her tender bundle of nerves.

Her eyes immediately popped open. "Slate," she whined. "Don't stop!"

"Keep your eyes on me, and I won't," he said.

She nodded jerkily, and he moved his thumb once more.

Her hips began to flex and her thighs tightened around him as she got closer and closer.

"That's it, babe. Fuck, you're so hot and tight! You're strangling my cock and it feels so goddamn good. I'm gonna fuck you hard as soon as you go over. I'm barely holding on as it is."

"*Yes*," she sighed.

Their gazes were locked. Slate wanted to look down, see where his cock was buried deep within her, but he literally couldn't. Her pupils were dilated with lust, her lips shiny from his earlier kisses.

He pinched her clit hard, and she lost it, curling into him even more as she came.

Slate's hands moved to her hips and he lifted her slightly, then slammed her back down.

She cried out.

Slate did it again, but not getting the friction he needed, he rolled until she was beneath him. She was still shaking as he thrust into her over and over. Grunting each time he bottomed out inside her spasming pussy.

It didn't take long for his own orgasm to overtake him. He pressed himself as deeply inside her as he could get, arched his back and let go. He swore his vision went dark for a second, then he saw stars, pleasure like he'd never even dreamed consuming him.

After he regained some sense of cognition, Slate lowered himself, propping his body on his elbows so he didn't crush Ashlyn. He kissed her gently, loving how boneless she was under him. Her breath was still sweet from the mixed drink she'd nursed all night, and he swore he'd never forget this moment, that taste, as long as he liv—

Instantly, something occurred to him. And as much as he didn't want to ruin the mood, it needed to be addressed immediately.

"Babe?"

"Hmmm?"

She sounded completely undone, and Slate fucking loved it.

"We were so crazy for each other, I didn't have a chance to put on a condom." He didn't beat around the bush. But he held his breath, praying she didn't freak out.

"Mmmm...kay."

He waited for her to say something else, but when Ashlyn merely wrapped her arms around his back and eased him closer, he said, "Did you hear me?"

"Uh-huh. No condom. I'm on the pill. I'm clean. Hope you are too."

"On the pill?" he repeated dumbly.

She laughed and finally opened her eyes to look up at him. "No, *clean*."

"I am," he said seriously. "I haven't gone ungloved. Ever."

"Ever?" she whispered.

"No."

"God...I'm sorry."

Slate frowned. "For what?"

"I basically attacked you. Didn't give you a chance to even grab one before I jumped on."

Slate chuckled. "Jumped on?"

"You know what I mean," she said, her cheeks heating with a blush. "I didn't mean to make you do something you don't want to do."

"I didn't say that I don't want you bare," Slate said. "I just wasn't sure if you'd be upset about it."

"We agreed to let each other know if we were seeing anyone else, and since you haven't said, I figure I'm the only person you've been with. It felt safe, and I'm protected against pregnancy. So no, I'm not upset."

Slate couldn't stop his hips from shifting if his life depended on it. He slid in and out of her body easily, both their orgasms easing his way. The feeling of being inside her raw was indescribable. His cock twitched and began to recover.

"Oh my God, you can't be ready to go again. I'm a pile of mush here, and you're already getting hard?"

"Can't help it," he gasped. "I can feel every twitch of your muscles. And your amazing heat. And you're so wet and slippery..."

Ashlyn giggled, and he felt that in his dick too.

"Oh my God, you're like a kid with a new toy."

Slate kind of felt just like that. "Don't worry, you don't have to do anything. I'll do all the work."

"It's a good thing, because I'm in an orgasm coma. And the room is still kinda spinning."

"You gonna puke?"

"No."

"Good." Slate slowly pulled his cock all the way out of her body until just the tip was inside her, then steadily pushed back in until his balls were flush against her once more. "Don't mind me then, I'll just be doing this for the rest of the night."

Ashlyn laughed and, once again, Slate felt it deep within her.

"Right, carry on then."

So he did.

Thirty minutes later, they were both sweaty again, and this time it was Ashlyn lying on *his* chest.

"That's it. I'm dead."

"But what a way to go," Slate breathed, still overwhelmed by the way she'd felt on his bare cock.

Ashlyn turned her head, kissed the skin of his upper chest, then rested her cheek against him once more. "Slate?"

"Yeah, babe?"

"I had a good time tonight."

"Me too," he said without hesitation. Before long, he felt her body relax against his as she fell asleep.

He lay under her for a long time, thinking of their day. He

replayed Mustang's words. Remembered how, even though Ashlyn was having fun with her friends, her gaze still sought his every few minutes. How good she felt against him when they danced. How generous and giving the woman was. How happy and content he felt when he was with her.

How amazing the sex was.

It seemed a little juvenile to add that into the pro category, but he couldn't deny that they had some killer chemistry. He'd never forgotten to put on a condom in his entire life. But he'd been just as anxious to get inside her body as she'd been to *have* him inside. And the feel of taking her bare...it was better than he could've ever imagined.

The bottom line was that the last few months had been some of the best of his life. Slate felt balanced. In the past, he'd been all about his work, and when he dated, he usually got annoyed with the women fairly quickly. Usually when they started demanding more of his time than he was willing to give.

But Slate couldn't remember one time when he'd truly been irritated with Ashlyn. She was so easy to be with. Didn't pester him about what he did at work, didn't pester him to spend time with her. In fact, he'd say *he* was the one who couldn't get enough of Ashlyn. Of course, she also seemed to completely enjoy herself when they were together.

He ran a finger up the delicate curve of her spine as she lay on top of him, and smiled when she arched into his touch and tried to snuggle even closer to him in her sleep.

Did he want more with her? More than what they had? Something deeper...more long term? It was a scary thought. As he'd thought after his talk with Mustang, trying to change the nature of their relationship might ruin everything. Ashlyn had made it clear that she was perfectly content with things as they were. The last thing he wanted to do was rock the boat.

Regardless, he was heading out on a mission in a few days. Now wasn't the time to have any in-depth conversations about changing their relationship.

For now, they'd continue to take things one day at a time. They didn't have to make any decisions right this moment.

CHAPTER SEVENTEEN

Three days later, Ashlyn was doing her best to keep herself from completely losing it. Slate was leaving for another deployment, and this one was more dangerous than the last. He hadn't told her that, of course, but she could tell. He came home late from work the last two nights with a furrow in his brow that hadn't been there before the last mission. He was stoic as he packed his bag, and also when they'd spent time cleaning out his fridge, collecting food to bring to Food For All that would spoil while he was gone.

He seemed more serious in other ways too. Their lovemaking last night had been more desperate. At least the first time. As if he knew there was a chance he might not come back.

Ashlyn couldn't even think about that as a possibility. Slate would come back. He had to.

"Don't know how long I'll be gone, babe," he told her now, as they stood next to his front door. "Appreciate you keeping an eye on my place for me."

All Ashlyn could do was nod against his chest. She couldn't pick her head up to look at him, knowing she'd burst into tears if she did, and that was the last thing he needed right now. She needed to be strong, to see him off with a smile and the reassurance that she'd be fine.

But she wasn't fine. She was scared to death. The seriousness of their mission had seeped into her, and she had a bad feeling about him leaving.

"Ash?" he asked softly.

Taking a deep breath, she knew it was time. Time for her to suck it up and let her boyfriend go kick ass like he was trained to do. She lifted her head and bravely met his gaze. "Yeah?"

His expression softened.

Shit. She hadn't hidden her fears and anxiety as well as she'd hoped.

"Have to admit, as much as I hate seeing that expression on your face, it feels damn good to know you're gonna miss me."

Ashlyn frowned at him. "Of course I am. Did you think I wouldn't?"

Slate shrugged. "Haven't had anyone to miss me before."

"Well, you do now," she said a little huffily.

He chuckled. "For the record, gonna miss you too, babe."

The tears she'd held back threatened to make an appearance. Ashlyn kept her composure. Barely. "Yup, because I'm awesome," she said as brightly as she could muster.

Slate smiled, but it didn't quite reach his eyes. "Stay safe while I'm gone. You got any new clients on the schedule this week?"

"No."

"Good. Planning a sleepover with the girls?"

Ashlyn nodded. "Yeah, Saturday. We hated to wait that long, but we've all got stuff going on at work. I think Carly is spending the week with Kenna though."

"Sucks her honeymoon got delayed," Slate said.

"She's looking forward to Jag making it up to her," Ashlyn said.

She knew what they were doing. They were making small talk to prolong the moment. It was killing her. There was something to be said for taking a bandage off fast; the pain was still there, but at least the hard part was over quickly.

"Be careful," she whispered.

"I always am."

"I know, but...you haven't said, and I haven't asked, but this mission feels different from the last one."

He nodded, confirming her fears.

"I know you're a badass, and you have some great men at your back, but please don't take any chances."

"I won't," Slate said, resting his forehead against hers.

They stood like that for a moment, then Ashlyn knew he had to go before she completely lost it.

"Okay, enough. You need to go. I'll see you when you get back."

"Yes, you will," he agreed. He tilted her head up with a finger under her chin and lowered his head.

Ashlyn thought he might kiss her desperately...but instead it was slow, tender, and loving. Which made her want to cry even more.

"Take your time this morning. It's still early," he said as he pulled back and leaned down to pick up his duffle bag.

Ashlyn nodded. She wasn't staying at his house while he was away. That would be pure torture. But she'd agreed to stop by and check on things every now and then.

She stood stiffly in his foyer and swallowed hard, even as she did her best to smile.

"See you soon," he said quietly.

"Soon," she echoed, praying that was true.

Then he was gone.

And Ashlyn let the tears she'd been holding back flow down her cheeks.

She couldn't bear to watch Slate drive away, so she went back into his room, burying her face in his pillow. His scent only made her cry harder. She couldn't help but think of last night. They'd fucked hard, almost manically, the first time. But then they'd made love, Slate cherishing her. There was definitely a difference, and while Ashlyn enjoyed when they were out of their heads with lust for each other, she loved it even more when Slate was slow and tender.

It took a while, but she finally got control of her emotions. She was a grown-ass woman with responsibilities. Military partners and spouses did this all the time. They watched their men and women go off into danger with alarming regularity, while they got on with their lives at home.

Ashlyn got dressed, then took a deep breath, made sure all the lights were off in the house, and headed out to her car. As much as she loved that she worked with two women who knew what she was going through, since they were experiencing the same thing, Ashlyn was kind of glad she'd have time to herself while doing deliveries today.

It wasn't that she didn't want to talk to Elodie or Lexie, she just needed space to process her feelings.

Somewhere along the way, her friends-with-benefits arrangement had morphed. She wasn't sure into what, exactly, but the laid-back relationship she'd proposed, with both of them moving on after getting each other out of their systems, was no longer the position she found herself in. Instead of her feelings for Slate tapering off, they were only getting stronger.

Sighing, she headed for her apartment. She couldn't bring herself to shower at Slate's place. His bathroom had too many memories of the love and laughter they'd shared in that space. Her shower was too small for them to share, so it felt like the safer choice for her fragile frame of mind right now.

"Slate will be fine," Ashlyn said out loud as she drove. "He's a professional who does this kind of thing all the time." She didn't know what "kind of thing" she was talking about, but it didn't matter. "He'll be back, and we'll pick up where we left off."

Her words sounded a little desperate, even to her own ears, but since no one was there to listen to her talking to herself, she couldn't bring herself to care.

She turned on the music in her car, happy that an upbeat, snappy tune was on and not some sappy love song. She'd be okay. Slate would be okay. Things would be fine. Just fine.

Ashlyn knew she was trying too hard to convince herself, but it was what she needed to do to keep her emotions in check.

* * *

Slate and his team hadn't been in Afghanistan even one full day before the shit hit the fan. The threat of attacks on the base turned into reality, and the SEAL team's well-rehearsed plans were completely useless within hours.

They'd headed into the extremely hostile city to try to track where the RPGs were fired from, and to take down anyone who got in their way. That was two days ago, and their search had led them to the outskirts of the city and an extremely dangerous area.

The houses were rundown and looked as if they were put together with any kind of material the residents could get their hands on. Corrugated metal, four by fours, the hood of a car, even wire fencing. It would've been depressing if their lives weren't on the line. Slate couldn't take time to process the kids' faces looking out of broken windows and holes in walls as his team silently and steadily made its way toward the target.

Intel had pointed them to the leader of an extremist group of insurgents who were extremely loyal to Osama Bin Laden. Even though the man had been dead for years, various groups were doing their best to bring back his ideology, and the violent tendencies he'd espoused.

Somehow, this particular band of soldiers had acquired a lot of RPGs, which they'd been firing at the American base, and word was they'd kill any American they came across in the town, in the country, or anywhere else.

The house they were about to breach stuck out like a sore thumb in the dilapidated neighborhood. It was two stories, compared to all the squat, ramshackle dwellings on the streets nearby. It was made of brick instead of scavenged materials. The large, sturdy structure was smack in the middle of what had been deemed Taliban central.

It was an extremely dangerous place to be, but with intel saying another attack on the base was imminent, the leader needed to be taken out now, before more soldiers and local civilians were hurt or killed.

Mustang pointed at Midas and Aleck, then to the right side of a door. Next, he pointed at Pid and Jag, and to the left of the same entrance.

Slate nodded and took up position next to his team leader. The most dangerous position when entering any kind of building was point, but he had no problem taking his friend's side. The others would enter right on their heels and cover their left and right. His objective was to take out any opposition directly in front of them.

The vibe around them was making Slate uneasy. It was calm...*too* calm. As if everyone in the vicinity was holding their collective breath. They could be walking into an ambush or an empty house. It was dark outside—they'd planned the raid at a time when the leader would hopefully be at home and sleeping—but that was really their only advantage.

Mustang held up a hand and counted down on his fingers. Three. Two. One.

Slate and Mustang burst through the door without any issues, the heavy wooden surface banging against the wall, sounding like a shot in the quiet night.

Slate could feel his teammates at his back, moving silently as they'd been trained. They quickly cleared the first room, moving steadily through the other two on the first floor. Empty.

The hair on the back of Slate's neck stood up. Something wasn't right. Intel said the leader had four wives and eight children. Even if they didn't all live here, *someone* should be in the house.

"Watch for booby traps," he whispered to Mustang, who nodded and pressed his lips together grimly. Slate felt a little better that he wasn't alone in his uneasy feelings.

They made their way up the stairs, and Slate winced when the warped boards creaked under their boots.

Aleck and Midas had their backs as he and Mustang made their way to the second floor. Pid and Jag stayed below to make sure no one entered the house while they were inside.

While the rooms downstairs were almost barren, holding nothing but a few tables and chairs and rugs on the floors, along with a very basic kitchen, upstairs was a different story. There were clothes strewn everywhere and boxes stacked in every room. It made clearing them extremely difficult. They worked quickly and efficiently through the floor.

Just when Slate thought the raid was a total bust, he saw movement in the corner of the last room they were searching.

He held up his hand to Mustang and pointed. His team leader nodded, and they crept closer, weapons at the ready.

"US Navy. Hands up!" Mustang ordered in a low and deadly tone.

They immediately saw two hands appear from behind a large box.

"What the fuck?" Slate breathed. Those weren't adult hands. They were too small.

Mustang swept the box to the side as Slate kept his weapon trained on whoever was hiding behind it.

Sure enough, it was a child. A boy dressed in what looked like rags. His face was dirty and he was holding what seemed to be a flashlight.

But his wasn't the face of a scared little boy. His expression was one of clear hatred.

"What's your name?" Mustang asked.

The boy either didn't understand English or had no intention of telling them anything.

Before any of the four men could do anything else, the boy flicked on the light in his hand and pointed it toward the only window in the room.

He swiftly turned it off and on twice.

"Fuck!" Mustang swore. "He's signaling someone."

Slate came to the conclusion at the same time as his team leader. His only thought was to get out as quickly as possible.

"Go, go go!" he shouted to Mustang and the others.

They all turned in tandem to rush out of the room. They were well-trained soldiers, but they also knew when the odds were against them and retreat was the only option.

The house was empty because it was a trap.

At the last second, Slate hesitated. The boy had obviously been brought up to hate Americans. He didn't see any fear or regret in the kid's eyes when he'd been found. In fact, Slate would bet he'd moved on purpose so he would be discovered. He was a plant. And whatever the plan was, that boy was meant to die—along with Slate and his team.

But even if the kid wouldn't appreciate being saved, Slate had to try.

He turned and took three steps back into the room, reaching for the boy's arm. He cried out when Slate jerked him toward the door roughly. There was no time to be gentle, to try to convince the kid he wasn't making a noble sacrifice, that he was merely a pawn. The kid probably had a mother somewhere who was crying her eyes out right this second, knowing her son was going to die.

The rest of Slate's team had made it to the bottom of the stairs and were on their way out the front door, their weapons drawn and ready to fire on anyone who might be waiting for them to exit.

But before Slate took even one step down the stairs, his world exploded, and the entire building collapsed around him.

CHAPTER EIGHTEEN

It hadn't even been a full week since Slate had left, but to Ashlyn, it felt like a year. She was looking forward to the sleepover tomorrow, as she desperately needed to talk about how she was feeling with her friends.

She wasn't sure she could handle this. She'd thought she could. Thought Slate's job wouldn't be a big deal. He'd go off to save the world and she'd carry on like usual while he was away. But she wasn't dealing well with knowing he was in danger. She had no idea how the others managed to keep their shit together. Ashlyn was failing at this whole girlfriend thing, and she hated that she was so weak.

She wasn't the one in danger, Slate was. So why was she so on edge? And everyone she came into contact with seemed to feed off her negative energy. She got into a shouting match with a man at the grocery store because he had forty-nine items in the express lane, instead of twelve or less, like the sign stated. She flipped off a woman on the interstate who'd cut in front of her, and Ashlyn was *always* levelheaded behind the wheel.

The last straw was when she'd visited James. He'd seemed

upset, but when he wouldn't tell her what was wrong, Ashlyn had simply given up, turned around and left. Hadn't tried harder to convince him to talk to her, had just left his house without saying much more than, "See you next week."

It wasn't like her. Ashlyn felt horrible for how she'd treated him, and she knew she had to get a handle on her emotions.

She'd just gotten home after work and was standing in front of her microwave, waiting for her frozen meal to be done, when her phone rang. Ashlyn practically leaped on her phone, hoping to see Slate's name on the screen.

She nearly screamed in joy when she saw it *was* him.

"Slate!" she exclaimed when she answered.

"Hey, babe." He sounded exhausted.

"Are you back?"

"Almost."

"Are you okay?" Ashlyn asked. "You sound weird."

"Just gonna be blunt. I got hurt. But I'm okay."

"Hurt? How? Where?"

"Nothing major. Got my marbles knocked loose in my head. Didn't get out of a building before it was blown up around me."

Ashlyn could tell he was trying to make a joke, but she wasn't finding any of his words amusing. "*Seriously?*"

"Yeah, made an error in judgement. I basically rode the stairs falling down beneath me, except my helmet came off and I hit my head on something. The guys dug me out and got me back to base. When I woke up, I had a hell of a headache."

Ashlyn couldn't breathe. *When he woke up?* That meant he'd been knocked unconscious. "But you're okay?"

"Yeah. Got a concussion. Docs wanted to fly me to Germany, but there was nowhere I wanted to recover more than my own place. So they let me come home."

Ashlyn didn't know how the military worked, but she had a feeling it wasn't quite as easy to refuse treatment when you were a Navy SEAL as it was when you were a civilian. But at the moment, she was more concerned with how Slate was doing than how he'd convinced a doctor to let him fly home with a concussion.

Ashlyn started to move toward her bedroom. When she got home, she'd immediately changed into a T-shirt of Slate's that she'd been sleeping in, which was all she currently wore.

"I'm gonna change so I can meet you at your house," she told him.

"No."

The single word froze Ashlyn in her tracks in the middle of her hallway. "What?"

"I'm exhausted, babe. And Mustang is gonna stay with me. I'll call you when I get up tomorrow morning."

If Mustang was going to be at Slate's house, that meant Elodie would probably be there too. Slate was all right with his friend and his wife being there...but not her? That hurt more than she thought it would.

In fact, the pain she felt at that moment was so sharp, so deep, she actually brought a hand up to her chest to try to contain it.

"I can look after you," she said, in a voice that was weaker than she wanted it to be. "Wake you up every hour or so, that's what you do for someone who has a concussion, right?"

"Mustang's got this," he told her. "We're pretty used to looking after each other when we get banged up. I called because I figured you'd hear from the others that we were back. Didn't want you to worry about me."

Not worry about him. Right.

"Okay," she said after a moment or two. What else *could* she say? She could beg him to let her come over, but that felt...desperate. And if he didn't want to see her, then she wasn't going to force herself on him.

"Gotta go. Mustang's giving me the evil eye. Mr. Doctor has been a pain in my ass with all his 'don't do this,' and 'you can't do that.' I'll talk to you tomorrow, babe. It's good to be home."

"Yeah. Okay. Glad you're all right."

"Later."

"Bye."

As soon as she clicked off the phone, Ashlyn's shaky legs gave out and she sank to the floor in her hallway. Then she dropped to her side, where she curled into a little ball.

Slate had been hurt on a mission—and he didn't want her to take care of him.

Like a bolt of lightning crashing through the roof of her apartment, Ashlyn realized that she loved him.

She hadn't meant for it to happen. He'd just snuck under her radar. She'd wanted this to be a casual thing...and it was anything *but* casual for her.

But apparently, he was perfectly happy with the status quo.

If he loved her, even just a little, wouldn't he be eager to see her? Wouldn't he want her at his side when he was recuperating? Understand that she *needed* to be with him, to see for herself that he was okay?

And Ashlyn couldn't even be mad at Slate. He'd done exactly as she asked...kept things easy and casual. Friends with benefits. Wasn't that what she'd said she wanted?

Whimpering, she curled into herself tighter. She was an idiot. So stupid. She should've known she couldn't do casual. She never had in the past. Had always jumped into relationships head first. But no rejection had ever hurt this badly before.

How long she lay in the middle of her hallway, Ashlyn

didn't know. Eventually, she got herself up and went into her bedroom. She knew she should go throw away the frozen meal she'd nuked, but she'd deal with it tomorrow. All she wanted to do right now was sleep. She couldn't even cry any more.

She knew what she had to do now. She needed to slowly pull back from her relationship with Slate. Needed to protect what was left of her broken heart. And she'd do what she could to stay friends with him, even though it would hurt like hell.

For tonight, though, she'd mourn the loss of what they'd never have.

* * *

Slate did his best to hide the hammering in his skull from Mustang. If his friend knew how much pain he was in, he'd drag his ass to the base hospital. But the only place Slate wanted to be was in his own bed.

The RPG that had taken out the house, that was meant to kill his entire team, had somehow miraculously only done half its job. He had no idea what happened to the boy he'd tried to save. Mustang and Midas said they hadn't seen him when they'd dug Slate out of the rubble. His helmet had been crushed by the collapse, forced off his head at some point, but he'd somehow ridden the debris when the house exploded, instead of being killed.

Jag and Pid had carried his passed-out ass back to the extraction point, and when he woke up, he was lying on a table in the base hospital. The doctors hadn't been happy in the least when he'd insisted on getting up. And they *really* hadn't been thrilled when he'd insisted Mustang get clearance for him to go home to recuperate.

He'd been lucky, and Slate knew it. Hell, everyone knew

it. He'd felt like shit but wanted to get the hell out of the country. He was trying to keep his pain from his teammates, though Slate had a feeling they knew exactly how awful he felt. Every muscle in his body hurt. His head throbbed. He was nauseous. His torso was covered in dark purple bruises, but miraculously the scans hadn't shown any internal bleeding.

It was a fucking miracle he hadn't been crushed beneath the rubble of that brick building.

Pid said the RPG hadn't made a direct impact. In fact, whoever was operating it had almost missed the house altogether. It had skimmed the far side of the building, making the bricks kind of collapse in on themselves rather than shooting in all directions.

He was sitting between Jag and Pid on the plane, and Slate could feel their worried gazes on him. It was taking all his concentration to stay conscious.

Vaguely, he realized the plane was descending. They would land within minutes. In the back of his fuzzy brain, it occurred to him that he could probably get cell reception even though they weren't on the ground yet. He pulled out his phone and dialed a familiar number.

A minute or two later, Slate hung up and closed his eyes just as the plane touched down.

"You good?" Jag asked from next to him.

"Yeah," Slate said softly, even though the pressure in his head was threatening to make him barf all over his lap at any second.

"Are you sure you made the right decision?"

Slate couldn't think straight. What decision was Jag talking about? But instead of asking, he just slurred, "Yeah."

His friend harumphed, obviously not pleased with his answer. Slate didn't care. All he could think about was lying down. He had to get off the plane, walk to Mustang's car, and hopefully get to his bed before doing something that would make Mustang drive him straight to the emergency room.

Finally, an hour later, Slate gingerly sat on the side of his bed. The trip home had been hell. And without Mustang there to help him into his house, he never would've made it.

"You need to go to the hospital, Slate," he said quietly now, obviously knowing how badly his friend's head hurt.

"No. I just need to lay down," Slate told him. "Can you help me find the pills the doc gave me for pain?" he asked. He'd taken one before he'd gotten on the plane, and it had promptly knocked him out for most of the flight. Slate didn't like how the medicine made him feel, but at this point, he'd prefer to be unconscious than endure the pain he was going through at the moment.

Mustang was right. He probably should've gone to the hospital, but he was home now, and he wasn't going anywhere. If he still felt this terrible tomorrow, he'd concede and go.

His friend left the room and came back with Slate's duffle bag. "You care if Elodie comes over?" Mustang asked as he dug into a side pocket of the bag.

"No."

Slate barely knew what Mustang was talking about. The throbbing in his head seemed to match his heartbeat. He felt as if he was a hundred and twenty years old. His muscles hurt. His joints hurt. Hell, his fucking bones hurt.

"Here," Mustang said. "Give me your hand."

Slate held it out and closed his eyes.

"Give me a second to get some water," Mustang said, but Slate ignored him. He popped the two pills into his mouth and swallowed them dry. Then he slowly shifted his body up and onto his mattress, and sighed in relief as he finally lay flat on his back.

"Shit," Mustang swore, but Slate didn't open his eyes.

He felt his friend working on unlacing his boots, but he didn't have the strength to thank him as he removed them.

"If you don't look like you're two seconds from turning into a fucking zombie in the morning, I'm dragging your ass to the hospital whether you like it or not," Mustang said in a low tone.

"Okay."

"Okay?" Mustang asked.

"Yeah."

"Good. I'll be in here waking your ass up on the hour, every hour, so don't bite my head off when I do it."

"I won't," Slate whispered.

He heard fabric rustling and figured Mustang was headed for the door.

"Mustang?" Slate said before his friend left. "Thank you. Not just for tonight, but for getting me out of there."

"You would've done the same for me," his team leader said.

"Damn straight. SEALs don't leave a SEAL behind," Slate said.

"Exactly. See you in an hour."

Slate wasn't looking forward to being woken up repeatedly, but knew it had to be done. For now, he forgot about everything but closing his eyes and letting the medicine he'd taken do its job.

* * *

The next morning, Slate was better. Marginally.

Mustang had done exactly as he promised, had woken Slate up once an hour throughout the night. It meant both men were exhausted the next morning, since neither got any uninterrupted sleep.

Slate slept off and on throughout the day on Saturday,

barely aware of the comings and goings of Mustang and Elodie. He ate whenever Elodie stuffed something in his hand, drank when Mustang ordered him to, but generally slept through the day, and again Saturday night.

By the time Sunday came around, Slate was feeling much more like himself. He refused the pill Elodie tried to convince him to take that morning and forced himself to get up, shower, and put on some clean clothes.

The last forty-eight hours were pretty much a blur. Slate barely remembered arriving at his house and had no recollection of any conversations he might've had with Elodie or Mustang.

He slowly wandered out of his room, noticing that it was past noon. The sun was bright in the sky, and he wasn't all that surprised to see Mustang sitting on his couch.

He *was* surprised to see Midas and Aleck there as well. Elodie was nowhere to be seen. She could be up on his rooftop deck, but Slate doubted it.

"Hey," he said as he entered his living room.

"Holy hell, you look like shit," Midas said.

"Thanks a lot," Slate said. "Thought I'd go for a ten-mile run this morning, you know, to stretch my muscles."

His friends stared at him in disbelief.

"Shit, I'm kidding. Jeez," he said with a small shake of his head. Slate wandered into his kitchen and realized he was starving. He didn't remember when or what he last ate, all he knew was that he would eat just about anything right that second.

"Go sit down," Aleck ordered, coming up behind him. "I'll make you some eggs and a protein shake."

Both sounded awesome, and Mustang turned to go join his other teammates. Then a memory niggled at his brain, and he stopped in his tracks. "Fuck. Ashlyn. Where's my phone?"

"Sit," Aleck ordered. "Before you fall on your face."

Slate ignored him. "Where's my fucking phone?" he asked again.

"I've got it," Mustang said, coming up next to him. But instead of handing him the phone, he put his hand on Slate's shoulder. "Sit down. You can call Ashlyn in a minute."

A feeling of dread descended. "What's wrong?"

"Come. Sit. Down," Mustang repeated, making it clear he wasn't fucking around. "We'll talk, then you can call Ash."

"Is she okay?" Slate asked as he let his friend lead him toward the couch.

Looking at Midas for any kind of clue about what the fuck was going on only made Slate more anxious. If he wasn't mistaken, there was a look of pity on his friend's face.

Shit shit shit!

"Okay, so...what do you remember from the moments before the RPG hit?" Mustang asked.

Slate took a deep breath. "Yelling at you guys to get the hell out, turning back to grab the kid. I couldn't in good conscience leave him there."

"Even though he was the one who gave the signal to blow the house?" Midas asked.

"Yeah. It was fucking stupid, I know," Slate said. "But he was a *kid*. What, seven or eight?"

"A kid raised to hate Americans and with the ideology that it's better to die for the Taliban than to live as a coward," Mustang added.

Slate pressed his lips together. His team leader was right, but Slate knew if he had to do it all over again, he probably would've done things exactly the same.

"Right, moving on. Then what?" Mustang asked.

"Waking up in the clinic. Arguing with the doctor about going to Germany. Bits and pieces here and there about the flight. Concentrating on getting here. On lying down. Then you and Elodie prodding me awake, feeding me. That's about it."

Midas and Mustang shared a look that Slate did *not* like.

"What am I missing?" Slate asked.

"I talked to Pid. He was sitting next to you on the plane, making sure you kept breathing, shit like that," Mustang said.

Slate winced. He should've stayed in the base clinic longer. Should've gone to Germany. He hated the position he'd put his friends in. But Mustang was still talking, so he didn't have time to dwell.

"He said that as soon as the plane started to descend, you pulled out your phone and called Ashlyn."

Slate stiffened. He'd called Ash? *Fuck.* He didn't remember that at all. She must've been freaking out. "What'd I say to her?" He hated that he had to ask, but his friends already understood he didn't remember much of the last two days.

"Pid said that you told her you were back, or almost back, and that you'd been hurt, but were okay. Said you were going home, that I'd be looking after you, and you'd talk to her later."

Slate waited, but when Mustang didn't continue, he mentally sighed in relief. That didn't sound so bad. The way his friends were acting, he thought maybe he'd told Ashlyn he never wanted to see her again or something.

Aleck walked into the room and braced his hands on the back of the couch. "He doesn't get it," he said to nobody in particular.

"If you'd all quit beating around the fucking bush and just spit out what the hell you think I said that was so bad, maybe we can get this over with so I can call my girlfriend," Slate seethed. The throbbing in his head was back, but he ignored it.

"You told your *girlfriend* you'd been hurt on a mission. That you had a concussion. And that Mustang would be looking out for you," Midas repeated. "From what Pid understood from your side of the conversation, she volunteered to come over and nurse you back to health, and you said no. That you'd call her tomorrow...which, by the way, was yesterday. And in case it's escaped your notice, you didn't call her. You were knocked the fuck out because your brains had been scrambled in your skull, and you were too stubborn to get the proper care for yourself."

Slate stared at his friend. Over the years, he and his teammates had gotten into plenty of arguments, but he couldn't remember ever hearing any of them sounding as pissed at him as Midas was at the moment.

"I tried to call her, hoping to explain, but she didn't answer. You and Ashlyn might only be fuck buddies, but that was a shitty way to treat her," Midas finished.

Slate clenched his hands into fists. He didn't like Ashlyn being referred to that way.

"If I had been hurt, and I'd called Elodie and told her Jag would be looking after me, how do you think that would make her feel?" Mustang asked in a far more mild tone. "And don't give me any bullshit about us being married either," he continued.

"She hasn't called," Midas informed Slate. "She hasn't texted Lexie. As far as we know, she hasn't gotten in touch with anyone. Probably because her boyfriend, who she'd been friends with for months before the change in relationship status, was deployed, and he called to tell her he was hurt but that no, he didn't want her to come see him. That his friend would be there for him instead."

"And she had to know that Elodie wasn't going to sit at home and wait for me," Mustang added quietly. "That she would rush over here to see me...and thus would help take care of you."

Slate swallowed hard and closed his eyes. *Fuck.*

"He's finally getting it," Midas sighed.

Slate opened his eyes and met Midas's gaze. "Give me my phone."

"Slate, most of us have tried to call her. To explain that you made light of your injuries and what happened, but she's been...evasive." Midas spoke far more gently now.

"If I have to ask one more time for someone to give me my fucking phone, I'm not gonna be happy," Slate said between clenched teeth. He wasn't happy *now*, but that was beside the point.

Mustang held out Slate's cell phone.

He leaned forward and grabbed it. Slate immediately saw a whole string of text notifications from the last day and a half. Lexie, Kenna, Monica, Carly, his other teammates...hell, even Baker wanted to know if he was all right.

There was one from Ashlyn. Just one. And it was short and impersonal, saying that she hoped he was feeling better.

Swallowing hard, he clicked on Ashlyn's name. He stood up and walked back toward his bedroom. He loved his friends, but the last thing he wanted was them eavesdropping on this conversation.

Slate wasn't sure whether to be surprised or pissed when Ashlyn didn't answer. The sound of her voice on her voice mail made him long to see her even more. After the beep sounded, Slate left a message. "It's me, Ash. I need to talk to you. Please call me back as soon as you get this."

He hung up and paced restlessly back and forth across his room. He needed to fix this. He'd fucked up. Yes, he'd been out of his mind with pain and didn't even remember much that happened after he'd hit his head, but if Ashlyn had been injured, he'd be going crazy with worry for her. The fact that she hadn't stormed his castle, so to speak, let Slate know just how upset she was.

He clicked on her name once more and quickly typed out a text.

Slate: Hey, I need to talk to you. See you. Will you come by?

He waited a full minute, but the gray check mark didn't turn green, meaning she hadn't opened his message.

Worried now, Slate sent another text.

Slate: I fucked up. It's not an excuse, but I had a concussion. I don't remember calling you. Please let me know you're all right, if nothing else.

Nothing. No three dots telling him she was responding to his text and no indication that she'd even read it.

Panicking, thinking the worst, Slate finally remembered the tracking app. He could see where she was. She might be at home, injured or sick with a migraine again, and not able to get to the phone. He clicked on the app...and couldn't quite understand what he was seeing at first.

Ashlyn wasn't home. If the app was correct, she was currently down in Waikiki at a place called Arnold's Beach Bar. It wasn't far from Duke's.

It was Sunday afternoon, and Ashlyn was at a bar? What the absolute fuck was going on?

Slate: If you don't answer me and let me know that you're okay, I'm gonna head down to Arnold's to check for myself that it's actually you down there, and not someone who's kidnapped you and stolen your phone and is using your credit cards to get shitfaced.

He held his breath, praying that she answered, but at the same time knowing if she did, it meant she was avoiding him...which would suck.

The gray check marks flicked to green on his screen and the three dots he'd prayed to see finally appeared.

Shit.

Ashlyn: I'm fine. I hope you're feeling better.

The words were polite but distant. And Slate wanted to fucking throw his phone across the room. Goose bumps broke out on his arms.

He wasn't ready to lose her.

Slate: What are you doing at a bar?
Ashlyn: Having lunch with a friend.

Every muscle in Slate's body froze as he stared down at the words on his screen. She was out to lunch while he was recuperating from almost dying? Yes, he'd apparently told her not to come over, but still. He wasn't being dramatic by thinking he could've been killed. In fact, he knew how close he'd come to being blown into a thousand pieces in that house. It was a miracle that he was still alive and kicking.

And his girlfriend was in a *bar*? With a "friend"? Her

friends were *his* friends, and he was pretty damn sure she wasn't out with Elodie, Lexie, or any of the others.

Was she out with a guy?

The thought made him nauseous.

And furious.

And disappointed.

And insanely fucking jealous.

In a moment of blazing clarity...Slate realized he'd been kidding himself for the last three months.

He'd agreed to Ashlyn's ridiculous friends-with-benefits suggestion because he wanted her any way he could get her. Maybe at first he'd done his best to not let her get under his skin, keeping their relationship mostly about sex, not staying the night, calling only periodically...but as the weeks passed, things had changed. She was *his*.

His, dammit! And he wasn't going to let this misunderstanding—okay, his colossal fuck-up—break them apart.

Casual be damned. There wasn't a single casual thing about their relationship. And he was going to make sure Ashlyn knew it. He was changing things up, big time, and she was just going to have to accept it.

He was being irrational, but Slate didn't give a shit.

He loved Ashlyn Taylor. She was everything he'd ever wanted in a woman. Smart and sexy and kind and loyal. She was *his*. Just as he was hers.

Thinking back over the last month or so, Slate had no doubt that Ashlyn loved him just as much. They were both desperately ignoring what was right under their noses.

She was hurt right now, and he couldn't blame her, but if she thought she could go out with another guy and just forget about him that easily, she was kidding herself.

Slate didn't bother responding to her message. He was too mad. Too jealous. Too upset. Hurting too badly. Besides, he wasn't going to say what he needed to say in a text. He wanted to be face-to-face in order to apologize properly. He needed to be able to read her expression, to see if his unintentionally callous actions had destroyed everything they'd been building for the last year.

Determination rising within him, Slate headed back out to his living room.

Mustang, Midas, and Aleck all turned their heads to look at him when he appeared.

"I need someone to drive me to Ashlyn's house."

Mustang grinned slowly.

Midas nodded in approval.

Aleck said, "Not until you eat something."

The last thing Slate wanted to do was eat, but he also didn't want to fall flat on his face when he was convincing Ashlyn to forgive him for being an inconsiderate asshole...and when he told her that he wanted to renegotiate the terms of their relationship.

Clicking on the app in his phone, Slate saw that Ashlyn was still in Waikiki at that fucking bar. He had time to eat. He nodded at Aleck.

CHAPTER NINETEEN

Ashlyn sighed in relief when she closed the door of the Uber she'd called to pick her up from the bar. It was Jack's birthday, another full-time employee who worked at Food For All, and a group of people had gotten together to celebrate at Arnold's.

Natalie, the manager of the downtown location, had texted, asking Ashlyn if she would come. She didn't want to. Had wanted to wallow in her misery all alone. But she'd forced herself to shower, change, and leave the apartment. Sitting around waiting for Slate to call wasn't on the top of her list of fun things to do. In fact, it was torture.

Mustang had called, as had some of the others, but she didn't feel strong enough yet to endure the pity in their voices while they tried to explain why Slate hadn't wanted her help when he wasn't feeling well. She didn't know exactly what had happened on his mission—not that she'd given anyone a chance to explain—but Slate telling her in no uncertain terms that his friends would be there for him, instead of asking her to come over, repeated in her head like a broken record.

She'd waited all day Saturday for his call, with no luck, and with every hour that passed, she got more and more depressed. It sucked to be head over heels in love with a man, then have it made very clear that he didn't feel the same. But she'd be okay. She always was.

The first step was staying busy and not moping around her apartment. So she'd told Natalie she'd be there. Not sure if she was going to drink anything or not, she'd called for an Uber. The afternoon had been fun...as fun as it *could* be when she was so damn heartbroken...but now Ashlyn was more than ready to go home.

Admittedly, she'd been relieved to finally hear from Slate. She didn't hate him. Could never hate him. And despite everything, she'd been crazy worried. So getting that first text made the stress and worry dissipate a bit.

He claimed he didn't remember calling her, and she supposed that could be the case. But he'd gotten home Friday. And it was now *Sunday*. Knowing he'd been home for almost two days, and he hadn't reached out to her, was a reminder of where she stood in his life.

She'd forgotten he had the tracking app until his third message. If she was a different kind of person, she would've ignored that text too, but she had a feeling he really *would* march his ass down to Arnold's to see if she was there, and the last thing she wanted was a confrontation in a public place.

Ashlyn wanted to see him. To see for herself that he was all right. Only after knowing for certain that he was truly uninjured would she explain that she thought it'd be better if they were just friends. It would hurt...absolutely kill...but she had to do it.

So she'd replied to his text. Reassuring him that she was fine. She'd planned to leave it at that, but Stupid Ashlyn couldn't *not* ask how he was feeling.

Instead of responding to her question, he'd asked what

she was doing at Arnold's. She should've said she was at a work thing, but she'd been vague...it was too hard to type with tears in her eyes. He hadn't replied back. Which was another blow. But whatever. She was steeling herself to move on.

Ashlyn hadn't realized how lost in her head she'd been until the driver said, "Here you go. Have a nice rest of the day."

Opening her eyes, Ashlyn saw that they were in the parking lot of her apartment complex. She thanked the woman and climbed out of the back seat. She slowly entered her building and walked up the stairs. She was digging in her purse for her key when something caught her eye.

Looking up, she paused halfway down the hall and stared at a frowning Slate, standing with his arms crossed over his chest, leaning against her door.

Ashlyn drank in the sight of him. He looked good. A few scratches on his face. A little pale, but in one piece. The overwhelming relief swept through her so fast, it made her knees weak, and she had to put a hand on the wall to steady herself.

Slate pushed off her door and stalked toward her. He reached for her elbow, clasping it gently. "Are you drunk?" he asked.

Blinking in surprise, Ashlyn shook her head. "No."

"Good. Because for the conversation we're about to have, I need you to be stone-cold sober."

"I didn't have anything to drink."

Slate jerked his chin down in a short nod and pulled on her arm, getting her to walk once more. Not protesting, and hating herself for how her stomach fluttered at his touch, Ashlyn walked next to him without a word. When they got to her door, she fumbled once more for her key. He took it from her as soon as she pulled it out of her purse and unlocked her door.

She dumped her purse on the small table in the foyer and walked into her apartment. She winced at the condition it was in. Dirty dishes piled in the sink, her trash needed to be taken out. She'd slept on her couch the last two nights, not wanting to go into her bedroom because it reminded her too much of Slate, and the blanket she'd used was on the floor. That, and her pillow on the end of the couch made it very clear she'd slept in her living room.

Used cups were on the coffee table, and she hadn't bothered to pick up the many crumbled and used tissues on the end table and floor before she'd left for Arnold's.

When she glanced at Slate, his gaze was locked on her, not on the shape of her apartment.

"You look tired," he said gently.

Ashlyn shrugged. She wasn't about to admit that she'd slept like shit, too busy worrying about him and crying her eyes out.

The stern look on Slate's face faded away, and Ashlyn could've sworn she saw nervousness take its place.

"You look good. Glad you're okay," she told him.

"Me too. Although my head still feels kind of fuzzy. If what I just went through was even half of what *you* felt when you had that migraine, I don't know how you got through it."

"I didn't really have a choice," she told him.

"True. Can we talk?" he asked.

Ashlyn's brows furrowed. "We *are* talking."

"I mean...I need to apologize. Explain what happened."

"It's fine. I understand."

"I don't think you do," he countered. "I need to go back to Wednesday and Thursday in Afghanistan. Explain what led up to me calling you Friday night."

"I didn't think you were allowed to talk about your missions," Ashlyn said in confusion.

"I'm not."

Her mind was spinning. She wasn't sure she wanted to hear details about what happened to him, because it would scare the shit out of her, but at the same time she was desperate for more information. "Okay."

Slate gestured to the living room. "Can we sit? I hate to admit it, but I'm still really shaky."

Ashlyn immediately nodded. God, she was a horrible person. While she hadn't been ready to see Slate at her door, and she definitely wasn't looking forward to breaking up with him, she didn't want to cause him any pain.

He followed her into the living area, and she was glad he didn't comment on the tissues and general disarray. She sat on one end of the couch, further relieved when Slate didn't sit right next to her. He gave her space, sitting on the other end.

"Things went to shit right when we arrived in Afghanistan. The insurgents were targeting the base, and everyone was on edge. We headed out into the city a couple nights in, trying to track down the leader of a group of Taliban fighters. We got intel about where he lived and went to check it out. Long story short, he wasn't there, but while we were inside his house, he, or one of his followers, shot an RPG at it, hoping to kill my entire team."

Ashlyn gasped.

Slate continued. "But whoever it was, they were a shit shot, or maybe they weren't prepared for the kickback of the weapon, because instead of hitting the building dead center, the shot went wide. The shitty construction of the house also probably saved me.

"I remember kind of trying to surf a bunch of bricks and boards as they slid under my feet...but that's all. I was knocked unconscious. I woke up at the base. The guys had dug me out of the rubble and got me to the base clinic. I guessed I was super aggressive—I don't really remember—and refused to stay there, and got *really* pissed when they suggested sending me to Germany. I don't know how he did it, but Mustang talked the doctors into releasing me into his care, and we left to come home.

"I don't remember calling you, babe," Slate said quietly. "I don't remember getting off the plane, into Mustang's car, or to my house. I don't remember anything but bits and pieces until around noon today, when I woke up a little more clear-headed. I just know I hurt you—and that kills me."

Ashlyn stared at the man she loved more than anyone she'd ever dated...and shrugged. "It's okay."

"It's not," Slate said firmly. "You should've been there."

"And I would've," Ashlyn said, hurt and anger rising a bit at his words. "But you made it clear that Mustang could take care of you just fine. It doesn't really matter that you don't remember saying it, Slate. It might actually mean more that you don't."

"What does that mean?"

"Just that maybe your subconscious was saying what you were truly thinking."

Slate shook his head. "No, you're wrong."

"Am I?" Ashlyn asked with a tilt of her head. "I'm just the chick you're having sex with," she said, trying to keep the sadness from her tone. "Mustang's the one who saved you. Who's been with you through thick and thin. You knew deep down that he'd protect you while you couldn't protect yourself. And you know him far better than you know me. It's only natural you'd want his help instead of mine."

"I know you," Slate said firmly.

Ashlyn didn't say anything.

"I do," he insisted. "You're the most generous person I've ever met in my life. And I'm not talking monetarily. Anyone can donate money and forget about it the next minute. You give *yourself*. To everyone who's smart enough to recognize how valuable you are. You babysat Jazmin's baby for two hours, giving her one of the first breaks she'd had in months. You praise Brooklyn when she's at the end of her rope with her toddlers. You've encouraged and supported her dreams of going back to school, something she never thought she could do until you started delivering meals to her and her family. You care about whether a handicapped woman is getting enough sunshine in her life. Enough to encourage her to sit outside and laugh with you for twenty minutes every time you visit. And let's not forget James. You've made that man feel less lonely, and like part of the world again. Not everyone would invite someone like him to their friend's wedding. You give every bit of yourself to everyone you meet, Ashlyn, and you've made *my* life a hundred percent better."

Ashlyn could only stare at him. She had no idea where he was going with this, but she couldn't get one single word out in response.

"You've made me a better man simply by existing. I'm not as impatient as I used to be. If you don't believe me, ask any one of my teammates. I laugh more. I'm actually taking an interest in the people around me, not just analyzing them to determine if they might be a threat. Hell, I got caught in the damn house for that very reason.

"There was a kid. Maybe seven or eight years old. He signaled to whoever had that RPG, letting them know that we were inside. Everyone ran like hell to get the fuck out of there because we all knew what was coming. But I couldn't leave that boy. He hated me. Was willing to die if it meant killing my team...but just as I turned to run, my conscience made me hesitate. I turned back to grab him.

"It was what *you* would've done. I knew it. Deep in my soul, I knew you wouldn't have left without trying to save that boy. Even as I was dragging him toward the stairs, I realized I wasn't going to make it. You know what flashed through my mind then?"

247

"What?" Ashlyn whispered. She was crying now, but she couldn't stop.

"I hoped the guys were clear. I wished the boy would stop clawing at my hand, trying to get me to let go. But more than anything else, I thought about you."

"Me?"

"Yes, babe. *You*. I was pissed that you'd never know just how much I cared about you. That I'd never get to explain our casual dating thing is total bullshit. There's nothing fucking *casual* about our relationship. Not for me."

Ashlyn's eyes widened. Was she hearing him wrong? Maybe she was so desperate for him to feel the same as her, she was hallucinating.

"I truly don't remember calling you. In my defense, my brain had gotten knocked around pretty good inside my skull. It's really not an excuse...but the first thing I wanted to do this morning, when I finally woke up and felt slightly normal, was talk to you. Then you told me you were on a date..."

Slate took a deep breath. "I fucking *hate* that I hurt you so badly that you went out with someone else—but I'm not giving up on you. On us. I'll do whatever it takes to regain your trust. If you want to continue to see other people while we're fixin' what we had, I'll deal with it. I won't like it, but I'll prove to you that I'm not only your friend, I'm the man who loves you. The man who will throw a temper tantrum in front of a military doctor like a three-year-old so he can get his way and come home to see the woman who owns his heart."

Ashlyn felt as if she was going to pass out. Instead of admitting she loved him back, all she could think to say was, "I wasn't on a date."

"Babe, you were at a bar, and you said you were with a *friend*."

"I was. But...it wasn't with a guy. I mean, there were guys

there, but it was a group thing. Today's the birthday of one of the guys from Food For All. A bunch of us went out to help him celebrate."

Slate sat up straighter. "You weren't on a date?"

"No."

His entire body slumped, and he closed his eyes and bowed his head.

"Slate?"

"Give me a second," he whispered.

Ashlyn wasn't sure what to do. A week ago, she would've climbed into his lap and reassured him the best way she knew how that he was the only man in her life...

And the moment she had that thought, Ashlyn wondered what was holding her back.

He'd apologized. He had a concussion. He didn't even remember the last two days.

He said he loved her.

She was moving before she realized what she was doing. Walking the couple of steps it took to stand in front of him. Then she put her knees on either side of his thighs.

The second he felt the cushion give beneath him, Slate's eyes popped open and his hands went to her hips. He held her steady as she scooted closer.

Ashlyn put her hands on his cheeks and met his gaze. She was scared to death, but this was too important to beat around the bush about. "You love me?" she whispered.

"Yes," Slate said without hesitation.

"I love you too."

He didn't move for a nanosecond after the last word left her mouth. Then he let out a long breath, pulled her close, and buried his nose in the space between her shoulder and neck.

"*Fuck me,*" he whispered.

Ashlyn was crying...again...but she smiled.

"Fuck!" Slate repeated.

"Not sure you're up to that yet," Ashlyn teased.

His head moved back, and she saw his eyes were shiny with tears. "Say it again," he ordered.

"I love you. Have for a while now but I was too chicken to admit it, even to myself. When I heard you were hurt...I've never been so scared. Then you said you didn't want to see me, that Mustang could look after you, and all that fear morphed into agony. I couldn't even talk to our friends because it just hurt too much."

"I'm so damn sorry," Slate said softly.

Ashlyn shook her head. "I didn't say that to make you feel bad or to get you to apologize again or anything. We're moving on from that. I messed up too. I should've ignored you and gone to your house anyway. I should've listened to what our friends had to say. I should've admitted long before now that I wanted so much more than a friends-with-benefits thing. I was too scared that was the only way I could have you."

"If there's ever a next time," Slate said, "I don't give a shit *what* I say, you get your ass to my side. Okay?"

Ashlyn swallowed down the fear that spiked through her at the thought of him getting hurt in the future. But she wasn't an idiot. Her man was a SEAL. His job was dangerous. She just had to hope and pray that his team would have his back and the bad guys wouldn't get lucky a second time. "Okay."

His hands framed her face. "You weren't out with someone else." It wasn't a question.

"No. You're the only man I've been remotely interested in for more than a year. I've had a crush on you forever."

"Yeah?"

"Yeah."

"I don't know if I can claim the same...but I know I

couldn't stop thinking about you. Worrying about you. Needling you so you'd go off on me."

Ashlyn rolled her eyes even as Slate wiped the lingering wetness from her cheeks with his thumbs. "So you acted like a grade-school kid picking on the girl he likes because he didn't know how else to get her attention."

"Pretty much," Slate agreed. Then he slowly leaned toward her.

His kiss was light, almost hesitant. As if it was the first they'd ever shared. And in many ways, it was. The first of their new, serious, very committed relationship.

When he pulled back, Slate rested his forehead against hers.

"How in the world are we gonna tell everyone, after all these months of insisting that we're nothing but casual, that all of a sudden we love each other and we're in a serious relationship?" she mumbled.

In response, Slate moved a hand to her hip to hold her steady, then leaned enough to reach into his back pocket with the other. He brought out his phone, using both hands to type something.

"Slate? What are you doing?"

"Give me a second."

"Seriously, Slate, what—"

"There. It's done. Everyone knows, so no more worrying about it."

"What's done? What did you do?"

He turned his phone around, and Ashlyn stared at the group text he'd just sent.

Slate: Ash and I are in love. We're gonna get married someday in the hopefully not-too-distant future. The first person who says "I knew it" or "I told you so" isn't gonna be invited to the wedding.

"Oh my God! I can't believe you just sent that. Who did you send it to?" Ashlyn asked, torn between being mortified and laughing hysterical.

"Everyone."

"You did not!"

"Yup."

Just then, his phone started vibrating in his hand as people responded to the message. Not only that, but Ashlyn could hear her own phone, still in her purse by the door, dinging with notifications.

"You're impossible."

"And you love me anyway."

She smiled. "I do."

His facial expression turned serious. "I'll do my best to never hurt you like that again, babe. But if I do, don't just take it. You give as good as you get. Always. I can't deal with the thought of you sleeping on your couch, crying your eyes out over something I did or said, ever again."

Figures he didn't miss that was exactly what she'd been doing for the last two days. "I will."

"I mean it. I'll always get my head out of my ass, but you calling me on my shit will help that happen sooner."

"Okay."

"Now that we're good—we *are* good, right?"

"We're good, Slate."

He nodded. "Okay. Now that we're good, I'm thinking I need to lie down for a while."

Ashlyn frowned in alarm. "Why? Does your head hurt? Should I call a doctor? Maybe Mustang should come over.

Since he's been looking after you, he'll know if you need to go to the hospital, right?"

"Shhhh. I'm all right. I'm just tired. And my head still hurts a bit. But nothing like before."

"Are you sure? You're not just telling me that so I don't freak out?"

"I'm sure."

Ashlyn breathed out a sigh of relief. "When was the last time you ate?"

"Before I came over here. Aleck made me eat eggs and a shake."

"How about you go lie down and I make you something for dinner. Maybe some lasagna? I'll put lots of meat in it for more protein. And the carbs will probably do you good."

"How about I lie here while you cook?" he countered.

"Okay. That's better. I can keep an eye on you," Ashlyn agreed. Then said sheepishly, "And there's already a blanket and pillow out here anyway."

Slate frowned. "Hate that I hurt you, babe."

"It's okay. Done and over with. We're moving on. I mean, apparently we're getting married at some point, even though I don't remember you asking, or me saying yes."

Slate grinned and leaned forward and kissed her deeply. "I know when I've found something good, and you, babe, are the best fucking thing to ever happen to me. We're getting married. Maybe not tomorrow, or next month, but it's gonna happen."

"You that sure we'll work out? That we won't get tired of each other?"

"I'm that sure," he said without a shred of doubt in his voice. "I didn't live through that RPG attack to continue being a dumbass."

Ashlyn couldn't help but smile, even though she still hated

to even think about what he'd been through. Then something else hit her. "Do you think he's okay?"

Proving they were on the same wavelength, Slate didn't have to ask who she was talking about. "I don't know. My gut says no, but my heart hopes that since I survived, maybe he did too. Maybe his parents came and dug him out after we left. The guys didn't find him while they were searching for me."

"It's all so sad," Ashlyn said.

"It is. Kids are innocent. I hate that someone twisted his little mind into harboring such hate so early in his life."

Ashlyn leaned forward and rested her body weight against Slate. His arms went around her and they sat like that for a few minutes.

"Food," she said, eventually sitting back with a sigh. When she looked into Slate's face, she could see the way he furrowed his brow as if his head was hurting. She climbed off him, leaned down, kissed him briefly, picked up the blanket that was still on the floor and pointed at the pillow. "Lie down."

"Yes, ma'am."

"And to think you could've had this excellent bedside service for the last couple of days," she joked as she spread the blanket over him when he settled on his back.

"Yeah."

Except he didn't sound as if he found her words funny.

"I was joking," she said.

"I wasn't. I made you cry. And almost lost you. It won't happen again."

"I know." And she did. "Nap, Slate. When you wake up, we'll eat, then get you settled into bed. Wait, do you need to work tomorrow?"

"No. I've got the week off."

"Okay, cool. I'll call Lex and see if she can get someone to cover for my delivery route for a few days."

"I'll be okay hanging out while you do your thing," he protested.

"Nope. I'm putting my foot down. I almost lost you," she said, whispering that last part. "Give me a few days."

"Done," he said without hesitation. "I'd love to have you look after me while I'm recuperating."

Ashlyn nodded, then reached for the lamp next to the couch. She turned off the light, then went to the curtains on the windows and shut those too. She knew how painful sunlight could be when she had a headache. Slate probably felt the same. His relieved sigh told her she was right.

"Oh, by the way, I'm not answering any of the texts from our friends. You sent the message, *you* can deal with them."

"No problem. I'll deal by ignoring them," he said with a small smile, even as he shut his eyes.

Ashlyn watched him for a while. Even if she was slightly overwhelmed by how she'd gone from wanting to break up with Slate to admitting that she loved him, she couldn't help but smile. She'd totally be talking to the other women about everything that happened. They would be thrilled for her, and probably smirk and say they knew all along she and Slate were gonna end up together...*for real* together.

Taking a deep breath, Ashlyn turned to the kitchen to start getting the lasagna ready. She needed to build Slate's strength back up. Get him back to the bossy, slightly annoying, protective man she knew and loved. She didn't like it when he was unsure and hurting.

Somehow a day that had started out miserable had ended up as one of the best of her life. Being in a relationship with Slate wouldn't be without its ups and downs, but as long as they said they loved each other at the end of each day, and promised to deal with the bumps in the road, they'd be okay.

CHAPTER TWENTY

The last four days had been some of the happiest of Ashlyn's life, for no other reason than she'd spent them with the man she loved.

They'd stayed at her apartment Sunday night into Monday, then had gone back to Slate's house the rest of the week. When she'd carefully removed his shirt Sunday night, before settling him into bed, the bruises covering his body shocked her. Slate had *way* downplayed his injuries. Ashlyn had refused to let him push himself too much after that, insisting he give himself time to heal.

But it was obvious yesterday that he was mostly back to his old self. He insisted on working out Thursday morning, lifting some light weights and doing sit-ups and pullups—no running yet.

It was Friday morning, and time for them both to return to their normal routines. Even though he didn't have to go back into work until Monday, Slate was anxious to talk to his commander and give his account of what happened in Afghanistan. Her man was damn stubborn, but also, luckily, a fast healer.

They'd finally made love last night. Ashlyn had attempted to keep things slow and easy, but it wasn't long before they were both too desperate to continue that route.

Slate had been insatiable, telling her over and over how much he loved her as he made her orgasm three times with his mouth and fingers before taking pity on her. She tried to roll over so he could take her from behind—she freaking *loved* when he fucked her that way—but he wouldn't allow it, forcing her onto her back and sinking deep inside her while they were face-to-face.

"After everything that happened, the first time we *make love*," he said, emphasizing the words, "I want to see your face. Want to look into your eyes so you can see just how much I love you."

She'd melted. How could she say no to that?

And he'd done just what he'd said, thrusting over and over slowly, steadily, without taking his gaze from hers. He'd brought her to the edge once more, until she was begging him to let her come. The second she curled into him and began trembling, he'd lost it, pounding into her again and again, repeating *I love you, I love you,* to the beat of his thrusts.

Afterward, they'd clung to each other, their hearts racing a mile a minute.

Now she was in her car, trying to stop daydreaming about last night.

She was looking forward to seeing her clients again. Though, they were more than clients. They were her friends, and Ashlyn was excited to see what she'd missed in the last four days. It was hard to believe it was only Friday. It felt as if weeks had gone by. Her life had changed so much in the last few days...for the better.

Elodie, Lexie, Kenna, Monica, and Carly had been overjoyed at the change in her and Slate's relationship. And yes, Ashlyn had heard a lot of "not surprised" and "about time" from her friends, but she wasn't annoyed in the least. It was obvious they were all thrilled for her and Slate.

Everyone on her route was happy to see her as well. Jazmin was excited to show her Henry's first tooth peeking through his gums. Briar and Curtis showed off their latest drawings, and Brooklyn was bursting with happiness because Trey had gotten a new job that paid five dollars more an hour. Even Christi smiled more than usual as they sat in the sun on her back porch for twenty minutes.

The only person who wasn't happy was James.

Ashlyn had approached his house with a spring in her step, excited to see him. But the second she saw him when he opened his door, she knew something was wrong. He smiled when he saw her, but something was definitely...off.

It took a bit of cajoling to get it out of him. After some small talk, after putting the piece of key lime pie Elodie had made on a plate for him, and after telling him all about the change in her and Slate's relationship, she said, "So are you going to tell me what's wrong, or are we going to sit here for the rest of my visit and pretend nothing's up?"

James sighed. "I'm eighty-nine years old. You'd think I'd be used to people disappointing me by now."

"What happened?" Ashlyn asked.

"It's about Aiden."

"Your home health aide?"

"Yeah. I've had my concerns about him for a while, but I wanted to give him the benefit of the doubt. The boy hasn't had an easy life, and he's been extremely helpful," James said.

"But?" Ashlyn pressed when he didn't immediately continue.

"You know I'm not a fan of banks, right?" James asked.

Confused about the change of subject, Ashlyn nodded. "I keep telling you that things have changed since you were a kid. That it's safe to deposit your money now."

James gave her a small smile. "I know, but old habits are hard to break. My parents talked about the depression all the time when I was growing up. They lost a lot of money because of the situation with the banks, and until the day they died, they kept their savings in the house. And don't talk to me about interest," he said, holding up a hand. "The paltry amount banks give you is a slap in the face. They're making money hand over fist on our accounts, and yet they give us pennies on the dollar. It's a rip-off!"

Knowing James could get extremely worked up when talking about this particular subject, Ashlyn tried to redirect him. "What happened with Aiden?"

James sighed. "I got my retirement check yesterday. Aiden was happy to take me to the bank to cash it. I always wait until I'm alone to hide my money. After Aiden left for the day, I went into the kitchen to put the money in one of my hiding places. I saw movement in my peripheral vision. It was Aiden, looking in through the window. I don't think he knew that I saw him, but I can't in good conscience have him in my house anymore."

"Oh, James. I'm sorry," Ashlyn said. "Are you sure he was actually spying on you?" It was a silly question, but she couldn't help but ask anyway.

James simply looked at her with raised eyebrows.

She sighed. "Yeah, dumb question. Sorry."

"It's not just that," James said. "I mean, after I was sure he was gone, I could've easily switched up where I put my money...but there are other things he's done that have made me uneasy for a while now."

"Like what?"

James waved his hand in a dismissive gesture. "It doesn't matter. I called the agency just before you got here and told them I didn't need their services anymore." James then slowly pushed himself out of his chair. He walked over to a small table against the wall near the kitchen and picked up a cardboard box. It was about double the size of a shoebox. He carried it over to where Ashlyn was sitting and held it out.

Ashlyn took it from him. "What's this?"

"My life savings," James said calmly as he sat back down in his chair.

"What?"

"It's all the money I have in the world. Took a bit of time to remember all my stash spots in the house, but I think I got it all."

"I can't take this!" Ashlyn exclaimed.

"It's not a gift," James corrected gently. "I might be old, but I'm not senile...yet." He smiled, but Ashlyn wasn't finding anything about this situation funny.

"I want you to hold on to it for me. I know it's not fair of me to ask, but I'm asking anyway. I trust you, Ashlyn. You've given me no reason not to. I kept a thousand dollars for anything that might come up, but I don't want all that money in the house anymore."

Ashlyn tried to think of something to say, but she was too surprised. Too shocked to come up with anything.

"I'm missing money," James told her. "I don't know how much, but I suspect Aiden's been helping himself for a long while. I can't prove it, and if I tried, I know the police would think I just forgot how much I had and that I'm a crazy old man."

"Maybe now's the time to open an account at the bank," Ashlyn said gently.

James just shook his head. "I don't have a lot of time left on this Earth, and I'm okay with that. My Angie is waiting for me on the other side and I can't wait to see her again. But I'll be damned if I let someone else take what I've earned. It's not a lot, maybe twenty thousand or so, but I trust you to take care of it for me."

Ashlyn wanted to cry. She definitely didn't want the responsibility of James's money, but she had even bigger concerns about him keeping it in the house, especially if he thought Aiden was stealing. "Okay, James. I'll keep it safe for you."

One of the first things she was going to do was deposit it into her account. No way could she keep this much cash just sitting in her apartment. And she had a feeling Slate wouldn't be comfortable with that either.

She watched as James's shoulders seemed to relax at her words. It was obvious he'd been worried about this. He seemed a hundred times less stressed than when she'd walked in.

"Good. I trust you, Ashlyn," he said again.

"That means the world to me, James," she told him. "But what are you going to do about a home health aide? I don't want to offend you, but you still need help."

"I know. Next week I'll call the VA and see if they can recommend someone else. In the meantime, I'll still see you Monday, Wednesday, and Friday, right?"

"Of course," Ashlyn reassured him. "And I'll see if I can add you to my route on the other days of the week too." His house wasn't near the others she visited on the alternate days of the week, but she'd figure out a way to make it work.

"You're a good girl," James said. "I'm proud to know you."

Ashlyn smiled. "And I'm proud to know *you*."

"Now, if you have time, maybe you can tell me more about how you and Slate went from 'nothing serious' to dropping the L bombs on each other."

Ashlyn burst out laughing. "The L bombs?" she asked between chuckles.

"Isn't that what the young people call 'I love you' these days?" James asked.

All she could do was shake her head. "I have no idea," she

admitted. She bent over and put the box of cash on the floor, picked up the cup of water James had insisted she pour for herself when she got there, and told her friend everything.

Half an hour later, the ding of Ashlyn's phone sounded in the room. She pulled it out of her pocket and saw she had a text from Slate.

Slate: Tell James hello for me. Any idea when you'll be headed home?

Home. God, that sounded good. For all the protests she'd made over the last few months about how she and Slate weren't moving in together, it sure felt good to think of Slate's house as *their home*.

"I'm guessing that's your young man," James said.

"Yeah. He says hi, and was just wondering when I'd be home," Ashlyn told him.

"It's getting late," James said. "Go on, get home to your man."

Ashlyn couldn't wait to see him again. They'd spent every minute together for the last four days, and now it felt weird to have not seen him since this morning.

But for some reason, she was uncomfortable leaving James. "It's not that late."

"Ashlyn, go home," James said firmly. "Besides, I'm tired. I'm gonna turn on the tube and probably fall asleep right here in my chair."

"All right, I'm going," Ashlyn said. "But I'm gonna call you tomorrow to check on you."

"I'll be fine," he reassured her.

"Right. Then I'm gonna call tomorrow to say hello," Ashlyn retorted.

James chuckled. "It would be silly to continue to protest getting a phone call from a pretty young lady, wouldn't it?"

"Yup." Ashlyn stood and went over to James's chair. She knelt down next to it and put her hand on his arm. Because of his personality, most of the time she forgot how old and frail he really was. But touching his thin arm and being up close to him like this, it hit home how vulnerable he truly was. "I'm sorry about Aiden. I know you liked him."

James pressed his lips together and nodded. "He's changed lately. I didn't realize it at first, but now that I look back, I can see it."

Ashlyn gently squeezed his arm. "It's better to be safe than sorry. I'll see what I can find out about another home aide service too. We'll get you set up in no time."

"You're a good woman," James said.

"I try," Ashlyn said. "Now, don't eat the other two pieces of pie for dinner. Elodie worked hard on the chicken, rice, and hummus meatballs she made yesterday. I brought enough for two dinners. There's also fruit and some bread in the kitchen too."

"You're too good to me," James said, lifting his hand and putting it on her cheek, much as Slate did.

For a moment, Ashlyn could picture her friend as a young man, wooing his wife and being protective and bossy, just as Slate was with her. It made her smile.

"Love seeing you smile," James said. "Now git. Go home to your man and have a wonderful weekend."

"I'll talk to you tomorrow."

James rolled his eyes, and it made Ashlyn smile.

"And call me if you need anything. I mean, it, James."

"Yes, ma'am. I will. And..." His voice lowered. "Thanks for taking care of that for me." He nodded to the box sitting by her chair.

"Of course." Ashlyn leaned forward and kissed James's cheek. "Talk to you soon."

"Lookin' forward to it."

Ashlyn stood, grabbed her cup and brought it into the kitchen, putting it into the sink. Then she went back out into the small living room, picked up James's life savings, smiled at him once more, and headed out to her car. She walked a little faster than she usually would, paranoid because she was carrying so much cash.

Thinking about how unhappy Slate would be, knowing she was walking around with twenty thousand dollars, Ashlyn picked up her phone when she was safely inside her car with the doors locked.

Ashlyn: Headed back to Food For All now. I should be home in forty-five minutes or so.

Slate: Sounds good. I'm making pasta with roasted veggies for dinner.

God, the conversation was so...domestic. Ashlyn loved it.

Ashlyn: Sounds great. Got a lot to talk to you about when I get there.

Slate: Everything okay?

Ashlyn: Yeah. Had a good day.

Slate: Okay. Gonna let you go so you can drive. Be safe.

Ashlyn: I will. See you soon.

Slate: Love you.

. . .

Ashlyn smiled and stared at the two words on her screen. It was amazing how good they could make her feel.

Ashlyn: Love you too.

Then she started her car and pulled away from the curb. It was almost scary how well things were going in her life. For a moment, she wondered when the other shoe would drop. It always seemed as if when things were going good for her, something usually happened to mess everything up.

But she wasn't going to think about that. Everything was fine. Great. Even if she and Slate inevitably faced problems at some point in the future, right now, everything was wonderful.

* * *

Aiden hung up the phone, threw his head back, and screamed in frustration.

He'd just been informed that James Mason no longer needed his services.

That old bastard couldn't fire him! Not now. He *needed* that job. Needed the money from the hidden stashes around his house. Without his dope, Aiden would literally die. Or at least it would feel like it when he went through withdrawal.

He'd had to take more and more heroin lately to maintain his high. And the only way he could afford to get as much as he needed was by supplementing his income. James's money was the fastest and easiest way to accomplish that.

The guy got free food delivered, he never left the house. He got retirement money from the Navy and social security. He hadn't missed a dime of what Aiden had already taken, so why should he even fucking care if Aiden needed a few bucks?

He'd been a little careless yesterday. After they'd returned from the bank, he knew James would hide the cash as soon as he was alone...and Aiden needed some of it. So he'd snuck around the side of the house and watched as the old man hid his money. It was a good thing he did too, because James had put it in a new spot.

He didn't recall James looking at the window...but he *must've* been spotted. And now he'd been fired.

Fuck James! And fuck his job! He didn't get paid nearly enough to deal with old people's shit all day. They were smelly, boring, messy, and pathetic.

Aiden paced his empty apartment. The place he wouldn't be able to afford for much longer, without a job and with a habit to support. The thought of how much money could potentially be hidden around James's house made Aiden salivate.

Since taking a little here and there was no longer an option, he'd just go in and take it all. Surely there'd be enough to last him a good while. He just had to find it.

Plans swirled in his head. He'd make one more trip to the house. He'd apologize. He'd get back in James's good graces... then drug him one last time. He'd been dosing his water with sleeping pills for a while. It was easier to search for the money when the old man was knocked out cold and Aiden didn't have to worry about being caught with his hand in the cookie jar, so to speak.

He'd heard him talking on the phone with that goody two-shoes food delivery bitch about being tired and taking more naps than usual. By some weird stroke of luck, he didn't seem to suspect Aiden, despite literally catching him dosing a glass of water a while back. How dumb could the guy be?

Tomorrow, the asshole would take a *very* long nap. One he wouldn't wake up from.

Aiden didn't even feel guilty about deciding to overdose the bastard. He was fucking older than dirt. A waste of space. He would give him a triple dose of sleeping pills then search for all the hidden money. He'd make sure to leave the house exactly as he found it, so no one would suspect anything other than an old man lying down for a nap and never waking up again.

His fingerprints wouldn't make the cops suspicious because he came by three times a week. He'd park a few blocks over from the house, so no one would see his car parked out front. Aiden had also watched enough true crime to know to leave his phone in his apartment, as an alibi in case the police checked his cell phone records.

The more he thought about it, the more excited Aiden became.

This was going to work. If the old guy hadn't fired him, he would've continued to take a few hundred bucks here and there, and it wouldn't have been a big deal. But now, he was gonna get the mother lode of cash.

"Stupid asshole," Aiden muttered. He had no idea if a triple dose of sleeping pills would actually kill the old fart or not, but he wouldn't waste time worrying about it. At the very least, it would knock him out for hours, maybe even all day and night. And by this time tomorrow, Aiden would have his drugs and feel good again. Depending on how much cash he found, he could be set for a very long time.

Aiden's only problem right that moment was scrounging up enough dough for a hit that would last him through tomorrow. He thought about breaking into his neighbor's apartment, which he'd done once before, but decided something less risky was smarter. He could hit up the chick he knew who sometimes took pity on him, throwing him a few bucks after he screwed her...or maybe he could work out an exchange of some sort with his dealer. He didn't like doing that, it was way too dangerous, but at this point, he'd do whatever it took to get his drugs.

"Last time," Aiden said out loud. "This'll be the last time I have to beg from someone else." Then he headed for his car. Luckily, he'd filled up the gas tank with part of the money he'd taken from James's house last time, so he had plenty of fuel to get him to Waikiki and back. He'd call his dope dealer, shoot up, and plan exactly how things would go down tomorrow.

Feeling better than he had in ages, Aiden smiled as he climbed into his car. He hit a mailbox on his way out of the neighborhood, but didn't even notice as he headed for the interstate.

CHAPTER TWENTY-ONE

Slate lay awake Saturday morning, simply watching Ashlyn sleep. Yesterday had been a tough day. He'd gone to the base and watched the body cam footage of what had happened a little over a week ago in Afghanistan. He'd definitely fucked up by trying to save the boy, but ironically, his actions had likely saved his life.

If he'd followed his team down the stairs, he likely wouldn't have made it out of the house before the RPG hit. And he would've been closer to the side of the house that collapsed first, buried under far more rubble. As it was, being on the top floor, on the opposite side of the point of contact, had allowed him to escape the worst of the explosion.

It hadn't been easy to watch his teammates frantically digging through the rubble, trying to find him, or to see them carrying his unconscious body through the hostile streets of the city as they retreated.

Slate had always known Mustang, Midas, Aleck, Pid, and Jag had his back, but seeing it firsthand, hearing the stress in their voices, and their absolute confidence in getting him back to the base safe and sound, made an already tight bond even tighter.

He had a different take on missions now. Yes, the bad guys still needed to be taken out, innocent civilians still needed to be rescued, captured comrades in arms needed to be liberated...but now, for the first time in his career, Slate was a little less willing to die in order to do any of those things. He'd still give his all to every mission, he still loved his country, but he now loved something, *someone*, even more.

Ashlyn lay curled against him, her breathing slow and deep. The love he felt for the woman seemed all consuming. How he hadn't admitted it earlier, Slate had no idea. It was ridiculous that he hadn't recognized his feelings for what they were, especially since he'd never felt like this before.

It had taken him getting hurt, and his jealousy, to finally make them both open their eyes and see what was right in front of them. Having Ashlyn come through the door last evening had been exactly what he'd needed to put the stress of the day behind him. He wanted them to come home to each other every single day.

He hadn't been thrilled that James had given her twenty thousand bucks to take care of for him, but he was relieved the old man didn't have that much cash in his house anymore. Today, despite James's opinion on banks, he and Ashlyn would deposit the money into an account for safekeeping. He'd talked her into opening a separate account for James's money, so there wouldn't be any conflict of interest or questions about it.

Afterward, they had no plans other than to enjoy each other's company. Slate was feeling surprisingly good after the slight swelling in his brain had subsided, and he'd be going back to work next week. But before that, he and Ashlyn had two full days to themselves.

It was hard to remember the time when he and Ash had

done nothing but snipe at each other. But Slate thought of those days fondly. She stood up for herself, stood up to him, and stood up for what she believed in, and he loved that about her...just as much as it drove him crazy.

She'd give away the clothes on her back if it meant helping someone else. She'd keep an old man's life savings safe if it made him feel more comfortable. She would always bend over backward to help others...which meant Slate had to make sure he always had her back. That helping someone else didn't mean she put herself in a vulnerable position. Slate was more than willing to let her do her thing, but he'd pull her back when the situation warranted it.

He felt guilty for the flash of relief that went through him at the knowledge she didn't have any vindicative ex-boyfriends. She wasn't wanted by the mob. They didn't have to worry about anyone wanting to hurt her because of something she'd done in the past. Slate didn't think she had an enemy in the world, which was a relief. He couldn't bear to think about her being in any of the situations her friends had been through.

Their life together would be as boring as he could make it, and they'd both be perfectly happy.

Ashlyn stirred against him, and Slate smiled as she slowly came awake. Her eyes opened a crack, and she looked from him, to the clock on the table behind him, then back to him. "It's early. You sleep okay?"

"It's not that early, and yeah, slept like a rock with you in my arms."

She smiled sleepily. "Me too."

Slate couldn't help but snort. She slept like a rock *every* night. She was one of those lucky people who fell asleep fast and stayed that way. He loved that for her.

"Okay, I sleep like a rock every night," she said, correctly reading his snort. "But I slept even better because you're with me."

Slate ran a finger over her nose and kissed her gently.

"Do we have plans today?"

"Other than going to the bank, no," Slate said.

"And they don't open until like, ten on a Saturday, right?" she asked.

"I think that's right."

One of her hands flattened on his belly and slowly inched downward. "So we have time to be lazy this morning."

"Lazy?" he asked with a smile. "Oh no, no laziness for you. I did all the work last night."

Her hand stilled and she frowned up at him. "No, you didn't. I distinctly remember being on top and being in charge."

Slate burst out laughing. "I think your memory is faulty, babe," Slate told her. "You started out being in charge, but after that first orgasm, you couldn't do anything but lie there, lost in a pleasure stupor, and I had to take over. You might've been on top, but it was *me* lifting your body up and down on my cock as I fucked *you*."

Instead of getting mad, Ashlyn merely grinned. "Yeah, okay, you might have a point," she said as her hand slipped into his boxers and she began stroking his morning woody into a full-fledged erection. "So this morning, you can be lazy and I'll for sure do all the work." She shifted, getting up on her knees and scooting down until she was between his legs. She pulled his boxers off, then bent above his very awake cock.

She smiled at him as she licked from base to tip.

If this was her idea of him being lazy, he was a damn lucky man. He shoved his hand into her hair as she lowered her head. Groaning, Slate refused to close his eyes as his woman went down on him. He loved her so damn much. He had no idea how he'd gotten so lucky.

* * *

Ashlyn smiled at Slate a couple hours later. Being *lazy* with Slate was awesome. She had a feeling she'd burned more calories in an hour that morning than she would the rest of the entire day. It wasn't often Slate could stay in bed with nowhere to be, so they'd milked it for all it was worth. Next week, he'd be up at the ass-crack of dawn, working out with his team once more, so Ashlyn had to enjoy every second of their lovemaking and cuddling.

They'd just enjoyed a late breakfast, and were washing dishes together before heading out to the bank when Slate's phone rang.

He frowned, dried his hands, and went to the counter to pick it up.

"Slate here," he answered. "Yes, Sir. No, it's okay, I can talk. Give me a second though? Thanks."

He put the phone against his chest and turned to her. "It's Commander Huttner. He has some questions about my statement of what happened last week."

"It's okay," Ashlyn said without hesitation. "Why don't I go to the bank now? I'll pick up lunch on the way home and we can spend the rest of the day hanging out."

Slate frowned. "I don't like the idea of you driving around with all that money."

Ashlyn rolled her eyes. "It'll be fine, Slate. I'm going to go straight to the bank, open an account, and that'll be that. I won't advertise the fact that I'm carrying a shit ton of money. No one's gonna know."

He only frowned harder.

"Seriously, talk to your commander. I'll probably be back

before you're done. I'll even stop and get Hawaiian for your lunch," she cajoled.

"You being able to sweet-talk me doesn't bode well for this relationship," he semi-growled.

Ashlyn giggled. "Actually, I think it says great things for this relationship." She leaned in and kissed him briefly. "Love you," she said softly.

"And I love you," he said, apparently not caring that his commander might be able to overhear. "Be careful—and don't get Hawaiian. You don't like it, so that means you'd have to make two stops to get yourself something too."

"It's not a big deal," she said.

"Babe. I have two more days off, and I want to spend as much of that time with you as possible. Bank, lunch, then get your ass back here so we can relax."

He was being bossy again, but since he was also being sweet about wanting to spend time with her, she couldn't complain. "Okay, Slate."

"Okay."

Ashlyn felt his eyes on her as he brought his phone back up to his ear. "I'm back, Sir."

He kept watching her as she slipped her feet into a pair of flip-flops and grabbed her purse, sunglasses, and the two manila envelopes they'd put James's money into after they'd counted it and bundled it into neat stacks. She took a moment to admire Slate while he was distracted speaking to his boss.

He had on a pair of jeans, which molded to his muscular thighs. He was wearing a Helena's Bakery T-shirt, his hair mussed, and his bare feet peeking out beneath the hem of his pants. All in all, her man was crazy hot. It didn't matter if he was in his uniform, a pair of jeans like today, gray sweats, or butt-ass naked, he was a fine specimen of a man.

"Be back soon!" she mouthed as she headed for the door.

"Be safe," Slate mouthed back.

Nodding, Ashlyn opened the door and headed out to her car.

As she drove to the bank, she glanced at the manila envelopes. James had been right, he had twenty thousand, two hundred dollars hidden around his house. It wasn't a ton of money for someone his age, but he seemed content with his lifestyle.

The visit to the bank went smoothly. She opened a new account, making a mental note to add James's name to it at some point. The clerk behind the counter didn't seem fazed about depositing over two hundred one-hundred dollar bills. She did check a few to make sure they weren't counterfeit, but once assured they were real, she quickly completed the transaction and handed over a receipt.

Feeling much better now that the money was safe, Ashlyn left the bank, relieved to no longer be carrying around that much cash.

As she got into her car, she thought about her promise to call and check on James and figured now was as good a time as any. She had a feeling she and Slate would be preoccupied later, and she wanted to make sure she didn't forget to check on her friend.

She dialed James's number and waited for him to answer. He didn't. The phone rang five times and went to voice mail. Ashlyn didn't bother leaving a message. James had admitted once that he had no idea how to access the message system on his landline and wasn't able to check them anyway.

She called back, only for the phone to go unanswered once more. A little worried now, Ashlyn called again, and then one more time. The phone only rang and rang.

She frowned, visions of all sorts of horrible things flew through her brain. James lying on the floor after having fallen, unable to get up. James becoming sick and unable to get out of bed. Living alone, and being so frail, there were so many things that could happen.

Ashlyn made the split-second decision to pop by his house just to check on him.

She quickly clicked on Slate's name and typed out a text.

Ashlyn: Money's deposited. Since you're probably still on the phone, I'm gonna stop by James's house real quick. He was kind of off yesterday, and I want to make sure he's good. I'll still get lunch on my way home. Love you.

She was probably overthinking the situation. James was likely sitting outside, enjoying the morning, and hadn't heard his phone ring. She'd swing by, they'd laugh at her paranoia, then she'd get lunch and head back to Slate's house.

If something *was* wrong, she'd get help for James, then call Slate. There was no use worrying him yet over probably nothing.

Her mind made up, and not surprised Slate hadn't immediately responded to her text, Ashlyn started her car and headed for James's house.

She got there in about ten minutes, the traffic being lighter since it was a Saturday. There were no cars parked at his house, which wasn't a surprise. Grabbing her phone, Ashlyn slipped out of her RAV4 and headed up to his front door. She knocked, but wasn't surprised when James didn't answer. She tried the knob. It was locked.

Biting her lip, Ashlyn took a deep breath and headed around to the side of the house. She'd see if James was in the backyard, scold him for scaring her, they'd share a laugh, and she'd head out.

But before she could get to the backyard, the kitchen

door caught her attention. It was at the side of the house, and while the screen door was shut, the inner door was not. It was unusual enough to stop Ashlyn in her tracks.

James *never* used this door, partly because there were two steps that led down to a sidewalk that definitely needed some repair work. Since he wasn't quite steady on his feet, he always preferred to enter and exit through his front door, where there weren't any stairs and the sidewalk wasn't cracked and uneven.

So why was the kitchen door open? Had he gotten hurt and tried to go outside to get some help, and hadn't made it? Her heart beating a million miles an hour, Ashlyn didn't hesitate to go up the two steps and open the screen door.

When she stepped inside James's kitchen, she stared around in disbelief at the mess that greeted her.

It looked like every cabinet had been opened and emptied. There were containers and dishes everywhere. Even the pantry had been ransacked. There was flour and sugar all over the floor, their containers lying on their sides on top of the mess.

"James?" she called out, then mentally smacked her head in exasperation. It was stupid to call attention to herself when it was obvious the house had been burglarized—and she had no idea if the perpetrator was still in the house or not. She needed to call the police. But she couldn't leave without checking on James first.

She stepped over the worst of the mess and looked into the living room.

To her surprise, it wasn't James who came out of one of the bedrooms.

It was Aiden.

Their eyes met...and Ashlyn knew instinctively that she'd messed up big time. As soon as she saw the mess in the kitchen, she should've backed out of the house and called the police. It was too late now.

"What the fuck are you doing here?" he growled.

"What are *you* doing here?" Ashlyn countered, suddenly pissed. She knew she should be scared, and she was, but her anger overcame everything else at the moment. "James told me he fired you."

"He did. I came by to apologize, and to ask him to reconsider," Aiden said.

Ashlyn didn't believe a word he was saying. The living area was in as much disarray as the kitchen. It even looked as if the cushions had been sliced open with a knife! The stuffing was scattered all over the floor.

It hit her then—Aiden was looking for James's money. The cash he'd given to her just the day before for safekeeping. The older man had obviously known what he was doing by entrusting his life savings to her. Aiden wasn't going to find the cash he was so obviously searching for.

They stared at each other for a long moment. Then both jumped when the phone in Ashlyn's hand rang.

"Fuck!" Aiden stalked toward her surprisingly fast. He grabbed her arm in an iron-tight grip and squeezed. *Hard.* "Don't answer that."

Looking down, Ashlyn saw Slate's name on the screen. "It's my boyfriend. If I don't answer it, he's going to know something's wrong. I always answer his calls."

"No," Aiden growled as he reached for her other hand.

Ashlyn held on to her phone with a death grip. She knew it was her link to the outside world. To help. She had no idea where James was, or what Aiden had done to him, but she had a feeling it was nothing good.

And now that she was face-to-face with Aiden, she suspected he was on something. His pupils were tiny in his eyes and his cheeks were flushed. Even as he tried to get her phone, he kept looking around nervously, as if expecting someone else to appear out of nowhere. Not exactly an idle threat, since *she'd* done just that.

"Give me your goddamn phone!" Aiden shouted, prying it out of her hand. He pulled her into the living room and flung her down onto James's favorite chair. The cushion was missing, but Ashlyn barely noticed as she kept her eyes locked on Aiden.

He glared down at the phone. "What's your password?"

Ashlyn pressed her lips together. She wasn't giving this asshole the password to her phone.

Aiden took two steps forward, leaned over her, and hissed, "Give me the password or I'll fucking kill you!"

"Three, two, one, four, five, six," she said immediately. It hit her at that moment just how precarious her situation was. Aiden was desperate and backed into a corner. He'd done something to James, was in the process of robbing him, and now she was a witness. This wasn't good. Not good at all.

Aiden unlocked her phone and began to type.

"What are you doing?" she whispered.

"Answering your fucking boyfriend," he spat out.

Ashlyn thought about the tracking app for the first time. Slate would know where she was if he looked at it. But she'd already told him where she was going in her earlier text. So he'd have no reason to think anything was wrong if he saw her location.

Shit. She was in big trouble—and she had no idea what to do about it.

"Where's James?" she asked quietly.

"He's fine."

"Where is he?" she asked again.

"He's sleeping," Aiden said as he scowled at her phone once more, then threw it onto one of the shelves of a bookcase near Ashlyn. She stared at it for a moment. If Aiden got distracted, and she moved fast enough, she could grab it and dial 9-1-1. Or call Slate.

"Don't even think about it," Aiden said. "You won't make it. I would've broken the damn thing but I need it to work."

Ashlyn couldn't help but ask, "Why?"

"Because I need a patsy," Aiden said. He went to a table near the front door and grabbed something. He walked back toward her, spinning the object in his hand...and if Ashlyn had thought she was scared before, now she was *terrified*.

The object in his hand was a gun. Aiden having it made an already bad situation downright deadly.

"You're my patsy," he repeated, when Ashlyn didn't respond to his last statement. "Your phone records will show that you were here. Neighbors will have seen your car. You drugged James, ransacked his place, then left. The cops'll be all over your ass...and I won't even be a thought in their head."

"Aiden, you don't—" she started, but he laughed, cutting off her words.

"I *do* have to do this," he told her. "You don't get it! But it doesn't matter. Once I find his stash, we'll be on our way. I'll take care of you and be set for a good long while."

Ashlyn didn't even want to think about what "take care of you" might entail. She also wasn't going to say a damn word about his search for James's money being futile. The longer he searched, and the longer they were there, the better the chance Slate would figure out something was wrong and come looking for her.

Ashlyn had no doubt whatsoever that her overly protective boyfriend would eventually come. She had no idea what Aiden had said in the text he'd sent, but Slate was smart. He'd figure out it wasn't her and come to check on her. She knew that as well as she knew her name. She just hoped she'd still be there when he showed up.

"What? No comment?" Aiden sneered.

Ashlyn simply shook her head.

"Good. I'm sick of hearing you talk anyway. Sit your ass there and be good," Aiden ordered, pointing the gun at her head.

Ashlyn froze. She'd never looked down the barrel of a gun before and wasn't enjoying the experience. She gripped the arms of James's chair tightly and did her best to stay calm. Slate would come, she just had to be smart until he showed up.

Aiden stared at her for a second over the sights of the pistol, then laughed. He shoved the gun in the front waistband of his jeans and said, "Sit. Stay. Good dog." Then he smirked and resumed his search for James's money. Money he'd never find.

CHAPTER TWENTY-TWO

Slate frowned down at his phone, reading the text from Ashlyn. She hadn't answered his call, which was somewhat surprising. He couldn't remember a time when she hadn't picked up when he called. It might not be *too* surprising if she was in the middle of a conversation with James, even though that had never stopped her in the past. But it was the text that convinced him something wasn't right.

Ashlyn: bsy cnt talk will cu soon I love you

Again, she'd never been too busy to talk to him. But that wasn't what had the hair on the back of Slate's neck standing straight up.

Ashlyn didn't abbreviate words when she texted. *Ever.* It was a small thing, and there was always the chance she was distracted and had done so this time for brevity. But Slate didn't think so.

He checked the tracker app once more and saw that she was at James's house. At least her phone was.

He was moving before he'd thought about what he was doing.

Slate needed to head over...just to make sure everything was all right. If he was overreacting, so be it. Ashlyn would complain that he was being overprotective and he needed to tone it down, and he'd apologize. But if he *wasn't* overreacting...

Slate had no idea what could go wrong during a visit to James's house. He just knew that if he didn't act, and Ashlyn needed him, he'd never forgive himself. For all he knew, she sent that text to make it clear that something *was* wrong. As a message. Or it might not have been Ashlyn who'd sent it at all. Either option wasn't good.

He was grateful there wasn't a lot of traffic on the roads, because Slate drove a little recklessly, his intuition pushing him to get to Ashlyn as soon as possible.

He was five minutes from James's house when it occurred to him that he shouldn't be going in alone. He'd been too preoccupied thinking about what could be wrong, and why Ashlyn didn't answer her phone, and why she'd sent that odd text. He hadn't even thought about calling his teammates.

He rectified that now.

"Hey, Slate. What's up?" Mustang asked.

"I'm on my way to James Mason's house. I need backup," Slate told his team leader.

"What's the situation?" Mustang asked in a no-nonsense tone that actually helped calm Slate a fraction.

"I don't know. I'm going in blind. Ashlyn's not answering her phone, and I just got a text that didn't sound like her. There might not be anything wrong...but James gave her twenty grand yesterday that he'd been hiding around his house because he hates banks. Told her to keep it safe for him. He also fired his home health aide because he caught him spying on him after he'd supposedly left. I'm not getting warm and fuzzy feelings."

"You call anyone else?"

"No. Just you."

"I'll take care of calling the team. Where are you?"

"I'll be on location in three."

"Wait for us," Mustang ordered.

Slate didn't like disobeying a direct order, but there was no way in hell he could wait outside when Ashlyn could be in danger. "You know I can't do that," he told his team leader.

"Fuck," Mustang swore, but didn't reprimand Slate. "Right. Get the lay of the land, gather intel, and pass it on before you go in then."

If something was wrong, Slate wasn't sure he'd be able to do that either, but he said, "Ten-four."

"We're comin', Slate. No way we're gonna let anything happen to your woman. Hear me?"

He did, but Slate knew better than most that sometimes shit happened no matter what preparations were made. No matter how deadly and accomplished the team was. "I hear you," he said belatedly. "I hope like hell I'm overreacting," he said, fear threatening to overwhelm him.

"You aren't," Mustang said. "I know you, and you might be an impatient son of a bitch, but your instincts are spot on. Watch your six and try not to shoot us when we make entry," Mustang said before clicking off the connection.

His team leader wasn't joking, it had happened in the past, team members getting caught in friendly fire incidents in chaotic situations, but that wouldn't be an issue today—as Slate realized he'd left his house without a weapon. It was a dumbass move, but he'd been more concerned about getting to Ashlyn than arming himself.

Slate prayed he hadn't made a deadly decision by leaving

without his gun, but tried to reassure himself that he was just as lethal without one. He'd been trained by the best of the best, knew how to kill with his bare hands and how to use things in his surroundings as weapons if necessary. And if Ashlyn was in danger, nothing would prevent him from eliminating the threat.

A few minutes later, Slate pulled onto James's street, and was actually relieved to see Ashlyn's car parked in front of the house. That didn't necessarily mean she was there, but it was a hell of a lot better than her phone being there and her car missing.

Slate threw his car into park a few houses down from James's and got out, leaving the keys in the ignition. He went into SEAL mode and did his best to make himself invisible as he made his way toward his target.

Avoiding the front entrance, Slate continued around the house until he reached the side door, which led into the kitchen. The screen door was shut, but the inner door was wide open. He listened for a moment and didn't hear anyone, which he didn't consider a good sign. But more disturbing was the state of the kitchen. There was food and debris everywhere. It looked as if the contents of the cabinets had been thrown out and left lying all over the counters, table, and even the floor.

Swearing to himself, he moved to the window beyond the door. He glanced in carefully, and saw James lying still on his bed. It looked as if he was sleeping.

Praying the door didn't squeak, Slate backtracked and entered the house. He stepped over as much of the broken ceramic and glass as he could, sticking to the wall. When he was just steps from the entryway that led into the living room, he finally heard someone speaking. But it wasn't Ashlyn.

"Fuck! This is bullshit! Where the hell is it?"

Slate didn't recognize the voice, but it didn't matter. Peeking around the entry, he breathed a sigh of relief when he saw Ashlyn. She was sitting in the chair James usually occupied. Her hands were gripping the arms of the chair and she had her gaze locked on the other side of the room. On a man with his back turned.

All of his training flew out the window. Mustang would kick his ass when he heard about this, but Slate's only thought was getting to Ashlyn.

He quickly stepped into the living area, his hands held out to his sides, indicating that he was unarmed.

Ashlyn's eyes widened when she saw him, but she didn't make a sound. The man in the room chose that moment to turn around.

Slate immediately recognized him as Aiden, the recently fired home health aide.

"What the fuck?" Aiden exclaimed. Ashlyn sprang up from the chair, even as Aiden barked, "No! Sit down!"

Ashlyn acted as if she didn't hear him, racing to Slate.

He wrapped his arms around her and immediately turned his back to the room. If Aiden had a weapon, any shots fired would likely go right through him and into Ashlyn, but getting her out of the direct line of sight was instinctual.

He could feel her trembling against him, but other than being scared, she seemed to be uninjured. A huge weight lifted from Slate's shoulders. She was upright, breathing, and seemed to be fine. He could work with that.

"Get away from her!" Aiden shouted.

Turning his head, Slate saw the man had taken a step closer. And he'd indeed produced a pistol. He could only assume he'd had it on his person somewhere.

"No," Slate said, trying to stay calm as he assessed the situation.

"I knew you'd come," Ashlyn whispered.

"Of course," he said.

"Shut the fuck up!" Aiden yelled, a little hysterically now.

Tensing, Slate peeled Ashlyn away and pushed her farther behind him as he turned to face the man.

"Thought you were fired," Slate said before he thought better of it. Agitating the man further wasn't smart. He was just so damn relieved to see Ashlyn alive that he wasn't thinking clearly. He had to get his shit together.

"Yeah, well, thought I'd come by and thank the old man personally for ruining my life," Aiden sneered.

It was then Slate realized the guy was under the influence of some sort of drug. It was going to be very hard to reason with him. And it made the weapon he was brandishing all the more threatening. Aiden was obviously desperate and not thinking clearly.

"Shit!" he seethed, not lowering the weapon. "This is not going the way I'd planned!"

"Knew that text wasn't from Ashlyn," Slate said, wanting to keep the man talking. He had to give Mustang and his team time to get there. "It was a good attempt, but I know my woman. She never uses abbreviations in her texts."

"Whatever. Get away from her! Go sit over there on the couch," Aiden ordered.

"No."

Aiden frowned. "What?"

"No. I'm staying here with Ashlyn," Slate said. What he really wanted to do was push Ashlyn into the kitchen and tell her to run, but even though they weren't that far from the entrance, the route was still in the direct line of fire. He'd have to keep her behind him for the time being.

"Damn it!" Aiden exclaimed. "I'm the one with the gun! Do as I say!" He was seriously agitated.

"Are you looking for James's money?" Slate asked. "Maybe

we can help you search. The sooner you find it, the sooner you can leave."

Aiden looked confused for a second, then he sneered. "Sure, right, you'll help me look. I'm not an idiot! The second my back is turned you're gonna jump me. I know who you are. The old man talked about you all the time. You're a fuckin' bigshot Navy SEAL. I'm not taking my eyes off you for a second!"

"If you know who I am, you know this isn't going to end well for you," Slate said in a deadly tone.

"You're wrong!" The words came out shrill.

"There *is* no money," Ashlyn told Aiden softly.

"Hush, Ash," Slate said, a little more harshly than he'd intended.

"No, don't fucking hush! What do you mean? I was with James when he cashed that check a couple days ago. And I know for a fact he's got bills all over this fucking house," Aiden said, waving the gun around as he spoke.

"He saw you spying on him," Ashlyn told him. "He realized you were stealing. He gathered all his cash and gave it to me for safekeeping. You looked at my texts. You had to have seen one of the last ones I sent to Slate. I deposited it in the bank this morning. There's nothing here to find."

Slate tensed as he saw Aiden's eyes widen in disbelief. "No..." he whispered.

"I'm sorry," Ashlyn said, and she truly sounded as if she regretted there being no money in the house for Aiden to steal. "Your best bet at this point is to leave. Just go out the door and get the hell out of here."

"I *need* that money! I have to have it," Aiden said, sounding seconds away from breaking into tears.

Slate subtly pushed Ashlyn more firmly behind him, preparing to rush Aiden, when the other man said, "Then I'll just have to take you with me. We'll go to the bank and get it back. Once I have it, I'll drop you off somewhere and we'll both go about our business."

He was seriously delusional. There was no way Slate was going to let him leave the house with Ashlyn. And there was no way *any* of them believed he'd just drop her off somewhere, safe and sound.

"Go, Aiden. It's over. You'll have a head start before we call the police," Ashlyn urged. "You can be far from here by the time they arrive."

"No!" Aiden yelled. "*No, no, no!* You don't understand!"

Slate understood that time was running out. Aiden was quickly becoming unhinged. He couldn't wait for his team to get there. He thought about James lying still on his bed. It was possible he wasn't sleeping, that Aiden had killed him, and the thought gutted him.

This needed to end. Now.

He shifted, getting ready to make his move—

A crash sounded from the back of the house...from the direction of the bedroom.

Aiden turned automatically to look toward the sound, the hand holding the gun dropped slightly—and Slate lunged.

Aiden reflexively pulled the trigger, shooting wildly in different directions as Slate charged, tackling him around the waist.

They both went flying backward, slamming into a bookshelf against the wall with their combined weight. The crack of Aiden's head hitting the edge of a shelf was loud, despite the ringing in Slate's ears from the gunshots. He could also hear Ashlyn yelling behind him, but his concentration was on mitigating the threat.

They crashed to the floor amid piles of books. When they were on down, Slate grabbed Aiden's wrist but the gun was no longer in his hand. Looking around, he saw it lying nearby.

Aiden wasn't even fighting him, but Slate wasn't taking

any chances. His adrenaline pumping through his veins, he lurched sideways and shoved the weapon out of arm's reach. Then he reached for Aiden's other wrist and pinned the man as he tried to catch his breath.

"Slate! Oh my God, you're bleeding!" Ashlyn cried.

It wasn't until that moment that Slate realized his arm was on fire. Looking down, he saw a dark red stain on the upper sleeve of his shirt and felt the blood begin to run down his biceps.

"Shit!" he exclaimed, flexing his arm. It hurt like hell, but the blood wasn't spurting out, which was a good sign. "Lift my sleeve, Ashlyn. I don't want to let go of him to look at it."

Ashlyn stepped toward them, her face white as a sheet, and gingerly pulled up the sleeve of his T-shirt as he'd asked. There was a strip of flesh missing from his upper arm. It was painful and messy, but not life threatening.

"Is he..." Ashlyn's words tapered off as she looked down at the unmoving man beneath him.

Slate finally realized that Aiden still wasn't struggling. A pool of blood under his head was growing at an alarming rate.

"Fuck," Slate said. He slowly let go of the man's wrists and scooted back until he was sitting on his heels. Aiden remained still, exactly as he'd landed. His eyes were closed, and when Slate studied him closer, he couldn't see his chest moving up and down.

"Not much we can do for him," Slate said. "You want to go check on James?" He wanted her out of this room. Didn't want her to have to look at Aiden's dead body any longer than she already had.

When Slate turned to look at Ashlyn, he was alarmed to find her swaying on her feet. He didn't think it was possible, but her face looked even more ashen now than it had a moment ago.

"Um...I don't feel good," she whispered.

Slate was moving even before her legs collapsed under her.

"Ash!" he cried as he caught her and lowered her to the floor. He put her on her back and ran his hands over her body frantically, trying to figure out what was wrong. When he brushed the left side of her chest, she let out a small moan.

She wore a black shirt, and he couldn't see any blood, but he didn't hesitate to lift the cotton to find the source of her pain.

For a second, Slate had a hard time wrapping his mind around what he was seeing.

There was a small hole in her chest, just below her breast.

Way too fucking close to her heart.

As he watched, blood pulsed out of her body, as if in time with her heartbeat.

"Slate?" she whispered. "I can't breathe very well."

Lowering her shirt, he clamped his hand over the wound. Hard.

This time, Ashlyn cried out in pain, arching into him, trying to dislodge his hand.

"No, stay still," he ordered. His words sounded weird to his own ears.

Ashlyn stopped moving, bringing a hand up to grip his wrist tightly. "He shot me?" she asked.

"Looks that way. But don't worry, you'll be fine." Slate knew he was talking out his ass. He had no idea if that was true or not. If the bullet nicked her heart, she'd bleed out in a matter of minutes. He rose on his knees and pressed harder on the wound, desperate to keep that from happening.

"Oh, God, Slate!" she wheezed in an anguished tone.

"No!" he practically barked at her. "Do not go there. You're going to be fine!"

But a tear escaped her eye, sliding down into the hair at her temple. "I love you."

"I love you too, but don't you think this is the end. I just found you, I'm not losing you now!" Where the fuck was his team?

He knew it probably wasn't a fair question; it felt as if hours had gone by since he'd arrived, but in reality it had only been a matter of minutes, not enough time for his team to get here yet. But the truth was, he needed them more now than he ever had before.

A sound behind him had Slate whipping his head around, but he didn't let up on the pressure on Ashlyn's chest. If Aiden hadn't actually died when his head busted open after hitting that shelf, and he'd been able to get a hold of the gun once more, Slate still wouldn't lift his hands. Someone would have to fucking shoot him to get him to leave Ashlyn's side.

But it wasn't Aiden. He was still lying motionless where he'd fallen. It was James. He looked tired, and definitely not one hundred percent all there. He'd propped himself up against the doorjamb of his kitchen.

"I called the police," he said. "They're coming."

As relieved as he was to see the older man alive, Slate couldn't do anything but nod and turn his attention back to Ashlyn. "Hear that, babe? Help is on the way. No, don't close your eyes! Keep them on me."

He could tell she was trying to cling to consciousness but was losing the battle.

"Slate," she whispered.

His throat closed up, and Slate swallowed hard. Ashlyn needed him to be strong right now. He couldn't lose his shit.

He opened his mouth but before he could say anything, he heard footsteps in the kitchen. Then his team was there. Slate had never been so relieved to see anyone in his entire life.

"Mustang...!" he said, not hiding the anguish he felt as he looked up at his team leader.

Mustang and Midas immediately knelt by Ashlyn's side.

Aleck and Pid went to James, and Jag headed for Aiden. Simply having his team with him gave Slate hope.

"Gunshot wound to the left chest," Slate told them.

"Okay, just stay where you are, keep that pressure on and don't let go no matter what," Mustang ordered.

Slate nodded jerkily and stared back down at Ashlyn. She hadn't taken her gaze from his face. She was laboring to breathe but wasn't panicking.

"You're doing great, babe. Just keep breathing, no matter what. Hear me?"

"I hear you," she said on a gasp.

Slate could hear Pid on the phone, most likely talking to a dispatcher about what was going on. He knew he needed to give his team a rundown of what had happened, but he couldn't. All he could do was stare at Ashlyn and try to lend her his strength.

"You're doing so good," he praised.

"Am I going to die?" she asked.

"No fucking way," he said, a little harsher than he'd intended.

"But he shot me..."

"He got me too," Slate reminded her. "But I'm gonna be fine, and so are you."

"I think...being grazed in the arm is...different than... being shot in the chest," she wheezed.

"That's my girl. Always disagreeing with me," Slate said.

"Because I'm right and you're wrong," she said weakly.

Slate wanted to yell at the unfairness of what was happening. Intellectually, he knew this was a freak incident. She couldn't have known Aiden would be at James's house today. Hell, none of them had a clue he could be dangerous. And yet, here they were.

Sirens sounded in the distance, and Slate said, "Hear that,

babe? They're almost here. The EMTs will get you all fixed up and you'll be as good as new."

There was no color in Ashlyn's face whatsoever now, and she was gasping for air. "No matter...what...happens," she said between gasps. "I'll never...regret asking you...to be my friend-with-benefits."

"Best day of my life," Slate told her honestly. "Took me too long to get my head out of my ass and see the treasure I had right in front of me, but I've never met a woman as perfect for me as you." He kept talking because he was afraid if he didn't, she'd close her eyes and stop fighting. "You made me less grumpy, less impatient, and more appreciative of what I have in my life."

"But you still drive...too fast," she said, attempting to smile. Then she closed her eyes.

"No! Look at me, babe," Slate ordered frantically.

It took her a moment, but she forced her eyes back open.

"I love you. More than I ever thought I'd love anyone in my life. Don't you leave me!" he begged, the tears finally breaking free of his iron control and slipping down his cheeks. "You've made me a better man, a better SEAL, a better friend. I need you!"

"It hurts, Slate," she whispered.

"I know, and I'm sorry. But as the SEALs say, the only easy day was yesterday. Fight, Ash. For you, for me...for us."

"I will."

"I know it hurts, but the pain means you're alive. Don't give in, please!"

Ashlyn licked her lips and nodded. Then her eyes closed once again, and the tight grip she had on his wrist slackened before her hand fell to the floor.

"Fuck," Slate whispered, tears steadily falling off his cheeks and onto her shirt, soaking into the material as he hovered over her.

"Everyone put your hands where we can see them!" a loud voice ordered, but Slate ignored it. He wasn't moving his hands from Ashlyn's chest. The cop who'd just entered the house would have to shoot him first.

It took a short while for the police to secure the scene and reassure themselves that the men in the house weren't a threat. Not long after that, the first paramedics entered. And still Slate didn't remove his hands. Mustang spoke for him, explaining Ashlyn's condition and as much about the situation as he could.

"You need to scoot back," one of the paramedics said. "We'll take over from here."

Slate couldn't move. He was frozen in fear.

It was Jag who convinced him to let the paramedics do their job by saying, "You've done all you can, Slate. If you want to give her a chance, you need to let them do their thing."

Slate looked up and met the gaze of the nearest paramedic. Staring him in the eye, he said, "She's my everything! Please don't let her die."

He could've sworn he saw a look of determination creep into the other man's eyes. "I've never lost a patient before, and I'm not starting today," he replied.

Nodding, Slate moved. He lifted his hands and quickly scooted backward, giving up his place by Ashlyn's side to the two men. They worked fast, cutting off her shirt, getting a quick look at the wound in her chest, then putting pressure on it once again.

"Load and go," one of the young men said. With the help of his team, they got Ashlyn onto a stretcher and were headed out the front door before two more minutes had passed.

Slate tried to follow but one of the police officers stopped him. "We're gonna need you to explain what happened."

Without taking his eyes off the stretcher holding the woman who was his entire world, currently lying motionless, Slate said, "Then you better get your ass in gear, because I'm going to the hospital with my woman."

Luckily, Aleck stepped in and finessed the situation. Slate was well aware that there was a dead man on the floor behind him, and a good possibility he could be charged with manslaughter, but nothing was going to keep him from being at the hospital with Ashlyn.

"Slate?"

The only thing that could've stopped him from following the ambulance right that second was James. Slate turned. Pid had gotten the older man to the couch. He looked at Slate with conviction.

"She's gonna be all right."

James didn't know anything more than Slate did at that point. He wasn't a psychic. Couldn't tell the future. But for some reason, those five words settled in Slate's soul. "I know," he said, nodding at the man. Then he turned and headed for the door.

Pid was on his heels, keys in hand. "I'm driving."

Slate nodded again. He was in no condition to drive, and he knew it. The last thing he wanted was to get into an accident and be unable to take care of Ashlyn when she was allowed to come home. And she *would* be coming home. He wouldn't accept anything less.

CHAPTER TWENTY-THREE

Slate sat in the private waiting room the nurses had unlocked for all of Ashlyn's supporters. Everyone was there. Elodie, Lexie, Kenna, Monica, Carly, his team and Commander Huttner. Elodie's friend Kai, from the fishing charter she'd worked for once upon a time. Theo, a regular at Food For All, not to mention several coworkers from the food bank: Jack, Pika, Courtney, Natalie, and Richard. Even Kaleen, one of the bartenders from Duke's, had heard about what happened and had come to show her support. Then there were the men, women, and children who Ashlyn delivered food to each week...Lori, the handicapped woman's sister; the Turner family; Jazmin and her baby; and several others who Slate didn't know.

James was there too. He'd been brought in for tests to make sure he was all right after being drugged by Aiden. He'd refused to go home after he was cleared, and was now sitting amongst Ashlyn's friends, praying and worrying about her.

It was more than obvious how loved Ashlyn was. She'd touched all these people with her kindness and open spirit.

Slate knew he should be talking to everyone, reassuring them, but he couldn't find it within him to do anything but sit and stare into space, lost in his thoughts.

All the time he and Ashlyn had spent together spun through his head. The times they'd playfully argued. How excited she'd been to show him some of the moves she'd learned at self-defense training. Her frequent laughter. The expression on her face when she was irritated with him. The way her cheeks flushed when she was angry, or upset, or turned on. Her enthusiasm in bed, her willingness to give all of herself even for a casual fling...that wasn't so casual on either of their parts. He thought about how good she felt in his arms as they slept. How she loved to cuddle. How she could sleep like a freaking rock.

He couldn't lose her. He *couldn't*.

Slate had no idea how he'd function without her. The panic he'd felt when he thought she was on a date was *nothing* compared to the soul-deep dread he was feeling right now.

"Duncan Stone?" a man asked, entering the waiting area.

"That's me," Slate said, standing so fast he wavered on his feet. Mustang was immediately on one side to steady him, Pid on the other.

Slate had no idea how much time had passed since he'd arrived at the hospital. But his team had been with him for every second. Pid had convinced him to wash his hands and had bought him a T-shirt at the gift shop so he could throw away the bloody one he had on.

When Aleck had arrived, he'd forced Slate to allow a doctor to look at his arm. As he'd thought, it was simply a graze, and a nurse had cleaned and bandaged it. Then Mustang arrived with two police officers, and Slate had told them everything he knew about what had happened. How Aiden had threatened them with a weapon, how he was looking for money to steal, and was planning on kidnapping Ashlyn. He admitted that he'd tackled Aiden, and that the man had cracked his head open on a shelf.

Slate told the officers about the money James had given Ashlyn, and that she'd deposited it into an account for safe-keeping.

He held nothing back, only wanting to get the interview done so he could find out something, anything, about Ashlyn's condition. Instead, he'd waited anxiously for hours.

Aleck told him a short while ago that everything he'd said matched up with the evidence at the scene, and with what James had told the police. Apparently, Aiden had tried to give James a quadruple dose of sleeping pills, but the older man was suspicious of the way his former aide was pushing him to drink his glass of tea. He told the police that Aiden had drugged him in the past without his consent, and realized too late that he'd probably been doing it for weeks.

James had still ingested some of the drugs when he'd reluctantly sipped the tea, but not enough to kill him or keep him asleep for long. He'd heard Aiden's yelling in the other room, had attempted to get up, and had fallen against his bedside table, knocking the lamp to the floor. That was the noise that had distracted Aiden long enough for Slate to tackle him.

The entire situation was fucked up. From what they'd gathered from talking to coworkers, his boss, and a couple others who knew him, Aiden used to be a dedicated employee and a hard worker. But he'd been hurt on the job about a year ago, and took painkillers to manage his back pain. When his doctor stopped prescribing them, he'd apparently turned to harder drugs, quickly spiraling into addiction, desperate for more of the dope to manage his pain and to keep from going through withdrawal.

The doctor gestured for Slate to step out of the room with him...and for just a second, he hesitated. If he didn't go with him, the doctor couldn't give him bad news about Ashlyn. But then again, he couldn't tell him good news either. So Slate took a deep breath and followed.

Mustang exited the room with him, and Slate was once again grateful his team leader was there. It had been his idea to tell the hospital staff that Slate was Ashlyn's husband. Slate didn't think anyone believed him, but since Ashlyn had no other relatives on the island, the staff didn't call them on it.

The doctor didn't hesitate. "Ashlyn is out of surgery. The bullet missed her heart by millimeters. She was very lucky. It hit her lung, which was why she was having a hard time breathing. She'll be moved to ICU shortly."

"She'll be okay?" he whispered.

"Barring infection or any other complications, yes," the doctor said.

Every muscle in Slate's body seemed to go lax. Mustang wrapped an arm around his shoulders, giving Slate the strength to stay on his feet. "When I can I see her?" he asked.

"It'll be a few hours. She's sedated right now, and we'll keep her that way until we're sure she can breathe on her own."

"Will you let me know the second I can visit her?" Slate asked.

"Of course. I don't usually tell family members this kind of thing, but...the surgery wasn't easy for her. Her blood pressure tanked twice, but both times she managed to rally without us having to resort to medical intervention. Your wife is a fighter."

Instead of getting upset at the doctor's words, for the first time, complete relief swept through Slate. His Ashlyn was tough as hell, and she'd done just what he'd begged her to do.

Fought for her life. She didn't give in when it would've been easier and less painful to do so.

"I'm not surprised. She's *definitely* a fighter," Slate said.

"And very well loved, if the number of people in that room is any indication," the doctor said, gesturing to the waiting room behind them. "I'm gonna go check on my patient. Why don't you go in there and let everyone know the good news."

"Thank you," Slate said, gratitude lacing the simple words.

"You're welcome." Then the doctor nodded at both Mustang and Slate and headed back down the hall.

Slate turned to Mustang and hugged him. Tightly. His friend returned the embrace. There was a time, not terribly long ago, when Slate never would've shared this kind of intimacy with his friends. But the women in their lives had slowly but surely broken down their walls when it came to showing affection.

"Thank you for being there for us," Slate said quietly. "For saving my life in Afghanistan and every other damn time I've needed you...and for believing me when I said I thought something was wrong earlier today."

Mustang pulled back and put his hands on Slate's shoulders. The two SEALs' gazes met, and they shared a long look of understanding. "I'll *never* not believe you," Mustang said after a moment. "You're my brother in all the ways that count, just as Ashlyn's my sister. I'd give my life for either of you. I hope you know that."

"I do, and I'd do the same for you and Elodie."

Mustang nodded. "I'm so damn relieved she's gonna be all right."

"Me too, brother. Me too," Slate said.

"How about we go let the others know what the doctor said. Ashlyn's got a lot of friends who would probably really like to hear some good news right about now."

Slate nodded and took a deep breath. His shoulders dropped, and suddenly he was exhausted. He'd been operating on pure adrenaline for hours. Now that the danger had passed, he felt exactly as he did after a long and dangerous mission.

"After we share the news, I'll see if I can't find a place for you to crash," Mustang said, seeing that Slate was at the end of his rope.

"I need to see Ash as soon as the doc says it's okay," he protested.

"And you will," Mustang replied. "But you don't need to look like you've been awake for three damn days when you do. You need to be her strength for a while, and you can't do that if you can barely stand. I know you're an impatient asshole, but you're gonna listen to me this one time."

Slate chuckled. "This *one* time?"

"Okay, you have to listen to me *all* the time since I'm your team leader. But you're gonna have to put that impatience aside for once and get some sleep for Ashlyn."

That, Slate could do. He nodded.

"Shit, I pray getting you to do what I want is this easy in the future," Mustang muttered.

"Don't count on it. I'm still a brooding, impatient asshole."

"Wouldn't want you any other way. Come on, let's go share the news."

Slate walked back into the waiting room, once again awed by everyone who'd dropped everything to come to the hospital and show their support for Ashlyn. It took him way too long to see how perfect she was for him, but he'd finally pulled his head out of his ass. It was a miracle that she'd ever been interested in him in the first place. He was kind of a jerk to her when they'd first met. Condescending, always assuming he knew better than she did when it came to her safety.

The bottom line was that Ashlyn was a giving soul, and he vowed right then and there to do whatever it took to give her the space and support she needed to keep being the kind of person she was. What happened today had been a fluke. Yes, they both probably needed to be a bit more aware of what was going on in the lives of the people she helped, but Slate wouldn't use injury as an excuse to stifle her. She'd wither away and die if she couldn't give assistance to others.

He'd always be overprotective and bossy, but for the woman he loved, he'd do what he could to help her spread kindness, and never stand in her way.

The room filled with sighs of relief and plenty of tears as everyone learned that their friend was going to be all right. As Slate hugged each and every person who'd come to show their support to Ashlyn, he couldn't keep the smile off his face. Ashlyn would love this. Would love seeing all her friends together like this...all of them supporting each other.

* * *

Later that night, after almost everyone had left, knowing they wouldn't be able to see Ashlyn that evening, and after Slate had rested for a short while, it was now just him and Mustang in the waiting room. A nurse opened the door and said that Ashlyn was stable and could have a visitor.

"I'll wait here and drive you home after," Mustang said.

Slate wanted to protest. Wanted to say that he'd stay here with Ashlyn. But since she was in ICU, he knew he wouldn't be allowed to stay by her side. It was practical for him to go home, shower, change, get some more sleep and something to eat, before coming back in the morning.

"Thanks."

"Stop thanking me. It's annoying," Mustang told him. "I think I prefer the crabby Slate."

303

"Oh, I'm sure he'll be back sooner rather than later. Especially once Ashlyn is on the mend and wants to go back to work before she should, making me crazy."

Mustang laughed. "True. Okay, then, you're welcome. Go see your woman. Give her my and Elodie's love."

Slate nodded and followed the nurse out of the room. He was led to a set of locked double doors, and they were buzzed in by a nurse in the ICU. He put on a sterile gown someone handed him and booties over his shoes. Itchy to see for himself that Ashlyn was all right, he did his best to control his impatience.

Finally, they led him to a cubicle, and drew back the curtain. The nurse was saying something, but Slate didn't hear her. He only had eyes for his woman.

Ashlyn was lying on the white sheets, and she had more color in her cheeks than the last time he'd seen her, being wheeled away toward the ambulance. She had IVs in both arms and an oxygen cannula in her nose. But she wasn't intubated, and almost looked like she was just resting peacefully, instead of like a woman who'd almost died.

Slate didn't bother with the chair, he took her hand in his and leaned in close.

"Hey, babe," he whispered.

To his surprise, her eyes immediately popped open. Her mouth moved, but no words escaped her lips.

"I've never seen anything as beautiful as your brown eyes," Slate told her.

"Slate," she whispered.

"I'm here," he reassured her.

"Tell me," she ordered.

"Tell you what?" Slate asked.

"What happened. I'm okay?"

"You're okay," he quickly said. "You were shot, but the

bullet missed your heart. Did some damage to your lung though. The doctors patched you up, and you'll be as good as new soon."

Ashlyn smiled. "I think you're leaving a lot of stuff out."

He was and he wasn't. "Nope. Just summing it up as quickly as possible for you."

"James?" she asked.

"He's fine. Ingested some sleeping pills, but not enough to keep him down for long. The guys arranged for him to stay at a hotel while the police finish with the investigation at his house, and they'll make sure it's cleaned up and ready for him to return as soon as possible."

"Good. Aiden?"

Figured she'd be worried about the asshole who'd shot her.

"Dead," Slate said succinctly.

"Don't care. Will you get in trouble?" she asked.

Slate's lips twitched. All right then, guess she wasn't worried about Aiden, after all. "No. It was self-defense."

"Okay." Then she croaked, "You're bossy."

Slate's brows came down in confusion. Not because he *didn't* think he was bossy, he definitely was, but he wasn't sure why Ashlyn had mentioned that *now*. "Yeah," he agreed.

"You yelled at me when I was in the operating room. I was asleep, but wasn't. You told me to fight. I didn't want to. I hurt. But you wouldn't get out of my head. Ordering me to suck it up and come back to you. I think I'm mad at you..."

Tears immediately welled in Slate's eyes. He'd cried more today than he could ever remember crying in the past. But he wasn't ashamed. How could he be? "You can be mad, babe. But I'm proud of you for not giving in. You're gonna be all right now. I'm here, and I'm gonna make sure of it."

"Love you, Slate."

"And I love you, Ashlyn. Go ahead and close your eyes and get some sleep. I'll be back later to check on you."

Ashlyn nodded and her eyes slid closed. Then they popped open, as if she'd thought of something.

"What? What is it, babe?"

"You sure it's okay for me to close my eyes? You said I couldn't."

"That was before. You're good now," Slate said, trying to control the wavering of his voice.

His reassurance seemed to be all she needed to hear, because her eyes closed again and she sighed before her breathing deepened.

Slate stood over her for several minutes, watching her breathe, and silently crying as he did so. Then he took a deep breath, rubbed his face on his sleeve, and leaned over Ashlyn once more. He kissed her gently on the lips before standing. He placed her hand on the bed and turned to leave the small cubicle area.

Slate stopped short at seeing three nurses staring at him from the entrance.

"The second she woke up from the surgery, she was asking for you," one said.

"She wouldn't settle until we reassured her over and over that you were all right," another added.

"Her heart rate is slower now," the third observed, nodding toward the monitor.

Slate nodded at them, not surprised in the least. His Ashlyn was one hell of a fighter, and it was so like her to want to make sure he was all right when *she* was the one who'd been shot and had almost died on the surgical table.

She was going to be all right. So was he. They had the rest of their lives to spend together, and Slate vowed not to squander one day of it.

He left the ICU in a much better mood than he'd entered

it. Seeing Ashlyn had done wonders for his psyche. The next couple of weeks would be tough, her recovery wouldn't be easy, but together they'd get through it, stronger both mentally and as a couple for the experience.

A smile crossed his face for the first time since he'd said goodbye to her that morning.

EPILOGUE

Four months later

Ashlyn lay in the dim bedroom, waiting for Slate to come to bed. She was determined to get their lives back to normal. And normal meant *sex*. She was ready. More than ready. But Slate was being overly cautious, not wanting to do anything that might cause her pain.

She'd had a checkup with the doctor today, and he'd told them both that she could resume normal activities...including sex. He'd followed up that statement with a warning that he wouldn't recommend sky diving or scuba diving for a while still, but since neither of those things were on Ashlyn's agenda, she was more than happy to agree.

While she more than appreciated Slate's attentiveness over the last few months, she was done being treated like she was made of glass.

During the last few weeks, Slate had relented a fraction, allowing her to use her hands to get him off, and giving her slow, easy orgasms with his fingers. But he'd refused to make love with her, saying that if he did anything to cause her an iota of pain, he'd never forgive himself.

But tonight, after the doctor had officially cleared her, Ashlyn was done waiting. She wanted her man.

Slate entered the room quietly, obviously thinking she was already asleep. He went into the bathroom and came out a couple minutes later wearing nothing but a pair of boxer shorts.

The second he climbed under the covers, Ashlyn moved. She threw one leg over his hips, straddling him. She'd purposely stripped off all her clothes before climbing under the covers.

Arching her back a bit, Ashlyn stared down at Slate and dared him to refuse her.

Slate inhaled deeply, and his hands came up to grip her hips.

"I love you," she said softly.

"I love you too," Slate returned immediately.

"It's time, Slate. What happened sucked...but I'm fine. Perfect. You heard the doctor today. I want to make love with my boyfriend."

"Fiancé," he corrected.

Ashlyn rolled her eyes. Whenever he introduced her to anyone, he always called her his fiancée. But he'd yet to make that status official.

She held up her left hand and made a big deal out of looking at her bare finger. "Huh, look at that," she said in mock-amazement. "My finger seems to be naked."

It was a running joke between them. Ashlyn had every intention of marrying the man, but it was fun to give him shit for *assuming* she'd marry him before he'd even popped the question.

He suddenly moved under her, and Ashlyn let out a girly screech. But she didn't have to worry about falling off Slate, because he kept one hand firmly on her hip as he reached for the drawer in the small table next to the bed.

He grabbed something, then reached for her left hand. Without a word, Slate slid a ring down her finger.

"There, now it's not naked anymore," he said with a satisfied grin.

Ashlyn could only stare at the ring he'd put on her finger. It was a princess-cut diamond solitaire that winked in the muted light from the lamp on Slate's nightstand. Her mouth opened, then closed, then opened again. She couldn't seem to form any coherent thoughts.

"I've rendered you speechless," Slate said with a small chuckle. "Mark this day down."

Ashlyn swallowed hard and blinked fast to keep from crying all over him.

"It's not huge," Slate said after a moment. "I wanted to get you the biggest diamond I could find, but that would just put you in danger. The last thing I want is someone seeing it and thinking they can steal it from you. So I went conservative."

"It's perfect," Ashlyn said after a moment.

"*You're* perfect," Slate countered. "I thought I wanted casual. But from the moment I touched you, I think I knew that was impossible. You crawled under my skin from the get-go, babe...and I've never been happier."

She waited a beat, but when he didn't say anything else, she raised an eyebrow and rested her palms on his chest. Seeing the ring on her finger made her want to smile in glee, but she forced herself to look serious. "You put a ring on it, but I still didn't hear you *ask* me anything," she told him.

In response, Slate lifted his hands and palmed both her breasts.

Inhaling sharply, Ashlyn let her head fall back.

He kneaded her sensitive nipples, and she felt his thumb brush over the scar under her left breast. She wanted to reas-

FINDING ASHLYN

sure him yet again that she was all right. That she was alive and Aiden's bullet hadn't killed her, but Slate moved a hand to her back and encouraged her to lean down.

His mouth closed over one of her nipples, and Ashlyn couldn't think about anything other than how good he was making her feel.

Slate spent a good bit of time worshiping her breasts before gently turning her onto her back. He immediately scooted down her body and kissed both inner thighs before turning his attention between her legs.

This wasn't the fast and desperate sex they used to have. While Ashlyn adored their rougher sex, and couldn't wait until they were both so out of control they felt like they had to have each other or die, she also craved this.

It felt like a reaffirmation of their love. It was so different from where they'd started, just wanting to feel good without the deeper complication of affections.

Slate worshiped her as he slowly brought her closer and closer to orgasm. But instead of pushing her over, he stopped when she was right at the precipice. He stripped off his boxers and scooted up until the tip of his cock brushed against her clit. Slate took hold of the base of his dick with one hand and balanced himself over her with the other.

He gently pressed himself against her, sliding inside inch by inch.

Ashlyn moaned and gripped his ass cheeks. "Faster," she begged.

But Slate ignored her. His gaze was locked on hers as he took her. When it felt as if he'd melded their souls, not just their bodies, Slate eased down onto his elbows.

Ashlyn could feel the slight hair on his chest rub against her nipples. She felt surrounded by him, and never wanted to move.

"I love you," Slate said softly. "I want to spend the rest of

311

my life with you. I want to wake up with you next to me, and go to sleep with you curled into my side. I want to laugh, cry, and watch annoying chick flicks with you."

Ashlyn wrinkled her nose at him.

He smiled. "I'm gonna be a pain in your ass a lot. I'm probably going to be even more overprotective than I was before."

"Probably?" Ashlyn quipped.

"But I can promise you that while on missions, I won't take risks. I won't do anything stupid that will take me from you. You're it for me, Ash. I'm never gonna want another woman. Ever."

Ashlyn took a deep breath and nodded.

"Will you marry me? You could do so much better, but I'm not letting you go. I mean, I would if you hated me, because I'm not a psycho stalker, but it would literally kill me. I'd probably waste away into a shell of the man I am now. I'd stop eating, lose a ton of weight, the Navy would have to kick me out because a ninety-eight-pound weakling as a Navy SEAL isn't exactly a good thing."

Ashlyn couldn't help but giggle. Leave it to her man to make her want to laugh instead of cry.

"And now she's laughing at me," Slate said with a sigh.

Ashlyn reached up and put her hands on her man's cheeks. The engagement ring winked at her, and she couldn't help but smile. "Of course I'll marry you."

Slate beamed. "Good."

"I mean, the Navy would probably be really pissed if I said no and they had to replace you."

This time, Slate chuckled. "Right. Any other reason why you want to marry me?"

"Well..." Ashlyn pretended to think about it. "That's a tough one. You like gross Hawaiian food and you definitely drive too fast. You also have a tendency to stalk me on that tracker app. I'm thinking maybe it wasn't a good idea to give you access."

Slate's hips shifted, and he began to slowly rock in and out of her.

Ashlyn's thoughts scattered. All she could think about was how good he felt inside her.

"True, although I might have some redeeming qualities," he said as he continued to make love to her.

Ashlyn's hands clutched his sides as he continued to slowly fuck her. She dug her nails into his skin. "Faster, Slate," she moaned.

"No."

"No?" she echoed, frowning at him.

"I know what the doctor said, but there's no way in hell I'm gonna fuck you the way I've dreamed about for months. That's gonna wait until I'm completely satisfied you're one hundred percent healthy."

"Slate," Ashlyn whined. "What's that gonna take? Me running a 10K? Doing a thousand jumping jacks? I'm *fine*."

"You're gonna have to humor me," he told her with a straight face. "I lost twenty years off my life when I realized you were shot. For now, I'm gonna make love to you. Slow and easy. You don't like this?"

Ashlyn did like it. A lot. She swallowed. "I like it," she admitted. "But I like when you fuck me too."

His lips twitched. "You're insatiable."

"For you."

"Damn straight. You want to come?"

"Duh," she fired back.

His lips spread into a full-fledged grin. "Right. How about you do that then? Touch yourself, babe."

Ashlyn didn't hesitate. She slipped one hand between their bodies, grateful when Slate lifted his hips a bit to give her room. Then she began to flick her clit as he gently moved in and out of her.

"I love you and can't wait to marry you," Slate said as she got closer and closer to exploding.

"I love you," she returned with a gasp. "Name the time and place, and I'm there."

"Come on my cock, babe," he replied. "I can't hold back much longer."

It took her mere seconds. It had been too long since she'd had her man inside her, and he'd already primed her with his tongue.

She hunched into him as the orgasm overcame her, digging the nails of the hand still clutching him harder into his skin.

He groaned and lost some of his control, slamming into her once. Twice. Then a third time before he exploded and held himself deep inside her.

Slate's head dropped and he sealed his mouth to hers, kissing her passionately.

When his body stopped shaking, he turned them without taking his lips away.

When she finally pulled back, Ashlyn felt as if she'd run a marathon. She was panting and pleasantly sore between her legs. She could feel Slate still deep within her body.

"Love you," she murmured as she rested her head on his shoulder.

One of his hands gripped her ass, holding her to him, and the other rested on her back. "You good? No pain?"

"Not like you mean."

"You're hurt?" he asked sharply.

"It's been months. And you're thick, Slate. But it's a delicious pain. And you're gonna have to work hard to get me used to you again." She felt him relax under her when he realized she wasn't in pain from her healed gunshot. "I'm thinking you need to make love to me at least once a day for the next month so I get used to you again."

"You do, huh?" he asked.

"Yup."

Slate chuckled. "You need me to get up and get you some painkillers? Run you a bath?"

"If you move, I'm gonna have to hurt you," Ashlyn warned.

"Right."

"All I need is you. Holding me. Loving me."

"That I can do. For the rest of our lives."

Ashlyn smiled. It was funny how life turned out sometimes. She'd come to Hawaii to be with another man, but had ended up meeting the one person she couldn't live without.

"Sleep, babe," Slate ordered. "Tomorrow's gonna be long."

Ashlyn smiled against him. "'Kay."

He picked up her left hand, kissed the ring he'd put there earlier, then curled his hand around hers as he rested it back on his chest.

Ashlyn fell asleep with a huge smile on her face. Getting shot sucked, but she'd go through it all again if it meant she'd end up right here, with the man she loved more than life.

* * *

Ashlyn squeezed Slate's hand as he led her toward the spot Baker had commandeered for them, overlooking Waimea Bay. The surf spot was known for its deep water and big swells.

Surprisingly, Baker, the former SEAL who'd been such a big part of helping when the other women in their group needed it, was ridiculously pissed about what had happened to Ashlyn. When he'd come down to visit and check on her, he'd asked what he could do to help her heal. Ashlyn had jokingly told him that she wanted a front-row spot to watch one of the big surfing competitions.

He'd more than come through on that. He'd convinced a local with a house on the northeast side of the bay to let them use his yard to watch the competition. Ashlyn shouldn't be too surprised, since Baker seemed to have connections everywhere.

The traffic on Kamehameha Highway had been horrendous—it always was during surf competitions at the North Shore—but Slate didn't even seem to mind that it took them an hour to drive a mile and a half.

They were the last ones to arrive. She and Slate had gotten carried away in the shower that morning, and one thing had led to another, and they'd spent way too long demonstrating how much they loved each other. Slate was still very cautious with her, but Ashlyn was thrilled that he seemed to finally realize she was truly all right, and they could resume their normal love life.

"Hi, everyone," Ashlyn said, refusing to be embarrassed about their lateness. It wasn't as if the others hadn't shown up late to some outing or another because they couldn't keep their hands off each other.

"You're here!"

"Oh my God, you aren't going to believe the size of these waves!"

"This one guy wiped out so hard, but amazingly he popped back up and was fine."

"I saved you a front-row seat."

The last came from Carly.

Ashlyn beamed at her friends. She'd never forget how supportive they'd all been while she was in the hospital. Someone was always with her. If it wasn't Elodie sneaking in chocolatey homemade treats, it was Lexie bringing her a romance novel. Kenna, Monica, and Carly had also been constant companions, as had their husbands.

Not only that, but the other employees from Food For All had all shown up, as had her clients.

James had made it a point to be at her side in the hospital anytime Slate couldn't be there. He eventually had to return to work, so James settled himself in the chair in her room most days, refusing to budge until Slate came by in the late afternoons.

He'd gushed over Mustang and the rest of Slate's team, how they'd hired people to clean his house and arranged for new furniture...free of charge, of course. He had a new home health aide, who came from the best agency in the area. He sounded happy, which was a huge relief for Ashlyn.

And Slate had spent every night in the crappy foldout bed the hospital provided for relatives. Ashlyn had tried to get him to go home, but he refused. All in all, Ashlyn felt blessed. And looking around at Slate's SEAL team, and their women, she was reminded once again how lucky she was.

"You want a drink?" Slate asked, leaning into her from behind and brushing her ear with his lips.

"Yes, please. A margarita?"

Slate snorted. "No fucking way. It's too soon. I'll get you some juice."

Ashlyn rolled her eyes. Despite the all-clear from the doctor to resume her normal routines, with no restrictions on food or drink, Slate was taking it upon himself to be uber conservative about her food intake. He made her high-protein and low-carb breakfasts and dinners, insisting she eat more vegetables as well. It was cute...and beginning to border on annoying. But she tried to tell herself that Slate had suffered almost as much as she had that day. If it had been him lying on the floor with a gunshot wound to the chest, she'd be acting just like he was, so she let it go.

"Sit here," Elodie said, patting a chair between her and Carly.

Ashlyn walked over to where Elodie indicated and sat. She stared over the cliff at the bay, and gasped at what seemed to be the biggest wave she'd ever seen.

"Yeah, it's pretty amazing that there are people who voluntarily and eagerly go out in that, huh?" Elodie asked.

"It's downright terrifying," Ashlyn said. Then she looked around and said, "Is Monica coming?"

"I don't think so," Carly said. "She's having issues breast-feeding Charlotte. And of course, Pid was more than happy to stay home with his girls."

Ashlyn smiled. Monica had her baby a month ago, and Pid had basically lost his mind. He'd gone overboard, buying all sorts of outfits and taking a million pictures of his little girl. He was also very protective of her, including asking people to wear masks when they came to visit, which no one minded. Slate regularly bitched that Pid wasn't sharing his daughter like he should, which made Ashlyn laugh. Seeing her large, grumpy boyfriend holding the tiny little girl was so damn precious.

Slate returned with a glass and handed it to her. "You good? Need anything else?"

"No, I'm good, thanks."

"Don't sit in the sun too long, babe. You'll burn," he told her, then leaned down and kissed the top of her head. "I'm gonna go chat with the guys a bit."

"You aren't going to watch the competition?" she asked, looking up at him.

He smiled. "Not my thing," he said easily.

"Oh, you should've said something," Ashlyn said worriedly.

"I'm happy simply being with you, doesn't matter what we're doing. And if you want to see a surfing competition, I'll bend over backward to bring you to see a surfing competition."

"Even if the traffic drives you crazy? And all the tourists?"

"Yup. Let me know if you need anything," he said, nodding at Elodie, then heading for where Mustang, Jag, and the other guys were standing.

"The two of you are so cute," Elodie gushed. "I never would've thought it back when you guys first met. Considering how you were always at each other's throats."

"Yeah, well, he's still in his 'take care of Ashlyn' mode. I'm sure we'll go back to bickering soon," she said, taking a sip of the juice Slate had brought her.

"Wait a minute...is that a ring?!" Elodie exclaimed.

Ashlyn grinned and held up her hand for Carly and Elodie. "Yeah. He proposed officially last night."

"It's about time! He's been calling you his fiancée ever since you left the hospital," Elodie said.

"When are you getting married?" Carly asked.

Ashlyn shrugged. "No clue. We haven't talked about details. But honestly, it doesn't matter to me. I don't need a huge ceremony. I just want to spend the rest of my life with Slate."

"I know the feeling," Elodie said with a smile.

"Happy for you guys," Carly said.

"Thanks."

A comfortable silence fell over the women, then Elodie asked, "How's James doing?"

"He's good. He felt guilty about what happened for a while, but I think I've finally got him out of that funk. Slate getting him connected with that veterans group was one of the best things for him. The meetings get him out of the house more, and thinking about something other than what happened."

"And is the new home health aide working out?" Elodie asked.

"Yeah. James was very reluctant to have anyone come into the house at first, but it was Slate who actually talked him into it."

"How?" Carly asked.

"By personally interviewing each of the applicants and basically scaring the shit out of them. Telling them if they so much as laid a finger in anger on his friend, or took something as small as a Q-tip from the house, they'd have him to deal *with*."

"Oh, Lord," Elodie said with a laugh. "I'm surprised anyone took the job."

"I was too. But I guess after hearing what happened to James, and me, the guy who finally took the position looked Slate in the eye, and promised over his dead body would anyone ever hurt James again."

"Wow, yeah, okay, I guess that's good."

"Yeah. And the new guy is a Navy vet himself. And has a huge Hawaiian *ohana*, family, here on the island. He takes James over to his house every Sunday to hang out and eat with all of them. He's a sweetheart, and I'm thrilled for James."

"That's awesome," Elodie said with a smile.

Ashlyn nodded, then heard the guys calling out greetings to someone behind her. She turned to see a man she'd only met a couple times enter the yard. She put down her drink and got up to greet him.

Baker looked good, as usual. He wore a pair of board shorts and a T-shirt that didn't hide all the tattoos on his arms. His salt-and-pepper hair was messy as usual, as if he'd just stepped off the beach after surfing all day, which probably wasn't a huge stretch.

She had to wait her turn, as Baker was currently having

his back slapped and shaking hands with the guys. When the macho greetings were done, Ashlyn approached.

Baker hugged her gently, as if she was made of glass. Smiling, she tightened her hold, squeezing him hard.

"Easy, woman," he warned as he pulled back.

Ashlyn rolled her eyes. She felt Slate's hand on her back as he came up behind her.

"Thank you so much for all this," she said, gesturing to the yard and the view of the bay behind her.

"Of course. I know the family who owns the house. He used to be a famous surfer, and he owed me one."

Ashlyn wasn't surprised at that. She had no idea what it was Baker had done for the owner of the house, but she didn't really care. She was happy to be away from the large crowds of locals and tourists below, all competing for the best viewing spots on the beach to watch the competition.

As she stood back and watched Baker greet the other women, a thought occurred to Ashlyn. When everyone had finished saying their hellos, she asked, "Where's Jody?"

Ashlyn could feel her friends' eyes on her. They'd talked about it some, about the woman Baker seemed to like, but the man himself never discussed her. She supposed she probably should've been more discreet when asking, but she'd learned the hard way how short life was. And she wanted Baker to be as happy as his friends were.

To her surprise, Baker didn't blow off the question. "She's down at the beach, workin'."

"Working?"

"Yeah. Volunteering. Making sure the surfers get water and snacks when they need it. But more than that, she's keepin' an eye on her kids."

"Her kids?" Lexie asked.

"The high school surfers. Everyone comes out to the beach to watch on competition days, and they stay all day.

She makes sure they aren't getting into trouble, and no one messes with them," Baker said.

"That's good," Kenna said.

Baker snorted. It was obvious he had his own opinions on what Jody was doing, but he didn't share them. "Anyway, I just came up to make sure you all were good. I'm headed back down to the beach. If you need anything, Jonny will be happy to get it for you."

They'd all met Jonny, the homeowner, and he'd seemed genuinely happy to welcome everyone to his home and to make them comfortable.

"I want to meet her at some point," Ashlyn said.

Baker lifted an eyebrow.

"And don't look at me like that. I was shot, I'm entitled to speak my mind."

Slate's arm wrapped around her from behind as he said, "Don't like you being so blasé about being shot, babe."

"I mean it," she said to Baker, squeezing Slate's arm to let him know she heard him. "You like her, it's obvious. She sounds like a fascinating person. I love that she takes care of the high school kids. I've heard about how she brings snacks to them in the morning when they're surfing and makes sure they all get off to school. But I've never heard anyone say anything about her having help, or about her hanging out with her own friends. And since you obviously think highly of her, she must be amazing. I'm thinking maybe she wouldn't mind getting to know us."

"She's older than you are, Ash," Baker said.

"So?" she fired back. "I've got lots of friends of all different ages. James is eighty-nine, and he loves hanging out with me and my friends."

"True," Baker said with a small smile.

"Look, I get that you're secret and broody and all that, but that doesn't mean you can't at least introduce us."

"She's pushy," Baker said to Slate.

"I am," Ashlyn said before Slate could respond. "Because I have a feeling this friend of yours is pretty cool. And I need all the cool friends I can find to balance out my dorkiness."

Everyone around her laughed. Ashlyn knew she was pushing a bit hard, but for some reason, she felt like this was important.

"Look around you, Baker. These guys might not have been your SEAL team, but you've helped all of them when they've needed it most. You're their friend. And you're *my* friend, and Elodie's, Lexie's, Kenna's, Monica's, and Carly's. Letting us get to know Jody isn't going to reveal any of your deep dark secrets. So let us in...at least this little bit."

Baker stared at her so long, Ashlyn had the feeling she'd pushed *too* hard. But then his lips quirked, and he shook his head. "You aren't gonna be happy until everyone around you is too, are you?"

"Nope," Ashlyn said with a smile. "It's what I do...I'm the happy fairy, sprinkling everyone with my special glitter everywhere I go."

Everyone burst out laughing again, but it was Baker's response she was most concerned about.

"Fine. I'll see what I can do," he said at last.

Ashlyn beamed. "Great. And don't take too long either," she ordered.

"Now you're pushin' your luck," he said dryly. "If you'll excuse me, I'm gonna go wash off the fuckin' glitter all over me and get back to work."

Ashlyn wasn't offended in the least. She stepped out of Slate's hold and hugged Baker once again. "Thanks for being awesome. Grumpy, secretive, kinda scary and standoffish, but awesome."

She was rewarded with another smile.

"Later," he told the group with a chin lift, then he turned and walked away.

Ashlyn couldn't help but notice the man had one hell of an ass. He might be in fifties, but all the other women were right...he was hot as fuck.

"Are you ogling another man's ass?" Slate asked, once again wrapping an arm around her, pulling her against his chest.

"Yup," Ashlyn said without hesitation, then she turned in his embrace and stared up at the man she loved. "But he's not you, so I'm not interested."

"You better not be," Slate growled.

"You're the only one for me. Though it does seem I have a thing for broody, grumpy men."

"You forgot impatient," he said.

"Are you wanting to leave already?" she teased.

"Let's see, hang out in the hot sun watching a bunch of idiots taking their lives into their hands by trying to ride those insane waves, and talking with the same guys I see every day...or go home with my woman, lie in bed, naked, and show her how much I love her more with every second? Tough decision," he said sarcastically.

Ashlyn smiled and put her hand on his cheek. He immediately turned his head and kissed her palm. "Thank you for bringing me up here today." She knew he was just kidding. Yeah, he didn't like watching surfing and the traffic did suck, but he enjoyed hanging out with his teammates, even if he did see them every day.

"If you feel up to it, maybe we can stop and see Monica, Pid, and Charlotte on the way home," Slate suggested.

"Yes!" Ashlyn agreed. She'd never turn down the chance to cuddle with the newborn. She wasn't quite ready for her own, wasn't sure she ever would be, but she loved being able to snuggle Charlotte, then give her back when she cried or needed her diaper changed.

"Love seeing you like this," Slate said after a moment.

"Like what?"

"Happy."

"I am," Ashlyn said fervently.

"Good. Can I assume we'll be making more visits up here to the North Shore in the near future?" Slate asked.

Ashlyn smiled. "Yes. I'm determined to meet this Jody person and bring her into the fold of our girl posse."

"She's a lucky woman then," Slate said. Then he leaned down. He kissed her long, slow, and deep, not caring if anyone was watching. When he lifted his head, he licked his lips. "I love you, Ashlyn. More than you'll ever know."

"And I love you too, Slate."

"Go hang with your girls. Before I throw you over my shoulder and drag you home."

Ashlyn laughed. There was no way he'd throw her over his shoulder, not so soon after everything that had happened... but hopefully in the future she could egg him on enough to make him lose control and do just that.

"Go," he ordered, as if he could read her mind.

Ashlyn backed up, then turned and sauntered toward Elodie and the others, swinging her hips a little more than she normally would. When she looked back, she saw Slate's gaze glued to her ass, just as she'd intended.

Life was good.

* * *

Jodelle Spencer kept an eye on her high schoolers as she sat as far away from the crowds as she could get, but still close enough so she could see what was going on. She didn't like being here, it brought back too many bad memories, but because this was where the surfers were, this was where she had to be.

"Do you have any more sandwiches, Miss Jody?" one of her favorite kids asked a little shyly.

"Of course, Rome. You want one or two?"

"You have enough for me to have two?" he asked.

"When have I never had enough for my boys to fill their bellies?" she retorted.

Rome grinned. "Then two please."

Jody reached into the cooler she always had by her side and fished out two sandwiches.

"Thanks, Miss Jody. Later."

She closed the lid as the lanky boy walked away, back toward a group of kids he'd been hanging out with.

She'd made it her mission to keep an eye on the boys, and the occasional girl, who liked to surf before school in the mornings, and in the afternoons as well. If someone had been there watching out for—

No. She wasn't going there.

Looking around, she searched for her kids, spotting most of them. Brent and Felipe were hanging out on the sand watching the surfers, Rome was eating the sandwiches she'd given him and flirting with a girl barely wearing a bikini. Iwalani, who went by Lani, one of the few females who surfed nearly every morning, was getting the autograph of one of the professional surfers. Kalama was hanging out with a bunch of older kids from the high school...

But as hard as she looked, Jody couldn't spot Ben Miller.

She'd been worried about him for a while now. He'd gone from a happy-go-lucky kid to someone who barely smiled lately, and even though he still showed up to surf in the mornings, he didn't seem to enjoy it as much as he used to.

Last week, when she'd shown up in the morning to the beach where the high school kids usually congregated to surf before school, she'd seen him sleeping in the back seat of his older-model Kia. He was too tall to fit in the seat. When she'd tried to ask him what was up, why he was sleeping in his car, he'd blown her off and refused to talk about it.

Which was another worry. Ben used to sit and talk her ear off about nothing in particular before he'd head out to the waves. Now he kept his head down and barely looked at anyone. It was worrisome, and him not being here today, at the surf competition, didn't make her feel any better.

"Hey, Jodelle," a deep voice said from behind her.

Smiling—and telling herself not to act like a dork—Jody turned. "Hey, Baker."

"Everything good?"

She wanted to tell him that, no, everything *wasn't* good. That she was lonely. That she missed her son more with every day. That she was worried about Ben. That she was running low on sandwiches and knew she'd never find a parking spot if she left and tried to come back. That it scared her to watch the surfers in the huge waves. That she thought Baker was so damn good-looking, it was hard to keep her hands to herself. That she both craved and dreaded being alone back at her house...

She said none of that. She simply replied, "Yeah."

But Baker had a way of looking at her that made Jody suspect he saw through her nonchalant responses. That he could see straight through to the heart of who she was. It was scary...and exhilarating at the same time.

He'd never once given her any indication he wanted to be anything but casual friends in all the time she'd known him. So Jody always did her best to hide her feelings. About him... about everything.

"You get your friends settled?" she asked. He'd told her earlier that his friends were going to be coming to watch the competition from up on the bluff.

"Yeah. They want to meet you," he said.

Jody blinked in surprise. "Me?"

"Yeah."

"Why?"

"Why not?" Baker countered.

"Um...because?"

Baker's lips quirked upward, and Jody's knees literally went weak at seeing that smile. He'd just started to respond when Lani came running up to them.

"Miss Jody! Something's wrong with Ben!"

All thoughts about how attractive Baker was flew from her mind. "Where is he? I haven't seen him."

"His car was parked at the back of the lot and someone saw him sleeping in it. Because it's so hot, he's got heat exhaustion. The medics are looking at him now!"

Jody turned to look at the medical tent, but didn't see any excessive commotion. She immediately headed for the parking lot.

She jerked in surprise when Baker reached out and took her elbow in his hand.

Looking up at him, she frowned. "You don't have to come."

He stared back with a look she'd never seen before on his face. "I know, but I am."

"Why?" she couldn't help but ask.

"Because as a friend recently reminded me, life is short, and I'm done being noble. I'm doing what I should've done a long fuckin' time ago."

Jody was confused. She had no idea what in the world Baker was talking about. But she didn't have time to worry about that right now. She had to figure out what the hell Ben was doing sleeping in his car in the middle of the day. Something was going on with him, and she was going to figure out what it was, no matter what it took.

* *

FINALLY! It's Baker's turn! He meets his match with Jodelle! Get the final book in the SEAL Team Hawaii series, *Finding Jodelle* now!

Want to talk to other Susan Stoker fans? Join my reader group, Susan Stoker's Stalkers, on Facebook!

The Lumberjack (TBA)

SEAL of Protection: Legacy Series

Securing Caite
Securing Brenae (novella)
Securing Sidney
Securing Piper
Securing Zoey
Securing Avery
Securing Kalee
Securing Jane

Delta Force Heroes Series

Rescuing Rayne
Rescuing Aimee (novella)
Rescuing Emily
Rescuing Harley
Marrying Emily (novella)
Rescuing Kassie
Rescuing Bryn
Rescuing Casey
Rescuing Sadie (novella)
Rescuing Wendy
Rescuing Mary
Rescuing Macie (novella)
Rescuing Annie

SEAL of Protection Series

Protecting Caroline
Protecting Alabama
Protecting Fiona
Marrying Caroline (novella)
Protecting Summer
Protecting Cheyenne

ALSO BY SUSAN STOKER

Protecting Jessyka
Protecting Julie (novella)
Protecting Melody
Protecting the Future
Protecting Kiera (novella)
Protecting Alabama's Kids (novella)
Protecting Dakota

Delta Team Two Series
Shielding Gillian
Shielding Kinley
Shielding Aspen
Shielding Jayme (novella)
Shielding Riley
Shielding Devyn
Shielding Ember
Shielding Sierra

Badge of Honor: Texas Heroes Series
Justice for Mackenzie
Justice for Mickie
Justice for Corrie
Justice for Laine (novella)
Shelter for Elizabeth
Justice for Boone
Shelter for Adeline
Shelter for Sophie
Justice for Erin
Justice for Milena
Shelter for Blythe
Justice for Hope
Shelter for Quinn
Shelter for Koren
Shelter for Penelope

Ace Security Series

Claiming Grace
Claiming Alexis
Claiming Bailey
Claiming Felicity
Claiming Sarah

Mountain Mercenaries Series

Defending Allye
Defending Chloe
Defending Morgan
Defending Harlow
Defending Everly
Defending Zara
Defending Raven

Silverstone Series

Trusting Skylar
Trusting Taylor
Trusting Molly
Trusting Cassidy

Stand Alone

Falling for the Delta
The Guardian Mist
Nature's Rift
A Princess for Cale
A Moment in Time- A Collection of Short Stories
Another Moment in Time- A Collection of Short Stories
Lambert's Lady

Special Operations Fan Fiction

http://www.AcesPress.com

ALSO BY SUSAN STOKER

Beyond Reality Series
Outback Hearts
Flaming Hearts
Frozen Hearts

Writing as Annie George:
Stepbrother Virgin (erotic novella)

ABOUT THE AUTHOR

New York Times, *USA Today* and *Wall Street Journal* Bestselling Author Susan Stoker has a heart as big as the state of Tennessee where she lives, but this all American girl has also spent the last fourteen years living in Missouri, California, Colorado, Indiana, and Texas. She's married to a retired Army man who now gets to follow *her* around the country.

She debuted her first series in 2014 and quickly followed that up with the SEAL of Protection Series, which solidified her love of writing and creating stories readers can get lost in.

If you enjoyed this book, or any book, please consider leaving a review. It's appreciated by authors more than you'll know.

www.stokeraces.com
www.AcesPress.com
susan@stokeraces.com

facebook.com/authorsusanstoker

twitter.com/Susan_Stoker

instagram.com/authorsusanstoker

goodreads.com/SusanStoker

bookbub.com/authors/susan-stoker

amazon.com/author/susanstoker

CPSIA information can be obtained
at www.ICGtesting.com
Printed in the USA
BVHW050031030223
657752BV00010B/118